On the day the end begins,
the sea will reveal a mystery.

DEEP FATHOM

"[Rollins] will make your toes curl and
your free hand clutch the armchair
as you speed through the pages."
Tampa Tribune

"Rollins writes with intelligence, clarity,
and a refreshing sense of humor."
Kirkus Reviews

"[Rollins] kept me turning pages
well into the night."
John Saul

"While Clive Cussler maintains
the gold standard in action lit,
Rollins has a firm grasp on the silver."
Publishers Weekly

JAMES ROLLINS

DEEP FATHOM

HARPER

An Imprint of HarperCollins*Publishers*

This is a work of fiction. Names, characters, places, and incidents are products of the author's imagination or are used fictitiously and are not to be construed as real. Any resemblance to actual events, locales, organizations, or persons, living or dead, is entirely coincidental.

HARPER

An Imprint of HarperCollins*Publishers*
10 East 53rd Street
New York, New York 10022-5299

First Harper paperback printing: March 2007
First HarperTorch paperback printing: July 2001
First HarperTorch special printing: January 2001

HarperCollins® and Harper® are trademarks of HarperCollins Publishers Inc.

Printed in the United States of America

Visit Harper paperbacks on the World Wide Web
at www.harpercollins.com

30   29   28   27   26   25   24

For Steve and Judy Prey . . .
teachers, friends, and founders of the Spacers

Acknowledgments

No man is an island, and certainly no writer. There are so many good people and friends who have helped hone this novel. First and foremost, I wish to express my appreciation to Lyssa Keusch, my editor, and to Russ Galen, my agent.

For technical assistance, several individuals have been invaluable in the research behind the novel's science and history: Stephen R. Fischer, Ph.D., for his background in Polynesian languages; Dr. Charles Plummer of CSUS, for his knowledge of geological sciences; Vera Rubin, for her articles on astronomy; both Dr. Phil Nuytten of Nuytco Research Ltd. and the folks at Zegrahm Deep Sea Voyages, for the details of submersible dynamics; Laurel Moore, librarian of the Woods Hole Oceanographic Institution, for her assistance in deep-sea biology; and David Childress, for his book *Ancient Micronesia,* an invaluable resource. Finally, a marked recognition must be made to two other authors whose books inspired this story: Colonel James Churchward, *Books of the Golden Age,* and Charles Berlitz, *The Dragon's Triangle.*

Of course, I must never forget my posse in words who helped pick apart and polish the first draft: Chris Crowe,

Michael Gallowglas, Lee Garrett, Dennis Grayson, Penny Hill, Debra Nelson, Chris Koehler, Dave Meek, Chris Smith, Jane O'Riva, Steve and Judy Prey, Caroline Williams—and for critical analysis and a decade of friendship, Carolyn Mc-Cray.

And lastly, a special thanks to Steve Winters of Web Stew, for his internet skills, and Don Wagner, for his ardent and accomplished support.

DEEP FATHOM

The Day
of the Eclipse

Tuesday, July 24

i

Before

On the morning of the eclipse, Doreen McCloud hurried from Starbucks with the *Chronicle* tucked under her arm. She had a ten o'clock meeting across town and less than an hour to ride the train to her offices near the Embarcadero. Clutching her mocha and shivering at the morning chill, she strode briskly toward the underground station at Market and Castro.

Glancing toward the sky, she frowned. The night's blanket of fog had yet to burn off, and the sun was only a pale glow through the mists. The eclipse was due to occur just after the four o'clock hour today—the first solar eclipse of the new millennium. It would be a shame if the fog marred the sight. She knew from the inundation in the media that the entire city was poised to celebrate the event. San Francisco could not pass up such an auspicious occasion without the usual fanfare.

Doreen shook her head at all the nonsense. With San Francisco's damned eternal fog, why did a few extra moments of gloom warrant such fervency? The event was not even a *total* eclipse.

Sighing, she pushed aside these stray thoughts as she snugged her scarf tighter about her neck. She had more important concerns. If she could land the Delta Bank account, her track to partnership in the firm was assured. She allowed this thought to buoy her across Market Street toward the BART station.

She reached the station just as the next train approached. Fumbling her transit card through the reader, she hurried down the steps to the platform and waited for the train to come to a stop. Content she would make her meeting in plenty of time, she raised the cup of mocha to her mouth.

A yank on her elbow pulled the cup from her lips. Hot mocha splashed in a chocolate arc as the cup flew from her hands. Gasping, she swung around and faced her attacker.

An elderly woman, dressed in mismatched rags and a tattered blanket, stared up at Doreen with eyes that looked somewhere other than here. Doreen had a flashback to her mother in bed: the reek of urine and medicines, slacken features, and those same empty eyes. Alzheimer's.

She stepped back, reflexively guarding her handbag under an arm. But the old woman, clearly homeless, seemed no immediate threat. Doreen expected the usual inquiry about spare change.

Instead, the woman continued to stare at her with those empty eyes.

Doreen took another step away; a twinge of sorrow pierced through her anger and fear. The eyes of the other commuters slowly turned away. It was the way of the city. *Don't look too closely.* She tried to follow suit but could not. Maybe it was the flash upon her own long-buried mother or some twinge of sympathy, but either way, she found herself speaking. "Can I help you?"

The old woman shifted. Doreen spotted a half-starved terrier pup hidden among the drape of rags about her ankles. It stuck close to its master. Doreen could count every rib on the thin creature.

The homeless woman noticed Doreen's gaze. "Brownie knows," she said hoarsely, her voice graveled by age and the streets. "He knows, all right."

Doreen nodded as if this made sense. It was best not to provoke the mentally ill. She had learned that with her mother. "I'm sure he does."

"He tells me things, you know."

Doreen nodded again, suddenly feeling foolish. The train doors opened with a *whoosh* behind her. If she didn't want to miss the train, she'd best hurry.

She began to turn away when a withered arm shot out from under the tattered blanket; bony fingers clutched her wrist. Instinctively, Doreen yanked her arm away. But to her surprise, the old woman hung on.

With a shuffle of rags, the woman moved closer. "Brownie's a good dog." The harsh voice was thick with spittle. "He knows. He's a good dog."

Doreen broke the woman's grip. "I . . . I must be going."

The woman did not resist. Her arm vanished under her blanket's folds.

Doreen backed her way into the open door of the train, her eyes still on the old woman. Left alone, the woman seemed to recede into her rags and tormented dreams. Doreen found the pup's eyes staring back at her. As the train doors closed, Doreen heard the homeless woman muttering, "Brownie. He knows. He knows we're all goin' to die today."

1:55 P.M., PST (11:55 A.M. Local Time)
Aleutian Islands, Alaska

On the morning of the eclipse, Jimmy Pomautuk worked his way up the icy slope with practiced care. His dog Nanook trotted a few paces up the trail. The large malamute knew the trail well, but, always the loyal companion, he still kept wary watch for his master.

Trudging after the old dog, Jimmy led a trio of English tourists—two men and a woman—toward the summit of

Glacial Point atop Fox Island. The view from there was spectacular. His Inuit forefathers had come to this same spot to worship the great Orca, building wooden totems and casting worship stones off the cliffs into the sea. His great-grandfather had been the first to take him as a boy to this sacred spot. That had been almost thirty years ago.

Now the spot was listed on countless tour maps, and the Zodiac boats from the various cruise lines offloaded their human cargo onto the docks of the picturesque village of Port Royson.

In addition to the quaint port, the other prime attraction to the island was the cliffs of Glacial Point. On a clear day like today, the entire Aleutian chain of islands could be seen spreading in an infinite arc. It was a sight considered priceless to his ancestors, but to the modern world it was forty dollars a head off-season, sixty dollars during the warmer months.

"How much bloody further is this place?" a voice behind him said. "I'm freezing my arse off here."

Jimmy turned. He had warned the trio that the temperature would grow colder as they neared the summit. The group was outfitted in matching Eddie Bauer coats, gloves, and boots. Not a stitch of their expensive outwear showed any use. A price tag still dangled from the back of the woman's parka.

Pointing an arm toward where his dog had just vanished, Jimmy nodded. "It's just over the next rise. Five minutes. There's a warming shack there."

The complainer checked his watch and grunted.

Jimmy rolled his eyes and continued his march up the hill. If it weren't for the tip as their guide, he'd be tempted to heave the whole lot of them over the cliffs. A sacrifice to the ocean gods of his ancestors. But instead, like always, he just trudged onward, reaching the summit at last.

Behind him he heard gasps from the trio. The view had that effect on most people. Jimmy turned to give them his usual speech about the significance of this site, but he found his companions' attention was not on the spectacular views, but on their hurried attempts to wrap every square inch of exposed flesh from the mild winds.

"It's so cold," the second man said. "I hope my camera lens doesn't shatter. I'd hate to have trekked all the way up to this cursed place and have nothing to show for it."

Jimmy's fingers clenched into a fist. He forced his tone to an even level. "The warming shack is nestled among that group of black pines. Why don't you all go on in? We've got a bit of a wait before the eclipse."

"Thank God," the woman said. She leaned into the man who had first complained. "Let's hurry, Reggie."

Now it was Jimmy's turn to follow. The English trio raced toward the scraggled copse of pines protected in a hollow. As he marched, Nanook joined him, nosing his hand for a scratch behind the ear.

"Good boy, Nanook," he mumbled. Ahead, Jimmy's gaze caught on the trail of smoke in the blue sky. At least his son had completed his chores and set the coals this morning before leaving for the mainland, off to celebrate the coming eclipse with friends.

For the oddest moment, a melancholy wave washed over Jimmy at the thought of his only son. He couldn't identify why this sudden mood overwhelmed him. He shook his head. This place had that effect on him. There always seemed a presence here. Maybe the gods of my forefathers, he thought, only half jokingly.

Jimmy continued his way toward the warmth of the shack, suddenly wanting to escape the cold as much as the tourists had. His eyes followed the smoke trail up to the sun near the eastern horizon. An eclipse. What his ancestors described as a whale eating the sun. It was due to occur in the next few hours.

At his side, Nanook suddenly growled, a deep-throated rumble. Jimmy glanced to his dog. The malamute stared out toward the south. Frowning, he followed the line of his dog's gaze.

The cliffs were empty, except for the wooden totem. It was a mock-up for the tourists, tooled by machines somewhere in Indonesia and shipped here. Not even the wood was native to these parts.

Nanook continued his deep-chested growl.

Jimmy did not know what had spooked his dog. "Quiet, boy."

Always obedient, Nanook settled onto his haunches, but he still trembled.

Squinting, Jimmy stared out at the empty sea. As he stood, an old prayer came to his lips, taught to him by his grandfather. He was surprised he even remembered the words, and could not voice why he felt the need to speak them now. In Alaska, to survive, one learned to respect nature and one's own instincts—and Jimmy trusted his own now.

It was as if his grandfather stood at his shoulder, two generations watching the sea. His grandfather had a phrase for moments like now. "The wind smells of storms."

4:05 P.M. PST (10:05 A.M. Local Time)
Hagatna, Territory of Guam

On the morning of the eclipse, Jeffrey Hessmire cursed his bad luck as he hurried through the corridors of the governor's mansion. The first session of the summit had broken for an early brunch. The dignitaries from the United States and the People's Republic of China would not reconvene until after the scheduled viewing of the eclipse.

During the break, Jeffrey, as the junior aide, had been assigned to type and photocopy the Secretary of State's notes from the morning's session, then distribute them among the American delegation. So while the other aides enjoyed the pre-eclipse buffet in the garden atrium and networked with the members of the presidential senior staff, he would be playing stenographer.

He cursed his bad luck again. What were they all doing out here in the middle of the Pacific anyway? Hell would freeze over before any nuclear pact would ever be settled be-

tween the two Pacific powers. Neither country was willing
to bend, especially on two critical points. The President had
refused to halt the extension of the country's new state-of-
the-art Missile Defense System to include the protection of
Taiwan, and the Chinese Premier had squashed any attempt
to limit the proliferation of its own intercontinental nuclear
warheads. The entire week's summit had succeeded only in
managing to escalate tensions.

The single bright spot was on the first day, when President Bishop had accepted a gift from the Chinese Premier: a
life-size jade sculpture of an ancient Chinese warrior atop a
war horse, an exact replica of one of their famed terra-cotta
statues from the city of Xi'an. The press had a field day taking pictures of the two heads of state beside the striking figure. It had been a day full of promise that, so far, had not
borne fruit.

As Jeffrey passed into the suite of offices assigned to
their delegation, he flashed his security clearance at the
guard, who nodded coldly. Reaching his desk, he collapsed
into the leather seat. Though he resented such a menial task,
he would do his best.

Carefully stacking the handwritten notes by his computer, he set to work. His fingers flew over the keyboard as
he translated Secretary Elliot's notes into clean, crisp type.
As he worked, his frustration fell away. He became intrigued by this peek at the behind-doors politics of the
summit. It seemed the President was actually willing to
bend on Taiwan, but he was haggling for the best price
from the Chinese government, insisting on a moratorium
on any future nuclear proliferation and Chinese participa-
tion in the Missile Technology Control Regime, which limited the export of missile knowledge. Elliot seemed to
think this was attainable if they played their cards right.
The Chinese did not want a war over Taiwan. All would
suffer.

Jeffrey was so caught up in the Secretary's notes that he
failed to hear someone approach until a small cough from
behind startled him. He swiveled his chair around and saw

the tall, silver-haired man. He was dressed casually in shirt and tie, with a suit jacket hung over one arm. "So what do you think, Mr. Hessmire?"

Jeffrey stood up so fast that his chair skittered backward across the floor, bumping into a neighbor's vacant desk. "M-Mister President."

"At ease, Mr. Hessmire." The President of the United States, Daniel R. Bishop, leaned over Jeffrey's desk and read the partial transcription of the Secretary's notes. "What do you think of Tom's thoughts?"

"The Secretary? Mr. Elliot?"

The President straightened, giving Jeffrey a tired smile. "Yes. You're studying international law at Georgetown, aren't you?"

Jeffrey blinked. He had not thought President Bishop knew him from the hundreds of other aides and interns who labored in the belly of the White House. "Yes, Mr. President. I graduate next year."

"Top of the class and specializing in Asia, I hear. So what is your take on the summit? Do you think we can wrangle the Chinese into an agreement?"

Licking his lips, Jeffrey could not meet the steel-blue eyes of Daniel Bishop, the war hero, the statesman, and the leader of the free world. His words were mumbled.

"Speak up, lad. I won't bite your head off. I just want your honest opinion. Why do you think I asked Tom to assign you to this task?"

Shocked at this revelation, Jeffrey could not speak.

"Breathe, Mr. Hessmire."

Jeffrey took the President's recommendation. Taking a deep breath, he cleared his throat and tried to organize his thoughts. He spoke slowly. "I . . . I think Secretary Elliot makes a good point about the mainland's desire to economically integrate Taiwan." He glanced up, pausing to take another breath. "I studied the takeovers of Hong Kong and Macau. It seems that the Chinese are using these regions as test cases for the integration of democratic economies within a Communist structure. Some suggest these experiments are in preparation for China's attempt to negotiate Taiwan's reintegration, to demonstrate how such a union could benefit all."

"And what of the growing nuclear arsenal in China?"

Jeffrey spoke more rapidly, warming to the discussion. "Their nuclear and missile technologies were stolen from us. But China's current manufacturing infrastructure is well behind their ability to utilize these newest technologies. In many ways, they are still an agrarian state, ill-suited for rapid nuclear proliferation."

"And your assessment?"

"The Chinese have witnessed how such proliferation bankrupted the Soviet Union. They would not want to repeat the same mistake. In the next decade, China needs to bolster its own technological infrastructure if it hopes to maintain its global position. It can't afford a pissing contest with the United States over a nuclear arsenal."

"A pissing contest?"

Jeffrey's eyes grew wide. He turned crimson. "I'm sorry—"

The President held up a hand. "No, I appreciate the analogy."

Jeffrey suddenly felt like a fool. What nonsense had he been spouting? How dare he think his views warranted President Bishop's time?

The President straightened from the desk and slipped into his jacket. "I think you're right, Mr. Hessmire. Neither country wants to finance a new Cold War."

"No, sir," Jeffrey mumbled softly.

"There may be hope to settle this matter before our relations sour further, but it'll take a deft hand." The President strode toward the door. "Finish your work here, Mr. Hessmire, and join us for the festivities in the atrium. You shouldn't miss the first solar eclipse of this new millennium."

Jeffrey found his tongue too thick to reply as the President exited the room. He fumbled for his chair and sank

into it. President Bishop had listened to him . . . had agreed
with   him!

Thanking the stars for such good fortune, Jeffrey sat up
straighter and returned to his work with renewed vigor.

This day promised to be one to remember.

ii

During

From the balcony of her office building, Doreen McCloud stared out over San Francisco Bay. The view extended all the way to the piers. She could even see the crowds gathered at Ghirardelli Square, where a party was under way. But the crowds below failed to hold her attention. Instead she gazed above the bay at a once-in-a-lifetime sight.

A black sun hung over the blue waters—the corona flaming bright around the eclipsing moon.

Wearing a sleek set of eclipse goggles purchased from Sharper Image, Doreen watched as jets of fire burst in long streams from the sun's edge. Solar flares. The astronomy experts on CNN had predicted a spectacular eclipse due to the unusual sunspot activity coinciding with the lunar event. Their predictions had proven true.

On either side of her gasps of delight and awe rose from the other lawyers and secretarial staff.

A long flare blew forth from the sun's surface. A radio playing in the background burst with a stream of static, proving true another of the astronomers' predictions. CNN had warned that the sunspot activity would cause brief interference as the solar winds bombarded the upper atmosphere.

Doreen marveled at the black sun and its reflection in the bay. What a wonderful time to be alive!

"Did anyone feel that?" one of the secretaries asked with mild concern.

Then Doreen sensed it—a trembling underfoot. Everyone grew deathly quiet. The radio squelched sharply with static. Clay flower pots began to rattle.

"Earthquake!" someone yelled needlessly.

After living for so many years in San Francisco, temblors were not a reason for panic. Still, at the back of all minds was the fear of "the Big One."

"Everyone inside," the head of the firm ordered.

In a mass, the crowd surged toward the open doorway. Doreen held back. She searched the skies above the bay. The black sun hung over the waters like some hole in the sky.

She remembered, then, the one other prediction for this day. She pictured the old homeless woman dressed in rags— and her dog.

We're all going to die today.

Doreen backed from the balcony rail toward the open door. Under her heels the balcony began to rock and buck violently. This was no minor quake.

"Hurry!" their boss commanded, taking charge. "Everyone get to safety!"

Doreen fled toward the interior offices, but in her heart she knew no safety would be found there. *They were all going to die.*

4:44 P.M. PST (2:44 P.M. Local Time)
Aleutian Islands, Alaska

From the cliffs of Glacial Point, Jimmy Pomautuk stared at the eclipsing sun. Nanook, paced restlessly at his side. Off to the left the trio from England shouted to one another in awe, the cold long forgotten in the excitement. The flash and whir of cameras peppered their exuberant outcries.

"Did you see that flare!"

"Bloody Christ! These pictures are going to be fantastic!"

Sighing, Jimmy sank to his seat on the cold stone. He leaned back against the wooden totem as he stared out at the black sun above the Pacific. The quality of the light was strange, casting the islands in a starkness that seemed unreal. Even the sea itself had turned glassy with a bluish-silver sheen.

At his side, Nanook again began a soft growl. The dog had been spooky all morning. He must not understand what had happened to the sunlight. "It's just the hungry whale spirit eating the sun," he consoled the dog in a low whisper. He reached for Nanook but found the dog gone.

Frowning, Jimmy glanced over his shoulder. The large malamute stood trembling a few paces away. The dog did not stare at the sun above the Pacific, but off to the north.

"My God!" Jimmy stood up, following Nanook's gaze.

The entire northern skies, darkened by the eclipse, were lit with waves and eddies of glowing azures and vibrant reds. They spread from the northern horizon to climb high in the sky. Jimmy knew what he was viewing—the aurora borealis, the Northern Lights. In all his life, he had never seen the magnitude of this display. The lights swirled and churned in sweeping waves, like a glowing sea in the sky.

One of the Englishmen spoke, drawn by Jimmy's shocked outburst. "I thought the borealis wasn't seen this time of year."

"It's not," Jimmy answered quietly.

The Englishwoman, Eileen, moved closer to Jimmy, a camera glued to her face. "It's beautiful. Almost better than the eclipse."

"The solar flares must be causing this," her companion answered. "Showering the upper atmosphere with energized particles."

Jimmy remained silent. To the Inuit, the appearance of the Northern Lights was fraught with omens and significance. A borealis in the summer was considered a harbinger of disaster.

As if hearing his inner thought, the totem trembled under Jimmy's palm. Nanook began to whine, something his dog never did.

"Is the ground shaking?" Eileen asked, finally lowering her camera with a look of concern.

As answer, a violent quake suddenly shook the island. With a stifled scream, Eileen fell to her hands and knees. The two Englishmen went to her aid.

Jimmy kept his feet, fingers still clutching the wooden totem.

"What are we going to do?" the woman screamed.

"It'll be fine," her friend consoled. "We'll ride it out."

Jimmy stared at the islands, bathed in that otherworldly light. *Oh God.* He whispered a prayer of thanks that his son had left for the mainland.

Out in the Pacific, the most distant islands of the Aleutian chain were sinking into the depths, like gigantic sea beasts submerging under the waves. At long last the gods of the sea had come to claim these islands.

4:44 P.M. PST (10:44 A.M. Local Time)
Hagatna, Territory of Guam

In the garden atrium of the governor's mansion, Jeffrey Hessmire stared in awe at the total eclipse of the sun. Though he had seen partial eclipses during his twenty-six years, he had never witnessed a total one. The island of Guam had been chosen for the summit because of its position as the only American territory in the path of full totality.

Jeffrey was thrilled at the chance to witness this rare sight. He had finished typing and photocopying the Secretary of State's notes with enough time left over to catch the tail end of the solar spectacle.

Wearing a pair of cheap eclipse-viewing glasses, Jeffrey stood with the other U.S. delegates by the west entrance to the gardens. The Chinese faction huddled on the far side of the atrium. There was little mingling between the two groups, as if the Pacific still separated them.

Ignoring the tension in the atrium, Jeffrey continued to watch the sun's corona flare in violent bursts around the shadowed moon. A few of the flares jetted far into the dark sky.

A voice spoke at his shoulder. "Wondrous, isn't it?"

Jeffrey turned to find the President directly behind him again. "President Bishop!" Jeffrey began to take off his glasses.

"Leave them on. Enjoy the view. Another is not expected for two decades."

"Y-Yes, sir."

Jeffrey slowly returned to his study of the sky.

The President, also staring up, spoke softly at his side. "To the Chinese, an eclipse is a warning that the tides of fate are about to change significantly—either for the better or the worse."

"It will be for the better," Jeffrey answered. "For both our peoples."

President Bishop clapped him on the shoulder. "The optimism of youth. I should have you speak to the Vice President." He finished the statement with a derisive snort.

Jeffrey understood this response. Lawrence Nafe, the Vice President, held his own views on how to handle one of the last Communist strongholds. While outwardly supporting Bishop's diplomatic attempt to resolve the Chinese situation, behind the scenes Nafe argued for a more aggressive stance.

"You'll succeed in ironing out an agreement," Jeffrey said. "I'm sure of it."

"There's that damned optimism again." The President began to turn away, nodding at a signal from the Secretary of State. With a tired sigh, he clapped Jeffrey on the shoulder again. "It seems it's time once again to try mending fences between our two countries."

As President Bishop stepped away, the ground started to shake underfoot.

Jeffrey felt the President's grip on his shoulder tighten.

Both men fought to keep their feet. "Earthquake!" Jeffrey yelled.

All around them the sound of breaking glass rattled. Jeffrey looked up, shielding his face with an arm. All the windows of the governor's mansion had shattered. Several members of the delegation, those nearest the walls of the atrium, were on the ground, lacerated and bleeding amid the shower of shards.

Jeffrey thought to go to their aid, but he feared abandoning the President. Across the atrium, the Chinese members of the summit were fleeing inside the governor's mansion, seeking shelter.

"Mr. President, we need to get you to safety," Jeffrey said.

The rumbling grew worse underfoot. An ice sculpture of a long-necked swan toppled.

Flanked by two burly Secret Service agents, the Secretary of State fought his way through the terrified crowd to join them. Once there, Tom Elliot grabbed the President's elbow. He had to yell to be heard above the rumbling and crashing. "C'mon, Dan, let's get you back to Air Force One. If this island's coming apart, I want you out of here."

Bishop shook off the man's hand. "But I can't leave—"

Somewhere to the east there was a loud explosion, drowning out all conversation. A fireball blew into the sky.

Jeffrey spoke up first. "Sir, you have to go."

The President's face remained tight with concern and worry. Jeffrey knew the man had served in Vietnam and was not one to run from adversity.

"You must," Tom added. "You can't risk yourself, Dan. You don't have that luxury anymore . . . not since you took the oath of office."

The President bowed under the weight of their argument. The temblors grew worse; cracks skittered up the brick walls of the mansion.

"Fine. Let's go," he said tightly. "But I feel like a coward."

"I ordered the limo to meet you out back," the Secretary said, then turned to Jeffrey as the President strode away with the pair of Secret Service agents in tow. "Stay with Bishop. Get him on board that plane."

"What . . . what about you?"

Tom backed a step away. "I'm going to round up as many of our delegation as possible and herd them to the airport." But before he turned away, he fixed Jeffrey with a stern stare. "Make sure that plane takes off if there is even the slightest risk of trapping the President here. Don't wait for us."

Jeffrey swallowed hard and nodded, then hurried off.

Once at the President's side, Jeffrey heard the man mumble as he stared at the eclipsed sun, "It seems the Chinese were right."

iii

And the Aftermath

As night neared, Doreen McCloud worked her way through the broken asphalt toward Russian Hill. Rumors told of a Salvation Army refugee camp up there. She prayed it was true. Thirsty, hungry, she shivered in the cold as the eternal fog of the bay crept over the ravaged city. The earthquakes had finally ended, except for the occasional aftershock, but the damage had been done.

Exhausted, legs trembling, Doreen glanced over her shoulder and stared out at what once had been a handsome city shining above the bay. The stench of smoke and soot clung to everything. Fires underlit the mists, creating a reddish halo over the devastation. From here, San Francisco lay shattered all the way to the water. Huge chasms cracked the city, as if a giant hammer had struck.

Emergency sirens still echoed, but there was nothing left to save. Only a handful of buildings were undamaged. Most others lay toppled or stood with their facades fallen away to reveal the ravaged rooms within.

Doreen had grown numb to the number of bodies she had crossed on her way to higher ground. Bleeding from a scalp wound, she had escaped almost unscathed, but her heart ached for the families gathered around burned homes and broken bodies. But she shared the one feature she saw in all she passed—eyes deadened from pain and shock.

A flare of light appeared atop the next hill—not fire, but clear, white light. Hope surged. Surely this was the Salvation Army's camp. She continued onward, her stomach growling, her pace hurried.

Oh please . . .

She climbed and crawled her way forward. Rounding an overturned bus, she came upon the source of the bright light. A crowd of men, dirty and ash-fouled, were digging through the remains of a hardware store. They had a crate of flashlights open and were passing them around.

As night rapidly approached, a source of light would be essential.

Doreen stumbled toward them. Perhaps they would give her one.

Two of the men glanced her way. She met their gazes, mouth open to ask for aid, then saw the hardness in their eyes.

She stopped, realizing that the men wore identical clothes. There were numbers stitched across their backs under the words: CALIFORNIA MUNICIPAL PENAL SYSTEM. Convicts. Wide grins spread across the men's faces.

She turned to flee but found one of the escaped prisoners standing behind her. She tried to strike him, but he knocked her arm aside and slapped her on the face, hard, driving her to her knees.

Blinded by pain and shock, Doreen heard the approach of others behind her. "No," she moaned, curling into a ball.

"Leave her," one of them barked. "We don't have time. We wanna be out of this fuckin' city before the National Guard hauls in here."

Grumbles met this response, but Doreen heard the scuff of heels as her attackers backed away. She started crying, relieved and terrified.

The leader stepped in front of her.

Teary-eyed, she lifted her face, ready to thank him for his mercy. Instead, she found herself staring into the muzzle of a handgun. The leader yelled back toward the ravaged store, "Grab any extra ammo! And don't forget the camp stoves and butane!" Without ever looking down at her, he pulled the trigger.

Doreen heard the crack of the weapon, felt her body flung backward, then the world was gone.

8:15 P.M. PST (6:15 P.M. local time)
Aleutian Islands, Alaska

As night approached, Jimmy Pomautuk clung to the totem pole depicting his ancestors' gods. Where once it had stood proudly atop the heights of Glacial Point, it now floated in the sea, bobbing in the waves. Jimmy clung to it. He tried his best to keep his body above the waterline, but the waves constantly tried to wash him from his perch atop the totem.

Hours ago he had hacked the totem from its cement base as the water rose up the cliff face of Glacial Point. The island had sunk surprisingly smoothly, giving him plenty of time to use a hand ax from the warming shed to free the length of wood. Once the waters had neared the summit, he flung it over the edge. The trio of English tourists had long since fled down the path toward Port Royson. Jimmy had tried to stop them, but they wouldn't listen. Panic had made them deaf.

Alone, he had leaped from the cliff and swam out to the floating totem. Only Nanook, the large malamute, had remained at the cliff's edge, unsure what to do, stalking back and forth. Jimmy could not save his old dog. He knew it would be hard enough for him to survive.

With a heavy heart he had straddled the totem and begun paddling toward the distant mainland. Nanook's bark echoed over the waters until the island vanished fully behind him.

As if his guilt plagued him now, he heard the barking

again. But it was no ghost. Twisting around, he saw something splashing toward him from several yards away. Jimmy spotted the flash of black and white fur.

Joy and concern mixed in his heart. The old dog had refused to give up, and as much as Jimmy tried to remain practical, he knew he would do what he could to rescue it. "C'mon, Nanook!" he yelled through chattering teeth. "Get your wet butt over here."

A smile cracked his blue lips as a bark answered him.

Then he saw something rise from the waves behind his paddling dog. A long black fin, too tall for a shark. *Orca*. Killer whale.

Jimmy's heart clenched. He reached a hand toward his dog, but it was useless. The fin sank away. Jimmy held his breath, praying to the old gods to spare his companion.

Abruptly, a burst of whitewater erupted around the dog. Nanook whined, sensing his doom. Then the great dog vanished into a surge of bloody froth. The black fin rose briefly, then sank away.

Motionless, Jimmy floated on his man-made log, fingers clinging to images of his ancestors' gods: Bear, Eagle, and Orca. Silence loomed over the sea. The ocean had quickly settled, leaving no evidence of the savage attack.

Jimmy felt hot tears flowing down his frozen cheeks. In grief, he rested his forehead against the wood.

The character of the light changed then. Jimmy lifted his face. The darkening skies now blazed an unnatural red. Craning his neck, he saw the source off to the left. A rescue flare high in the sky. And in the glaring brightness, he spotted a Coast Guard cutter gliding through the waters.

He sat up, waving an arm and yelling. "Help!" He fought to keep his balance on the bobbing wood.

A short beep of a horn answered him. Then faint words reached him from a megaphone. "We see you! Stay where you are!"

Lowering his arm, Jimmy settled closer to his pole. He let out a long sigh of relief. Then he sensed it. The presence of something nearby. He turned his head to stare forward.

Another long black dorsal fin surfaced directly in front of

him, its forward edge brushing the end of the wood, nudging it, testing it.

Jimmy slowly pulled his feet from the water.

Then on his left, another fin arose . . . and another. The pod of killer whales slowly circled him. Jimmy knew the cutter would never arrive in time. He was right. Something struck the underside of the totem, jolting it a full yard into the air, and he went flying, fingers scrambling for wood.

He struck the ocean and sank. He was already so cold that he barely felt the icy chill. He opened his eyes under the water, salt burning. In the flare's fiery light, Jimmy saw the huge shadows still circling. He tried not to move, though his frozen lungs screamed for air. He allowed his natural buoyancy to float him toward the surface.

Before he reached the waves, one of the shadows moved nearer. For a moment he stared back into a fist-sized black eye. Then his head broke the surface. Jimmy bent his neck and gasped for a breath of air.

The Coast Guard cutter bore toward his position at full speed. The crew members must have seen the attack.

Jimmy closed his eyes. Too far.

Something clamped on his legs. No pain, only a fierce tightness. His limbs were too frozen to feel the teeth. As the Coast Guard spotlight swept over him, his body was yanked away, dragged into the depths by the gods of his ancestors.

10:56 P.M. PST (6:56 P.M. local time)
Boeing 747-200B, cruising at 30,000 feet, en route from Guam

In the paneled conference room aboard Air Force One, Jeffrey Hessmire watched the President respond to the worldwide emergency. Gathered around the table were his senior staff and advisors.

"Give me a quick summary, Tom. How extensive were the quakes?"

Secretary of State Elliot, his left arm splinted and carried in a sling, sat to the President's right. Jeffrey noticed the morphine glaze to Tom Elliot's eyes, but the man remained remarkably alert and sharp. One-handed, he shuffled through the ream of printouts atop the table. "It's too early to get any clear answers, but it appears the entire Pacific Rim was affected. Reports are coming in from as far south as New Zealand and as far north as Alaska. Also from Japan and China in the east, and from the entire western coast of Central and South America."

"And the United States? Any further word?"

Tom's face grew grim. "Reports remain chaotic. San Francisco is still experiencing hourly aftershocks. Los Angeles is burning." Tom glanced down at one sheet and seemed unwilling to report what lay there. "The entire Aleutian Island chain of Alaska is gone."

Shocked murmuring rose from around the table.

"Is that possible?" the President asked.

"It's been confirmed by satellite," Tom said softly. "We're also finally getting reports from Hawaii." He glanced up from his pile of papers. "Tidal waves struck the islands forty minutes after the initial quakes. Honolulu is still underwater. The hotels of Waikiki lay toppled like dominoes."

As the litany of tragedies continued, the President's face drained of color; his lips drew in, to tight lines. Jeffrey had never seen President Bishop look so old. "So many dead . . ." Jeffrey heard him mutter under his breath.

Tom finally finished his report, detailing the explosion of a volcanic peak near Seattle. The city lay under three feet of ash.

"The Ring of Fire," Jeffrey whispered to himself. He was overheard.

President Bishop turned to him. "What was that, Mr. Hessmire?"

Jeffrey found all eyes turning to him. "Th-The Pacific Rim has also been nicknamed the Ring of Fire, because of its extensive geological activity—earthquakes, volcanic eruptions."

The President nodded, swinging back to Tom. "Yes, but why now? Why so suddenly? What triggered this geologic explosion throughout the Pacific?"

Tom shook his head. "We're still a long way from investigating that question. Right now we must dig our country out of the rubble. The Joint Chiefs and Cabinet are convening by order of the Vice President. The Office of Emergency Services is at full alert. They just await our instructions."

"Then let's get to work, gentlemen," the President began. "We've—"

The plane bucked under them. Several members of the staff were thrown from their seats. The President kept his place.

"What the hell was that?" Tom swore.

As if hearing him, the captain came on the intercom. "Sorry for that little bump, but we've run into some unexpected turbulence. We . . . we may be in for a rough ride. Please secure your seat belts."

Jeffrey heard the false cheer in the pilot's voice. Worry rang behind his words. The President, whose eyes were narrowed, glanced at Tom.

"I'll check on it." Tom began to unbuckle his seat belt.

The President put a hand on Tom's injured arm, restraining him. He turned instead to Jeffrey and motioned to a member of his security team. "You boys have better legs than us old men."

Jeffrey unsnapped his seat buckle. "Of course." He stood and joined the blue-suited Secret Service agent at the door.

Together they left the conference room and worked their way forward, past the President's suite of private rooms and toward the cockpit of the Boeing 747. As they neared the cockpit door, Jeffrey caught a flash of brilliance from out one of the side windows.

"What was—" he started to ask when the plane tilted savagely.

Jeffrey struck the port bulkhead and crashed to the floor. He felt his eardrums pop. Through the door to the cockpit, he heard frantic yells from among the flight crew, screamed orders, panic.

He pulled himself up, his face pressed to the porthole window. "Oh my God . . ."

11:18 P.M. PST (2:18 A.M. local time)
Air Mobility Command, Andrews Air Force Base, Maryland

Tech Sergeant Mitch Clemens grabbed the red phone above his bank of radar screens. He keyed in for the hard-link scrambled and coded to the base commander. With Andrews on full alert, the phone was answered immediately.

"Yes?"

"Sir, we have a problem."

"What is it?"

Sweating, Mitch Clemens stared at his monitor, at the aircraft designation VC-25A. Normally it glowed a bright yellow on the screen. It now blinked. Red.

The tech sergeant's voice trembled. "We've lost Air Force One."

1

Nautilus

Jack Kirkland had missed the eclipse.

Where he glided, there was no sun, only the perpetual darkness of the ocean's abysmal deep. The sole illumination came from a pair of xenon lamps set in the nose of his one-man submersible. His new toy, the *Nautilus 2000*, was out on its first deep-dive test. The eight-foot titanium minisub was shaped like a fat torpedo topped by an acrylic plastic dome. Attached to its underside was a stainless steel frame that mounted the battery pods, thruster assembly, electrical can, and lights.

Ahead, the brilliance of the twin lamps drilled a cone of visibility that extended a hundred feet in front of him. He fingered the controls, sweeping the arc back and forth, searching. Out the corner of his eye he checked the analog depth gauge. Approaching fifteen hundred feet. The bottom of the trench must be close. His sonar reading on the computer screen confirmed his assessment. No more than two fathoms. The pings of the sonar grew closer and closer.

Seated, Jack's head and shoulders protruded into the acrylic plastic dome of the hull, giving him a panoramic view of his surroundings. While the cabin was spacious for most men, it was a tight fit for Jack's six-foot-plus frame. It's like driving an MG convertible, he thought, except you steer with your toes.

The two foot pedals in the main hull controlled not only acceleration, but also maneuvered the four one-horsepower thrusters. With practiced skill Jack eased the right pedal while depressing the toe of the left pedal. The craft dove smoothly to the left. Lights swept forward. Ahead, the seabed came into view, appearing out of the endless gloom.

Jack slowed his vehicle to a gentle glide as he entered a natural wonderland, a deep ocean oasis.

Under him, fields of tubeworms lay spread across the valley floor of the mid-Pacific mountain range. *Riftia pachyptila*. The clusters of six-foot-long tubes with their bloodred worms were like an otherworldly topiary waving at him as he passed, gently swaying in the current. To either side, on the lower slopes, giant clams lay stacked shell-to-shell, open, soft fronds filtering the sea. Among them stalked bright red galatheid crabs on long, spindly legs.

Movement drew Jack's attention forward. A thick eyeless eel slithered past, teeth bright in the xenon lamp. A school of curious fish followed next, led by a large brown lantern fish. The brazen fellow swam right up to the glass bubble, a deep-sea gargoyle ogling the strange intruder inside. Minuscule bioluminescent lights winked along the large fish's sides, announcing its territorial aggression.

Other denizens displayed their lights. Under him, pink pulses ran through tangles of bamboo coral. Around the dome, tiny blue-green lights flashed, the creatures too small and translucent to be seen clearly.

The sight reminded Jack of flurries of fireflies from his Tennessee childhood. Having lived all his young life in land-locked Tennessee, Jack had instantly fallen in love with the ocean, enthralled by its wide expanses, its endless blue, its changing moods.

A swirl of lights swarmed around the dome.

"Unbelievable," he muttered to himself, wearing a wide grin. Even after all this time, the sea found ways to surprise him.

In response, his radio earpiece buzzed. "What was that, Jack?"

Frowning, Jack silently cursed the throat microphone taped under his larynx. Even fifteen hundred feet under the sea, he could not completely shut out the world above. "Nothing, Lisa," he answered. "Just admiring the view."

"How's the new sub handling?"

"Perfectly. Are you receiving the Bio-Sensor readings?" Jack asked, touching the clip on his earlobe. The laser spectrometer built into the clip constantly monitored his blood-gas levels.

Dr. Lisa Cummings had garnered a National Science Foundation grant to study the physiological effects of deep-sea work. "Respiration, temperature, cabin pressure, oxygen supply, ballast, carbon dioxide scrubbers. All green up here. Any evidence of seismic activity?"

"No. All quiet."

Two hours ago, as Jack had first begun his descent in the *Nautilus*, Charlie Mollier, the geologist, had reported strange seismic readings, harmonic vibrations radiating through the deep-sea mountain range. For safety's sake he had suggested that Jack return to the surface. "Come watch the eclipse with us," Charlie had radioed earlier in his Jamaican accent. "It's spectacular, *mon*. We can always dive tomorrow."

Jack had refused. He had no interest in the eclipse. If the quakes worsened, he could always surface. But during the long descent, the strange seismic readings had faded away. Charlie's voice over the radio had eventually lost its strained edge.

Jack touched his throat mike. "So you all done worrying up there?"

A pause was followed by a reluctant "Yes."

Jack imagined the blond doctor rolling her eyes. "Thanks, Lisa. Signing off. Time for a little privacy." He yanked the Bio-Sensor clip from his earlobe.

It was a small victory. The remainder of the Bio-Sensor system would continue to report on the sub's environmental status, but not his personal information. At least it gave him a bit of isolation from the world above—and this was what Jack liked best about diving. The isolation, the peace, the quiet. Here there was only the moment. Lost in the deep, his past had no power to haunt him.

From the sub's speakers the strange noises of the abysmal deep echoed through the small space: a chorus of eerie pulses, chirps, and high-frequency squeals. It was like listening in on another planet.

Around him was a world deadly to surface dwellers: endless darkness, crushing pressures, toxic waters. But life somehow found a way to thrive here, fed not by sunlight, but by poisonous clouds of hydrogen sulfide that spewed from hot vents called "black smokers."

Jack glided near one of these vents now. It was a thirty-meter-tall chimney stack, belching dark clouds of mineral-rich boiling waters from its top. As he passed, white clouds of bacteria were disturbed by his thrusters, creating a mini-blizzard behind him. These microorganisms were the basis for life here, microscopic engines that converted hydrogen sulfide into energy.

Jack gave the chimney a wide berth. Still, as his sub slid past he watched the external temperature readings climb quickly. The vents themselves could reach temperatures over seven hundred degrees Fahrenheit, hot enough, he knew, to parboil him in his little sub.

"Jack?" The worried voice of the team's medical doctor again whispered in his ear. She must have noticed the temperature changes.

"Just a smoker. Nothing to worry about," he answered.

Using the foot pedals, he eased the minisub past the chimney stack and continued on a gentle dive, following the trench floor. Though life down here fascinated him, Jack had a more important objective than just admiring the view.

For the past year, he and his team aboard the *Deep Fathom* had been hunting for the wreck of the *Kochi Maru*, a Japanese freighter lost during WWII. Their research into its manifest suggested the ship bore a large shipment of gold bullion, spoils of war. From studying navigation and weather maps, Jack had narrowed the search to ten square nautical miles of the Central Pacific mountain range. It had been a long shot, a gamble that after a year had not looked like it was going to pay off—until yesterday, when their sonar had picked up a suspicious shadow on the ocean's bottom.

Jack was chasing that shadow now. He glanced at the sub's computer. It fed him sonar data from his boat far overhead. Whatever had cast that shadow was about a hundred yards from his current position. He flipped on his own side-scanning sonar to monitor the bed's terrain as he moved closer.

A ridge of rock appeared out of the gloom. He worked the pedals and swerved in a wide arc around the obstruction. The abundant sea life began to dissipate, the oasis vanishing behind him. Ahead, the seabed floor became a stretch of empty silt. His thrusters wafted up plumes as he passed. *Like driving down a dusty back road.*

Jack circled the spur of rock. Ahead, another ridge appeared, a foothill in the Central Pacific range. It blocked his progress. He pulled the sub to a hovering halt and released a bit of ballast, meaning to climb over the ridge. As he began to drift upward, a slight current caught his sub, dragging him forward. Jack fought the current with his thrusters, stabilizing his craft. *What the hell?* He nudged the craft forward, skirting toward the top of the ridge.

"Jack," Lisa whispered in his ear again, "are you passing another smoker chimney? I'm reading warmer temperatures."

"No, but I'm not sure what—Son of a bitch!" His sub had crested the ridge. He saw what lay on the far side.

"What is it, Jack?" Fear quavered in Lisa's voice. "Are you okay?"

Beyond the ridge a new valley opened up, but this was no oasis of life. Ahead was a hellish landscape. Glowing cracks crisscrossed the sea floor. Molten rock flowed forth, shadowy crimson in the gloom as it quickly cooled. Tiny bubbles obscured the view. Jack fought the thermal current. The flow kept trying to roll him forward. From the hydrophone's speakers a steady roar arose.

"My God . . ."

"Jack, what did you find? The temp readings are climbing rapidly."

He needed no instruments to tell him that. The interior of the sub grew warmer with each breath. "It's a new vent opening."

A second voice came on the horn. It was Charlie, the geologist. "Careful, Jack, I'm still picking up weak surges from down there. It's far from stable."

"I'm not leaving yet."

"You shouldn't risk—"

Jack interrupted, "I've found the *Kochi Maru.*"

"What?"

"The ship is here . . . but I don't know for how long." As the sub hovered atop the ridge, Jack stared out the acrylic dome. On the far side of the hellish valley lay the wreck of a long trawler, its hull cracked into two sections. In the dull glow, the shattered windows of the pilothouse stared back at him. On the bow were printed black Japanese letters. He was well-familiar with the name: KOCHI MARU. Spring Wind.

But the name no longer fit the wreck.

Around the ship, molten rock welled and flowed, forming ribbons and pools of magma, steaming as it quickly cooled in the frigid depths. The forward half of the ship lay directly over one of the vents. Jack watched as the steel ship began to sink, melting into the magma.

"It's smack dab in the middle of hell," Jack reported. "I'm gonna get a closer look."

"Jack . . ." It was Lisa again, her voice hard with a pending command. But she hesitated. She knew him too well. A long sigh followed. "Just keep a watch on the external temp readings. Titanium isn't impervious to extreme temperatures. Especially the seals—"

"I understand. No unnecessary risks." Jack pushed both foot pedals. The sub shot off the ridge, climbing higher at the same time. As he glided toward the wreck, he watched the temperature continue to rise.

Seventy-five . . . one hundred . . . 110 . . .

Sweat pebbled Jack's forehead and his hands grew slick. If one of the sub's seals should weaken and break, the crushing weight at this depth would kill him in less than a second.

He climbed higher, until the temperature dropped below a hundred again. Satisfied he was safe, he goosed the sub, passing over the valley. Soon he hovered over the wreck itself. Tilting the sub on its side, he circled the broken ship.

Leaning a bit, Jack stared down at the wreck. From this vantage point, he could see the broken stern resting a full fifty yards from the bow. The hollow cavity of the rear hold was turned away from the vents. Across the silt, lit by the fiery glow of the nearby vents, lay a scattering of crates, half buried, wood long turned to black from the decades it was submerged.

"How's it looking, Jack?" Lisa asked.

Narrowing his eyes, he studied the spilled contents of the wreck. "Ain't pretty, that's for damn sure."

After a studied pause, Lisa came back on. "Well . . . ?"

"I don't know. I mortgaged the ship and the old family ranch to finance this trip. To come up empty-handed—"

"I know, but all the gold in the world's not worth your life."

He could not argue with that. Still, he loved the old homestead: the rolling green hills, the whitewashed fences. He had inherited the hundred-acre ranch after his father died of pancreatic cancer. Jack had been only twenty-one. The debts had forced him out of the University of Tennessee and into the Armed Services. Though he could have sold the place and finished school, he had refused. The land had been in the family for five generations—but truthfully it was more personal than that. By the time his father had passed away, his mother was already long in her grave, succumbing to complications from a simple appendectomy when he was a boy, leaving no other children. Jack hardly remembered her, just pictures on the wall and a handful of memories tied to the place. No matter what, he refused to lose even these slim memories to the bank.

Lisa interrupted his reverie. "I could always try extending

my NSF grant and scrounge up more funds." It was her government money that had allowed them to lease the *Nautilus* and test its patented Bio-Sensor system.

"It won't be enough," Jack grumbled. Secretly he had hoped to garner sufficient funds from a successful haul here to clear his debts, with a stash left over to finance a lifetime of treasure hunting.

That is, if the *Kochi Maru*'s manifests were accurate. . . .

Jack ignored caution and obeyed his heart. He shoved both foot pedals. The submersible dove in a tight spiral down toward the broken stern of the *Kochi Maru*. What would it hurt to take a fast peek?

The temperature gauge began to climb again: *110 . . . 120 . . . 130 . . .*

He stopped looking.

"Jack . . . the readings . . ."

"I know. I'm just going to take a closer look at the ship. No risks."

"At least replace your Bio-Sensor clip so I can monitor you."

Jack wiped sweat from his eyes and sighed. "Okay, Mother." He slipped the sensor to his earlobe. "Happy now?"

"Ecstatic. Now don't kill yourself."

Jack heard the worry behind her light words. "Just keep one of those Heinekens in the cooler for me."

"Will do."

As he neared the seabed, Jack lowered the sub behind the wreck's stern and edged toward the open rear hold. The giant prop and screw dwarfed his vehicle. Even here life thrived. The old hull, draped in runnels of rust, had become an artificial reef for mussels and coral.

Clearing the keel, he spun the sub and aimed his lights into the hold. He glanced at the temperature reading. *One forty*. At least the rising heat had stabilized in the shadow of the ship's bulk. Beyond the dark ship, the seas radiated a fierce crimson, as if an abysmal sun were rising nearby. Jack ignored the heat, his back and seat now slick in his neoprene suit.

Lifting the sub's nose, he pointed the xenon lamps into the heart of the dark hold. Two large eyes glared back at him from the hold's cavern.

His heart jumped. "What the hell . . . ?"

Then the monster was upon him. It sprang out of its manmade den. Long, sinuous, silver. The sea serpent shot toward him. Mouth open in a silent scream of rage.

Jack gasped, scrambling for the controls to the sub's hydraulic manipulator arms. He waved the titanium arms, trying to defend himself, but mostly just flailing in his shock.

At the last moment the creature shied from his frantic waving and flashed past him. Jack watched its long silver-scaled body rush past like a sinewy locomotive. It had to be at least seventy feet long. His tiny craft was buffeted by the creature's passage, spinning in place.

Jack craned his neck around and watched the creature flee, disappearing into the midnight waters with a flick of its tapering tail. Now he recognized it for what it was. A rare beast, but no serpent. It had clearly been as spooked by the chance encounter as he was. Jack forced his heart out of his throat, swallowing hard. "Goddamn!" he swore as he stabilized the sub, spinning in the creature's wake. "Whoever said there are no sea monsters?"

Static rasped in his ear. "Sea monsters?" It was Lisa again. "An orefish," he explained.

"God, your heart rate almost doubled! You must have—"

A new voice interrupted the doctor. It was Robert Bonaczek, the group's marine biologist. "An orefish? *Regalecus glesne*?" he asked, using the fish's Latin name. "Are you sure?"

"Yep, a big one. Seventy feet if it's an inch."

"Did you get any pictures?"

Jack blushed, remembering his panic. As a former Navy SEAL, he knew his response to being attacked by a deep-sea monster had been less than heroic. He wiped his damp forehead. "No . . . uh, there was not enough time."

"A shame. So little is known. No one suspected they lived so deep."

"Well, this one was living large, that's for damn sure.

Made its home in the hold of the wreck." Jack moved his ship forward, lights again delving into the interior. Crates lay stacked and broken everywhere. The *Kochi Maru* had been heavily laden. Jack spotted where the orefish had nested. A cleared-out cubby near the back. Carefully, he eased his sub into the open hold.

Static buzzed in his ear. "Jack, I'm . . . don't know, *mon* . . ." Jack recognized the geologist's voice, but the transmission was blocked by the walls of the hold as the sub glided inside. It seemed even the vessel's patented deep-water radio could not pierce three inches of iron.

Jack touched his throat mike. "Say again."

He received just static and garble.

Frowning, he eased off the thruster pedals, meaning to retreat clear of the hold's walls. Then his eyes caught a bright glint from deeper in the hold. He glided the craft gently forward, nose down. His lamps now splayed the floor.

Amid the crates, against the far wall, was a sight that drew a sharp whistle from him. The swipe of the orefish's tail as it lunged from its nest had brushed free a few bricks, black with algae, from the top of an impressive pile. The exposed section revealed the bricks deeper in the pile.

Gold, shining brighter than a Caribbean sun in the reflection of the xenon lamps.

Jack inched closer, not believing his luck. Once in range, he settled his hands on the controls to the external hydraulic manipulator arms. Having practiced at length, he was familiar with their use. Manning the controls, he extended the left arm's pincers to their full length of fifteen feet. He gripped one of the black bricks, bringing it up to the light. With the other arm, he carefully scraped the surface.

"Gold." There was no doubt. He grinned widely and used the other arm to grab another brick, then tapped his throat mike. He had to tell topside. Static squelched sharply. He had forgotten about the interference by the hull. He backed the sub slowly, careful not to get hung up on the debris, meanwhile running through several different salvage scenarios. Float bags wouldn't work. They'd have to hook a dredge to the sub and make a few hauls.

The sub finally cleared the hold and reentered open water. He was instantly assaulted by someone yelling in his ear. "Get out of there, mon! Now! Jack, get your ass away from there!" It was Charlie. Panicked.

"What is it?" Jack yelled back. He glanced at the external temperature reading. It had climbed almost fifty degrees. In the fever of discovering the gold, he had failed to notice the rising temperature. "Oh shit!"

"The seismic readings are spiking, Jack. Radiating out from your location. Haul ass! You're sitting on the goddamn epicenter!"

Jack's Navy training kicked in. He knew when to obey orders. He swung the submersible up and away, chasing after cooler waters, pushing the *Nautilus* to its maximum speed of four knots. Jack craned his neck around. "Damn."

The forward section of the *Kochi Maru* had melted halfway into the magma pool. The crisscrossing of magma cracks had widened. But the most ominous sight was how the seabed now bulged, like a bubble about to burst.

Jack had both pedals to the floor, jerking the nose of the submersible toward the distant surface. He blew all his ballast. The thruster motors whined as he pushed them to the extreme.

"Damn, damn, damn . . ." he swore in a continuous litany.

"Jack, something's happening. The readings are—"

He heard it before he felt it. A monstrous roaring from the hydrophones, like thunder rolling through hills. Then the sub caught the shockwave's edge, tumbling end over end.

Jack's head struck the optical acrylic dome. As he spun he caught fleeting glimpses of the seabed.

A flaming wound gaped below him. Magma blew forth, spattering upward. A volcano had opened directly under him. As he flew upward, spinning without control, the seas around him began to boil. Bubbles as big as his sub bombarded his ship, striking like fists.

He fought the thrusters to maintain some semblance of direction, but was shaken and jarred about. He tasted blood on his tongue. He tried to raise the *Deep Fathom*, yelling. But static was his only response.

For what seemed an endless time he rode the chain of bubbles toward the surface, fighting for control of the sub. He had to get clear of the volcanic stream. As his ship tumbled, an idea came to him. To survive a riptide a swimmer had to stop fighting it.

He lifted his foot off the right pedal and tapped only the left thrusters. Instead of trying to stop his spin, he made the vehicle spin faster. He was soon pinned to the port side of the sub by the centrifugal forces. Still, he kept engaging just the left thrusters. "C'mon . . . c'mon . . ."

Then one of the monster bubbles struck the undercarriage of the submersible. The spinning sub tilted nose-up. The sudden shift pitched the craft end over. Like a skipping stone, the *Nautilus* shot free of the bubble stream.

As the sub's tumble slowed, Jack pulled himself back into his seat. His feet worked the pedals and halted the spin. Sighing in relief, he aimed for the surface, noting that the midnight waters had already lightened to a weak twilight. Craning his neck upward, he saw the vague glow of the distant sun.

The static in his ear cleared. "Jack . . . answer us . . . can you hear us?"

Jack replaced the throat mike. The adhesive had torn away during his assault. "All clear here," he said harshly.

"Jack!" The relief in Lisa's voice was like a cool spray of water. "Where are you?"

He checked the depth gauge. *Two hundred twenty feet.* He couldn't believe his rate of ascent. It was lucky his sub was a sealed one-atmosphere vehicle, maintaining a constant internal pressure. If not, he would have died of the bends before now. "I'll be surfacing in about three minutes."

Glancing at his compass, Jack frowned. The needle spun around as if still dizzy from the tumble. He tapped at it, but the needle continued to spin. He gave up and touched his mike. "Compass is fried. Not sure how far off I am, but once up, I'll hit the GPS beacon so you can track me."

"And what about you? Are you okay?"

"Just bruised and battered."

Charlie came on the line. "For someone who just survived a volcanic eruption under the seat of his pants, you are damn lucky, *mon*. I wish I could've seen it."

Jack grinned. The birth of an undersea volcano was surely a geologist's wet dream. Jack fingered the hard knot atop his head, wincing. "Believe me, Charlie, I wish you had been here instead of me, too."

Around Jack, the waters grew from a deep purple to a lighter aquamarine. "Coming up," he said.

"What about the *Kochi Maru*?" a new voice asked, hopeful. Jack was surprised to hear from Professor George Klein, the ship's historian and cartographer. The professor seldom left the *Deep Fathom*'s extensive library.

Jack suppressed a groan. "Sorry, Doc. She's gone . . . so is the gold."

With disappointment, George finally responded, "Well, we can't even be certain the *Kochi Maru*'s manifests were accurate. During the war, the Japanese often falsified records to mask their gold shipments."

Jack pictured the tall pile of bricks. "It was accurate," he said gloomily.

Charlie came back on the line. "Hey, Jack, it seems you were not the only one shaken up. Reports are coming in from all over. Earthquakes and eruptions have been rattling the entire Pacific, coast-to-coast."

Jack frowned. What did he care? Since leaving the world behind twelve years ago, he had little interest in the rest of the planet. All that mattered was this single eruption. It had cost him not only a huge fortune, but possibly even his ship. "Signing off," he said with a long sigh. "Be topside in one minute."

He watched the water grow lighter. Soon the bubble of his dome broke the surface. The brightness of the afternoon sun stung. He shaded his eyes. Off to the west, the seas burbled with steaming bubbles, marking the site of the undersea volcano. But off to the southeast, he spotted a dark blip. The *Deep Fathom*.

He hit the distress beacon, activating the GPS locator, then leaned back to wait. As he stared out over the water, a glint caught his eye. Curious, he sat up straighter. He reached and fingered the RMS controls to lift the two external arms. As they were raised, seawater dripped from the titanium limbs.

Jack sat straighter, bumping his head again. "It can't be. . . ."

Sunlight shone brightly off two large bricks, one clamped in each pincer. He'd forgotten about grabbing them before fleeing the hold of the *Kochi Maru*. The gold bars had been scrubbed clean by the rough flight to the surface, but luckily, they had remained clamped in the hydraulic grips.

He whistled appreciatively. "Things are suddenly looking brighter."

George's voice came on the line again. "Jack, we've got your GPS signal."

"That's great!" Jack said, jubilant, barely hearing the words. "And make sure you have the champagne chilled!"

George's response was clearly puzzled. "Oh . . . okay . . . but I thought you should know we just received a call on the Globalstar."

Jack sobered, sensing an undercurrent of tension. "Who's calling?"

A long pause. "Admiral Mark Houston."

Jack felt as if he'd been slugged in the stomach. His former naval commander. "Wh-What? Why?" He had hoped never to hear that name again. He had put that life behind him.

"He's ordered us to a set of coordinates. About four hundred nautical miles from here, and—"

Jack clenched his fists, interrupting. "Ordered us? Tell him to take his order and shove it up—"

Now George interrupted. "There's been a plane crash. A rescue operation is being gathered."

Jack bit his lip. It was the Navy's right to ask for his aid. The *Deep Fathom* was a registered salvage ship. Still, Jack found his hands trembling.

Old memories and emotions flared brighter. He remembered his awe at seeing the shuttle *Atlantis* shining brightly in the Florida sunshine, and the pride he felt upon learning he would be the first Navy SEAL to fly in that bird. But shadowing these pleasant memories were darker ones: flames, searing pain . . . a gloved hand reaching for him, voices screaming . . . slipping, tumbling . . . an endless fall.

Seated in the *Nautilus*, Jack felt as if he were still falling.

"Did you hear me, Jack?"

Shaking, he could not breathe, let alone answer.

"Jack, the plane that crashed . . . it's Air Force One."

2

Dragons of Okinawa

Crouching behind an alley trash bin, Karen Grace tried her best to avoid the military patrol. As she hid, two armed servicemen sauntered into view, flashlights in hand. One of them stopped to light a cigarette. Holding her breath, Karen prayed for them to pass. In the light of the match, she noticed the insignia on a sleeve. U.S. NAVY.

After yesterday's earthquakes, a state of martial law had been declared throughout the prefectures of Japan, including the southern island chain of Okinawa. Looters had been plaguing the city and outlying areas. The island leaders, overwhelmed by the level of destruction and chaos, had requested support from the local American military bases, to aid in clean-up, rescue, and protection of the damaged city.

The city's leaders had set a curfew for Naha from dusk to dawn, and Karen was breaking that new law. The sun was still a half hour from rising.

Move . . . keep walking, she silently urged them.

As if hearing her, one of the men raised his flashlight and

shone it down the alley. Karen froze, closing her eyes, afraid any movement would draw his attention. She wore an embroidered dark jacket and black slacks, but she wished she had thought to cover her blond hair. She felt exposed, sure the two servicemen would spot her. At last the light vanished.

Karen opened her eyes. A mumble followed by a bark of laughter echoed back to her. A crude joke. The pair continued on their patrol. Relieved, she sagged against the metal Dumpster.

From deeper in the shadows a voice whispered at her, "Are they gone?"

Karen pushed up from her knees. "Yeah, but that was too close."

"We shouldn't be doing this," her accomplice hissed, climbing out of the shadows.

Karen helped Miyuki Nakano up. Her friend swore under her breath, convincingly, considering English was Miyuki's second language. On leave from her Japanese university professorship, Miyuki had worked for two years at a Palo Alto Internet firm and had grown fluent in English. But the petite teacher was clearly out of place here as she crawled from under a pile of old newspapers and rotted vegetables. Miyuki seldom left her pristine computer lab at Ryukyu University, and was rarely spotted without her starched and pressed lab coat.

But not this morning.

Miyuki wore a dark red blouse and black jeans, both now prominently stained. Her ebony hair was tied back into a conservative ponytail. She plucked a spinach leaf from her blouse and flung it away in disgust. "If you weren't my best friend—"

"I know . . . and I apologize for the hundredth time." Karen turned away. "But, Miyuki, you didn't have to come along."

"And leave you to venture through Naha alone, meeting with who knows what manner of scoundrel? It's just not safe."

Karen nodded. At least this last statement was true.

Sirens echoed throughout the ravaged city. Searchlights from temporary camps cast beacons into the night skies. Though the curfew had been ordered, shouts and gunfire could be heard all around. Karen had not expected to find the city in such chaos.

Miyuki continued to complain about their predicament. "Who knows what type of men will be waiting for us? White slavers? Drug smugglers?"

"It's only one of the local fishermen. Samo vouched for the man."

"And you trust a senile janitor's word?"

Karen rolled her eyes. Miyuki could worry a hole through tempered steel. "Samo is anything but senile. If he says this fisherman can take us to see the Dragons, then I trust him." She lifted the edge of her jacket to reveal a black leather shoulder harness. "And besides, I have this." The .38 automatic fit snugly under her arm.

Miyuki's eyes widened. Her skin lost a touch of its rich complexion. "Carrying a gun is against Japanese law. Where did you—"

"At times like this, a girl needs a little extra protection." Karen crept to the alley's entrance. She glanced down the street. "It's all clear."

Miyuki slid beside her, hiding in her shadow.

"C'mon." Karen led the way, excited and anxious at the same time. She glanced to the skies. True dawn was still about an hour away. Time was running short. Curfew or not, she was determined not to miss the rendezvous. This was a once-in-a-lifetime opportunity.

Three years ago she had traveled all the way from British Columbia to study at Ryukyu University and complete her doctoral thesis on Micronesian cultures, searching for clues to the origins and migration patterns of the early Polynesians. While studying here, Karen heard tales of the Dragons of Okinawa, a pair of submerged pyramids discovered in 1991 off the island's coast by a geology professor at Ryukyu, Kimura Masaaki. He had compared the pyramids to those found at ancient Mayan sites in Central America.

Karen had been skeptical—until she saw the photographs: two stepped pyramids with terraced tops rising twenty meters from the sandy sea floor. She was instantly captivated. Was there some ancient connection between the Mayans and the Polynesians? Throughout the last decade new, submerged structures continued to be discovered in the waters off neighboring islands, trailing as far south as Taiwan. Soon it became hard to separate fact from fiction, natural topography from man-made structure.

And now the newest rumor floating among the fisher folk of the Ryukyu island chain: *the Dragons had risen from the sea!*

Whether this was true or not, Karen could not pass up the opportunity to explore the pyramids firsthand. A local fisherman, scheduled to transport medical supplies and other aid to outlying islands, had offered to take her to see the structures. But he planned on sailing at dawn, with or without her. Hence, the early morning bike ride from the university to the outskirts of Naha, then the game of cat and mouse with police and patrols.

Karen continued along the street. It felt good to be moving again. The morning sea breeze tousled her loose blond hair as she walked swiftly. Using her fingers, she combed the stray locks from her face. If the two women were caught, both risked expulsion from the university. Well, maybe not Miyuki, Karen thought. Her friend was one of the most published and awarded professors on the campus. She had accolades from around the world, and was the first woman nominated for the Nobel Prize in computer science. So Karen had not argued against Miyuki coming along. If the pair were caught, Miyuki's notoriety on the island might soften any legal repercussions for her as well.

Or so she hoped.

Karen checked her watch. It would be close. At least the roads through here were relatively clear. This section of the city had survived the quakes mostly unscathed: broken windows, cracked foundations, and a few scorched buildings. Meager damage when compared to other districts, which had been leveled to brick foundations and twisted metal.

"We'll never make it in time," Miyuki said, cinching her

photo bag higher up her shoulder. Though Karen had pocketed a disposable Kodak camera in her jacket, Miyuki had insisted on bringing full gear: digital and Polaroid cameras, video equipment, even a Palm handheld computer. All stuffed into a promotional bag stenciled with the logo from *Time* magazine.

Karen took the bag from her friend and slung it over her own shoulder. "Yes, we will." She increased the pace.

Miyuki, a head smaller, had to jog to keep up.

They hurried to the end of the street. Naha Bay was only a hundred yards down the next avenue. Karen peeked around the corner. The street lay empty. She continued with Miyuki trailing. The smell of the sea grew stronger: salt and algae. Soon she saw lights shining off the bay. Encouraged, Karen continued at a half run.

As she neared the end of the street a harsh command startled her. "*Yobitomeru!* Halt!" She froze as the bright beam of a flashlight blinded her.

A dark figure stepped forth from the shadows between two buildings. The light lowered enough for Karen to recognize the uniform of a United States sailor. He cast the beam briefly at Miyuki, then searched up and down the street. A second and third sailor stepped from their shelter in a building entryway. The group was clearly one of the American wandering patrols.

The first sailor stepped nearer. "Do you speak English?"

"Yes," Karen answered.

He relaxed slightly, flashlight now pointing toward the street. "American?"

Karen frowned. She was used to this response. "Canadian."

The sailor nodded. "Same thing," he muttered, and gestured his companions to continue down the street. "I'm heading back to base," he said to them. "I've got this covered."

Rifles were returned to shoulders, and the other two strode past, but not before glancing up and down the two women's figures. One of the men mumbled something, eliciting a laugh and a final salacious glance toward Miyuki.

Karen ground her teeth. Though not native to this soil, the Navy's casual assumption of control here rankled.

"Ladies, don't you know about the curfew?" the sailor asked them.

Karen feigned confusion. "What curfew?"

The sailor sighed. "It's not safe for two women to be out here alone. I'll walk you back. Where are you staying?"

Karen crinkled her brow, trying to think of an answer. *Time to improvise.* She unslung Miyuki's camera bag and pointed to the large insignia for *Time* on its side. "We're working freelance for the magazine," she said. She pulled out her Ryukyu University identification card and flashed it at the man. It looked official, and the Japanese lettering was clearly unreadable. "Our press credentials have been approved by the local government."

The sailor leaned closer, comparing Karen's face to the card's picture. He nodded as if satisfied, too macho to admit he could not read the Japanese script.

Karen pocketed her card, maintaining an officious attitude. She introduced Miyuki. "This is my local public relation's liaison and photographer. We're gathering pictures throughout the Japanese islands. Our ship leaves at dawn for the outer islands, on its way to Taiwan. We really must hurry."

The sailor still wore a suspicious look. He was close to buying the story, but not completely convinced.

Before Karen could press on, Miyuki reached over and unzipped the bag. She pulled out the digital camera. "Actually, it's somewhat fortunate we ran into you," she said in crisp English. "Ms. Grace was just mentioning how she wanted to try and capture a few of the servicemen on film. Showing how the United States is helping to maintain order in this time of chaos." Miyuki turned to Karen, nodding back at the sailor. "What do you think?"

Karen was shocked by the sudden brazenness of the tiny computer teacher. She cleared her throat, thinking fast. "Uh . . . yes, for the sidebar on the American peacekeepers." Karen tilted her head at the man, her expression thoughtful.

"He does have that all-American look we were searching for."

Miyuki lifted the camera and pointed it at the sailor. "How would you like to have your picture in magazines across the country?"

By now the sailor's eyes had grown large. "Really?"

Karen hid a smile. She did not know a single American who was not enthralled with the mystique of celebrity. And for the opportunity to join such ranks, common sense was often cast aside.

Miyuki stepped around the sailor, eyeing him from several angles. "I can't make any guarantees. It'll be up to the editors at *Time*."

"We'll take a few pictures," Karen said. "One of them will surely pass muster." She framed the man between her fingers, sizing up a shot. "'American peacekeeper' . . . I think this really will work."

Miyuki began to take a few pictures, ordering the sailor into several poses. Once done, she bagged up her camera and collected the serviceman's name and number. "We'll fax you a photo release form. But Harry, we'll need it returned to New York before the end of the week."

The man nodded vigorously. "Of course."

Karen glanced to the brightening skies. "Miyuki, we really must be going. The press ship is scheduled to leave any minute."

"I can take you to the marina. I'm heading toward the bay anyway."

"Thank you, Harry," Miyuki said. "If you can take us as far as Pier Four, that would be wonderful." She smiled brightly at him, then turned to Karen, rolling her eyes. "Let's go. We don't want to be late."

Led by the sailor, they hurried to the bay. The gray dawn cast the waters in dull silver. Gulls dove and screeched among the piers' pilings and boats. Throughout the bay, wrecks dotted the water, ships and boats that had scuttled against the docks and reefs during the quakes. Already, cranes and heavy equipment had been moved into position.

The bay was the lifeline of the island and had to be cleared as quickly as possible.

As the sun crested the eastern sky, they reached the entrance to the marina. Miyuki and Karen again thanked Harry and said their good-byes. Once the sailor left, the two hurried down the long planks.

Karen glanced over her shoulder to make sure the sailor had truly gone. There was no sign of him. She relaxed and turned to Miyuki, who was cinching the camera bag higher on her shoulder. "I can't believe you."

Miyuki smiled, her face flushed. "That was fun. It's lucky I got that free tote bag with my subscription to *Time*."

Both women started laughing, tears at the corners of their eyes.

Karen led the way to berth twelve. Ahead, she spotted a small fishing boat still docked at the berth. The twenty-meter wooden craft was piled high with boxes displaying prominent red crosses. A pair of men were already loosening ropes in preparation for leaving. Karen hurried forward, waving an arm. *"Ueito!"* Wait!

One of the workers glanced their way and yelled to another on the boat. A grizzled Japanese man left the wheel and met them near the ship's stern. He was dressed in Levi's and a green slicker. Offering his hand, he helped them on board.

"S-Samo sent us," Karen said in broken Japanese.

"I know," the old man answered in English. "The American."

"Actually, I'm Canadian," she corrected him.

"Same thing. I must get the ship going. I wait too long already."

Karen nodded and unslung her bag. She and Miyuki were guided to a stained wooden bench beside a folded mat of net. The reek of fish entrails and blood from the wooden planks of the boat almost overpowered her.

Around her, the two-man crew had freed the ropes from the dock and jumped on board. At the wheelhouse, the ship's captain barked orders. The motor roared. Water began to churn, and the boat slowly edged forward. The crewmen took up posts near the bow, one on the starboard, one on the port side, watching the waters ahead. Sunken debris made the bay treacherous.

It was clear why the captain insisted on leaving with the dawn. As the morning tide receded, these waters would become even more treacherous.

Past the pier's end, they sailed toward the center channel of the bay and slowly edged by a pole sticking crookedly up from the water, a flag flapping at its tip. Karen glanced over the rail and realized it was the mast tip from a submerged sailboat. The fishing boat with its shallow draft cut around and over the debris.

Across the bay, the United States military base lay burning. Fires still glowed from the refinery blaze, set off during the quakes as underground tanks had been ripped open. A smudge of oily smoke climbed high into the morning sky. Helicopters circled the area, hauling dredges of seawater and sand in an attempt to stanch the fires. So far with little luck.

A thick-bellied transport plane, military gray, passed low over them, its engine roaring. The fishing boat's captain shook a fist at it. The United States presence here, especially this base, still rankled the locals. Back in 1974 it had been agreed that the land would be returned to the islanders, but that transition had yet to be realized.

Finally, the fishing boat sailed free of the bay and headed toward open water. Clear of the smoke, the breeze freshened. With the open sea all around them, the captain nodded for his first mate to take the wheel, then sauntered over to them. "My name is Oshi," he said. "I take you to Dragons. Then we come back before sun go down."

Karen nodded. "Perfect."

He held out his hand, awaiting payment.

Karen stood and pulled a wad of bills from her jacket's inside pocket. She noticed the fisherman eye her holstered gun. Good. Just so things were clear. She counted out the appropriate number of bills, half the prearranged fee, then returned the rest to her pocket. "The other half when we return to Naha."

The man's face remained hard for a heartbeat, then flashed a quick scowl. He mumbled something in Japanese and shoved the bills into his jeans.

Karen sat back down as he left. "What did he say?"

Miyuki wore a grin. "He says you Americans are all alike. Never stick to your own agreements, so you don't trust anyone else."

"I'm not American," she said in an exasperated voice.

Miyuki patted her knee. "If you speak English, have blond hair, and carelessly throw that much cash around, you're American to him."

Karen tried her best to sulk, but she was too excited. "C'mon. If this American is paying for this excursion, I want better seats."

She stood and led Miyuki toward the bow. They crossed to the forward rail as the boat rounded the southern tip of Okinawa and passed the tiny island of Tokashiki Shima. The Ryukyu chain of islands spread south in an arc almost stretching to Taiwan. The Dragons were located near the island of Yonaguni, an hour's journey but still within Okinawa's prefecture.

One of the sailors bowed his way into their presence. He placed two small porcelain glasses of green tea and a small plate of cakes on a nearby bench.

"*Domo arigato,*" Karen said. She took the tea and let the hot cup warm her hands. Miyuki joined her, nibbling on the edge of a cake. They stared in silence as green islands drifted slowly past. The coral reefs colored the nearby shoals in shades of aquamarine, rose, and emerald.

After a time Miyuki spoke, "What do you really hope to find out there?"

"Answers." Karen leaned on the rail. "You read Professor Masaaki's thesis."

Miyuki nodded. "That once these islands were part of some lost continent, now sunk under the waves. Pretty wild conjecture."

"Not necessarily. During the Holocene era, some ten thousand years ago, the ocean levels were three hundred feet shallower." Karen waved an arm. "If so, many of these separate islands would have been joined."

"Still, you know from your own research that the islands of the South Pacific were populated only a couple thousand years ago. Not ten thousand."

"I know. I'm not saying you're wrong, Miyuki. I just want to see these pyramids for myself." Karen gripped the ship's rail tighter. "But what if I can find proof to support Professor Masaaki's claim? Could you imagine what this revelation would mean? It would change the entire historical paradigm for this region. It would unite so many disparate theories—" She hesitated, then continued. "—even explain the mystery of the lost continent of Mu."

Miyuki crinkled her nose. "Mu?"

Karen nodded. "Back in the early 1900s Colonel James Churchward claimed he had stumbled upon a set of Mayan tablets that spoke of a lost continent, similar to Atlantis, but in the central Pacific. He named this sunken continent Mu. He wrote a whole series of books and essays about the place . . . until he was discredited."

"Discredited?"

Karen shrugged. "No one believed my great-grandfather."

Miyuki's brows rose, her voice shocked. "Your great-grandfather!"

Karen felt a blush blooming. She had never explained this to anyone. She spoke softly, embarrassed. "Colonel Churchward was my great-grandfather on my mother's side. When I was a child, my mother used to tell me stories of our infamous ancestor . . . even read sections from his diaries to me at bedtime. His stories first drew me to the South Pacific."

"And you think the Dragons might prove your relative's wild claim?"

Karen shrugged. "Who knows?"

"I still say this is all a wild goose chase."

Karen shrugged. Wild goose chases? They ran in her family, she thought sourly. Twenty years ago her father had left his wife and baby girls to chase the dream of oil and wealth in Alaska, never to be heard from again—except for a sheaf of divorce papers arriving in the mail a year later. After his disappearance, hardships drained the life from the remaining household. Her mother, abandoned with her two young daughters, had no more time for dreams and worked herself into a dull job at a secretarial pool and an even duller second marriage. Karen's older sister, Emily, had moved to the small town of Moose Jaw after graduating from high school, her belly full of twin boys.

Karen, however, had inherited too much of her father's wanderlust to settle down. Between tips as a waitress at the Flying Trout Grill and a few small scholarships, she was able to put herself through an undergraduate program at the University of Toronto, followed by graduate work in British Columbia. So it was no particular surprise to those who knew her that Karen Grace had ended up on the far side of the Pacific. Still, she had learned from her father's abandonment—each month she mailed a chunk of her paycheck back home to her mother. Though she may have inherited her father's blood, she didn't have to accept his cold heart.

A call from the wheelhouse drew her attention. *"Yonaguni!"* the captain yelled above the motor's roar. He pointed off the port side to a large island. The fishing boat made a wide turn around the isle's southern coast.

"This is the place," Karen said, shading her eyes with a hand. "The island of Yonaguni."

"I don't see anything. Are you—"

Then from around the high cliffs of the island, they appeared, no more than a hundred meters off the coastline, shrouded in morning sea mists: two pyramids, towering above the waves, their terraced sides damp with algae. As the boat drew closer, details emerged. Among the pyramids' steps, white cranes clambered, picking stranded urchins and crabs from the debris.

"They're *real*," Karen said.

"That's not all," Miyuki said, her voice full of awe.

As the small boat continued to circle around the island, the deeper mists parted and the view opened wider. Past the pyramids, rows of coral-encrusted columns and roofless buildings rode above the waves. In the distance a basalt statue of a robed woman stood waist-deep in the sea, draped in seaweed, a stone arm raised as if calling for their aid. Farther yet, piles of tumbled bricks and cracked stone obelisks marched deep into the Pacific.

"My God," Karen exclaimed in shock.

Along with the Dragons, an entire ancient city had risen from the sea.

3

Wreckage

On the bridge of the *Deep Fathom*, Jack lounged in the pilot's chair, sprawled out, his bare feet propped up on a neighboring seat. He wore a white cotton robe over a pair of red Nike swim trunks. The morning had started warm and had only grown warmer. Though the pilothouse was equipped with air-conditioning, Jack hadn't bothered. He enjoyed the moist heat.

As he sat, one hand rested on the wheel of the ship. The *Fathom* had been on autopilot since it left the site of the sunken *Kochi Maru* yesterday, but Jack felt a certain comfort with his hand on the wheel. A twinge of mistrust for automated equipment. He liked to keep things in his immediate control.

As he sat, he chewed on the end of the cigar hanging from his lips. A Cuban El Presidente. The smoke trailed in a lazy circle toward the open window nearby. Behind him, Mozart's Clarinet Concerto in A Major wafted gently from a

Sony CD player. This was all he wanted: the open sea and a handsome ship to travel her.

But that was not to be. Not today.

Jack glanced at the reading from the Northstar 800 GPS. At their current cruising speed they should arrive at their destination in another three hours.

Exhaling out a stream of smoke, he stared out the windows across the upper deck of his salvage ship. He understood why his ship had been summoned to aid the search for the wreckage of Air Force One. The *Fathom* was the closest salvager with a deep-sea submersible on hand, and they were contractually obligated to lend the sub's services during an emergency.

Still, though he knew his duty, he did not have to like it. He spit out his cigar and ground its fiery end into the ash tray. This was *his* ship.

Twelve years ago, using money from his settlement against General Dynamics after the shuttle accident, Jack had purchased the *Deep Fathom* from a shipyard auction house. The eighty-foot *Fathom* had originally been built as a research ship for the Woods Hole Institute back in 1973. In addition to the purchase price, he had been forced to take out a large loan to convert the aged research vessel into a modern salvage ship: adding a hydraulic cargo crane, upgrading to a five-ton capacity A-frame, and overhauling the Caterpillar marine diesel engine. He had also updated the navigation equipment and outfitted it so the *Fathom* could operate without outside assistance for weeks at a time. He added Naiad stabilizers, a Bauer diving compressor, and Village Marine water makers.

It had cost him his entire savings, but eventually the *Fathom* had become his home, his world. Over the years, he had gathered a team of scientists and fellow treasure hunters to his side. They became his new family.

Now, after twelve years, he was being called back to the world he had left behind.

The door to the pilothouse squeaked open behind him and a fresh cross-breeze blew in. "Jack, what are you still doing here?" It was Lisa. The doctor from UCLA scowled at him as she entered. In shorts and a bikini top, she did not look the part of an experienced medical researcher. Her limbs were deeply tanned, and her long blond hair had been bleached white by the months under the sun. She looked like she belonged on a beach, hanging on the arm of a muscled surfer. But Jack knew better. There was no sharper doctor on the high seas.

Lisa held open the door to let in another member of the crew. A lanky German shepherd loped inside the cabin and crossed to Jack's side for a scratch behind the ear. The dog had been born aboard the *Fathom*, from a litter whelped during a storm in the South China Sea. Underweight and sickly, the pup had been abandoned by the bitch, and Jack took him in, nursing the pup back to health. That had been almost nine years ago.

"Elvis here was worried about you," Lisa said. She sidled to the chair next to him, shoving Jack's feet off.

Jack patted the large dog's side and pointed to the cedar pillow in the corner. "Bed," he ordered. The old dog crossed and collapsed into the thick pillow with a long sigh.

"Speaking of bed," Lisa said, "I thought you were supposed to be relieved at sunrise. Shouldn't you be trying to catch a nap?"

"Couldn't sleep. Thought I might as well be useful."

Lisa pushed away the ashtray to make room for the mug she brought in with her. She glanced at the navigation array. After five years on and off the *Fathom*, she had become a fairly skilled pilot herself. "Looks like we'll be at the rendezvous site in less than three hours." She faced Jack. "Maybe you should try to get some sleep. We've a long day ahead of us."

"I've still got to—"

"Get some sleep," she finished with a frown. She shoved her mug toward him. "Herbal tea. Try it. It'll help you relax."

He leaned over the steaming mug and sniffed. The medicinal tang was sharp after smoking his cigar. "I'll pass."

Lisa pushed the mug closer. "Drink it. Doctor's orders."

Jack rolled his eyes and picked up the cup. He took a few

sips to placate her. It tasted as bad as it smelled. "Needs sugar," he said.

"Sugar? And taint my healing herbs?" Lisa feigned shock and nudged the ashtray. "As it is, you have enough bad habits."

He took another sip and stood. "I should check on Charlie. See how the tests are going."

Lisa turned, her lips firm, her eyes hard. "Jack, Charlie and the gold aren't going anywhere. Go to your cabin, shut the drapes, and try to sleep."

"It will only—"

She held up a hand. Her expression softened, as did her words. "Listen, Jack. We all know what's got you so anxious. Everyone's been walking on eggshells around you."

He opened his mouth to protest.

Lisa stopped him with a touch. She stood, parted his robe, and raised a hand to his chest. Jack did not flinch at such casual intimacy. Lisa had seen him naked many times. On such a small ship, privacy was limited. But more than that, years ago, when Lisa first arrived onboard, the two of them had played at being lovers. Eventually it became clear their feelings were more physical than heartfelt. Without a word, their trysts had eventually ended, settling into a warm companionship. More than friends, less than lovers.

"Lisa . . ."

She traced a finger down from his collarbone, trailing through the coarse black hair on his chest. Her finger was warm on his skin. But as it moved below his right nipple, the feeling vanished. Jack knew why. Across the middle of his chest lay a swath of trailing scars. Old burns. The scars were pale against his bronzed skin. Numb and dead.

Jack shivered as he felt Lisa's touch return, past the scarring, just above his navel. Her finger traveled still lower and crooked into the waistband of his trunks. She pulled him nearer. She whispered, "Let it go, Jack. The past can't be changed. Only forgiven and forgotten."

Gently pushing her hand away, he stepped back. Those were easy words for Lisa to say, a girl who had led a charmed life in Southern California.

She stared up at him, her eyes slightly wounded. "You weren't found at fault, Jack. You were even offered the goddamn Medal of Honor."

"I turned it down," he said, swinging away. He headed toward the door. The shuttle accident was a private matter, a subject he did not want to share and discuss. Not with anyone. He had enough of that from the Navy's psychiatrists. Free of the pilothouse, he hurried down the steps to the boat deck.

Her heart heavy, Lisa watched the large man retreat out the door.

In the corner, Elvis had lifted his head from the bed, and watched his master storm out. The big dog grumbled under his breath, a throaty complaint.

Lisa settled into the pilot's seat, still warm from its previous occupant. "My words exactly, Elvis." She sagged into the chair. Though their fiery relationship had died to ash, Lisa could still touch the warmth of her old feelings: Jack's hard body holding her tight, the heat of his mouth on her breasts and neck, his lovemaking both rough and tender. He was an attentive lover, one of the best she had ever experienced. However, strong hands and legs couldn't build a relationship by themselves. It took an even stronger heart. Jack loved her. She never doubted this, but there was a part of Jack's heart that was as dead and numb as the scars on his chest. She had never found a way to heal this old wound—and doubted she ever could. Jack would not let it heal.

Lisa reached for the mug of herbal tea and dumped its contents into the trashcan. She had spiked the tea with Halcyon before climbing up here. Jack needed to sleep, and the sleeping pill hidden in her elixir should help him relax.

At least, she hoped. She had never seen Jack this bad before. He was normally outgoing, quick to smile and joke, full of an energy that shone from his skin. But there had been times in the past when he would sink into a funk, drift away from the others, hole up in his cabin or pilothouse. They had all learned to give Jack the space he needed during these times. But the past twenty-four hours had been his worst.

The door on the opposite side of the pilothouse suddenly crashed open. Lisa jumped at the noise, caught off guard by her reverie. From his corner, Elvis let out a warning bark.

Lisa swung around as two people shoved their way inside, still in mid-argument.

Charlie Mollier's face was darker than its usual Jamaican mocha. The geologist's eyes were lit with an inner fire. "You can't be serious, Kendall. Those gold bars weigh fifty stone each. They're worth a half-million U.S. easy."

Kendall McMillan simply shrugged, unimpressed by the larger man's tirade. McMillan was an accountant from Chase Manhattan Bank, assigned to be present here when the wealth of the *Kochi Maru* was brought to the surface, to watch after the bank's investment. "Perhaps, Mr. Mollier, but as your laboratory results proved, the bullion is full of impurities. Not even sixteen carat. The bank has offered a good deal."

"You're a bloody thief!" Charlie sputtered angrily. The geologist finally seemed to see Lisa. "Can you believe this *mon*?"

"What's going on?"

"Where's Jack?" Charlie answered. "I thought he was up here."

"Gone down below."

"Where?" Charlie crossed to the opposite door. "I need to tell him—"

"No, you don't, Charlie. The captain has enough on his plate right now. Let him be." Lisa glanced at McMillan.

Where Charlie was dressed in his usual deckwear—a baggy set of trunks hanging down to his knees with a floral Jamaican shirt—McMillan wore Sperry deck shoes, khaki slacks, and a smart shirt buttoned to the top. The middle-aged accountant had been on board the *Fathom* for almost two months now, but he had yet to relax into the casual routine of the ship. Even his red hair was carefully trimmed and combed.

"What's this all about?" Lisa asked.

McMillan drew himself straighter under her gaze. "As I was explaining to Mr. Mollier after reviewing his laboratory analysis, there is no way the bank will pay current market price for the gold. The old bullion is full of impurities. I've used the satellite phone to confirm my own estimates with the bank's experts."

Charlie threw his hands in the air. "It's high seas piracy."

McMillan's face tightened. "I take affront at your allegation that I'd—"

"I can't believe you two," Lisa finally interrupted. "The entire Pacific Rim is trying to recover from a day of horrible disasters, and you two are arguing over pennies and percentages. Can't this wait?"

Both men hung their heads. McMillan pointed toward Charlie. "He started it. I just gave him my numbers."

"If he hadn't—"

"Enough! Both of you get out of here! And if I hear that you dump any of this on Jack, you'll be sorry you ever stepped on board the *Fathom*."

"I'm already sorry," McMillan grumbled under his breath.

"What was that?" Lisa asked fiercely.

The accountant backed up a step. "Nothing."

"Get off my bridge," she demanded, pointing toward the door.

Both men retreated quickly.

Quiet returned to the pilothouse. The German shepherd settled back to his bed, eyes closing. Soft classical music returned to fill the space. Lisa combed her hair back with her fingers. *Men!* She had enough of all of them.

Swiveling in her seat, she popped out the classical music CD. *Why does Jack like this stuff?* She shuffled through the stack and found one of her own. After inserting the disk, she hit the Play button, and the all-girl band, Hole, blared from the speakers. Backed by a strident guitar and a mean drum riff, the lead singer's harsh voice echoed through the cabin, singing of men's inadequacies and faults.

Lisa sank back into her seat. "That's more like it."

* * *

In his cabin, Jack lay sprawled atop his bed on his back, still in his robe. He snored softly, mouth hanging open. He sank deeply into a Halcyon-colored nightmare.

Floating in his EVA suit, tethered to the shuttle Atlantis, *he was surrounded by the unrelenting darkness of space. Below him, the payload bay doors were open. In the orbiter's workspace, he saw other crew members manhandling the large satellite into position using the shuttle's manipulator arms.*

The stenciled logo of the Navy's seal gleamed unnaturally bright on the satellite, as did the weapon's name: Spartacus. In slow motion, the satellite, a half-billion-dollar test model outfitted with an experimental particle-beam cannon, was lifted from the bay on a system of lever arms. Clear of the bay doors, the satellite's solar wings and communication array unfolded.

It was a wondrous sight as sunlight reflected off its solar cells. A butterfly climbing from a cocoon.

Beyond the shuttle, the blue globe of Earth loomed bright.

He thanked the stars around him for this opportunity. He had never imagined anything so beautiful—especially knowing he was sharing it with the one woman whose eyes outshone even these stars.

Jennifer Spangler was the mission specialist for this trip, and as of last night, she was also his fiancée. He had first met her six years ago, when one of his fellow SEALs introduced him to his younger sister. He ran into her again as a fellow astronaut in training. They had quickly and passionately fallen for each other: furtively meeting in empty closets and wardrooms, sneaking off to dance at the Splashdown pub, even sharing midnight picnics on the acres of tarmac around the center. During those endless nights, under these very stars, they had planned their lives together.

Still, when he had corralled her alone aboard the flight deck last night and held out a small gold band between them, he was as nervous as a schoolboy. He did not know what her answer would be. Was he moving too fast? Did she share the depth of his feelings? For an eternal moment the gold ring had hung between them, weightless, shining in the moonlight—then she reached out and accepted his offer, her smile and tears answer enough.

Grinning at the memory, he was interrupted by Jennifer's all-business voice over his comlink, drawing his attention back to the satellite. "Unlocking arms. One, two, three. All go. I repeat, go for spring launch. Jack?"

He answered. "Visual check confirmed."

Colonel Durham, commander of this flight, chimed in from the flight deck. "All clear here. Green lights all around. Releasing payload in ten seconds . . . nine . . . eight . . . seven . . ."

Time slowed as the work crew retreated from under the satellite. Wrench in hand, he maneuvered along his tether to the port side, out of the way. They had practiced the release a hundred times.

As he drifted, he pictured Jennifer's body and wondered what it would be like to share a bed out here, with the whole blue Earth looking on. What could be a better honeymoon?

". . . six . . . five . . . four . . ."

As he daydreamed he was slow to see the mistake. One of the three locking boom arms, built by General Dynamics, had failed to release completely. From his position, he saw the satellite drift a few degrees to the starboard side. Oh, God! He took one second to confirm the error. It was one second too many.

". . . three . . . two . . ."

"Stop the launch!" Jack screamed into his com.

". . . one . . ."

He saw the springs release, catapulting the satellite out of the bay. The springs had been engineered to thrust the satellite gently into proper orbital insertion, but instead the releasing mechanism snagged.

In dream-time slow motion, he watched in horror.

The five-ton satellite slammed against the starboard bay doors. One of the satellite's solar wings smashed into the shuttle's side. Soundlessly, the bay door bent. Hundreds of ceramic tiles cracked from the shuttle's surface and spun away, like playing cards cast into the wind.

Spartacus spun out into space, its broken wing flailing. It tumbled toward a higher orbit.

He witnessed a brief explosion on the underside of the satellite as it passed overhead. A small panel blew out as its axial guidance system was overloaded.

Spartacus floated away, dead in space.

Hours later he found himself strapped to a seat in the mid deck, wearing his Advanced Crew Escape Suit. Overhead, in the flight deck, he heard the pilot and shuttle commander conferring with NASA. The bay door had been repaired, but the loss of protective heating tiles made reentry risky.

The plan: get as far through the upper atmosphere as possible—then eject if there was any mishap. But the new emergency evacuation system, installed after the Challenger *tragedy, had yet to be tested.*

Whispers of prayers echoed over the open comlink.

Jennifer sat beside him, in the mission specialist's chair. His voice sounded far away as he tried to reassure her. "We'll make it, Jen. We have a wedding to plan."

She nodded, offering a weak smile, but she couldn't speak. This was her first shuttle mission, too. Her face remained pale behind her faceplate.

He glanced to either side. Two other astronauts shared the mid-deck seats, backs tense, fingers clutching the seat arms. Only the commander and pilot were on the flight deck above. The commander insisted all the crew be as near the mid-deck emergency hatch as possible.

At the controls, Colonel Jeff Durham checked one last time with Houston as he began their descent. "Here we go. Pray for us."

A static-filled reply from Shuttle Mission Control. "Godspeed, Atlantis."

Then they hit the atmosphere hard. Flames chased them. Their ship rocked and bucked. No one spoke, breaths were held.

Sweat pebbled his forehead. The heat grew too rapidly

for his suit's air-conditioning unit to compensate. He checked the cooling bib connection, but it was secure. He glanced at Jennifer. Her faceplate had misted over. He wished he could reach her, hold her.

Then he heard the best words of his life from the pilot. "Approaching sixty thousand feet! Almost home, folks!"

A whoop of joy echoed through all their comlinks.

Before their jubilation died down, the shuttle bucked violently. He saw the Earth spin into view as the ship hoved over on its side. The pilot fought to right the ship but failed.

Only later would he learn that the damaged patch of the shuttle's exterior surface had overheated and burned through a hydraulic line, igniting the auxiliary oxygen tank. But at that moment all he knew was terror and pain as the orbiter tumbled through the upper atmosphere.

"Fire in the bay!"

He knew it was futile as the pilot continued to wrestle his controls. Another violent quake shook through the bones of the ship.

"Fifty thousand feet!" the pilot yelled.

The commander's voice came over the intercom. "Prepare for bailout! Depressurize on my count!"

"Forty-five thousand!" the pilot yelled. "Forty thousand!" They were falling fast.

"Close your visors and activate emergency oxygen. Jack, open the pyro vent valve."

He found himself rising from his seat, his personal parachute assembly strapped to his back. He lumbered across the bucking mid-deck and reached the T-handle box. He tugged the vent handle and twisted it. The valve would slowly depressurize the cabins to match external pressures.

"Get ready!" Colonel Durham ordered. "Switching to autopilot!"

The orbiter bucked more violently and he flew up, striking his head savagely. One of the other astronauts, who had been unbuckling from his seat, struck an overhead support bar. His helmet split and the man fell limp.

He started to cross to the man's aid, but the second astronaut waved him off. "Man your station!"

"Autopilot's off line!" the commander screamed. "Gonna have to stay on manual!"

He glanced over his shoulder at Jennifer. She was struggling out of her seat, meaning to assist with the injured crewman. But she was clearly having some trouble. She tugged at something by her left arm.

"Thirty-five thousand!" the pilot announced. The shuttle continued to rock viciously. "I can handle it! I can handle it!" The pilot sounded as if he were arguing with himself, then—"Jesus Christ!"

A litany of swearing erupted from Colonel Durham. "Bailout!" he screamed over their comlinks. "Get your asses out of here!"

He knew they were still too high, but he obeyed the direct order. He twisted the second T-handle. The side hatch blew out. Winds exploded out of the cabin. The depressurization had not been complete. He found himself almost sucked out the hatch, only saving himself by clutching the T-handle in an iron grip.

Screams filled the com system. The shuttle rolled on its back. The floor buckled.

He caught movement out of the corner of his eye and turned to see Jennifer slide past him, belly first, her fingers scrabbling for a hold. Her parachute assembly was missing.

Oh, God . . .

He lunged out, snagging her hand. "Hang on!" he screamed.

A huge explosion sounded from behind him. The mid-deck hatch blew out with a screech of metal. A whirlwind of flames tore into the cabin, burning all the way to the flight deck. He lost sight of the other astronauts. The fires rolled toward him and Jennifer.

"Help!" he yelled into his communication unit. But there was no answer. The shuttle had become a plummeting rock. He began to slip.

"Let go of me!" Jennifer gasped at him, struggling to free her hand. "I'm pulling you loose—"

"Goddamn it! Hang on!"

"I'm not taking you down with me!" Jennifer reached her

other hand and unlocked the metal flange that mated her suit's glove to its sleeve.

"No!" He clenched his hand, but he was too late. He clutched only an empty glove. Jennifer slipped beyond his grip.

As in all nightmares, he found himself unable to move. In slow motion he watched Jennifer slide away from him . . . so slowly. He struggled to reach out to her, but his limbs refused to obey. He could only watch.

His last view was not of Jennifer's panicked face . . . but of a small gold band, blazing brightly on her hand, shining with the promise of undying love as she fell away.

Deaf to his own screams, he dove after her, chased by a wall of flame. He tumbled through the hatch just as the shuttle flipped end over end. The huge wing of the orbiter sliced through the air over his head. Darkness harried the edges of his vision as he twisted and spun uncontrolled. He could not breathe.

Still, he searched as best he could for some sign of Jennifer, but the blue skies were empty. Only a flaming trail marked the path of the burning shuttle.

Tears in his eyes, he fumbled for the manual parachute release. The eighteen-inch pilot chute deployed, instantly drawing out the four-foot drogue chute, stabilizing his spinning tumble. But the small chutes did little to stop his rate of descent. They were not meant to. Not in this thin air. Later, a third chute would automatically engage as he descended, but he never saw it.

Darkness finally claimed him.

Jack fell all the way back to Earth, back to his own bed aboard the *Deep Fathom*. With a jolt, his eyelids popped open. Too bright. It took him a second to recall where he was. He struggled to sit up, his robe soaked with sweat. He shivered and shrugged out of the garment. Half naked, he stood on wobbly feet.

He shuddered again and crossed to the wall safe. He thumbed the combination and pulled open the door. Amid the ship's papers and a few thousand dollars in American currency lay a crumpled glove. Jack pulled it out. The fingers and edges were scorched, but he had not been able to part with it. No matter how much he wanted to forget the past. He couldn't.

"I'm sorry, Jennifer," he whispered, pressing it to his lips. When the rescue crew had found Jack's unconscious body amid the billowing parachutes, they had found this glove still clutched in his hand. He had been the only survivor. Even now he could still feel Jennifer's frightened and panicked grip on his hand.

Behind him a rapid knocking shook his cabin door.

Jack returned the glove slowly to the safe, his eyes closed against the tears. "What?" he growled irritably.

"Just thought you should know, Jack. We're about to reach the rendezvous point."

He recognized the marine biologist's voice and glanced to his clock. Three hours had passed. "All right, Robert. I'll be up in a moment."

Crossing to his room's head, Jack splashed cold water on his face. As he straightened, he stared up at his reflection. Water dripped off his hard features and strong chin. His black hair, though still dark, was now dusted with gray at the temples. He wore it long, to his shoulders. No longer the military crew cut. He shoved the damp hair behind his ears and toweled off his sun-bronzed skin. He turned away, unable to face his own reflection.

Tuned to his ship, Jack recognized the slight change in the engines' constant rumble. They were slowing down. Hurrying, he slipped into a loose shirt, left it unbuttoned, and crossed barefoot to the door. As he exited he found Robert Bonaczek still waiting for him.

The marine biologist seemed nervous, shifting his feet, unable to meet Jack's eyes. Robert Bonaczek was only twenty years old, the youngest on the crew, but also the most serious and dour. He seldom smiled. He had graduated with a master's degree in marine sciences at the tender age of eighteen and had been on board the last two years, working toward his doctorate. Lisa called him "an old soul trapped in a young body." This assessment was compounded by the fact that the man's thin blond hair was already balding.

"What is it, Robert?"

The biologist shook his head. "You need to see it for yourself." The young man turned and headed for the door to the open deck.

Jack followed, shoving through the door after the biologist.

The sun, now lower in the sky, blinded Jack. He blinked against the glare and raised a hand to shield his eyes. The other members of the team were all on deck, except for the geologist, Charlie Mollier. Jack spotted his large frame behind the windows of the pilothouse. Charlie gave him a short wave.

Jack joined the others at the rail; Robert, on one side, Lisa on his other. "How'd you sleep?" the doctor asked.

"You slipped me something, didn't you?"

She shrugged. "You needed sleep."

He thought to reprimand her. What right did she have to treat him like a child? He was the goddamn captain of this boat. But instead his eyes were drawn forward.

Ahead, the normally empty stretch of ocean was crowded with ships: fishing trawlers, cargo ships, military cutters. Flags from various countries flapped above the ships. Overhead, a pair of Jayhawk helicopters buzzed by. Jack followed their path, guessing they had been sent from the Air Force base on Wake Island. Near the horizon, a wide-bodied C-130 swept back and forth over the scene, a search pattern. The plane had probably been scanning the area all night with its sonar. The U.S. National Transportation Safety Board had clearly mobilized its "go-team" on this crash.

George Klein stepped up behind Jack, reading his mind. "The NTSB has been busy. An impressive mobilization, considering how far out we are."

The professor puffed on a pipe as he stared out at the turmoil. Except for the thick pipe, George looked nothing like a sixty-something Harvard professor. The older man was muscular, wearing a pair of trunks and nothing else. His wispy white hair fluttered in the thin breeze. Jack had always thought George bore a striking resemblance to Jacques Cousteau.

"What's that smell?" Kendall McMillan asked, wrinkling his nose.

Brought to his attention, Jack caught the acrid taint in the ocean breeze. "Fuel spill." He finally noticed the slight stain on the ocean's surface off the port bow. The oil slick spread in a black bloom. There was no question that some sort of crash had occurred here.

Within the oil slick, Jack spotted a few bobbing red buoys. Data buoys, he realized, dropped to give the searchers some indication where wreckage and bodies may have drifted. "Someone should have hauled my ass up here earlier," he said.

George glanced at Lisa, who suddenly bore a more intense interest in the ocean. "And bear Lisa's wrath? I'd rather face a Great White with chum hanging around my neck. Besides, Charlie contacted the head of operations here an hour ago." George glanced at Jack with his brows raised. "The Coast Guard vice admiral himself . . . flown in from San Diego last night. Not exactly a friendly fellow, from Charlie's description."

"How do they want us to help?"

"We're on standby until they localize the pinging of Air Force One's data recorders and initiate an action plan. It seems NTSB is really only interested in our *Nautilus*. We're to sit out here until our sub is called into play."

"And what about Admiral Houston?" Jack asked. His old Navy commander had been the one to order them to service. "Isn't he here?"

"Due to arrive tomorrow."

"What's taking him so long?"

"I guess it takes longer to grease the huge wheels of the U.S. military machine. He's due at daybreak in the USS *Gibraltar*." George waved his pipe forward. "All this malarkey is just preparation. Getting all the ducks in a row before the true deep-water search begins."

"The *Gibraltar*," Jack mumbled.

"You did a tour on that boat, didn't you?"

Jack nodded. He had served aboard the ship for seven years. The *Gibraltar* was a Wasp-class Landing Helicopter Dockship, one of the largest ships in the Navy, only dwarfed by the supercarriers themselves. The LHD was a part of the infamous 'Gator Navy, an amphibious task force combining the combat power of the Marines with the speed and mobility of the Navy.

Robert called out from nearby, pointing. "Look."

Off to the port, a bit of debris bobbed among the buoys. It hadn't been there a moment ago. It must have just surfaced. Jack squinted. "Get me a pair of binoculars."

Robert hurried away and returned with a set of Minolta glasses. Jack donned them. It took him a moment to find and focus on the piece of equipment. It was the back of an airline seat, the presidential seal bright blue against the red seat back.

A sudden swell rolled the seat over. A flash of pale flesh. An arm hanging limply. Then the sight vanished.

"Is it wreckage?" Robert asked.

Jack could not answer. He flashed to his own tumble through the air twelve years ago. The crash of the shuttle *Atlantis*. The sight struck too close to home.

"Jack, are you all right?" Lisa touched his shoulder.

He lowered his binoculars, pale, trembling. "We should never have come here. No good can come of it."

4

Blame

David Spangler waited outside the Oval Office. All around him, even at this late hour, the West Wing of the White House bustled with aides, underlings, and messengers. This current turmoil was not localized just to Pennsylvania Avenue. The entire Beltway remained in high gear: countless press conferences were convened, repeated emergency meetings atop Capitol Hill took place, and an endless amount of petty backdoor bickering occurred throughout the halls.

All the pandemonium over the loss of a single man—President Bishop.

David himself had been specially flown in this morning from Turkey. He and his ops team had been called back early from a mission along the Iraq border, but he had yet to be told why.

"Coffee, sir?" An aide approached David with a tray of mugs.

He gave the tiny-breasted girl the barest shake of his head.

Seated stiffly in an upholstered chair, David continued to study the room, not moving, just picking up everything around him: the casual banter, the half jokes, the faint scent of perfume. He breathed deeply. Opportunity was in the air.

His own boss, CIA Director Nicolas Ruzickov, was in conference with the new leader of the United States, Vice President Lawrence Nafe.

Each of Bishop's former Cabinet members was meeting in private with Nafe. Who would be axed? Who would retain their job? Rumors spread like wildfire through government halls. It was well-known that a deep political gulf separated the former President from his running mate. Nafe had been named to the ticket only as a ploy to gain the South; since then, their two offices often found themselves in conflict. Today, David suspected Nafe had been getting his ass kissed like it had never been before—but not from the CIA director. Nafe and Ruzickov had always been close friends, fellow students at Yale and fellow ideologues when it came to dealing with foreign aggression.

David had once shaken Nafe's hand at a White House function. He'd found the man as weak and dishonest as the next politician, all fake smiles and perpetual condescending air, but in his opinion Nafe was at least better than the former occupant of the White House. President Bishop had been too much of a dove, coddling the Chinese, while Nafe was willing to take a more hard-line stance.

Nafe's secretary typed at her computer, a dictation device hooked to one ear. As David waited for the conference to end, he caught her glancing in his direction, smiling shyly when she was caught looking. He was accustomed to this reaction from women. He was tall, his shoulders broad and muscular, his blond hair cropped to tight angles about his hard features, his skin tanned by years under the sun of many foreign lands. Prior to the aborted mission in Turkey, his last assignment had been to Lebanon, where he and his ops team had dispatched a Lebanese terrorist with the usual economy, taking out the man's family and fire-bombing the hotel, erasing all evidence of the assassination. It had been a clean operation.

Pride for his team fired his blood. They were men he had trained from the start. Handpicked. He knew each of them would die for him. They were one of the most successful covert ops teams, with a body count numbering over a thousand.

The phone at the secretary's desk buzzed. David's gaze twitched in her direction. She picked up the receiver. "Yes, sir. Immediately, sir." She put down the phone and turned to face David. "The President—" She blushed at her mistake. Nafe had not been formally sworn in yet, not without more concrete evidence of Bishop's demise. "The *Vice* President requests you join Mr. Ruzickov in the Oval Office."

David stood smoothly, a single line on his forehead marking his surprise at the invitation.

The secretary waved him toward the door, then returned to her typing. He crossed the room, unsure why he was being called into this conference. The door was opened by a Secret Service agent, whom David did not even acknowledge.

He took three steps inside, then snapped to attention at the edge of the circular rug bearing the presidential seal. The eagle icon on the carpet seemed to stare at him, as did the two occupants in the room. His boss sat in an armchair. The former Marine, though gray-haired and edging toward sixty, was as lithe and wiry as when on duty. As usual, his hard blue eyes remained unreadable. David respected Ruzickov deeply.

"Commander Spangler, please come join us," the Vice President said, waving him in as the door shut with a click behind David. Lawrence Nafe stood, leaning on the edge of the wide desk. In appearance, he was the opposite of the CIA director. His features were soft: thick lips, a hint of a double chin, cow eyes. His belly bulged slightly over his belt, and the dung-brown color of his hair, what remained of it, clearly came from a bottle. "Please take a seat."

Nodding curtly, David strode into the room, maintaining a stiff posture.

The Vice President came around the desk and settled easily into the chair, as if he had done so a thousand times before. The man nudged a folder on his desk. "Mr. Ruzickov has been telling me much about your team's exploits." His eyes rose to study David, who was still standing. "Please take a seat," Nafe repeated, with a trace of irritation.

David glanced to the CIA director, who gestured to a neighboring chair. He sank into the seat, spine straight, not leaning back. Suspicious, alert.

Nafe continued, "Omega team has served our country well, whether the public knows this fact or not."

"Thank you, sir."

Nafe leaned back in his chair, lacing his fingers over his belly. "I've read the report on Somalia. Fine job. We could not have a Communist newspaper starting in that volatile region."

David nodded. Fourteen deaths, staged like a mass suicide. It was artfully done, discrediting the Communist insurgents while ending their threat. Besides Omega team, only two other people knew the truth, and they sat in this room now.

"We have been discussing another mission for your team. We believe you and your men are ideally suited." The silent question hung in the air.

David answered it. "Anything, sir."

His response raised a small smile from Nafe, again with an icy hint of condescension. "Excellent." Nafe sat up straighter again, grabbed a folder and passed it to the CIA director. "Your orders and details are in here."

In turn, Nicolas Ruzickov passed the folder to David, maintaining the chain of command in these matters. If anything went wrong, David could honestly say the order came from the CIA director, not from the Vice President.

David placed the folder on his lap.

His boss spoke for the first time, outlining the mission, while Nafe sat silently, leaning back, hands over his belly again. "As you know, the Chinese have been a thorn in our side for decades. While we've helped drag them into the twenty-first century with aid and favorable trade status, they in turn have grown more belligerent and inflexible."

"Biting the hand that feeds them," Nafe interjected.

"Exactly. While our government has kowtowed to these Communist leaders, the Chinese have grown stronger—increasing their nuclear arsenal, stealing the secrets for intercontinental ballistics, growing and spreading their naval presence. In just ten years they've grown from a Communist nuisance to a global threat. This tide must be stopped."

David found his fingers tightening on the arms of his chair. No truer words had been spoken. He nodded, hard. "Yes, sir."

Ruzickov's eyes flicked to Nafe, then back to David. "But public sentiment does not favor such action. The average American is more interested in the value of his stock portfolio and what's on TV at night. Confrontation with China is not a priority. If anything, the opposite is true. We have grown complacent. If we are to stem this rising tide of communism, then this sentiment must be changed also."

David nodded his understanding.

Ruzickov studied him, then spoke again. "You know of the mobilization to recover Air Force One."

David didn't answer; the CIA director's words were not a question. Of course he knew of the mobilization. It was in the news. The entire world had turned its eyes to an empty stretch of ocean. Still, his nostrils flared. He almost smelled his boss's discomfort.

"We believe this is an opportunity not to be missed. A chance to gain some value for the loss of President Bishop."

"How so?" David asked, intrigued.

"You are to join the NTSB's go-team at the crash site."

David's left eye twitched in surprise. "To help in the recovery?"

"Yes . . . but also to help ensure that the information that comes from the crash site serves our end."

"I don't understand."

Nafe clarified. "We want the crash to be blamed on the Chinese."

"Whether the facts substantiate this claim or not," the director finished.

Both of David's brows rose.

Nicolas Ruzickov stood up. "With the Chinese blamed for the assassination of the President, there will be a public outcry for retribution."

"And we will answer it," Nafe added.

David appreciated the plan. With the world already in turmoil after the Pacificwide disasters, the moment was ripe for such a change.

"Does Omega accept this mission?" Ruzickov asked formally.

David stood. "Yes, sir, without question."

Nafe cleared his throat, drawing both their attention. "One other thing, Commander Spangler. It seems that a colleague of yours is already on site. A fellow SEAL . . . someone you once worked alongside."

Again David sensed a bomb was about to be dropped. "Who?"

"Jack Kirkland."

A gasp escaped David's throat. He barely heard the Vice President's next few words. His vision grew black at the edges.

"We know you still blame the man for the *Atlantis* accident. The entire country mourned the death of your younger sister."

"Jennifer," David mumbled. He pictured the girl's face full of pride on the day of the launch, her first mission with NASA—at her side, Jack Kirkland, her teammate, wearing a shit-eating grin. Jack had won the shuttle's military seat over David; both men had been up for the mission. But NASA had not wanted two siblings going up on the same mission— in case something happened. David closed his eyes. Jennifer's body had never been found.

"I'm sorry for your loss," Nafe said, drawing back David's attention.

He straightened, going cold. "Thank you, sir."

Ruzickov spoke at his shoulder. "We just want to make

sure Kirkland's presence isn't going to interfere with your mission."

"No, sir. The past is the past. I understand the importance of this mission and will let nothing stand in my way—not even Jack Kirkland."

"Very good." Ruzickov turned toward the exit. "Then gather your team. You ship out in two hours."

With a nod to the country's new leader, David swung around on numb legs. He would do as he had been ordered. Omega team had never failed in a mission. But on this journey, David intended to add a side objective of his own.

To avenge his sister's death.

5

Serpent's Heart

With the sun yet to rise, Karen was already at the docks, bartering for the rental of an outboard motorboat. She stared out across the water. The twin pyramids lay just a couple hundred meters out past the bay. After yesterday's discovery, she had refused to return to Naha and the university. Instead, over Miyuki's protests, she chartered a fishing boat to drop them off at the small town of Chatan on Yonaguni Island's coast.

"We should have returned to Naha yesterday," Miyuki said, scowling at the condition of the boat. The old fiberglass craft showed significant wear—the metal railings dented and bent, the vinyl seats cracked and fraying at the seams—but the hull itself looked seaworthy enough to cross the hundred or so yards to the nearby pyramids. "We could have struck a better deal in Naha."

"And lost half a day getting back here," Karen answered. "I could not risk looters damaging the Dragons—or what if the pyramids sank again?"

Miyuki sighed, her eyes tired. "All right, but you're driving."

Karen, bubbling with excitement despite a restless night, nodded and climbed into the stern.

Last night, she and Miyuki had talked late into the night, sharing a bottle of saki between them. From their hotel room's tiny balcony they had a clear view to the sea and the twin Dragons. Under the moonlight, the misted pyramids had shone damply, as if glowing with an inner light. Then, throughout the long night, Karen had risen many times from the cramped bed to stare out the window, afraid the sight might disappear. But the twin pyramids remained in the shallows off the coastline.

With the first blush in the eastern sky, Karen had hauled a grumbling Miyuki from her bedsheets. In the chilly predawn the two women had hiked the short distance to the docks and negotiated an expensive price for the day use of a fisherman's old motorboat. An entire month's pay. But Karen had no choice but to agree. There had been no other boat available.

She helmed the wheel, while Miyuki caught the ropes from the grinning fisherman, pleased with his profit.

"You know, of course, you're being robbed," Miyuki said.

"Perhaps," Karen responded. "But I would have been willing to pay ten times as much for this chance to be the first to explore the ruins."

Miyuki shook her head and settled into the passenger seat as Karen eased the throttle forward. The engine chugged harshly; the smell of burning oil wafted over them. Miyuki crinkled her nose. "It's plain piracy."

"Don't worry, if there are any other pirates . . ." Karen patted her jacket, where her .38 automatic rested in its shoulder harness.

Miyuki groaned dramatically and sank deeper in her seat.

Karen smiled. Despite her companion's protest, she had noted the twinkle in Miyuki's eyes. The stoic Japanese professor was secretly enjoying this outing. Yesterday, Miyuki had ample opportunity to return to the university, but instead had remained with her. It was what forged their friendship. Miyuki tempered her wilder streaks, while she added a bit of spice to Miyuki's professional routine.

Once clear of the marina, Karen sped up. The engine's whining chatter filled the morning. As they circled clear of the breakwater cliffs, the rest of the ancient city appeared, filling the seas in front of them. Both women stared at the sight and rode the waves in silence. Behind them the seaside village of Chatan dwindled in size, fading as a morning fog settled over the island and the nearby seas.

To the east, the sun finally crested the horizon, spreading a rosy glow over the ruins. "Who built this drowned city?" Karen wondered aloud.

"Right now all I care about is my own city, my own lab." Miyuki replied, waving a hand forward. "The past is the past."

"But whose past?" Karen continued to wonder in awe.

Shrugging, Miyuki searched through her bag and pulled free her handheld Palm computer. She leaned back in her seat and, began tapping at the small screen with her stylus.

"What are you doing?"

"Connecting to Gabriel. Making sure everything is okay at the lab."

A quiet voice rose from the handheld computer, synthetic and tinny: *"Good morning, Professor Nakano."*

Karen grinned. "You two really should think about tying the knot."

Miyuki just frowned at her and continued working.

"You're already connected at the hip," Karen teased.

"And you're just jealous."

Karen snorted. "Of a computer?"

"Gabriel is more than just a computer," Miyuki countered, her voice strained.

Karen held up a hand to ward off a diatribe. "I know, I know." Gabriel was a sophisticated artificial intelligence program designed and patented by Miyuki. The development of its theoretical base algorithms had won Miyuki the Nobel Prize. Over the past four years, she had turned theory into practice. Gabriel, named after the fiery Archangel, was the result. "How's he doing?"

"He's categorized all my e-mail and is still monitoring the Emergency Broadcasts across various international websites."

"Any news?"

"The quakes have ended throughout the Pacific, but there seems to be a massive mobilization effort by American forces in the Central Pacific, though the details are sketchy. He's been attempting to worm his way into the D.O.D. network."

"D.O.D.?"

The answer came from the small computer: *"D.O.D. is the acronym for the United States Department of Defense."*

Karen glanced in shock at her friend. Not only did it unnerve her when Gabriel answered one of her questions, but sniffing around a military computer network . . . that could bring down serious trouble. "Should Gabriel be doing that?"

Miyuki waved away her concern. "He'll never be caught."

"Why not?"

"You can't catch what doesn't exist. Though my mainframe birthed him, Gabriel lives within the framework of the Internet now. He has no specific address to trace back to."

"A ghost in the machine," Karen mumbled.

"More precisely, Dr. Grace. I am the ghost in the machine. I am the only one of my design."

A shiver traced up Karen's back. Miyuki had tried once to explain Gabriel's looping algorithms and self-learning subroutines—a form of synthetic intelligence—but it quickly went over her head. She had always felt uncomfortable around Miyuki's lab. It was as if invisible eyes were staring at her all the time. She felt that way now.

"Darn it!" Miyuki swore under her breath.

"What is it?"

"The university is shutting down for the month. The chancellor just sent e-mail to all the department heads. Students are being allowed to return home to help their families."

Karen's brows rose. "And how is this bad news?"

"With my aides gone, it's going to significantly set back my research. I'm supposed to complete a progress report on my grant in three weeks."

"Considering the circumstances, I'm sure you can file an extension."

"Maybe." Miyuki snapped her stylus back in place. "Thank you, Gabriel. I'll be streaming you digital video throughout the day. Please record the data to the mainframe's hard drive and back them up to the DVD drive."

"File name?"

Miyuki glanced at Karen. "Dragon."

"Opening data file Dragon now. I await your next transmission."

"Thank you, Gabriel," Miyuki said.

"Good-bye, Professor Nakano. Good day, Dr. Grace."

Karen cleared her throat, feeling awkward. "Good-bye, Gabriel."

Miyuki lowered the Palm unit to her belt, clipping it in place.

By now they had neared the edge of the half-sunken ruins. Karen slowed the boat. "Miyuki, can you get an overview shot of this for me?"

Her companion shuffled through her bag, removed and hooked a compact video camera to the Palm computer at her belt. Standing, Miyuki scanned the view of the ruins, feeding the digital image through her portable computer back to her office computers. "Got it."

Karen edged the motorboat slowly forward, the engine coughing as it idled. She knew she had to be careful. Near the risen ruins, the water was shallow, less than six feet deep. As she drifted forward, columns rose around them, green with algae. Pale crabs scuttled away as they neared. Drawn into this ancient world, she quickly forgot about Gabriel and advanced computer algorithms. "This is amazing."

In the distance, a few other boats wove among the ruins.

Excited voices echoed over the water, too distant to make out any words. As a nearby punt poled past, a trio of dark-complexioned men, Micronesian in heritage, stared out at the ancient columns and sea-drowned homes.

Could ancestors of these men have built this site? Karen wondered. And if so, what happened?

The punt vanished as Karen edged the boat slowly past a low roofless building, window openings gaping at them as they drifted along. All the structures seemed to be similarly constructed, of stacked and interlocked blocks and slabs. All the same dark stone. Volcanic basalt. Some of the slabs had to weigh several tons. Here was architectural skill seldom seen in the South Pacific. It rivaled the vaulted skill of the Incas and Mayas.

Rounding the building, a clear way led to the first of the Dragons.

"Get a picture," Karen said, hushed with awe.

"I already am." Miyuki held the camera in front of her.

Ahead, the pyramid's crown towered twenty meters above the waves. Eighteen terraced steps climbed from the sea, each a meter tall, leading to the flat plateau on top. Morning sunlight blazed on the partially tumbled summit temple, a small structure composed of flat slabs.

As they neared, a flock of white cranes took flight at their noisy approach. Turtles, basking on the steps, plopped into the surf. Karen circled the pyramid. On the far side, the second Dragon appeared. It was a twin of the first, except its flat-topped summit was empty of any sign of a temple.

"Let's take a closer look." Karen aimed their boat toward the first pyramid, bringing the craft up to the lowest step. A short basalt pillar at the northeast corner was a good place to tie a rope and secure their boat.

"Hold the wheel," Karen said as she throttled down. The waves bobbled the craft. Grabbing the aft mooring line, she crossed to the rail and used it to boost herself over the open water. Landing on the step of the pyramid, she slipped on algae and damp weed.

"Careful!" Miyuki yelled as Karen cartwheeled her arms. Recovering her balance, she swiped a few strands of hair away from her eyes and gave Miyuki an embarrassed grin. "Safe and sound."

With more care, Karen crossed to the meter-tall pillar, rope in hand. As she knelt she realized that the pillar was actually a sculpted figure of a robed man, its details eroded away by sand and sea, the nose gone, the eyes no more than shadowed depressions.

Karen hauled on the mooring rope until the boat's hull bumped the lower step, then she secured the line to the statue's base, cinching the hitch knot tight.

"Could you help me with my bag?" Miyuki asked, holding out her satchel filled with the photography gear. Karen relieved her of the bag so the petite professor could clamber over the rail.

Miyuki scrunched up her face as her heel squashed something bulbous and slimy. "You're buying me new shoes when we're through here."

"New Ferragamos, I promise," Karen quipped. "Direct from Italy."

Miyuki bit back a smile, still refusing to admit she was enjoying the adventure. "Well, then that's okay I guess."

"C'mon. I want to check out the ruined temple on the top."

Miyuki craned her neck. "That's a long climb."

"We'll take it slow." Karen pulled up onto the first step, then reached back to help Miyuki, who waved away her hand and clambered up on her own. But once up, she fingered a long strand of seaweed from her knee and tossed it aside in disgust, glowering at Karen.

"Okay, so we'll visit Nordstrom, too, when we get back. We'll buy you a new pantsuit."

This earned a true smile from Miyuki. "New shoes, new suit. Let's keep going. Before we're done here, you'll be financing my whole new spring wardrobe."

Karen patted her friend's arm and led the way up the steps, but she soon outpaced her companion. Halfway up, she stopped to give Miyuki time to close the distance, and meanwhile stared out at the spread of the drowned city. By now the sun had fully risen, a bright globe in the east. The columns and buildings cast long shadows across the blue water. From that height, she could see it had to be at least two kilometers until the ruins faded away. The surprising size of the city suggested it may have housed a population in the tens of thousands. *So where did they all go?*

Karen moved aside as Miyuki made her way up. "It's not much further," she assured her.

Miyuki, breathing hard, just flapped a hand. "I'm fine. Let's keep moving."

"We'd better rest," Karen said, though in truth she wanted to rush forward. "We should pace ourselves."

Miyuki sank down, ignoring the algae under her. "If you insist."

Karen dug out a water bottle and passed it over. Miyuki flipped the cap and drank greedily, but her eyes remained locked on the view. "It's so extensive. I would never have imagined it."

Settling next to her, Karen took a swig from the water bottle, too. "How could all this have been hidden for so long?"

"The water here is . . . or *was* very deep, the currents tricky. Only experienced divers could explore out here. But now! Once word gets out about this place, it'll be swamped."

"And trampled," Karen added. "Now's the best time to study the city."

Miyuki scooted up. "If you're ready to go on, so am I."

"We could rest a little longer. These ruins have waited centuries to be explored. A few more minutes won't make any difference."

Miyuki settled back.

Karen did, too. She stared out over the amazing view. "I appreciate your help, Miyuki. I couldn't ask for a better friend."

"Me, too," Miyuki said softly.

The two women had met at a Ryukyu University social function. Both were single, about the same age, and working in a male-dominated environment. They had begun socializing—trips to a local karaoke bar, late dinners while grading midterms, matinee movies on Saturdays—and had become close companions.

Miyuki said, "Did I tell you I heard from Hiroshi yesterday?"

"No! You didn't!" Karen sat straighter. Hiroshi Takata, a fellow university professor, had been engaged to Miyuki, but her success in her field had raised some professional jealousy and driven a wedge into their relationship. Two years ago he had abruptly broken off the engagement and transferred to Kobe. "The bastard! What did he want?"

Miyuki rolled her eyes. "He wanted me to know *he* was okay after the quakes. He didn't even bother to ask how I was doing."

"Do you think he wants to reconcile?"

"In his dreams," Miyuki snorted.

Karen laughed. "We do seem to attract the most obnoxious men."

"Spineless, more like."

Karen nodded knowingly. In Canada she had run through her own long series of bad relationships, from cold to abusive. And she was in no hurry to continue the pattern. It was one of the reasons she accepted the four-year position here on Okinawa. New city, new future.

"So what do you make of all this?" Miyuki asked, changing the subject. "Could this be a part of your great-grandfather's lost Atlantis?"

"You mean the lost continent of Mu?" she said slowly. "I doubt it. Hundreds of other megalithic ruins dot the Pacific: the statues of Easter Island, the canal city of Nan Madol, the Latte stones of Guam, the Burden of Tonga. All of them predate the oral histories of these islands. No one has been able to connect them together." She warmed with the mystery.

"And you hope to do that?"

"Who knows what answers may be found here?"

Miyuki gave her a crooked grin and pushed up. "There is only one way to find out."

Karen shoved to her feet, matching her friend's grin. "I should say so."

The pair continued their climb, staying together, each

helping the other up the high steps. In twenty minutes, with the sun climbing higher, they reached the summit. Karen scrambled up first, breathing heavily.

The plateau was a single monstrous slab. A long crack traversed the surface, but the split was clearly due to more recent damage, most likely from the seismic activity. Karen guessed that when the pyramid was built, the slab must have been lifted intact atop this structure. She slowly turned. Ten meters on each side, she estimated. The meter-thick slab had to weigh hundreds of tons. How did these ancient builders get it up here?

Miyuki clambered up behind her, then turned in a slow circle, appreciating the view, her eyes shining. "Simply amazing."

Karen nodded, too awestruck to speak yet. She crossed to the tumbled temple in the center of the roof. It had once been constructed of slabs and basalt logs. She could imagine how it must have looked. A squat, low building surmounted by a slab roof. She edged around it, viewing it from all angles.

Miyuki dogged her steps, video camera in hand.

Karen examined the temple. It was unadorned. Or perhaps any decorative carving had been worn away long ago. She straightened. "I'm going in."

"What?" Miyuki lowered her camera. "What are you talking about?"

Karen pointed to a pair of wall slabs that had fallen and were tilting against each other. A narrow crawl space lay between them, descending at a slant.

"Are you crazy? You don't know how stable those stones are!"

Karen chipped some coral that had taken root between the two slabs. Like living cement. "For coral to grow here, it means they haven't moved in ages. Besides, I'm just going to take a quick peek. If there's any carving or petroglyphs, they'll be inside. Sheltered from erosion." She slipped out of her embroidered jacket and dropped to her knees. "It's gonna be a tight squeeze."

She yanked off her belt so the buckle wouldn't snag, then

shrugged out of her shoulder harness, lowering her holstered pistol to the stones.

"Is that penlight still in your bag?" she asked.

Miyuki shuffled through her pack and pulled out a tiny fluorescent purple flashlight. Karen took it, twisted it on, then put the handle in her mouth as she lay flat on her belly.

"Are you sure you should do this?"

As answer, Karen snuggled into the hole head first, penlight pointed forward. Worming her way inside, she used her fingers to find imperfections in the rock to help pull her forward, but mostly it was her toes that edged her inch by inch into the crawlway. She ignored the thick slabs hanging over her. She had done some caving in her past, but nothing this tight. She kept her breathing calm, told herself to just keep moving, don't stop.

"There go your feet!" Miyuki called to her.

Her friend's voice was muffled. Karen's body fit snugly within the tunnel. She found it harder to breathe with the walls compressing her chest. An edge of panic set in, but she bit it back. She took quicker, shallower breaths. She would not suffocate.

She moved on. If she became stuck, she could always use her hands to propel her backward, plus Miyuki could pull her by the ankles. There was no real danger here. Still, her mouth grew dry and sticky as her toes began to slip on the damp stone.

"How you doing?"

Karen opened her mouth to answer and realized she did not have enough air to yell back to her friend. "I'm okay." It came out in a gasped whisper around the flashlight held in her teeth.

"What was that?"

Karen stretched her arms forward. The fingers of her right hand just caught the edge of the slab's end. The end was that close! She locked her fingers and pulled, shoving with her toes at the same time. Her body thrust forward. By now her pulse pounded in her ears. Her jaw ached from biting on the metal penlight. "C'mon, goddamnit!" she swore in a short gasp.

Fingers scrambling, she found a purchase for her left hand, too. Grinning, she heaved her body forward, pulling her head free of the tunnel. She paused to crane her neck around, the beam of light casting back and forth.

A cramped space lay open here. No bigger than a half bath. But what caught her eye was what looked like an altar on the far side. Barnacle-covered urns and broken pottery lay scattered about the floor, all frosted with algae. Around the edge of the altar wove a carved snake. Karen followed it with her light until she reached the serpent's nose. A mane of stone feathers surrounded its fanged head. Its eyes, red stones, reflected back her light. Most likely rubies.

Ignoring the jewels, she moved the light, more excited by the representation of feathers. It reminded her of Quetzalcoatl, the feathered snake god of the Mayas. Could this be a sign that the Mayas had built this site?

She spat out the penlight. Twisting and using her arms as leverage, she hauled herself out of the damp tunnel and into the chamber. Recovering her flashlight, she turned to the entrance. Miyuki should see this.

Karen bent by the tunnel as a shot rang out.

The sharp blast echoed in the small space, followed by a terrified scream.

Karen dropped to her knees, trying to peer down the tunnel. "Miyuki!"

6

Sounding the Depths

For the first time in over twelve years, Jack placed his foot aboard a United States military vessel—and it was no small tugboat. He stepped from the Sea Knight helicopter onto almost an acre of open flight deck. The USS *Gibraltar* was two football fields long and half a field wide, a monstrous beast powered by two boilers. Up and down the flight deck, huge painted numbers signaled, landing pads for up to nine aircraft.

Ducking his head, he strode from under the helicopter's rotors. Overhead, the roar of the blades was deafening. The rotorwash tore at his unzipped jacket. As he cleared the blades, he almost tripped over one of the many aircraft tiedowns. He caught himself, feeling foolish. A rookie's mistake. It truly *had* been a long time since he walked this deck.

Past the deadly blades, Jack straightened and glanced out to sea. Near the horizon, he could just make out the tiny dot that was the *Deep Fathom*. He had been flown here for an organizational briefing due to start at noon. Closer to the huge ship, flanking its two sides, were three smaller destroyers, support ships for the mighty behemoth.

Jack scowled at the sight. Talk about overkill. At least the Vice President hadn't deployed an entire goddamn battle group.

Turning, Jack eyed the bristling array of weapons systems near the *Gibraltar*'s superstructure. With that much firepower, he thought, who needed an entire battle group? The *Gibraltar* could probably take over a small country by itself. Its air contingent consisted of forty-two Sea Knight helicopters, five Harrier attack planes, and six ASW helicopters. Additionally, the vessel bore its own defenses: Sea Sparrow surface-to-air missile systems, Phalanx Close-in Weapons System, Bushmaster cannons, even a Nixie torpedo-decoy system. All in all, one hell of a big stick to shake at the enemies of the United States.

Motors whined on his left. A portside elevator lifted another Sea Knight helicopter from the hangar below. Men and women in red and yellow jackets buzzed around the deck. With the large ship approaching ground zero of the crash site, the great beast was stirring.

Near the stern, Jack noted new additions to the flight deck: three large cranes and winch assemblies. Now he understood one reason for the vessel's late arrival. Before steaming here, they had clearly readied the ship for the salvage operation.

"Mr. Kirkland," a stern voice barked from behind.

Jack turned. A trio of uniformed personnel strode toward him. He did not know any of them, but did recognize their credentials. Instinctively, he found himself straightening, throwing his shoulders back.

In the lead was the C.O. of the *Gibraltar*. "Captain John Brenning," the man said, introducing himself as he stopped in front of Jack. No hand was offered to shake. He gestured to his right and left, saying, "My executive officer, Commander Julie Knudson, and Master Chief Hayward Lincoln."

Both nodded. The woman eyed Jack up and down as if he were a bug. The black master chief remained stoic, barely acknowledging him.

"Rear Admiral Houston has requested a private meeting before the noon briefing. Commander Knudson will take you below to the officer's wardroom."

The captain and master chief turned away, meaning to cross toward the main deck and the rallying air wing. The female officer spun on her heel, ready to lead Jack away.

But Jack remained standing. "Why the private meeting?"

Three pairs of eyes swung his way. Clearly, their orders were seldom questioned. Jack met their stares, unmoving, awaiting an answer. The sun glared mercilessly off the metal flight deck. Jack knew he was no longer in their chain of command. He was a civilian, his own man.

Captain Brenning sighed. "The admiral did not elaborate on his reasons. He asked us only to deliver you to him ASAP."

"If you would please follow," the executive officer said with the barest trace of irritation.

Jack crossed his arms over his chest. He would not be bullied into a subordinate position here. When it came to dealing with the military mentality, it was best to let them know where you stood, to get the pecking order firmly established up front.

"I agreed to lend the use of my submersible in this search," he said. "Nothing more. I only accepted today's meeting so I could discharge this duty as swiftly as possible. I am in no way obligated to kiss a rear admiral's rear."

A gruff voice called from an open hatch behind him. "And who the hell would want you to, Jack?"

The three uniforms snapped to attention, hands raised in sharp salute. "Admiral on deck!" the master chief barked.

From the shadows of the open hatch a large man stepped into the sunlight. He wore a green flight jacket, casually loose. His battle ribbons were in plain view. He strode forward from the shelter of the doorway. When Jack had last spoken to Mark Houston, the admiral had been a captain. Otherwise, Houston had not changed. The old man had the same thick gray hair cropped short, the same weathered features. His frosted blue eyes were as keen as ever as they stared Jack down.

Houston acknowledged his people with a nod.

Captain Brenning stepped forward. "There was no need for you to come up here, sir. Mr. Kirkland was just on his way down to meet you."

The admiral chuckled. "I'm sure he was. But there's one thing you need to learn about Jack Kirkland, Captain. He doesn't take orders well."

"So I am learning, sir," the C.O. said stiffly.

Though Jack stood six-foot-three, the admiral still seemed to tower over him, fists on hips. "Jack 'the Flash' Kirkland," he muttered sternly. "Who would have ever thought to see you on the *Gibraltar* again?"

"Not me, sir. That's for damn sure." Though Jack hated to be aboard another Navy vessel, he could not shake a certain warmth at seeing the old man. Mark Houston had been more than his commanding officer. He had proved a friend and mentor. In fact, it was Mark Houston who had successfully campaigned for him to be awarded the seat on the military shuttle mission. Jack cleared his throat. "It's good to see you again, sir."

"I'm glad to hear you say that. Now maybe you'll cooperate and follow me down to the conference room."

"Yes, sir."

The admiral dismissed his officers with a nod. "Come. I have coffee and sandwiches below," he said to Jack, leading the way toward the hatch in the looming superstructure. "The NTSB people have had a long night, so we're catering this briefing."

"Thank you, sir." Jack held his breath as he ducked through the hatch and entered the ship's bowels. Out of the sun, the cold of the ship struck him immediately. He had forgotten how frigid the inside of the ship's "island" could be, but the smell of oiled metal triggered old memories. Voices echoed from deeper in the ship. It was as if he had entered a living creature. Jonah in the whale, he thought morosely.

The admiral led him down to Level 2, stopping periodically to bow his head with other officers, to share a joke or pass on an order. Mark Houston had always been a hands-on officer. Before becoming admiral, when Houston was the

C.O. here, he had never holed himself up in his room. He could be found as often as not down in the crew quarters as up in the officers' galley. It was what Jack liked best about the old man. He knew all his crew, and the crew were all the more loyal for it.

"Here we are," Houston said. He rested his hand on the latch to the door and glanced down the hall, a tired smile on his face. "The *Gibraltar*. I can't believe I'm back here."

"I know what you mean."

Houston snorted. "They've got me berthed up in Flag Country. Seems strange. Last night I almost returned to my old C.O.'s cabin by habit. Funny how the mind works." The old man shook his head and pulled open the door. He waved for Jack to enter first.

The conference room was dominated by a long mahogany table. It had already been set up for the briefing. Water glasses, notebooks, and pens were aligned precisely before each of the ten chairs. There were also thermoses of coffee and platters of small sandwiches.

Jack glanced around as he crossed to the table. Maps and charts hung on the walls, with tiny flagged pins poking out. He recognized a regional map of local currents on a nearby wall. Inked squares were checkered on it. The search parameters. It seemed that the admiral had not been lax on the ride here.

Jack took it all in quickly, then turned to find Houston directly behind him. Again the admiral seemed to study him. "So how've you been, Jack?"

He shrugged. "Surviving."

"Hmm . . . that's too bad."

Jack scrunched up his brows, surprised by this response. He did not think the admiral bore him any ill will.

But Houston clarified his statement as he sank into one of the seats and kicked another toward Jack. "Life isn't just about surviving. It's about living."

Jack sat. "If you say so."

"Any women in your life?"

Jack frowned. He did not understand this line of questioning.

"I know you're not married, but is there anyone special in your life?"

"No. Not really. Friends, that's all. Why?"

The admiral shrugged. "Just wondering. We haven't spoken in over a decade. Not even a Christmas card."

Jack wrinkled his brow. "But you're Jewish."

"Okay, a Hanukkah card, you ass. My point is that I thought you'd at least keep in touch."

Jack studied his own hands, rubbing at his chair's armrests in discomfort. "I wanted to put everything behind me. Start new."

"And how's that going for you?" Houston asked sourly.

Jack's discomfort welled toward anger. He bit it back and remained silent.

"Goddamn it, Jack. Can't you tell when someone is trying to help you?"

Jack glanced to his former C.O. "And how's that?"

"Whether you know it or not, I've been keeping tabs on you. I know the financial straits you're in. You're about to lose that rust bucket of yours."

"I'll manage."

"Yeah, and you'll manage a hell of a lot better with several thousand dollars from the Navy for assisting us in the search for Air Force One."

Jack shook his head. "I don't need your charity."

"Well, you need something, you goddamn stubborn fool."

Both men just stared at one another for several breaths. Houston finally clenched a fist on his knee, but his voice softened with old pain. "Do you remember when Ethel died?"

Jack nodded. Ethel had been the admiral's wife for over thirty years. A year before the shuttle accident, she had succumbed to complications from ovarian cancer. In many ways, Ethel had been the only mother Jack had ever known. His own mother had died when he was three years old.

"The day before she slipped into a coma, she told me to watch over you."

Jack looked up in surprise. The admiral would not meet his eyes, but Jack noticed a glint of tears.

"I don't know what Ethel ever saw in you, Jack. But I won't let the old broad down. I've given you enough time to yourself . . . to work through what happened on the *Atlantis*. But enough is enough."

"What do you want of me?"

He met Jack's eyes. "You've been hiding out here long enough. I want you to come in from the sea."

Jack just stared, dumbfounded.

"That's why I recruited you. Not just for your submersible. It's time you returned to the real world."

"And the Navy is the real world?" Jack snorted.

"Close enough. We at least come to port every now and then."

Jack shook his head. "Listen, I appreciate your concern. I really do. But I'm almost forty years old, not a child to be coddled. Whether you believe it or not, I'm happy in my current life."

His former commander sighed and lifted his hands in surrender. "You are a goddamn piece of work, Jack." He stood up. "The briefing should be under way shortly. I suppose you understand the importance of our work here."

Jack nodded, standing also. "Of course. It's Air Force One. The President."

"It's more than just the President, Jack. We've lost Presidents before. But never under such circumstances, in the middle of a worldwide catastrophe. As much as the rest of the world disparages the United States and its foreign policy, it still doesn't stop them from looking to us for leadership during a time of crisis—and now we are leaderless, rudderless."

"What about the Vice President? Lawrence Nafe?"

"I see you at least keep abreast of current events out here," Houston teased lightly, but his voice quickly grew sober again. His brows knit with worry. "Washington is screaming for answers. Before Nafe can be sworn in, we need to put the fate of President Bishop to rest. Already rumors are spreading. Some are claiming terrorists—Arabs, Russian, Chinese, Serbian, or even the I.R.A. Take your pick. Some are saying it's all a hoax. Some say it's a conspiracy tied to JFK." The admiral shook his head. "It's a friggin' mess. For order to be restored, we need concrete answers. We need a body we can bury with the usual pomp and ceremony. That's why we're here."

Jack had never seen Mark Houston look so worried. "I'll do my best to help," he said sincerely. "Just ask, and I'll do it."

"I never expected less of you." Before Jack could stop him, the admiral reached out and gave him a quick hug. "And whether *you* believe it or not, Jack, I'm glad to see you again. Welcome back to the *Gibraltar*."

Jack froze in the man's embrace, unable to speak.

Houston released him and headed toward the door. "I have a few last minute details to address, but help yourself to the sandwiches, Jack. The egg salad is especially good. Real eggs, not that powdered shit." The admiral gave him a tired smile, then left, closing the door behind him.

Alone, Jack sank into one of the seats. He wiped his damp palms on his trousers. The gravity of the situation began to press on him. For the first time in a decade, he sensed the eyes of the world again looking in his direction.

Three hours later Jack found himself back on the *Deep Fathom*, but not for long. Dressed in his blue Norseman dry suit, he climbed into the cockpit of the *Nautilus 2000*, squeezing into the cramped seat. Once settled, he hooked up the Bio-Sensor monitors and attached his microphone. He ran down the predive safety checklist with Lisa, who was in the *Fathom*'s pilothouse.

Charlie worked atop the submersible as it floated behind the *Fathom*, stomping around, visually checking seals, while Robert, in mask and snorkel, swam under the ship. Jack had done his own check, but his crew were taking no chances. "Check everything twice," he had drilled into them.

Charlie clambered over to Jack. He stared with concern at his friend. "You sure about this, *mon*? That's a long way down. Deeper than you've ever flown this girl."

"She's rated for this depth."

"On the drawing boards maybe, but this is real life. The ocean has a way of surprising you. She can be a real bitch."

Jack looked up at the Jamaican geologist. "I'm going, Charlie."

"Okay, *mon*. It's your funeral."

Jack reached out and clasped the large man's hand. Then Charlie lowered the acrylic dome over Jack's head and screwed it into place. Once done, Charlie gave Jack a thumbs-up and dove off the sub, joining the marine biologist in the water as Jack finalized his checklist.

Around the *Fathom*, the other search ships were spread in a wide circle. Off to the south, the *Gibraltar* filled the horizon. Overhead, a Sea Knight helicopter buzzed by. All eyes remained on Jack and his tiny sub.

Lisa came on the radio. "You're ready to go, Jack." The nervousness in her voice could not be hidden.

"Check and check. Diving now," he said dryly. He engaged the thrusters, the sub humming under him. He took on ballast and the *Nautilus* began to lower into the surf. The waterline climbed up the dome, swamping over Jack's head.

A brief flash of claustrophobia struck him. He ignored it. He knew it was just a base animal reaction, a triggered survival instinct against drowning. Divers had been experiencing it for ages. He breathed steadily past the momentary twinge of anxiety as the sub sank deeper. He had a long way to go.

Six hundred meters. More than a quarter of a mile.

Earlier, on the *Gibraltar*, the briefing had been curt and to the point. The overnight search had picked up the pinging of the flight's data recorder, and the NTSB team had localized the most likely dive spot—in water over six hundred meters deep. The Coast Guard's vice admiral had argued for deploying the Navy's *Deep Drone*, a remote-operated deep-sea robot, to explore the seabed. But the *Deep Drone*, presently stationed in the Atlantic, could not be flown onsite for another two days.

As the situation was debated, Jack had let the group know that his own ship's test submersible was rated for depths of eight hundred meters and that he would be willing to at least recon the site and attempt to retrieve the data recorders. The NTSB seemed reluctant to accept his help. "Too dangerous," the team leader had asserted. "We can't risk the loss of more lives."

But Jack's former commander had argued against such caution. "If Mr. Kirkland says he can safely explore the region, then I say let him."

Even now Jack could remember the flare of pride at Mark Houston's support. Without it, he wouldn't be diving to this new depth.

With his other teammates clear, Jack worked the pedals of the *Nautilus*. He descended in a slow spiral, his eyes on all his monitors, the *ping* of his own sonar echoing in his ears. The space between the ping and its return were still spaced far apart.

. . . *ping*. . . . . *ping* . . .

As he sank deeper, the waters grew darker around him. He flicked the battery switch and engaged the sub's headlights. Cones of brilliance shot forward, disappearing into the infinite blue. Slipping past the two hundred meter mark, the waters became inky, as if he were descending through oil instead of water. Already Jack heard the telltale groan and tick of stressed seals as pressure built outside the sub. But this was just the beginning. At a depth of six hundred meters the pressure would grow to half a ton per square inch, enough to crush him to pulp in a heartbeat.

He reached to his computer monitor and tapped up the sonar model for this region of the seafloor. The detail was poor. Scans had revealed only an odd fuzzy detail of the seabed. Even side-scanning sonar had failed to make much headway. The topography of the seabed here was too folded and broken with hills, scarps, seamounts, and other seabed aberrations. Any hope of discovering a telltale sonar ghost of the airplane had long been given up. It would be up to him to search from here.

. . . *ping*. . . . . *ping* . . .

Jack began to feed his own sonar information into the computer model. Slowly the fuzzy detail began to focus. Details emerged. "Are you getting this?" he asked, touching his microphone.

Lisa answered. "It's a mess down there. Be careful."

As the sonar image grew crisper, he could make out a maze of gigantic seamounts and flat-topped guyots on the floor below. Deep canyons and troughs wound around these towering mounts. It reminded Jack of the Badlands of the American West, a maze of crisscrossing canyons and river channels through a landscape of windswept mesas and red rock. He had once taken a horseback trip through those wild lands. Even with a map, it had been easy to get lost. He suspected the same was true here.

The radio hissed for a moment, then Charlie's voice came over the tiny speakers. "I don't like what I'm seeing, Jack."

"What do you mean?"

"Seamounts arise from volcanic activity. This dense clustering looks highly suspect to me."

"Any seismic readings?"

A long pause. "Uh, no . . . it's all quiet, but I still don't like it."

"Keep an eye out for me, Charlie." Jack remembered what happened the last time he had ignored the geologist's advice. A volcano opened up under him. He did not want to repeat the experience.

He continued to sink deeper in a widening spiral, slowing his descent. He watched his depth gauge climb from the four hundred mark toward the five hundred. Beyond the acrylic dome, tiny flickering lights caught his eye, drawing his attention away from his monitors. At first he thought it was just his imagination, then, as if he were caught in a snowstorm, a flurry of blue lights swelled and fluttered around his sub. Bioluminescent creatures, too tiny and transparent to see clearly.

"Coming up on life down here," Jack said. He hit the video button, swiveling around to appreciate the storm as it rolled and churned away into the darkness. "How's the new video feed?"

"Shaky, jittery . . . but we can make out pretty good detail."

As quickly as they had appeared, the flock of organisms were gone. Darkness closed in again. Jack settled into his seat. The experimental video system had been loaned to them by the Navy and installed quickly, so others could monitor his progress. He glanced to his depth gauge. He was already nearing the six hundred mark.

. . . ping . . . ping . . .

The sonar echo narrowed. He had to be near the floor. He slowed his descent from a spiral to a gradual slope, gliding smoothly down, lights spearing forward.

"Jack!"

"Oh shit!" He saw it at the same time. He slammed the left pedal, tilting thc sub and driving it in a sharp turn to the left. He just missed crashing into a tall gnarled pillar. It had appeared out of the darkness. Jack stabilized his sub, circled past the pillar and found himself in a forest of other twisted columns and spires. Some were spindly, only a hand span wide but tens of meters tall. Others were as thick as redwoods and towered just as high. He had almost crash landed into a stone forest.

Charlie's voice was full of delight. "Get as much on video as you can."

Jack had never seen their like. He rose a bit to avoid the densest patches, but still had to weave and wiggle around the larger pillars. "What are they?"

"Lava pillars! Fragile basalt columns formed where lava extrudes up tiny cracks in the mantle, then are cooled rapidly by the frigid waters."

Jack tilted to view the twisted tangle below and watched a huge octopus climb through the tangle. Fish darted from his light.

Charlie continued, "We still don't know much about them. They were only recently discovered."

Jack edged past a monster column that had to be three meters thick and vanished up into the darkness over his head.

"But be cautious, Jack. As I was warning you before, this clustering of lava pillars suggests the region is unstable. A tectonic hot spot. Not a place you want to be hanging around. But I've got your back. Any blip on the seismic scale and I'll send you an SOS."

"Please do." Jack cleared his throat. "Lisa, can you hear me?"

"Yeah, Jack."

"How am I positioned in reference to the NTSB's estimate of where Air Force One's black box is pinging?"

A short pause. "I'm feeding your computer the newest data. You should be almost on top of her. About a hundred and twenty meters due north."

Jack glanced to his compass. The needle jittered in a half arc back and forth. He futilely tapped the glass. It had been working perfectly ten minutes ago. "Lisa, you may have to guide me in verbally. The compass is malfunctioning. Can't get a clear reading."

"Fine. Turn the sub's nose about thirty degrees, then go straight."

Jack slowly turned the ship, estimating by using one of the pillars as a reference point. "How about now?"

"Perfect. Straight ahead slow."

Jack depressed the foot pedals, and the sub slid smoothly forward, lights drilling a path forward.

"Good, your trajectory is right on target."

Frowning, Jack watched his compass begin to swing wildly. It reminded him of the problem he had with his compass when he was caught in the volcanic eruption. "Topside . . . there's something screwy with—"

Suddenly, the submersible's lights reflected back at Jack, blinding him for a few blinks. "Holy—"

"Shit!" Lisa finished for him.

Ahead, a massive sleek triangle of whitewashed metal blocked the way forward, thrusting up from the jungle of lava pillars. The twin xenon lamps lit it up brightly. In the center, a huge American flag was prominently depicted, under it the designation BOEING 28000. It was the tail fin of Air Force One.

"The Eagle has been found," he whispered.

Jack slowed his sub, engaging the thrusters to lift him up

and over the gigantic fin. As he rose he dilated his lights to maximum diffusion, thrusting a fog of brilliance over the landscape below.

Past the tail fin, the remainder of the wreckage appeared. In a rain of destruction, the Boeing 747 lay scattered across the valley in a rough circle. Hundreds of the fragile lava pillars lay toppled amid the debris. Seamounts towered on the far side.

Jack slowly circled the site. Sections of torn wing and chunks of fuselage littered the seabed. He crossed over the crumpled nose of the great plane. Its glass had been shattered out, but Jack could see the instrument panel.

He tore his eyes away, afraid of what else he might find. It was a graveyard down here. Memories of the shuttle crash flashed across his mind. Another fall from the sky. Had this been all that was left of *Atlantis*, bits and pieces scattered across a seabed floor? Jack shuddered.

The admiral's firm desire to know the fate of President Bishop had been accomplished. All that remained now were the details.

Who to blame?

Jack closed his eyes for a moment, taking a deep breath. After the *Atlantis* disaster, he had experienced firsthand the feeding frenzy of blame, and he pitied the person who would bear the brunt of the coming accusations. Opening his eyes, he reached and gripped the controls to his exterior manipulator arms. He had one final duty down here. Retrieve the two black boxes—the flight's data recorder and the cockpit voice recorder—and bring them to the surface.

"Lisa, I'm going to need more guidance from here to find those boxes." Jack glanced at his compass, expecting to see it still spinning. Instead the needle remained fixed and steady, pointing toward the debris field. "Looks like I've got the compass back."

"Good, then what you want to do—"

Jack watched the compass needle slowly inch as the *Nautilus* circled the debris field. "Just a second, Lisa." Bunching his brows, he accelerated, gliding around the edge of the crash site. He completed almost a full turn, yet the compass needle continued to point toward the center of the destruction.

"That can't be right."

"What is it?" Lisa asked. "Do you have a problem?"

Jack slowed the sub, swinging its nose forward. He coned his lights back down to narrow spears. The concentrated light penetrated to the heart of the debris field. A towering pillar lay near the center, at least forty meters tall—but something wasn't right.

The pillar seemed to glow.

Jack blinked, thinking the seawater must be playing tricks.

He edged the *Nautilus* forward, passing for the first time into the graveyard. Small hairs at the back of his neck began to tingle. Not from any fear of the ghosts, but something more physical. Even the hairs on his arm began to vibrate.

Lisa's voice came over the radio, but interference drowned out her words. Not static. It was as if someone had recorded Lisa's voice and played it back at a higher speed.

"Say again, Topside."

He concentrated, and he could just make out Lisa's words. "Your heart rate . . . it's dropping significantly. Are you okay?"

Jack glanced to his own pulse reading. It was normal. "I don't understand."

Any response was lost in a high-pitched whine. Jack lowered the volume as it began to ache his ear. He thought there must be a glitch with the radio, and glanced to the compass. It still pointed toward the strange pillar.

The damned thing must be magnetic.

As he moved nearer the pillar, the tingling sensation was swept from his body, as if cool water were drenching him. Jack shivered and slowed the submersible. He hovered before the pillar.

Craning his neck, he examined its length. The column continued to glow, but not with its own light. It was simply an optical effect, a reflection and refraction of his own light, like sunlight on a diamond. Though the pillar was clearly stone, it was not black volcanic rock. Instead, it was made of some type of crystal, like a shaft of quartz thrust up from the seabed floor.

Under his lamplight, the crystal had a slight aquamarine hue to it, streaked with whorls of brilliant ruby. Though it stood as straight as an arrow, Jack sensed it was a natural structure. Not man-made. Some natural phenomenon, undiscovered until now. With only five percent of the ocean floor explored, such discoveries, like the lava pillars, were being made all the time.

Jack circled the crystalline obelisk. With the communications still garbled, he feared the video feed might also be affected, so he switched the cameras to local recording, saving it all on DVD disk. Once he was done, he turned the sub around and returned to the edge of the debris field.

The mystery would have to wait for now. He had a mission to complete. He would use his own hydrophones and sonar to search for Air Force One's data recorders. It would make the work harder, but not impossible. Whatever communication glitch had occurred would have to be worked out topside.

As he swung free of the debris field, Lisa's voice came over the radio, as clear as glass. "Jack . . . What the hell is going on down there?"

"Lisa?"

"Jack!" The relief in her voice rang clear. "You goddamn asshole. Why didn't you answer me? The readings we were getting were all frizzed, and the video feed became garbled nonsense. We didn't know what was going on."

"How are my readings now?"

"Uh . . . fine. Green lights across the board. What happened down there?"

"I'm not entirely sure. There's something here that I can't explain. It's screwing with my compass and must be affecting other systems, too."

"What is it?" Charlie asked, piping in. "I was getting tiny seismic readings just as you went off-line. You scared me good, *mon*."

"I'm not sure, Charlie. But I got it all on DVD. I'll show

you when I get topside, but right now I still have my mission to accomplish." Jack glided the sub near the jet's tail fin again. He had come complete circle. "Lisa, can you guide me to the boxes?"

"Y-You're right on top of them." Lisa's voice trembled. She was clearly still shaken. "Grab them and get your ass out of there."

Jack lowered the sub. "Will do." He glanced to his compass. It still pointed to the strange pillar thrusting up from the heart of the debris, a gigantic gravestone marking the resting place of the dead.

He began his search through the rubble with a quiet prayer for the men and women of Air Force One, especially one: *Rest in peace, Mr. President*.

7

Ancient Footprints

"Miyuki!" Karen yelled. A second shot blasted from beyond the short tunnel, muffled this time. But who? Karen knelt on both knees. She saw the passage to the outside blocked. Someone was crawling toward her.

She swung her tiny flashlight up.

From the tunnel, Miyuki's panicked face stared back at her. "Pull me to you," she hissed. "Someone's shooting at us." Miyuki extended her arms.

Karen dropped the flashlight and reached out to grasp her friend's wrists. Planting her feet, she hauled Miyuki inside the cramped heart of the pyramid's temple.

Miyuki, panting and wild-eyed, rolled off Karen and sat up. She reached down and unhooked two packages from her ankles: their tote bag of equipment and Karen's .38 automatic, still in its holster. "I didn't want to leave anything behind," she said, handing Karen the pistol.

Karen undid the snaps and shook the holster off her gun.

It reassured her to feel cold steel in her palm. "What happened?"

"Men . . . three of them. They must have spotted our boat and come to see what we had discovered."

"Looters?"

Miyuki nodded.

"So you crawled in here?"

"I didn't know what else to do."

"Did they see you slip in here?"

"I don't know."

Already, harsh voices echoed to them. Their attackers were climbing the pyramid. Karen did not have time to crawl back out and set up an ambush. She scanned around the cramped chamber for another exit. They were trapped. All they had to defend themselves were the eight remaining bullets in her pistol.

Miyuki backed away from the tunnel opening. "What are we going to do?" She crossed to the snake-adorned altar and crouched next to it.

The rasp of boots on stone approached, the voices louder. The looters were not speaking Japanese. It sounded like a dialect of one of the South Pacific islanders. Karen strained to understand, but the language was unfamiliar to her.

A pair of legs appeared at the tunnel's entrance.

Tensing, Karen flicked off her flashlight, plunging the chamber into darkness. She raised the pistol in both hands. Sunlight blazed beyond the tunnel. She had a clear shot. Three men, eight bullets. If she shot well, they might have a chance. But her hands shook. She was an excellent shot, but had never aimed at a human target before.

The man knelt at the exit, leaning on one palm. Karen noticed a pale tattoo scrawling up his dark arm: a winding snake. The man twisted, barking an order to a companion. As his forearm turned, Karen saw the sprout of feathers about the head of the snake. Its red eyes stared back at her.

Karen suppressed a gasp. It was the same as the altar's carving! The man's face leaned into view, flashlight in hand. In his other hand he held her embroidered jacket. He yelled something toward them. Though she didn't know the language, she knew he was ordering them to show themselves.

Karen ducked to the side as a beam of light pierced their hiding place. She clutched the gun to her chest. She would only shoot if forced. Maybe they would believe that she and Miyuki had fled.

The beam of light vanished and darkness reclaimed the chamber. Karen leaned against the damp rock wall. As long as they sat still, she thought, they were safe. If any of the men tried to crawl inside, she could easily dispatch them with a single shot.

The best defense right now was a waiting game.

The men outside had grown quiet. Karen could hear scuffling and scraping but could not discern what they were doing. Moving quietly, she shifted to peer out of the tunnel again.

In the bright sunlight, she saw a rusted metal canister being tipped and its contents splashed into the tunnel's entrance. The reek hit her nostrils at the same time understanding clenched her heart.

Kerosene!

Karen watched the trail of flammable liquid flow down the slanted tunnel toward them. She covered her mouth against the rising fumes. The looters meant to burn them out or kill them. She backed away from the tunnel, knowing she dare not shoot, not when a spark might ignite the kerosene.

Karen bumped into Miyuki behind her. Her friend had her handheld Palm computer. In the gloom, she saw Miyuki furiously tapping at its tiny glowing screen.

"I'm trying to reach Gabriel," Miyuki said sternly, all business. "A call for help, but there is too much interference."

Karen was surprised at Miyuki's resourcefulness. "What if you were nearer the entrance?"

Miyuki glanced toward the opening. "That might help," she said.

Briefly illuminated by the computer screen's glow, Karen's eye again caught on the ruby-eyed altar serpent. It was similar to the rendering on their attacker's arm. Was there some connection? But how? The pyramid had been submerged for centuries in these waters.

Miyuki had moved closer to the entrance, with Karen beside her. The flow of kerosene now trailed into the chamber. Karen peered out and saw the canister on its side. No men were in sight, but she could still hear them. Tilting her head, she listened. They were singing—or perhaps *chanting*.

Shivering, she gestured to Miyuki. "Hurry."

Her friend knelt into the stream of flammable liquid, her hands trembling. She dropped to her belly, extending her computer to arm's length down the tunnel, seeking a wireless signal. "I can barely see the screen."

"Just try. We have to—"

"Good afternoon, Professor Nakano." Gabriel's voice seemed explosively loud.

Miyuki froze, sprawled in the stream of kerosene. "Gabriel?"

"I am continuing to collect and correlate your data. May I be of additional assistance?"

The singsong chanting continued uninterrupted from beyond the tunnel. Their conversation had not been heard.

"Can you pick up our location?"

"Of course, my GPS is working perfectly, Professor Nakano."

"Then please contact the Chatan authorities. Tell them we are under assault by looters at this location."

Before Gabriel could acknowledge this command, the chanting outside abruptly ended. Karen clutched Miyuki's arm, warning her to silence. Miyuki yanked back her computer, and the two women rolled to the side. Karen saw the first man's face appear again at the tunnel's mouth. This time it was not a flashlight he held in his free hand, but a matchstick.

Time had run out.

He struck the match on the stone. A tiny flame sprouted. Holding the match aloft, the man again called toward them. His words almost sounded laced with regret. Then he tossed the flaming match down the tunnel.

Northwest of Enewak Atoll, Central Pacific

"You're running out of air, Jack," Lisa warned through the radio. Her voice had remained edgy since the glitch in communications. She had been calling him every other minute.

"I know," he snapped back at her. "I can see my oxygen gauge." Jack worked the pedals of his submersible while simultaneously manipulating the controls to the remote exterior arms. He dragged a large chunk of fuselage out of the way. Silt billowed up from his motion, clouding his view. He had been working now close to an hour, shifting through the debris, following the *ping* of the wreck's black boxes. Jack released the chunk of twisted metal and shifted the sub into reverse, using the thrusters to blow the silt clear. He didn't have time to wait for it to settle on its own.

The *Nautilus* glided backward, but he watched the water clear ahead of him. Once satisfied, he slowed the submersible and edged back to the work site. Tilting the sub, Jack examined the sandy seabed. A thick sea cucumber rolled across the empty space, disturbed by his passage.

C'mon, you bastard, where are you?

Then he spotted it. A squarish object half buried in the muddy silt. He swung his lights to focus on it and sighed in relief. *Thank God!* He wiped sweat from his eyes. The small space had grown humid from his labors. "Found it!" he called hoarsely into his microphone.

"Say again?"

"I found the second black box."

He inched the sub forward and settled it to the seabed. The characteristic orange and red box lay near the sub's nose. The term "black" box was a misnomer. The data recorders had never been black. Jack reached out with his titanium arms. Using the right pincer, he gripped the rectangular box and carefully pulled it from the mud. He lifted it into view and grinned in relief, suddenly giddy. He had done it! It was Air Force One's cockpit recorder.

"Got it!"

"Then get your ass up here, Jack. You're damn near the point of no return. Your CO_2 levels are already rising."

"I hear you, Mother," he said, checking his gauges. He had just enough oxygen to reach the surface—at least, he hoped so. Swinging around in a tight arc, he returned to where he had left the first box—the flight's data recorder—and collected it up in his left pincer.

"Got both prizes. Coming up!"

Jack had reached for the key to blow his ballast when a glint from the seafloor caught his eye. Frowning, he swung his lamps. A gasp escaped his throat. "Oh, God!"

"Jack, what is it?"

In the lamp's glare a *face* stared back at him from the seabed floor. It took Jack a couple heartbeats to realize the visage was not that of a dead body—instead, the face shone bright green under his light. It was hard, crystalline. Jade. As he adjusted the light, he recognized the distinct Asian features and ancient war crown. He'd been told about the gift given to President Bishop by the Chinese Premier—a full-sized replica of a terra-cotta warrior, done in jade. Jack nudged the *Nautilus* closer and bumped the bust with one of the sub's arms. The head rolled across the silty bottom. It was all that was left of the ten-foot statue.

"Jack, what is it?" Lisa repeated.

Jack swallowed hard. "Nothing. I'm okay. Coming up."

But before he could leave, his eyes returned to the green gaze of the jade bust. The features were so lifelike—the sole survivor of the tragedy. Switching both black boxes to one pincer, Jack used the freed-up arm to grab the piece of jade sculpture. It had been the last gift to a dead President. He would not leave it behind.

With his treasures in hand, Jack tapped a key and blew his ballast. The sub burst upward from the seabed with a goose of his thrusters.

Below, he watched the debris field fade away. Near its center, the strange spear of crystalline rock came into view again, jabbing up from the seabed. His gaze was drawn to it. He knew Charlie would sell his eyeteeth to catch a glimpse of the amazing structure. Jack hoped the video footage he had recorded to disk would come out.

As he climbed, the sight vanished beyond the reach of the

sub's searchlights. Jack settled back to his seat. Every muscle ached. He had not realized how the effort had worn on him: the tension, the cramped quarters, the meticulous work. While sifting through the debris, he had kept himself tight as a fist. Periodically as he'd worked, the strange tingling sensation had washed over him, quivering the tiny hairs all over his body. It was as if the eyes of the dead were studying him. Occasionally he would swear he caught movement at the corners of his eyes. But when he'd looked, all he found was wreckage and debris.

"Jack, there's someone here who wants to speak to you."

"Who?"

A new voice came over the radio. "How are you doing, Jack?"

"Admiral?" What was Mark Houston doing aboard the *Fathom*?

As if reading his mind, the admiral answered, "I was flown to your boat about ten minutes ago. I heard the good news en route. So you've recovered *both* data recorders?"

"Yes, sir. I should be up with them in about fifteen minutes."

"I knew you could do it, Jack."

Jack remained silent. As much as he wanted to distance himself from his naval past, praise from his old commander still affected him.

Admiral Houston continued, "How did your submersible handle?"

"Except for that glitch in communications, she handled like a dream."

"Good, because the NTSB team has been monitoring your video feed of the wreckage. The team has already targeted a few key pieces of the plane that they'd like to see brought to the surface."

"Sir?"

"Would you be willing to haul cable from the winches?"

Jack bit his lower lip, holding back a curse. He had hoped the retrieval of the flight's data recorders would end his obligation here. "I'd have to check with the rest of my team."

"Of course, you have the night to sleep on it. The NTSB

will have enough on its hands just analyzing the black boxes."

Jack grimaced. He did not want to return to the deep-sea graveyard. Though he had been searching wrecks for the past decade, this one was different. It reminded him too acutely of his own accident.

"I'll consider it, Admiral. That's all I'll say for now."

"That's all I'm asking."

Sighing, Jack leaned back and watched the depth gauge wind toward the two hundred meter mark. The seas around him began to lighten. It was as if dawn were approaching after a long moonless night. He had never wanted to see the sky so desperately.

A more familiar voice returned to the radio. "We have your GPS picked up," Lisa said. "Charlie already has the dinghy in the water."

"Thanks, Lisa. The sooner I get out of this titanium coffin and into a cold shower, the better."

"What about what the admiral wants us to do?"

Jack screwed up his face. He did not want this conversation. "What do you think? Should we do it?"

He could almost hear Lisa shrug. "It's up to you, Jack, but I don't like that communication glitch. The sub is still experimental. It was not meant to be tested so vigorously. I'd really like to see the sub dry-docked and inspected to make sure the seals are undamaged. You don't take chances at these depths."

"You're probably right, Lisa. This wreckage isn't going anywhere." Jack warmed to the idea. It would buy him time to sort through his feelings. "Could you have Robert prepare the A-frame? We'll haul the *Nautilus* out and give her a thorough going over before we consider the Navy's request."

"Good." Lisa sounded relieved.

The depth gauge crossed the hundred meter level. Jack craned his neck back. He could see the distant sun as a watery glow in the dim water. "I should be up in less than a minute."

"We're ready for you. Charlie is on his way."

Jack closed his eyes, allowing himself a few private moments. If the admiral was aboard the *Fathom*, he suspected this would be his last moment of peace for the remainder of the day. He knew he faced a long debriefing.

As sunlight suddenly burst around him, Jack peeked open his eyes. He fished into a side compartment and retrieved his sunglasses. After being submerged for so long, the light stung. As he snapped the side compartment closed his hand settled on the video DVD recorder.

Without a good reason, but unable to resist, he popped out the tiny disk, slipped it into a pocket of his wet suit, and zippered it closed. The video of the crystal spire had nothing to do with the crash, and Charlie would want to see it. If the investigators knew of it, they would just confiscate it and lose it among the thousands of other details—or so he rationalized to himself.

In truth, the bit of subterfuge was his way of exerting some control over the situation. He meant to keep something for himself from this adventure.

The sound of an outboard motor sounded, buzzing through the gentle slosh of waves against his acrylic bubble. Jack turned and spotted the *Fathom*'s Zodiac dinghy, its green pontoons bouncing through the small swells.

Grinning, he slipped on his sunglasses. He spotted Charlie at the wheel. The tall Jamaican waved a long arm in his direction. *Here comes the cavalry!* Then Jack saw someone standing beside the geologist. Someone in a black wet suit. He frowned. *Who's that?*

Charlie pulled alongside the bobbing sub and hopped over. As he secured the mooring lines, the dinghy's other occupant dumped over the side before Jack could get a better look at him.

Charlie clambered over and unscrewed the acrylic dome. Jack pushed from the inside and shoved the dome back. Fresh air swept into the cabin and he breathed deeply, not realizing until this moment how dead the air in the sub had become. He *had* shaved this dive a little close.

Pulling with his arms, Jack yanked himself from the compartment. "Who's with you?"

"One of those NTSB investigator boys. He's here to make sure the black boxes are secure."

Jack stretched, joints popping, then clambered over toward the nose of the sub. "I could have brought them in myself."

"They're not taking any chances. National security and all that. Someone had to be present."

Jack knelt and saw the man, in snorkel and mask, working at the grips of the submerged arms. He worked fast and efficiently. At least they sent someone who knew something about submersibles. The man loosened the first pincer and collected both data recorders into a bulky float bag. It bobbed to the surface, tied by a tether to the man's belt. The man did not even come up for air as he turned his attention to the second pincer. He freed the jade bust and collected it into another float bag.

Jack felt a twinge of respect. The man knew his stuff.

As the second float bag broke the surface, Charlie called to Jack, "Help me turn the dinghy!"

Jack left his observation point and assisted Charlie with the final preparations to haul the submersible back to the *Fathom*. Not that they would have far to go; the *Fathom* was already motoring toward their position. Jack squinted at his ship, a welcome sight.

The dinghy suddenly rocked under Jack's feet. He grabbed the back of the pilot's seat to keep his footing. Glancing over his shoulder, he saw the NTSB man haul himself over the leeward pontoon. Jack stumbled over to assist the man into the dinghy, but by the time he got there the man had rolled aboard and was hauling one of the float bags inside.

"Let me help you," Jack said, leaning over the side and grabbing the edge of the other float bag.

Jack found himself hip-checked and knocked onto his rear. "Leave it!" the man ordered. His words were harsh and carried a tone of command.

Jack pushed to his feet, his cheeks red, his blood up. No one shoved him around his own boat. He stepped nearer. "Who the hell do you think—"

The big man turned, ripped away his mask and pulled back the hood of his wet suit.

Jack gasped as he recognized the diver. It could not be. He had not seen his former teammate in over a decade. "David?"

The tall blond man's face was twisted with hatred. Before Jack could move, a fist flew toward his face. Hard knuckles struck his lower jaw and threw him backward. Sparks of light danced across his vision as he hit the floor.

Charlie was instantly there, stepping between the attacker and his captain. "What the hell do you think you're doing, *mon*?"

Jack sat up. "Stay out of it, Charlie." He pushed himself to his feet, tasted blood on his tongue. The tall Jamaican moved back a half step, ready to defend his friend if necessary.

David Spangler's thin lips sneered at Jack. "That was for Jen!" he spat.

Jack rubbed his jaw. He had no answer for that. In fact, he couldn't blame David for his reaction. "What are you doing here?" he simply asked, leaning back against a chair.

"I've been assigned to the investigation by the new President."

"What's the CIA have to do with this?"

David's right eye twitched.

"Yeah, I heard about your transfer," Jack said, tired. "It seems you've moved up in the world."

"And you should have stayed gone from it," David said. He turned and hauled the second float bag into the dinghy.

"It wasn't my idea to come here."

"Let me guess," David said harshly. "Admiral Houston called you in."

Jack shrugged.

David dumped the second black box into the boat, none too gently. "Houston always had a hard-on for you, Kirkland."

Jack's voice grew gruff. "He was a friend of Jennifer's, too."

"Yeah, and look what it got her."

Jack nudged Charlie toward the wheel. "Get us out of

here." Jack stared David down. In the other man's blue eyes, Jack saw all the blame he felt in his own heart. "I'm sorry about Jennifer—" he started.

"Fuck your apology," David spat back. "I have my job, you have yours. Just stay out of my way."

Jack knew no words would ever settle this old score. David would never forgive him for his sister's death. The chasm between them was unbridgeable. Giving up, Jack crossed to the stern to make sure the mooring lines remained clear of the motor. As he moved past the former SEAL, the man leaned close to him, his breath hot on Jack's face.

David's eyes shone with rancor and malice. It was like looking into the eyes of a rabid animal. He whispered so his words were heard only by Jack: "This isn't over, Kirkland."

Off the coast of Yonaguni Island, Okinawa Prefecture

"Get back!" Karen pulled Miyuki to her knees. Flames filled the narrow crawlway and spread rapidly along the trail of kerosene. On hands and knees the two fled behind the altar.

At the crawlway, flames swept into their hiding place, accompanied by a blast of searing heat and stinging smoke. Miyuki cupped her arm across her mouth, her eyes tearing.

Karen joined her, suppressing a choking cough, afraid to alert the looters outside. What were they to do? In the brightness of the flames, Karen's watery eyes were drawn to the sharp glint from the snake sculpture wrapped around the altar. Its twin eyes glowed at her, reflecting the fire. Rubies.

"Karen . . . ?" Miyuki reached out a hand to her.

Karen took it, and the women clung to one another. The wall of flames blocked escape, and the air grew smokier with each breath.

"I'm sorry," Karen mumbled.

"Could there be another way out?" Miyuki asked. "A secret passage."

Karen bit her lower lip, straining to think past her panic. "I don't know. If there was, it would probably be near the altar." Her eyes were again drawn to the altar's snake carving. Something had been bothering her about it, nagging for her attention. Her gaze caught again on the snake's ruby eyes. With her free hand, Karen touched the stone carving. Then she saw it, reflected in the firelight—a defect. One of the ruby eyes shone much brighter than the other. It was almost as if a hollow space lay behind it. Using a finger, she pressed against the faceted eye.

"What are you doing?" Miyuki asked.

The jewel pushed back into the snake's skull, she heard a sharp *click*, then felt the snake's head loosen in her grip. "It's a lock release!" She could now swing the figure's head back and forth. But nothing happened. What was its purpose?

The smoke, meanwhile, settled thicker in the chamber. Near the tunnel, the flames receded, the kerosene almost spent. Karen rubbed her sore eyes. Outside, she heard the attackers stir. Since their initial volley had failed to smoke them out, what might they do next?

The answer came quickly. A flaming glass bottle flew into the room and exploded against the front of the altar. A wave of fire burst up.

Karen fell backward, and Miyuki ducked farther behind the altar with a startled squawk.

"Goddamn them!" Karen swore. Ignoring the flames, she moved back to the altar. The secret release suggested the carving was more than decoration. *Could there be a hidden passage?* The heat burned Karen's cheeks as she studied the stone snake. The serpent curled fully around the edge of the altar, its tail not far from its raised head. A thought occurred to her. The worm Ourbourus. The snake biting its own tail. A symbol of the infinite. Many cultures had similar mythic images. It was even in Mayan astrology.

Beyond the tunnel, Karen heard the men's voices grow heated, argumentative, impatient. Then a bullet blasted into the chamber, ricocheting in a shower of stone shards. Ducking, Karen shoved the sculpture's head all the way around until the tip of the serpent's snout touched its own tail.

A loud grinding sounded under her toes, and Karen tensed.

"What's happening?" Miyuki whispered, waving the smoke away.

Karen backed up as the altar stone lowered, dropping into the slab floor. "C'mon!" Karen took the penlight from a pocket and flashed a long beam into the inky darkness. The altar had fallen down about two meters.

She sensed that a larger chamber lay below, and leaned closer, trying to get a better look. A bullet whizzed past her left ear. She felt the heat of its passage as she dropped to her belly. "There's no other way out of here," she said, glancing at her friend.

Miyuki's eyes were huge, but she gave a quick nod.

Karen popped the penlight in her mouth. "I'll go first," she mumbled. Swinging her legs into the pit, she probed with her toes. No footholds. With a glance below, she aimed for the top of the lowered altar and pushed off. Her feet hit hard, dropping her to one hand.

She flashed her light around the chamber. Pools of dank water dotted the floor. Pale ropes of algae hung from the roof. On the far side, a dark tunnel led away. She stood and shifted her light for a better look. No, not a tunnel—a *stairway*. It descended at a steep angle. Wherever it led, it was better than here.

A second shot blasted overhead, quickly followed by another.

Miyuki squeaked, laying flat.

Straightening, Karen called up. "Toss my gun and holster."

Miyuki's face disappeared for a moment. "Here!" She dropped the leather holster strap. The gun followed a second later. Karen caught it in one hand.

"Now you!" Karen urged.

"Not yet." Miyuki disappeared again.

What was she doing?

Miyuki's legs reappeared. Karen reached up and guided her friend's ankles. "Okay. You're clear."

Miyuki let go, landing almost on top of Karen, who held her friend steady. "Good job."

"Yeah, thanks," Miyuki muttered, clutching her satchel of equipment tight to her chest. She caught Karen's glance. "I wasn't leaving Gabriel behind."

Karen grinned, despite the situation. She bent and collected her pistol. It seemed each of them had their own security blanket. Holstering the gun, she tossed the strap over her shoulder. "C'mon."

She hopped off the altar, and Miyuki followed. As soon as the petite woman left the stone table, they heard gears grinding overhead. The altar stone and its platform thrust back up, rose on a basalt pillar and jammed back into place.

"Pressure sensitive," Karen said with awe at the keen counterbalance system. It astounded her that the mechanism functioned after being immersed for centuries in the salty sea.

Gloom settled over them. Distantly, the drip of water echoed up from the neighboring stairwell. Miyuki took a flashlight from her bag, clicked it on and shone it forward. She wore a determined expression. "You go first."

Karen nodded, and led the way. The stair was narrow, but the ceiling high enough to walk upright. Within the passage, the echoing drip of water grew louder. Karen splayed out her light, ran a finger along the damp wall. "The stone blocks are fitted perfectly. I can barely feel the seams."

Miyuki made a noncommittal noise. She kept glancing back over her shoulder as they moved slowly down the stairs. "Do you think they'll follow?"

Karen directed her light forward again. "I . . . I don't know. But if they do, let's be as far away from here as possible."

Miyuki was silent for several steps. Her breathing, though, was strained and tight. She finally asked the question uppermost in Karen's mind. "Where do you think this leads?"

"I'd guess some royal burial chamber. But I'm not sure. This passage is pretty steep. We must be close to the base of the pyramid by now."

Proving her theory true, the stairs ended at a tunnel. The

next passage led in a straight line away from there. A long way. Karen's light failed to find an end. She assumed the tunnel led beyond the pyramid itself.

Frowning, she moved down to the last step. Ahead, the tunnel lay partially flooded. At least a foot of water covered the floor. Within the beam of her light, Karen watched trickles of water drip and flow from cracks in the ceiling. "We must be underneath the pyramid . . . underneath the sea itself," she muttered. "Look at the walls here. They're not carved stone blocks, but solid rock. It must have taken decades to tunnel out this passage."

Miyuki leaned beside her. "Maybe not. It might just be a lava tube. Japan-is riddled with them."

"Hmm . . . maybe."

Miyuki stared over at the dripping water. "I don't know about this. Can't we just wait—"

A ringing sound cut her off, echoing down the stairs to them. Metal on rock. The two women's eyes met.

"They're trying to dig themselves inside," Karen said.

Miyuki pushed Karen toward the watery passage. "Get going!"

Karen splashed into the water and gasped as the cold clamped around her ankles. The tang of salt was sharp in the stagnant air. Miyuki followed, holding her equipment bag tight. They continued down the long tunnel, their splashes echoing up and down the passage. The noise made them both edgy.

Karen ran her fingers along the wall here, too. It was still smooth, almost glassy. Too smooth to have been carved by crude tools. It seemed a natural passage, as Miyuki had suggested. She tapped the wall with a knuckle.

"Don't do that!" Miyuki yelled at her.

The shout startled Karen. She dropped her hand.

"Do you want to drown us?" Miyuki said.

"This passage has been down here for ages."

"Still, don't knock on the walls. After the quakes and uplift, you don't know how fragile it might be."

"All right," Karen said, "I'll leave it alone." She turned her attention to the passage ahead, which seemed to widen.

She increased her pace. Could it be the end? She prayed for another exit. The ringing strike of metal on stone still echoed periodically behind them. Their pursuers were not giving up.

Splashing in water up to her knees now, Karen hurried forward, then stopped. She looked around, mouth gaping open. The passage continued, but here the tunnel ballooned out. The ceiling became a dome overhead, as glassy and smooth as the passage itself. If this was a lava tube, a bubble must have formed at this spot.

Karen wagged her flashlight around. Overhead, embedded bits of glittering quartz dotted the roof. At first she thought it was a random pattern, then she turned in a circle, neck craned back. "It's a starscape. See, there's the Orion constellation."

Miyuki looked less impressed. She glanced over her shoulder as another echoing strike sounded behind them. "We should keep going."

Karen lowered her light. She knew Miyuki was right, but her legs would not move. Nothing like this had ever been discovered among the islands of the South Pacific. Who had built this? Her light, now pointing forward, settled on a waist-high section of the wall. A sharp glint attracted her attention. She narrowed her eyes. A small niche had been dug out of the smooth wall. A cubbyhole. Something inside reflected back her light. Karen approached it.

Miyuki started to speak, but Karen stopped her with an upraised hand. She bent to peer into the tiny alcove. Resting inside was a palm-size crystal star. Five points glittered brightly under her penlight. It was as if a rainbow had exploded inside. As she shifted her light, she noticed deep scratches on the nearby wall and took a step back. She had almost missed it at first. She cast her light along the curved wall.

"My God!"

Meticulously carved into the stone were lines of small symbols. Three rows of them. Clearly some form of archaic language.

Bending closer, she touched the first symbol with a finger. The wall etchings were precise, carved deep, as if written with a diamond-pointed tool. But for all the precision, the symbols themselves were crude. Rough hieroglyphics. Pictures of animals and men in distorted shapes and postures. Strange icons and repeated symbols.

Karen tilted her head, moving the light. The rows continued, waist-high around the bubble in the tunnel.

She turned to Miyuki, her breath rushed. "I need a picture of this."

"What?" Her friend looked at her as if she were crazy.

Karen straightened, reaching for Miyuki's bag. "Video record it. Save it. I can't risk this being lost."

Miyuki scowled. "What are you thinking? We need to get out here."

"The looters might destroy this. Or the whole area might sink again."

"I'm more worried about it sinking with us in it."

Karen pleaded with her eyes.

Finally, Miyuki sighed and passed the satchel to Karen, who held it as Miyuki shuffled through it for her tiny digital camera. Freeing it, she passed Karen her own larger flashlight. "I'll need plenty of light. Follow as I record." Miyuki returned to the wall, camera raised. She slowly edged around the chamber, tracing the wrap of ancient writing until she made a complete circuit.

Karen realized something as they worked. "It's not three rows," she mumbled. "It's one continuous line—starting at the crystal star and wrapping around and around the room, like the groove in a vinyl record."

"Or a curled snake," Miyuki said, lowering the camera as she finished recording. She started to put it away. "Satisfied?"

Karen passed Miyuki the large flashlight. "Could you get a couple shots of the star map on the ceiling?"

Miyuki frowned but took the flashlight.

Snugging the equipment satchel over her shoulder, Karen

turned away. "I'm going to take the crystal artifact with me. We can't let the looters get it." She crossed to the cubbyhole and reached inside, grabbed the star and tried to pick it up, but failed. She gave it a cautious tug, but it didn't budge. "Goddamn. It's cemented in place."

Finished with the recording, Miyuki joined Karen. "Then leave it." She peered down the tunnel. The sound of digging had stopped a few minutes ago. "I don't like this quiet. Maybe they got through."

Karen scrunched up her brow. She didn't want to leave the crystal star behind. "Shine your light in here so I can see what I'm doing."

Miyuki moved closer and shone her light into the cubby. Again the rainbow brilliance sparked sharply. "It's beautiful," she conceded in a hushed voice.

Again Karen palmed the star and tugged hard. This time it popped free easily. Caught off guard, she stumbled back, bumping into Miyuki. Her friend's flashlight went flying and splashed into the water.

Miyuki bent to retrieve it. "I hope you're done," she said, fishing through the seawater. "Lucky the flashlight's waterproof."

Karen held the star against her belly. It was like cradling a bowling ball. She had to hold it with both hands. The star hadn't been cemented into the niche, she simply hadn't expected it to be so heavy. "This thing weighs a ton," she said. She lifted the star and dropped it into a side pocket of the equipment bag. The bag now pulled hard on her shoulder. "Okay. Let's keep going."

"We should hurry. I don't like how quiet—"

The explosion caught them by surprise. The two women were thrown to their knees as the tunnel shook. The ringing blast deafened them.

Karen twisted around, keeping her bag above the water. She fumbled for her pistol. Miyuki pointed her light back down the tunnel. Smoke billowed toward them from the far end.

"Dynamite," Karen said. "They must have lost their patience with a pickax."

As the ringing faded, a low groan filled the tunnel. The drip of water became a deep gurgle. A few meters away a spout of water erupted, spraying a thick stream of seawater. Closer, a crack opened overhead, weeping water over them.

"It's breaking apart!" Miyuki yelled in terror.

Up and down the passage, more and more spouts opened. Falling rocks splashed.

"Run!" Karen shouted. Already the water rose from knees to thighs.

Karen led the way down the next tunnel, Miyuki struggling behind her, fighting through the deepening water. "Where are we going?"

Karen had no answer. First fire—now water. If not for her numbing fear, she would have appreciated the irony. But not now. Ahead, the dark passage stretched beyond the reach of their lights . . . quickly filling with frigid seawater.

8

Endgame

In his usual red trunks and white cotton robe, Jack relaxed in a lounge chair on the bow deck of his ship. His hair was still wet from the long shower, but the late afternoon remained warm. It felt good to soak in the last rays of the setting sun. His dog, Elvis, lay sprawled beside the lounge.

Across the deck, the sleek contours of the *Nautilus 2000* reflected the light off its titanium surface. Robert worked under the dry-docked submersible, inspecting every square inch, while Lisa sat inside, doing the same. So far the sub seemed to have withstood the extreme pressures without a problem. The only concern: the radio glitch. Lisa had been troubleshooting the computer and com systems, trying to trace the gremlin in the works, but so far without success.

"How's your jaw?"

Jack turned his attention back to his companion. Admiral Mark Houston relaxed on a neighboring lounge. He puffed on a thick cigar, one of Jack's prized stock. With his other hand, the admiral scratched Elvis behind an ear, earning a slow thump of a tail.

"I've had worse." Jack rubbed his jaw. It still ached dully.

Houston held out his cigar, inspecting it with pleasure. "Cuban tobacco . . . I'm breaking so many laws . . ."

"But it's worth it, isn't it?"

He replaced the cigar, inhaling deeply. "Oh, yeah." His eyes narrowed with appreciation as he exhaled.

Except for the admiral and his two personal aides, Jack had the *Deep Fathom* back to himself, at least for now. With the two black boxes wrapped and under armed guard, David Spangler and the other government investigators had left immediately for the USS *Gibraltar*. The admiral had remained behind. He would be alerted as soon as any word came through on the flight data and cockpit recorders. Until then, everyone was holding their breath.

"So I take it," Houston said, "that your reunion with Commander Spangler didn't resolve anything."

"What did you expect?" Jack slumped in his lounge chair. First the *Gibraltar*, then Admiral Houston, now David Spangler. All together again. He had run from his past for over a decade, and ended up right where he started. He sighed. "Nothing changes. Even before the shuttle accident, David hated me. He resented that I took his place on the shuttle."

"It wasn't your decision. It was NASA's jurisdiction."

"Yeah, tell that to Spangler. We had a major blowout the night before the launch. I was almost scrubbed."

"I remember. He found out you were dating his sister during the year you spent at NASA training." Houston pointed his cigar at Jack's swollen lip. "And it seems that old grudge is still strong."

Jack shook his head. "He lost his sister. Who can blame him?"

"You should. We've lost other shuttles. Everyone knows the risks." The admiral sucked on his cigar. "Besides, there's something I just don't like about our Mr. Spangler. I never did. There's always been a lot of hatred buried beneath that cold surface. I'm not surprised he's fallen into the employ of

Nicolas Ruzickov at the CIA. Those two sharks deserve each other."

Jack was surprised at the admiral's words. His face showed it.

Houston's voice grew stern. "Just watch yourself around him, Jack." He pointed his cigar at Jack's swollen eye. "Don't allow your guilt to weaken your guard. Not around him."

Jack remembered the keen hatred in David's eyes: *This isn't over, Kirkland.* Perhaps he had better take his former commander's advice and steer clear of the man, he thought. Jack closed his eyes and leaned back. "If only I had spotted the glitch a few seconds earlier . . . or held her hand tighter."

"Hindsight is always twenty-twenty, Jack. But, you know what, sometimes shit happens. You can't see every bullet aimed at your head. Life just isn't that fair."

"When did you become such a philosopher?"

Houston tapped his cigar. "Age grants you a certain wisdom."

From across the deck Lisa called to him, perched at the sub's hatch. "Jack, come see this."

Groaning, Jack pushed himself up. "What?"

Lisa just waved to him.

"All right. Hang on." He got off his lounger, and the admiral sat up straighter, preparing to follow. "Relax," Jack said. "I'll be right back."

Elvis rolled to his chest, starting to push to his legs.

Jack held out a hand, stopping the dog. "You, too. Stay." The German shepherd sank back to the deck with a clearly irritated huff.

Houston patted Elvis's side. "We old men will keep each other company."

Jack rolled his eyes, then crossed the deck. He climbed down the stepladder to join Lisa. She lowered herself into the sub's seat, and Jack leaned over her. "What's up?"

"Look at the *Nautilus*'s internal clock." She pointed to the clock's red digital numbers. The seconds scrolled normally. "Now look at my wristwatch."

Jack studied the Swatch on her wrist, then looked back at the digital clock. It was off by a little over five minutes. "So it's slow by a few minutes."

"Before the dive, I synchronized the clock myself when I calibrated the Bio-Sensor program. It was exact to the hundredth of a second."

"I still don't understand the significance."

"I compared the time gap with the Bio-Sensor log. The difference in clocks exactly matches the length of time you were off-line."

Jack crinkled his brow. "So the glitch must have affected the clock, too. Must be a short in one of the batteries."

"No, the batteries checked out fine," she mumbled, and looked up at him. "When you were off-line, did you see the clock stop?"

Jack shook his head, frown lines creasing the corners of his lips. "No. In fact, I remember checking. The clock was running normally the whole time."

Lisa wiggled up off the seat. "It doesn't make any sense. The diagnostics of the systems are perfect. Jack, is there anything you're not telling me?"

He glanced over his shoulder. The admiral was lost in his appreciation of his cigar. Jack lowered his voice. During the postdive briefing, Jack had glossed over the details of the strange crystal pillar. No one seemed interested anyway. "That pillar I discovered down there . . ."

"Yeah. The one on the disk you gave Charlie."

Jack bit his lip. He didn't want to sound crazy. He ran a hand through his hair. "I don't know. The pillar was giving off some strange vibrations or harmonics. It screwed with my compass. I could even feel it on my skin, an itchy tingle like ants crawling all over."

Lisa furrowed her brow. "Why didn't you tell me this before?"

"I didn't want to prejudice your examination of the *Nautilus*. If there was any other explanation, I wanted you to find it."

Lisa's cheeks grew red. "Jesus Christ, you know me better than that. Either way, I would have been just as thorough."

"You're right. I'm sorry."

Lisa scooted out of the sub. Jack helped her onto the ladder. Her eyes flicked toward the admiral, then back to Jack. "Charlie is still holed up with George, studying that secret disk of yours. I'm going to find out if they've learned anything." She shoved past. "You really should have told me, Jack."

"What do you think it means?"

Lisa shrugged. "Beats me, but it's worth checking out."

"I'm coming with you."

Robert, the marine biologist, crawled from under the sub's tail. "All the seals check out fine, Jack. If you want to take her for another dive, you should have no problems."

Jack nodded, distracted. "Robert, could you keep the admiral company for a few minutes? I have some brandy in the cupboard under the microwave."

"Yeah, I know where it's at. But what's up?"

"We'll fill you in with the details as soon as we have any," Lisa answered, casting an angry look at Jack. She moved off.

Jack called across the deck to Admiral Houston. "I'll be right back!"

He was answered with a nod and a dismissive wave.

Jack followed Lisa to the lower deck hatch. She descended the steep stair ahead of him, back stiff. This first of the lower levels contained Robert's wet lab, the ship's library, and Charlie's tiny work station. Below were the crew's cabins.

Lisa led the way through the wet lab to Charlie's smaller compartment. She knocked on the steel door.

"Who is it?" Charlie called out to them.

"Lisa and Jack! Open up!"

After a short pause, Jack heard the locks unlatch and the door creak open slightly. Charlie peered out at them. "Just making sure you're alone." He sounded excited. The geologist pulled the door the rest of the way open. "C'mon inside . . . you have to see this."

"You found something?" Jack asked as he and Lisa entered.

"Oh, yeah, *mon*, you could say that."

The geology lab was no bigger than a single car garage, but every square inch was utilized. Equipment and tools were stacked neatly on shelves and counters: rock saws, drills, sieves, scales, magnetometers, even a complete ASC Core Analysis System. Jack was ignorant of most of the equipment's use. This was Charlie's domain.

With a dual doctorate in geology and geophysics, the Jamaican geologist could have taught at any university. But instead he ended up on Jack's boat, doing his own research. "I didn't earn my degrees to hole up in no classroom," he had explained seven years ago, eyes bright with excitement. "Not when there is so much to explore out here. The deep ocean seabed, Jack! That's where the Earth's history and future are written. Down there! It's waiting for someone to read it. And that someone is me!"

As Jack entered the lab now, he saw the same excitement in Charlie's eyes. The geologist waved them over to his worktable. A television and video recorder had been set atop it.

Crouched before it was the ship's historian. The professor leaned only a few inches from the video screen, squinting through his bifocals. George scribbled on a pad. "Amazing . . . simply amazing," he mumbled as he worked.

Jack and Lisa moved to either side of him, trying to get a better look at the monitor. "What did you find?" Jack asked.

George finally seemed to realize their presence. He turned, his eyes wide. "You have to go down there again!" he said in a rush, clutching Jack's sleeve.

"What? Why?"

"We should start at the beginning," Charlie interrupted. He pointed the remote, and the video image reversed. On the screen, Jack watched the view of the crystal spire vanish into the ocean gloom. Once he'd rewound it far enough, Charlie stopped the DVD and allowed it to play forward. The obelisk slowly reappeared as Charlie spoke. "You were right, Jack. The crystalline substance appears natural. I've analyzed the video closely, and from the fracturing of the planes and uniformity of light refraction, it must be a spike of pure crystal."

"But what type? Quartz?"

Charlie tilted his head, watching the video. "No. That's just it. I don't know. At least not yet. But I'd sell the *Fathom* for a sliver of it."

"So you think it's something new?"

The tall Jamaican nodded. "Nowhere on this planet is there an environment like the one down there." Charlie tapped at the screen. The sub slowly circled the spire, showing the brilliant shaft from every angle. The video image was crisp and detailed. Flawless. There was no sign of the interference that was described topside. "At these extreme pressures of seawater and salinity, who knows how crystals might grow?"

Jack sat on one of the stools. He leaned closer to the screen. "So what you're saying is that we're the first people ever to see such a crystal creation?"

Charlie laughed, drawing Jack's eye away from the screen. "No. I'm not saying that, *mon* . . . I'm not saying that at all." Charlie manipulated the remote's shuttle, slowing the recording.

Jack watched the spire slow its spin as the submersible finished its circuit. Charlie stopped the video just as the sub's xenon headlamps began to swing away. Jack remembered this was the moment when he had turned back to continue his search for the black boxes. He had been looking elsewhere and missed what his camera picked up next.

With the light cast at an angle across the nearest plane of the obelisk, slight imperfections could be seen marring its crystalline surface.

"What is that?"

"Proof that we're not the first to discover this crystal." Charlie played with the remote and zoomed in on the imperfections. The image swelled on the monitor. The imperfections grew into rows of tiny markings, too regular and precise to be natural. Jack leaned in closer. Though the en-

larged video image was fuzzy, there was no mistaking what
he was seeing.

George spoke it aloud, voice hushed with awe. "It's writing. Some type of ancient inscription."

"But at those depths?" Jack stared in disbelief. Etched
deep into the crystal were blocks and rows of tiny iconlike
images: animals, trees, distorted figures, geometric shapes.

Jack could not dismiss what he was seeing. Each symbol
was carved into the smooth surface, then filled with a shiny
metallic compound. It was no optical illusion.

It was ancient writing ... on a spire two thousand feet
underwater.

Off the coast of Yonaguni Island, Okinawa Prefecture

Karen held her penlight above her head as she fought the
growing depth of the water. She slogged forward, the water
now past her waist. She shrugged the equipment bag higher
on her shoulder, trying her best to keep it dry, but the heavy
weight kept pulling toward the rising seawater. When would
this passage end? How long was it? Up and down the passage the echo of pouring water filled the tunnel.

Behind her, she could hear Miyuki struggling. The Japanese professor was smaller than her, the water up to Miyuki's
breasts. She half swam to keep up.

At last Karen saw her penlight illuminate another wall ahead, something different than this endless passage. "I think we've reached the end."

She moved faster. The tunnel ended at a staircase, its steps climbing up. It reminded her of the staircase that had led them down here. She reached the first step, almost tripping over it since it was under the black water. Catching herself on the smooth wall, Karen stumbled up the steps and dragged herself out of the flooding passage.

She turned to help Miyuki, and both women climbed several steps until exhaustion dragged them down. They sat on the dry stairs, panting, shivering.

Karen pointed to the walls on either side. "Stone blocks," she said. Here the walls and ceiling were no longer bare rock, but stacked and carefully fitted basalt slabs and blocks. "We're above the lava tube."

"So we won't drown?" Miyuki looked pale, her ebony hair wet and clinging to her face.

"Not if we climb high enough. Get above sea level."

Miyuki stared up the staircase. "But where are we?"

"If I had to guess, I'd say these steps lead into the heart of the second Dragon, the twin pyramid to the one we entered." At least, she hoped so. But it made some sort of symmetrical sense. And if she wasn't mistaken, the passage had been heading in the direction of the other pyramid. The lava tube must connect the two structures.

"Will there be a way out?"

Karen nodded. "I'm sure there is." She left unspoken her own fear. What if they couldn't find it?

"Then let's go," Miyuki said, shoving herself to her feet. She reached toward Karen. "I'll carry the bag from here."

Karen pushed the strap off, only too glad to shed the burden, and passed the bag to Miyuki, who almost dropped it.

"You weren't kidding that it's heavy," she said, straining to heft it to her own shoulder.

"Nope. It's that crystal artifact. It must weigh close to ten kilos."

"But it was so small."

Karen shrugged and stood up. "Just one more mystery

about this place." Sighing, she led the way up, praying that the final mystery would not escape her: *the way out of this death trap.*

The climb up the steep stairs was a cruel torture for their aching limbs. It felt like they were climbing a ladder. But they plodded onward, silent, too tired to talk. At least the exertion served to warm their cold bodies. But soon even the warmth became a burden. With each step the temperature seemed to rise in the narrow stairway. By the time they neared the top of the stairs, it was stifling. It seemed to Karen that her damp clothes were steaming.

She wiped the sweat from her forehead and entered the next chamber. "Finally," she moaned as she shuffled into the room. Miyuki followed her, wheezing. Karen raised her small flashlight.

The bare walls of the inner chamber offered no clue to an exit. Stacked stones and a slab roof surrounded them. Both women gazed around. There were no adornments, no writing.

Karen moved along the margins of the walls. "Turn off your light," she ordered Miyuki. Karen flicked her penlight off, too.

Darkness plunged around them. The echo of splashing water from the passage below seemed to swell. With eyes wide, Karen looked for a chink in the solid walls and ceiling. Some evidence of an exit. By now she assumed the sun would be sliding toward the western horizon.

She mopped at her brow. It was so warm in there. Not a bit of air moved. With one hand on a wall, she edged around the room, searching for a telltale glow, some sign of an exit. But the darkness seemed complete.

"Are you finding anything?" Miyuki asked, hopeful.

Karen had opened her mouth to answer when her hand touched a stone warmer than the others. She paused, placing one palm on one stone and the other on its neighbor. There was a clear difference in temperature.

"I think I may have a clue here." She fingered the edges of the warmer stone. It was difficult in the dark. The blocks had been fitted snugly. She discovered the edges, but as she stared, found no sign of sunlight creeping through. She frowned. There had to be a reason for the warmer stone.

Karen thumbed on her penlight, and Miyuki moved to her side, resting her bag on the stone floor. She rubbed at her shoulder. "What did you find?"

Karen shoved hard on the stone. It didn't move. She backed up a step, head tilted, studying the stone block. It was featureless, about half a meter square. "This is warmer than the others, suggesting it must be more directly exposed to the sun."

"Is it a way out?" Miyuki turned on her own flashlight.

"I hope so. I just don't know how to open it." Karen closed her eyes. *Think, goddamn it!* She pictured the second Dragon in her mind. It was identical to the first, except for the collapsed temple. This second pyramid's summit had been bare. No clue.

"What are you thinking?" Miyuki asked.

Karen opened her eyes. "I'm not sure. In the other pyramid, the temple's altar was the access point. The sculptured snake head was the key."

"Yeah?"

"Think symmetry. Think larger. In the ruins of Chichen Itza on the Yucatan peninsula, the main pyramid casts a snake shadow during the equinoxes, a winding shadowy body that connects to a carved stone snake head at its base."

"I don't understand."

Karen kept talking, intuiting that she was close to an answer. "The serpent's head was the entry point. This connected to a long lava tube . . . perhaps representing a snake's body."

Miyuki nodded. "If you're right, then we're in the snake's tail."

"We were swallowed by a snake, traveled through its belly, and now must complete the digestive process."

"In other words, we must find this snake's butt."

Karen laughed at the dead seriousness with which Miyuki had spoken these last words. "Yep." Karen turned. The opening to the stairwell lay directly opposite her. She twisted around. The warm stone was in direct line with the opening. A straight line. She placed a hand on the stone. "This is the tip of the tail. The end of the snake."

"Right. You said that. It's the way out."

"No! We aren't paying attention to anatomy. A snake's butt isn't in the tip of its tail. It's on its underside!" Karen pointed to the floor. "Its belly!"

Miyuki stared at her toes. "To go up, we must go down."

Karen dropped to her knees on the stone floor. It wasn't a slab, but fitted blocks, like the walls. She crawled forward, starting at the warm brick and aiming for the stairwell, wiping the water and debris from the floor as she went. It had to be here!

Her fingers brushed over something rough on the smooth stone. She froze for a heartbeat, then rubbed the spot, praying.

Miyuki knelt near her. "What is it?"

Karen moved aside. "The snake's butt!"

Imprinted into the smooth block was a carving: a star-shaped depression.

"Get me the crystal!"

Miyuki rushed over and retrieved her bag. She dragged it back, then zipped open the side pouch and pulled the star-shaped crystal out. She had to use both hands. Grunting, she hauled it over to Karen. "Here."

Karen rolled to her belly and lugged the star into place in the depression. It was a perfect fit. She held her breath, ready for anything. Miyuki stood by her shoulder, a fist at her throat.

Nothing happened.

Karen sat up on her knees. "What's wrong? What aren't we doing right?"

"Maybe the mechanism is broken."

Karen did not even want to think of that possibility. She knew that by now the lower passage must be totally flooded. There was no way back. They were trapped here. She felt tears coming to her eyes. Her throat tightened.

"How was the crystal supposed to trigger the secret passage?" Miyuki asked, still pondering the riddle.

"I . . . I don't know."

"Didn't you say something about the other mechanism being pressure-sensitive?"

Miyuki's words sank through Karen's hopelessness. She remembered how the altar stone had moved back up into the ceiling after Miyuki had jumped off it. The mechanism must have been pressure-sensitive, responding to the change in weight.

Karen stared down at the crystal. It was heavy, unusually so. But if the secret door here was triggered by weight, then why hadn't it triggered when she'd first walked across it?

Then it dawned on her.

"Get off! Get off!" she yelled at Miyuki, waving her away from the stone block and crystal. "We weigh too much!"

"What?" Miyuki said, but backed away.

Karen moved beyond the edge of the block. "It must be balanced to the weight of the crystal. No more, no less."

Both women stepped away. Karen stared hard at the crystal. Still nothing. She felt a scream of frustration building in her chest. What were they missing?

She turned in a slow circle. The walls were blank and featureless. No answer—*or was there*?

She turned again. No wall sconces. No place to hook a torch. "Darkness," she mumbled. "The belly of a snake is hidden from the sun."

"What?"

"Turn off your flashlight!"

"Why?"

"Trust me!" Karen thumbed off her penlight.

Miyuki followed suit, plunging them into perfect darkness. "Now what are—"

A sharp grinding interrupted Miyuki. Rock on rock. Karen froze, praying she was right. In the hushed silence she reached out and fumbled for Miyuki's hand.

Then a spear of sunlight appeared, sprouting from the floor to strike the ceiling. Blinking against the glare, Karen dropped to her knees. The stone block with the crystal was sinking into the floor.

Karen crawled to the edge and peered into the deepening

hole. The shaft of sunlight came from a narrow crack in the left wall of the pit. As she watched, the block sank away and the crack grew wider, opening a side tunnel.

Light poured in.

Karen's vision blurred with tears of relief. It was the way out!

Below, the stone block finally stopped its descent with a grating sound, leaving the side passage wide open.

Karen rolled to her side and waved for Miyuki to go first. "Let's get out of here." It was only a drop of a couple meters.

Grabbing her satchel, the Japanese professor, smiling with relief, clambered into the pit. She landed and crouched down, peering through the side tunnel. "It's only a few feet! I see the sun!" Miyuki crawled into the passage, giving Karen room to come down.

Karen did not pause. She jumped into the pit. The sunlight blinded her for a moment, then she saw the blue sea beyond the short tunnel, shining bright. "Thank God!" She bent and entered the side passage. Twisting around, she grabbed the crystal star. She was not leaving behind her prize.

The star seemed much lighter now. She was able to pick it up with one hand. As she held it, the stone block ground up behind her and Miyuki, closing off the doorway back to the inner chamber. Turning to the exit, she shoved the artifact into her hip pocket. Free of her fingers, it sank like a lead weight, straining her pants' seams. *Damn, this thing is heavy.* But as she moved beyond the tunnel and into the sunlight, cold metal pressed against the back of her neck, and she forgot about her burden.

"Don't move!" someone ordered in Japanese.

She froze.

A second man jumped off the pyramid step behind her. With relief, she saw that he wore a police uniform with the Chatan emblem on his sleeve. It wasn't the looters. She was ordered to face the stone, palms on the rock.

To the side, Miyuki spoke rapidly to another officer. He

had her identification in his hand. He finally nodded, turned to the man holding Karen and waved him off.

Karen stepped away from the wall. "They got Gabriel's warning over the teletype about the looters and were just under way when they heard the explosion," Miyuki told her. "By the time they got here, the looters had already taken off. There was no sign of them, so they staked out this second pyramid, meaning to protect it."

"And they found us crawling out and thought *we* were the looters."

Miyuki nodded. "Luckily, Gabriel had transmitted our names, saying we were in danger." Miyuki put away her identification. "We'll have questions to answer, but there'll be no charges."

Karen took a deep breath. "Answers? I have more questions than answers." She pictured the looter's tattoo, a pale winding snake against his dark skin. Another serpent. In the light of the day, it seemed too much of a coincidence.

Karen wandered to the corner of the pyramid so she could see the other Dragon. Miyuki followed. Across the hundred meters, the Dragon's summit was a cratered ruin. Smoke curled into the sky, a man-made volcano.

Why had their attackers done that? It made no sense.

And where had they gone?

"What's wrong?" Miyuki asked. "We're safe."

"I don't know." Karen could not escape the feeling that the true danger was just beginning. "But let's go back to the university. I think it's time we tried to put a few pieces of this mystery together."

"No argument from me."

They turned away from the smoking pyramid and crossed back to the officers. The white and blue police motorboat waited in the water below, its lights blinking.

Karen sighed with shaky relief. "Remind me I owe Gabriel a great big hug."

"And you owe me a new pair of Ferragamos." With a tired grin, Miyuki swiped her hair from her damp forehead. "After all this, I'm holding you to your promise!"

Northwest of Enewak Atoll, Central Pacific

Ensconced in the ship's geology lab, Jack and the others sat staring at the frozen video image of the inscribed obelisk: metallic symbols etched crudely into the crystal's surface. "Who could have done this?" he asked.

George took off his bifocals. "I've never seen anything like it. But I'm going to get on-line and post some questions to various archaeology websites. See if I get any bites." He picked up a legal pad with a handwritten copy of the writing. "But it would help if we had more data." The historian glanced meaningfully at Jack.

Charlie clicked off the monitor. "I agree with the professor. We need more information."

Jack found all eyes on him.

George spoke first. "You've got to go back down there."

"I . . . I haven't made a decision on that yet." He was in no hurry to return to the deep-sea graveyard.

Lisa added her support. "We should just take the money and run. We've met our obligation to the Navy. We're not required to haul pieces of the plane to the surface . . . and I don't like what happened when Jack was near that pillar."

George crinkled his brow. "What do you mean? What happened?"

Lisa turned to Jack, allowing him to explain, but he remained silent. He felt foolish discussing his vague misgivings while down there.

"The *Nautilus* checked out fine," Lisa explained, filling in for him. "Instruments, computers, radios, power supply . . . all get clean bills of health. But during Jack's communication blackout, when he was near that pillar, he reports sensing vibrations coming off it."

Charlie offered a more plausible explanation. "If the sub's batteries were malfunctioning, the thrusters might have become misaligned, tremoring the vessel." He looked at Jack. "Or maybe you were picking up vibrations from the slight seismic readings. They occurred the same time as the blackout."

Jack, embarrassed, felt heat rising to his cheeks. "No, it

was not vibrations from the ship. It felt . . . I don't know, more electric . . ."

"Then a short in a system somewhere?" Charlie persisted.

Lisa shook her head. "I found no evidence of any electrical problems."

George pocketed his paper. "So what are you saying?"

By now Jack's face was red. He could not meet the others' gazes. "It was the pillar. I can't explain how I know this, but it was. The crystal was giving off some type of . . . I don't know . . . harmonics, vibrations, emanations."

George and Charlie stared at Jack. He recognized the doubt in their eyes. Charlie spoke first. "If you're right, it's even more of a reason to go down and do a little private snooping."

George nodded. "And if there's more writing, I'd like a complete copy."

A firm knock on the door saved Jack from having to answer. "It's Robert," the marine biologist called from beyond the door.

"What is it?" Jack asked, relieved at turning aside more questions from the others.

"Word has come over from the *Gibraltar*. They have news about the crash."

Jack unlocked the door. He hoped some concrete answer had been discovered, something that would dismiss the need to go back down.

Robert stood outside. He waved them all out. "They're faxing over a copy of the cockpit voice recorder."

"Then let's go," Jack said.

The marine biologist, excited, continued his explanation. "Whatever they found, it has everyone in a buzz. I saw the admiral's face when he was informed over a scrambled line. He did not look happy. He insisted that a full copy of the cockpit's final conversation be faxed over to him."

Jack hurried, climbing the stairs to the main deck, then up the steps to the pilothouse. As he opened the door, he found Houston's two personal aides inside, in uniform, armed, standing stiffly. They were twin bulldogs, old Navy.

Nearby, the *Fathom*'s accountant leaned on the pilot seat.

"Where's the admiral?" Jack asked.

Kendall McMillan pointed toward the closed door to the radio and satellite system. "He's in there. He told us to wait for him."

Jack frowned at the closed door. This was his ship. He did not like someone closing him out of his own ship's heart—even an admiral. He moved to the door, but the two burly aides blocked him, hands on holstered pistols.

Before any confrontation could flare, the door swung open. The first one out was Jack's dog. Elvis padded from the radio room, tail sweeping back and forth. The admiral followed him. Jack opened his mouth, about to scold the old man, but when he saw the pallor to Mark Houston's face, he remained silent. Deep wrinkles etched the admiral's forehead.

"What is it?" Jack asked.

Houston glanced around. The entire ship's crew was now crammed into the small pilothouse. "Is there a place to get a drink around here?"

Jack waved the others away and turned to his old friend. "Follow me. I have a bottle of twenty-year-old scotch in my stateroom."

"Just what the doctor ordered." The admiral smiled, but it came out sickly.

Jack led the way down to the main deck and to his stateroom. He held the door open for the old man.

Once both were inside, Houston nodded back at the door. "Lock it."

Jack did as ordered. He pointed toward a pair of leather chairs in front of his shelves of nautical memorabilia. Houston crossed to the shelves, touching an ancient sextant. "Is this the one I gave you?"

"After I was accepted to the shuttle mission, yep."

Houston turned and sank into one of the chairs with a long sigh. For the first time, Jack saw the man's age. He looked sunken, defeated. The admiral pointed back at the sextant. "So you haven't completely tossed away your past."

Jack moved to a cabinet and pulled out a bottle of scotch and two glasses. "Not the important things."

Houston nodded. He was silent for several moments. "Jack, have you made a decision yet on helping us retrieve sections of Air Force One?"

Jack sighed. He poured a couple fingers worth of his private stash into each glass. He knew Houston liked his scotch neat. "No, sir . . . we're still doing some diagnostics on the sub."

"Hmm . . ." the admiral mumbled, accepting the glass. He sipped thoughtfully, clearly thinking something through. Finally, he settled the glass on a teak captain's table. Reaching inside his flight jacket, he pulled out a folded sheaf. "Maybe this will help you decide." He held out the papers.

Jack gripped the proffered sheets, but the admiral did not release them. "This is confidential information. But if you're going to help us, you should be kept informed." Houston let go of the report.

Jack moved to his chair. "This is from the cockpit voice recorder?"

"Yes, the last minutes between the cockpit crew."

Jack sat down and slowly unfolded the papers. As much as he didn't want to be drawn further into this operation, his curiosity couldn't be ignored. He read the report.

BOEING 27-200B
(DESIGNATION: VC-25A)
Time: 18:56

CAPTAIN: Honolulu, this is Victor Charlie Alpha. Can you update our weather? We're hitting some heavy pockets out here.

FIRST OFFICER: Why aren't they answering?

CAPTAIN: Honolulu, this is Victor Charlie Alpha. Please answer. We're having trouble with our radar and compasses. Can you . . . Hang on!

[loud rumble and rattle]

NAVIGATOR: What the hell was that?

CAPTAIN: Another pocket. Try climbing higher.

FIRST OFFICER: Climbing to thirty-five thousand.

NAVIGATOR: I'm still getting conflicting readings here from the INS units. The Omega, the radar, the celestial sextant . . . it's making no sense. I'm going on dead reckoning.

CAPTAIN: Everyone keep your heads in the game here.

FIRST OFFICER: She's heavy, sir. Not able to climb.

CAPTAIN: What?

NAVIGATOR: This doesn't make sense. I'm picking up land ahead.

CAPTAIN: Must be Wake Island. I'll try to pick up something local on the radio.

[*pause*]

Wake Island, this is Victor Charlie Alpha, we need assistance.

[*silence for thirty seconds*]

NAVIGATOR: It's too big, sir. This can't be right. I'm going to check the manual sextant.

FIRST OFFICER: What are those lights?

CAPTAIN: Just glare off the windshield. Keep climbing.

NAVIGATOR: Where the hell are we?

[*deep rumble*]

NAVIGATOR: What is that? What is that?

FIRST OFFICER: Losing altitude. Controls aren't responding!

CAPTAIN: My God!

NAVIGATOR: We're over land!

FIRST OFFICER: I can't see! The light!

[*screech of metal, rush of wind*]

FIRST OFFICER: Engine number one is on fire!

CAPTAIN: Shut it down! Now!

FIRST OFFICER: Yes, sir.

NAVIGATOR: What the hell is going on!

CAPTAIN: Honolulu, this is Victor—

FIRST OFFICER: Something ahead of us! Something ahead of us!

NAVIGATOR: I'm not reading anything. Nothing on radar . . . nothing on anything!

CAPTAIN: Honolulu, this is Victor Charlie Alpha. Mayday, mayday!

FIRST OFFICER: The sky! The sky is opening up!

[roaring noise, then silence]

END OF COCKPIT VOICE RECORDING
Time: 19:08

Jack lowered the sheets. "My God. What happened up there?"

Houston shifted in his seat and reached for the fax sheets. "A chopper is on its way to collect me. I want to listen to the recording myself. But as to the true answer, there's only one way to find out. . . . The answer lies down below."

Jack reached a trembling hand to his glass of scotch. He swallowed its contents in one gulp. The expensive liquor burned all the way to his belly.

"Jack . . . ?"

Jack filled his glass one more time. He leaned back into his seat, sipping more gently at the smooth scotch, appreciating it this time. He met the admiral's gaze. "I'll go," he said simply.

Houston nodded and raised his scotch. Jack reached over and tapped his old friend's glass with his own. "To absent friends," Jack said.

9

Pieces of the Puzzle

Karen hurried across the staff parking lot, late for her lunch meeting with Miyuki. Her friend's office and lab were on the fourth floor of the old Yagasaki Building, once a government office complex. Ryukyu University had originally been founded by the United States Civil Administration in 1950, built upon the site of the ancient Castle of Shuri, but in 1972 the Japanese took over the administration. Since then the university had spread from its original site into the surrounding countryside and local buildings.

Dashing up the steps and through the double doors, Karen crossed to the stationed guard and flashed her identification card.

He nodded from behind his desk and waved her past, checking her name off his list. The president of Ryukyu University was taking no chances. Although the island of Okinawa was climbing out of the devastation, looting remained sporadic. The added security measures were the university's attempt to protect its assets.

Karen strode to the stairwell, passing a bank of elevators cordoned off with yellow tape declaring them "Out of Service." She imagined the companies that produced those rolls of ribbon were making a fortune. The same yellow tape was strewn like party streamers throughout the island.

Checking her watch, she picked up her pace on the stairs. Since returning from their harrowing journey to the ruins of Chatan, this was the first chance the two women had to consult one another. Miyuki had called this morning and urged Karen to join her at her lab. She had news about the crystal star but would say no more over the phone.

Karen wondered what her friend had learned. Over the past three days, Karen had been doing her own research—investigating the cryptic language, trying to trace its origin. But progress had been slow. The island was continually plagued by power failures that interfered with communication. For a while, she'd been sure the glyphs were similar to a script found in the Indus Valley ruins of Pakistan, but on closer inspection she realized the similarity was only superficial. This line of study, however, was not a total waste. It did send her down another path, to another similar language, one even more exciting. Still, she needed further study before she was willing to voice her theory aloud.

At the top of the stairs, Karen found Miyuki waiting, dressed in her usual crisp lab coat. "The guard buzzed me that you were on the way up," her friend said. "C'mon."

As they walked, Karen asked, "What have you found?"

Miyuki shook her head. "You have to see this for yourself." She led the way down the hall past other teachers' offices. "What about the hieroglyphics?"

Karen hesitated. "I may have a lead."

Miyuki glanced at her with surprise. "Really? I've been having Gabriel try to decode it, but he's had little success."

"He can do that? Decipher it?"

"One of his base algorithms is a decoding program. Ciphering is a useful model for building an artificial intelligence construct, and if you correlate—"

Karen held up a hand, surrendering. "Okay, I believe you. Has Gabriel learned anything?"

"Only one thing . . . it's part of the reason I called you. But he'd have more success with additional examples of the language. More data from which to correlate, cross-check, and build a language base."

Karen bit her lip, then confessed her own secret. "I may be able to supply that."

Miyuki looked over again, frowning. "How?"

"I wanted to confirm my idea before bringing it up. But the library was of no use, and I keep getting booted off the Internet by these hourly brownouts. I couldn't get an outside line all day yesterday."

"What were you looking for?"

"Examples of a written language found on the island of Rapa Nui."

"Rapa Nui? Isn't that Easter Island, the place with the big stone heads?"

"Exactly."

"But that island's on the other side of the Pacific."

Karen nodded. "That's why I need further information. It's not my area of expertise. I've been concentrating my studies on Polynesia and Micronesia."

The pair reached Miyuki's laboratories. Miyuki unlocked the door with a key card and held it open for Karen. They entered a tiny anteroom. Starched white "clean suits" hung on the wall. Beyond the glass doors ahead was Miyuki's lab, all stainless steel and linoleum. Under the fluorescent bulbs, every surface gleamed, dust-free and spotless.

Karen took off her sweater and slipped out of her Reebok sneakers. She took a clean cloth suit from a peg. It was stiff after being freshly dry-cleaned and pressed. She wriggled into the white one-piece jumpsuit, then sat down on a tiny bench to slip on paper booties.

Miyuki did the same. She insisted that her lab maintain a

sterile environment. She wanted no contaminants interfering with the large banks of computers lining the center of the room, the birthplace of Gabriel. "What's this connection to Rapa Nui?"

Karen fixed her short blond hair under a disposable paper bonnet. "Back in 1864, a French missionary reported the discovery of hundreds of wooden tablets, staffs, even skulls carved with an unknown hieroglyphic script. The natives called this language *rongorongo*, but they couldn't read the script. Some claimed the language came from the time before the natives arrived on the island in 400 A.D. Unfortunately, most of the artifacts were destroyed before they could be recovered. Only about twenty-five examples of the writing exist today in museums and universities."

"And you think this language is the same one we discovered?"

"I can't be sure. *Rongorongo* is the only known indigenous written language among all the peoples of Oceania. But its origin remains a mystery, and the text unreadable. Many epigraphers and cryptologists have attempted to decipher the language, but all of them have failed." Karen could not keep the excitement from her voice. "If we've discovered a new vein of this language, for the first time in centuries, we might have a chance not only to unlock the mysteries of *rongorongo*, but also to discover the lost history of Polynesia."

Miyuki stood. "So what's the next step?"

"I need to get on-line and hunt down the other examples of the language. Confirm my hypothesis."

Miyuki began to catch Karen's excitement. "And if you're right, we can add these other examples to Gabriel's database. With more information, he might be able to decipher it!"

"If so, it would be the archaeological discovery of the century."

"Then let's get to work. Gabriel can get you a line to the outside by hooking into the U.S. military's phone lines.

They're the most stable." Miyuki crossed to the glass door to her lab.

"He can do that?"

Miyuki nodded. "Of course. Who do you think is the main backer for my research? The U.S. military is very intrigued by artificial intelligence and its practical application. I have a Level 3 clearance." Using her key card again, she unlocked the inner door. There was a *whoosh* as the door seal broke. The next room was under a slight positive pressure, extra insurance against contaminants entering the lab.

Karen followed her into the clean room. "You go through a lot of trouble to avoid a bit of dusting," she mumbled with a smirk.

Miyuki ignored her and crossed to a half-arc bank of computer monitors. Two wheeled chairs rested nearby. Miyuki took a seat and waved Karen to the other. "Let me show you what Gabriel has been able to decode so far." She began tapping a keyboard while speaking aloud. "Gabriel, could you please bring up the images of the hieroglyphs?"

"Certainly, Professor Nakano. And good morning, Karen Grace." The artificial voice came from stereo speakers behind the two women.

"Good morning, Gabriel," Karen answered, still feeling awkward. She glanced over her shoulder at the speakers. It was as if someone stood behind her. "Th-Thank you for your help."

"It has been a pleasure, Dr. Grace. You have presented an intriguing conundrum." Across the long curved bank of monitors, the glyphs of the unknown language ran along the multiple screens in a continuous line: Birds, fishes, human shapes, geometric figures, and strange squiggles.

"What has he learned?" Karen asked.

"He was able to decipher a small section at the beginning."

"You're kidding!" Karen sat up straighter.

The line of script ran across the screen until a section appeared highlighted in red. Then the scrolling images stopped, centering on the highlighted section. It contained six symbols.

"Gabriel believes it's a lunar calendar designation. A date, so to speak."

"Hmm . . . those central symbols do look like the sickle shapes of a waning or waxing moon." Karen shifted back. "But if it is a date, what does it mean? The date when the inscription was written or some historical notation?"

"I'd guess the latter," Miyuki said. "Some ancient historical event being described."

"Why do you think that?"

Miyuki remained silent.

Karen glanced at her friend. "What?"

Miyuki sighed. "Gabriel came to his calendar conclusion by cross-referencing with the starscape etched on the ceiling of the inner chamber."

Karen recalled the quartz star map on the room's domed ceiling. "So?"

"He compared the chamber's starscape with an astronomical program, then tied it to the lunar calendar." Miyuki looked at Karen. "He's calculated the rough date noted in the inscription."

"Amazing . . . When? What's the date?"

"Gabriel?"

The program answered: *"The icons denote the fourth month of a lunar year."*

Karen noted the four moon sickles. "Early spring."

"Correct . . . and from the relative position of the depicted constellations, I can extrapolate the approximate year."

"Within a statistical error of fifty years," Miyuki elaborated.

"Of course, I could not be more precise."

"That's close enough!" Karen's mind spun. If Gabriel's

calculations were correct, this might be a clue to when the ancient ruins had been constructed. "What year? How long ago?"

"*According to the astronomical map—twelve thousand years ago.*"

Northwest of Enewak Atoll, Central Pacific

Aboard the *Nautilus* submersible, Jack drifted over the debris field. From his position several yards away, he watched the tail fin of the Boeing 747 rise from the silt, drawn up by two four-inch-thick steel cables. Disturbed clouds of silt wafted up as the fin was pulled like a bad tooth from where it was embedded. Six hundred meters overhead, the motorized winch aboard the USS *Gibraltar* hauled on the cables, slowly but efficiently drawing its catch to the surface.

"Going for the next fish," Jack called into his throat microphone. He worked the foot pedals and swung his sub around. He checked the *Nautilus*'s clock. He had been working for almost three hours, targeting the specific pieces of the plane the NTSB had picked out from the video feed of his first dive.

By now the salvage of Air Force One was becoming almost routine. Over the past three days they had hauled up almost forty sections of the plane. The recovered wreckage was now spread and numbered in the lower hangar deck of the USS *Gibraltar* like a macabre jigsaw puzzle.

Though the recovery of the plane was well under way, so far only four bodies had been recovered: two floaters discovered in the tricky currents, identified as two men from the press pool, and the pilot and copilot, found strapped to their seats. Jack drove away that memory. The plane's crumpled nose cone had been one of the first pieces to be hauled to the surface. He had diverted his eyes from the shattered window as he attached the cables, but had caught a brief look. The pressures at this depth had crushed their bodies to a pulp. They looked like flesh-colored clay molded into a vague approximation of the human form. The only way to identify them were by their uniforms and their seats in the cockpit.

Since then, as Jack sifted through the wreckage, he had held his breath, fearing what else he might chance upon, but no other bodies were found. The impact and currents had thoroughly scattered the plane's human cargo.

"We're ready with the second winch," the NTSB radioman announced.

"Aye. Ready on the second winch. Going for the next target."

Jack swung the sub around and edged to the opposite side of the debris field. Ahead, another cable appeared, seeming to hang on its own, its end disappearing into the gloom above. It connected to a second surface winch aboard the *Gibraltar*. Jack dove the *Nautilus* down to the electromagnet hook attached to its end.

Working the sub's external manipulator arms, he grabbed the hook and dragged it to one of the plane's engine sections. Then he lowered the cable's end and placed it against the metal nacelle.

"Okay," he called up. "Energize!"

On his signal, he watched the cable's electromagnetic terminal flip and attach to the engine's side.

"Fish is hooked. Haul away!"

Jack backed his sub with a whine of thrusters. He watched the slack in the cable tighten; then the engine cowling slid from the silt.

Jack swung around. The graveyard was now almost half cleared. Only smaller pieces and sections of fuselage and wing remained. Under his sub, he passed over a large chunk of landing gear, its tires collapsed under the pressure. Another day or two and nothing would be down here.

As he spun the sub in a slow circle he noted movement off to his left. A school of hatchet fish flashed past the bubble of his submersible. He had been noting more and more denizens of the deep attracted to the light and noise of the salvage operation: long pinkish eels, scuttling crabs, and one six-foot-long dogfish. Off to the left, he watched a vampire squid shoot out of a crumpled nest of debris and snatch a passing hatchet fish. In a flick of tentacles, it vanished away.

These were his only companions. Swiveling his sub's twin lamps, Jack observed the tall, flat-topped seamounts towering just at the edge of his light's reach, giants looming over the wreckage. Closer, a forest of twisted lava pillars enclosed the space. From his sub's hydrophones, the subsonic whistles and high-pitched clicks of the living sea called to him, a lonely sound.

As he waited, a twinge of isolation struck him. Down at these sunless depths, it was as if he had traveled to another world.

Sighing, Jack swung back around. He had a duty to perform and could not be distracted with stray thoughts. In another twenty minutes the pair of winch cables would drape back down once again, awaiting his help to snatch more wreckage. Until then, he turned his attention back to his own investigation.

He edged his sub toward the center of the debris field. Out of the silty gloom the crystal pillar appeared, glowing with the warmth of his reflected xenon lamps. The clear crystal shone with veins of azure and rose hues. Over the past days, he had recorded the spire from every possible angle, again saving it all to a secret DVD disk for review by his team. By now George had compiled a complete copy of the strange etchings on the crystalline surface.

Jack brought his sub near the pillar. Since the first exploratory dive, he had experienced no further radio interference or difficulties with his sub. The strange emanations had never returned. Jack was almost ready to admit that the odd sensation may have been due to something mundane, like a glitch in the *Nautilus*'s systems.

Hovering before the pillar, he reached out with his manipulator arm. Charlie had been hammering at him to try and clip a sample of the crystal. Jack reached with his titanium pincer and touched the pillar. From his hydrophones he heard a slight tinkle as metal struck crystal.

As the sound struck his ear, Jack felt every hair stand on

end, as if his body had become a living tuning fork. His skin tingled, his sight wavered, and the world began to spin. He felt as if he were going to pass out. He suddenly could not tell which way was up. It was as if he were weightless, in space again. His ears rang, and distantly he heard voices calling to him, as if down a long tunnel—garbled, in some strange language.

Gasping, he slammed his foot hard on the right pedal, driving his submersible away from the crystal. As he broke contact, Jack snapped back into his own seat, back into his own body. The tingling sensation vanished.

"—hear me? Jack!" Lisa yelled in his ear. "Answer me!"

Jack touched his throat mike, needing some physical contact with the world above. "I'm here, Lisa."

"What are you doing?"

"Wh-What do you mean?"

"You've been off-line for forty minutes! The Navy was about to launch one of their ROV robots to search for you."

Jack drifted away from the pillars. He widened the focus of his lights and saw the salvage cables hanging ahead. *How had the Navy hauled up the two plane sections so fast?*

He glanced at his clock. Only two minutes had passed since he'd hooked the tail fin and engine section to the cables. How was that possible? Frowning, Jack remembered the glitch Lisa had noted after his first dive.

"Lisa, what time do you have topside?"

"Three-fourteen."

Jack stared at the sub's computer screen. The digital clock was thirty-eight minutes slow.

"Jack?"

"I . . . I'm fine. Just another communication glitch." He glided toward the cables. Had he blacked out?

Lisa's voice came back tentative, full of suspicion. "Are you sure?"

"Yes, Lisa, nothing to worry about. I'm going for the next pieces."

"I don't like this. You should head up now."

"I can handle it. I've got green lights across the board. How are you reading now?"

Lisa's voice returned reluctantly. "Receiving you fine now."

A new voice interrupted. It was Admiral Houston. "Your doctor is correct, Mr. Kirkland. You had everyone in a panic topside."

"It's just a glitch, sir."

"I don't care. This mission is over for today."

Jack's grip grew hard on his controls. He glanced back at the crystal spire. His initial panic at the strange event had burned down to a deep-seated anger. He was determined to find out what had happened. "At least let me hook up these last cables. They're already down here."

A long pause. "Okay, Mr. Kirkland. But be careful."

Jack nodded, though no one could see him. "Aye, sir."

He swept his submersible up to the first cable and checked the computer screen for his next two targets—a cracked section of fuselage and a chunk of landing gear. Grabbing the cable's end, he dragged it over to the curved section of fuselage wall. He noted a portion of the plane's lavatory was still attached to the inside surface. Working rapidly, he attached the magnetic hook and called topside. "Ready on cable one."

The technician acknowledged, "Hauling away."

Jack swung toward the second winch line. As he turned the radio buzzed in his ear. It was Robert on the *Deep Fathom*. Jack was surprised to hear from the marine biologist. "Jack, I've got movement down there."

"What do you mean?"

"Something large just cleared the trough between two seamounts northwest of your position and is coming your way."

Jack frowned. For something to show up on sonar at this depth, it must be huge. "How big?"

"Sixty feet."

"Jesus . . . what is it? A submarine?"

"No, I don't think so. Its outline is too fluctuant, its movement too sinuous. Not artificial."

"So, in other words, a sea monster." Jack remembered the

serpent that had startled him in the hold of the *Kochi Maru*. "Is it another orefish?"

"No, too thick."

"Great," he mumbled. "How far off now?"

"A quarter klick. But it's picking up speed. Damn, it's fast! It must be attracted to your lights."

"Can I outrun it?"

"No. Not without a larger head start."

"Any suggestions?"

"Play dead."

"Say again."

"Settle to the seabed, turn off lights and motors. Abysmal sea life is attracted to sound, light, even bioelectric signatures. Turn everything off and you should be blind to whatever is coming."

Jack was not comfortable with this choice. As a former SEAL, he was trained for action, for a more proactive means of defense. But without an assault rifle and grenade launcher, he would have to listen to the expert here. Jack settled the *Nautilus*'s skids to the silty seabed.

After a short pause he flicked off the battery switch. The xenon lamps winked off. The constant whine of the thrusters went silent. Darkness swamped over the tiny sub. Even the internal lights dimmed and died.

His own breathing seemed so loud in the tiny space. His eyes strained for something to see. Distantly, he thought he could pick up flickers of winking lights. Was it just his eyes playing tricks? Bioluminescence? Ghost lights?

Robert whispered in his ear, "Don't communicate. It might be able to focus on you. We'll try pinging from above to scare it off."

"Where—"

"Quiet! It's just clearing the last ridgeline. It's huge! Here it comes!"

Jack held his breath, afraid even that would be heard. He craned his neck, searching the darkness around him. His eyelids were stretched wide.

"He's circling the area. Damn, what is it?"

Jack felt a trickle of sweat roll off his nose. The sub's cabin had grown humid. Without the carbon dioxide scrubbers working, he knew he had maybe thirty minutes of air before it became stale. He could not play possum forever.

Suddenly, he sensed something large move over him. He saw nothing, but something primal in his brain set off alarms. Jack's heart hammered. Fresh sweat broke out on his forehead, and he fought to see anything around him. What was out there?

"He's on top of you," Robert whispered.

The sub shoved a few inches across the silt. But Jack knew nothing had touched the tiny craft. The dragging movement was from the wake of something large sweeping past, close, the dead sub buffeted by its passage.

The *Nautilus* rolled onto one skid, twisting around slightly, caught in the wash of another wake. Jack froze, lifting both palms to brace against the acrylic dome. How big was this thing? The sub spun for two heartbeats more, then crashed again to the seabed with a screech of metal on metal, the left skid landing on a chunk of wreckage.

The sub now rested at a tilt, teetering slightly on the uneven perch.

"It's sticking near you, Jack. Our sonar pinging is not scaring it off."

Jack saw nothing beyond his own nose, but sensed something circling out there, stalking him. He breathed silently through clenched teeth.

Then he felt the sub move, tip forward. He heard something rasp across the acrylic dome, wet leather drawn over glass. The sub fell onto its side, and Jack sprawled, hanging in his straps. Before he could shift into a better position, something struck the sub, hard this time.

Jack was jarred into the seat harness, choked by the straps. The sub flipped and ground across the seabed. He heard something tear free from the framework.

Luckily, the sub settled back upright on its skids. Jack straightened. The damn thing out there was playing with him. Like a cat toying with a mouse.

He grabbed his controls. Before he was torn apart by

whatever was out there, he meant to fight. With his thumb, he flicked on the power. Spears of light lanced out. The darkness was driven backward. Closer, the whine of the battery-powered thrusters filled the space.

"Jack, what are you doing?"

"Where is it?"

"It's right *next* to you!"

He sensed the movement before seeing it. He twisted to his left. A huge black eye, the size of a garbage can lid, opened in a wall of flesh. Jack bit back a gasp. The eye blinked against the glare of the sub's lights.

The monster was lying beside the tiny sub, dwarfing it. Jack caught more movement. He craned his neck farther. Behind the sub's stern, a tangle of tentacles rose, twisting and churning as the behemoth awoke from its initial shock at its prey's brilliant display. Jack remembered the vampire squid snatching a hatchet fish, and now sympathized with the tiny fish.

Slamming both pedals, he shot his sub forward and away.

"Don't run!" Robert yelled in his ear.

"Who's running?" Jack hissed tightly. He spun the sub around, nose pointed at the gigantic beast. Grabbing the manipulator controls, he raised the sub's titanium arms and flexed the pincers. They could crush stone.

The creature rolled, tentacles scrabbling and twisting around toward Jack.

"What is it?"

"Video feed is fuzzy, but I think it's an *Architeuthis*," Robert said. "A giant squid of the cephalopod family. Only a few have ever been found. And those were dead, dragged up in the nets of deep trawlers. Nothing this big has ever been seen."

The beast shied slightly from the direct lances of the sub's xenon lamps. One tentacle, thick as a sewer pipe, came probing low along the seabed.

Jack backed away, all thrusters on full—but he wasn't fast enough.

The snaking limb shot toward him, slapping a wide blow. The sub bounced, its nose driven up. Jack's forehead struck the acrylic dome. With stars dancing across his vision, he fought the control pedals but found the submersible unresponsive.

At first he feared he was out of power. Then he noticed a platter-sized sucker clamped onto the acrylic dome. He was caught, trapped in its grip. The tentacle wound around the sub, drawing him toward the mass of the beast. The seals around him groaned with the strain.

Ahead, the creature was fully revealed in his lights. Eight muscular arms and two longer tentacles coiled out from its pale body. Its skin was almost translucent, its flattened head flanked by lateral fins. Its two longer tentacles probed the sub, dragging toothed suckers across its titanium frame.

The vessel suddenly jolted. His lights swung. Jack spotted the beaked mouth of the monster opening and closing— only a yard away. Through the hydrophones, he could hear the grind of its maw.

Swearing under his breath, Jack shifted the manipulator arms. He maneuvered the pincers and snatched at the nearest tentacle. The titanium grips tore into the leathery tissue. Black blood bloomed out.

Before Jack could savor his attack, the *Nautilus* was flung away, tumbling end over end. He released the manipulator controls and braced himself, tried to slow his tumble with his thrusters' foot pedals, but it was no use. The *Nautilus* struck the seabed, gouging a trough in the silt. Jack's shoulder bore the brunt of the impact. The sub lay on its side.

"Jack! Turn off your lights!"

"Playing dead didn't work before," he answered, and pushed up on one arm. He searched for the giant squid, but a cloud of silt enclosed the vehicle.

"Listen to me! We're going to try and draw the creature away."

"How?" Jack shifted as the silt settled around him. His lights began to pierce through the cloud. It was not an encouraging sight. A mass of tentacles twisted toward him. Rather than intimidating the beast, his attack had only succeeded in angering it.

Jack toggled down his power—but didn't shut it off. The

sub's lamps dimmed. He refused to go totally dead. He did not want to be blind down here again. "What's your plan?"

"I've just ordered the Navy to activate the second cable's electromagnet," Robert said. "The strong electric field might attract the beast away . . . but only if you disappear."

Jack bit his lip. He lowered his power further, flipping off the thrusters. The light was now just a weak glow. He could barely see the roiling mass of tentacles. Through the silt, the beast continued to crawl slowly toward him. "Okay. Try it," Jack ordered.

"We already have. We turned it on a minute ago. Is the *Architeuthis* taking our bait?"

The squid continued to roll toward him.

"No," he said with disgust. It wasn't working. He would have to fight, try to chase it off. Jack reached to power up again. Then a thought occurred to him. He remembered Robert's initial warning—*don't run*! "Robert, try moving the cable! Drag it along like a fishing line!"

"What? Oh . . . I get it. Hang on!"

Jack turned off all systems, except the sub's lamps. He searched for the cable, but the light was too weak to reach that far.

C'mon, Robert . . . c'mon . . .

The squid edged nearer, a wall of pale tissue, tentacles, and dinner-plate-sized suckers. He watched one of its huge eyes roll in his direction. Suspicion shone forth. He prayed the beast remained wary long enough for Robert's ruse to play out.

"Where are you, Robert?" he mumbled.

A tentacle lashed out toward the half-buried sub.

Jack reached for his manipulator controls. His thumb shifted to the battery toggle.

Then off to the left a new light suddenly bloomed in the inky gloom, its brilliance sharp.

Both Jack and the squid froze.

Slowly, the beast's huge eye rolled its attention toward the new source of light. Jack looked over, too.

Across the seabed, a spike of pure brilliance thrust up. It was the crystal spire, aglow with an inner fire.

In the gleam, Jack spotted the winch cable drifting only a few feet from the spire, its electromagnet swinging even closer.

Jack stared, slack-jawed. *What the hell . . . ?*

Under the sub the seabed began to tremble—at first mildly, then more vigorously. Bits of smaller wreckage began to dance atop the tremoring floor. Great, Jack thought, first a sea monster, now this!

He held on tight. The vibration traveled up his bones to his teeth.

Across the debris field the cable drifted away from the spike. As it moved farther, the brilliance of the crystal faded, and the trembling died away. As the light dimmed, Jack watched the electromagnetic lure float beyond his sight, disappearing into the dark water.

He stared at his adversary.

The giant squid remained near the sub. A hulk of tentacles. It seemed to hesitate, clearly spooked by the tremors and strangeness. Then, slowly, it crawled after the disappearing lure—away from the *Nautilus.*

"It's working!" Robert hailed from topside.

Jack remained silent, afraid of distracting the great beast. He watched the squid stalk its new prey. Soon the monster drifted beyond the reach of the sub's dimmed lamps. He dared not turn them brighter, having to remain satisfied with updates from Robert.

"We're drawing the cable both up and away. It's still following. . . ."

Jack allowed himself a long low sigh.

"It's far enough away. Maybe you'd better get the hell out of there."

Jack did not have to be told twice. He powered up the sub, dumped his ballast, and engaged the thrusters. Silt coughed up around him as the *Nautilus* pulled from the seabed. The tiny sub rose rapidly.

Robert's voice returned. "Damn."

"What?"

"We lost it."

Panic clutched Jack's throat. "What do you mean?"

"Don't worry. It's not heading your way." Robert's voice was distinctly disappointed. "It gave up on us and dove back into the deeper troughs. It's gone back home. Damn, I would've loved to see it up close."

"Trust me . . . the experience is not as fun as it looked on video."

"Uh . . . oh yeah, sorry, Jack."

"Coming up. Be topside in fifteen."

"We'll be waiting for you."

Jack leaned back into his seat. He wiped his face with a hand towel. Though the terror was still fresh, he grinned. He had survived.

Still, a nagging kernel of concern marred his perfect relief. He pictured the brilliant glow as the cable passed near the crystal spire. He remembered his own experience with the pillar: the odd sensations, the lost time. It seemed there were more mysteries down here than just the crash of Air Force One.

Ryukyu University, Okinawa Prefecture, Japan

"Twelve thousand years? That's impossible!" Karen exclaimed.

Miyuki pushed away from the bank of monitors. "It might be a mistake. The database of this new language is limited right now. If Gabriel had more information . . . more examples . . ."

Karen nodded. "It has to be a miscalculation. There is no way the date could be denoting a real incident twelve millennia in the past. Unless the event were some fable . . . some creation myth being recounted."

"Still, how would these people know how to map a snapshot of the night sky from twelve thousand years ago? Gabriel says the position of the constellations and stars is precise to a tenth of a millimeter."

"It's not impossible," Karen argued. "The Mayans of South America had astronomical calendars of such precision that they rival our abilities today."

"But to extrapolate that far back?"

"If the Mayans could do it, why not these folks? In fact, the builders might even be some lost tribe of the Maya. Who knows?"

"You're right," Miyuki said, shaking her head and standing up. "Who knows? There are too many variables. That's why I didn't bring it to your attention when Gabriel first told me of his discovery two days ago."

Karen frowned. "You knew this two days ago?"

Miyuki shrugged. "I didn't think it was that important. I was just testing Gabriel's decoding ability. Since you were studying the language, I figured we'd discuss it later."

"Then if it wasn't this bombshell, why did you call me over today?"

Miyuki sighed. "The crystal star. Didn't you listen when I phoned?"

Karen stood, remembering Miyuki's urgent call. She had indeed mentioned something about the crystal star. "What have you learned? Did you find someone in the geology department to help you check it out?"

"No. Most of the geologists are still out in the field, researching the quakes and studying their effects. Such a catastrophe is a boon to those in their field. They won't be back until the university reopens."

"Then what did you learn?"

"I thought to do a bit of basic checking on my own. I was curious about its abnormally dense mass." Miyuki led the way across the lab. "I borrowed an electronic scale and tools. I figured I'd do some simple measurements. Nothing complicated. Calculate its mass, density . . . that sort of thing."

"And?"

"I kept failing." Miyuki crossed to a workstation neatly arranged with graph paper, metal rulers, calipers, compasses, and a squat stainless steel box.

Karen scrunched up her nose. "You kept failing?"

Miyuki picked up a few leaves of graph paper. Neatly drawn on them were precise depictions of the five-pointed star, from multiple views. Each had tiny metric measurements denoted. It was clearly the work of many hours. "I calculated its volume both by geometry and water displacement. I wanted to be exact. I found it to occupy precisely 542 cubic centimeters."

"What about its weight?"

Miyuki adjusted her bonnet. "That's the strange part." She waved at the graph papers and tools. "I thought these calculations were going to be the hard part. I figured that all I'd have to do afterward was weigh the artifact, then divide the weight by the calculated volume to get the density. Simple."

Karen nodded. "So how much did it weigh?"

"That would depend." Miyuki crossed to the steel box. "I borrowed this electronic scale from the geology department. It's able to weigh an object down to a fraction of a milligram."

"And?"

"Watch." Miyuki switched on the power switch. "I left the crystal star in the sample chamber."

Karen watched the red digital numbers climb higher and higher, settling at last on one number. Karen stared in disbelief.

14.325 KILOS

"Amazing. That's over thirty pounds. I can't believe it. The star is that heavy?"

Miyuki turned to Karen. "Sometimes."

"What do you mean?"

Miyuki opened the door to the electronic scale. Karen bent closer. Inside the sample chamber, the crystal star shone brightly, fracturing the room's light into brilliant shards. Karen was once again stunned by its beauty.

She turned to Miyuki. "I don't understand. What?"

Miyuki pointed to the red analog numbers of the electronic scale. The number had changed. It was smaller.

8.89 KILOS

Karen straightened, frowning. "Is there a problem with the scale?"

"I thought the same thing." Miyuki picked up the flashlight from the table. "Watch." She flipped on the flashlight and pointed its narrow beam at the crystal.

The star shone more brilliantly. Karen had to squint against its glare. But her gaze did not remain long on the crystal artifact. She stared at the digital reading. It was smaller again.

2.99 KILOS

"How . . . ?"

Miyuki shadowed the flashlight's beam with her palm and the number climbed higher. "Now you know why I had trouble with my calculations. The weight keeps changing. The stronger the light, the less it weighs."

"That's impossible. There's no crystal on this planet that acts this way."

Miyuki shrugged. "Why do you think I called you?"

10

Thunder

David Spangler crossed the rolling flight deck of the *Gibraltar*. A southern storm had whipped up overnight, pelting the vessel with rain and gale force winds. This morning the worst of the storm had blown itself out, but the sky remained stacked with dark clouds. Drizzle swept across the deck in wicked spats. Safety nets that fringed the ship snapped and flapped in the gusts.

David hunched against the cold and headed toward the ramp tunnel that led down to the hangar deck below. Striding briskly, he approached the two men sheltered just inside the tunnel's entrance. Two guards. They were his men, members of his seven-man assault team. Like him, they wore gray uniforms, black boots, black belts. Even their blond crew cuts matched his. David had handpicked his team five years ago. He nodded as he approached. They snapped to attention, no salutes.

Though their uniforms were free of any rank or designation, the entire NTSB team knew David's men. A personal letter from CIA Director Ruzickov had made it clear to the investigators and the ship's command staff that Spangler's team was in charge of security for the wreckage until the ship left international waters.

"Where's Weintraub?" he asked his second-in-command, Lieutenant Ken Rolfe.

"At the electronics station. Working on the flight data recorder."

"Any news?"

"They're still having no luck, sir. It's tits up."

David allowed himself a grim smile. Edwin Weintraub was the lead investigator for the NTSB—and a prime thorn in his side. The man was thorough, keen-eyed and sharp-witted. David knew that his presence wouldn't make subterfuge any easier.

"Any suspicion?" he said in a lower voice, stepping closer.

"No, sir."

David nodded, satisfied. Gregor Handel, Omega team's electronics expert, had done his job well. As head of security, David had no trouble granting his man access to the recorder, out of sight of anyone in the NTSB. Handel had promised he could sabotage the recorder without any telltale sign of tampering. So far the lieutenant had proven as good as his word. After the revelation on the cockpit voice recording, David had not wanted the information on the flight's data box to pinpoint a simple malfunction of one of Air Force One's primary systems. It would be hard to blame the Chinese for an ordinary mechanical glitch. So he had ordered the second black box damaged.

"Do you know why Weintraub called me this morning?" David asked.

"No, sir. Only that something stirred up the hornet's nest in there an hour ago."

"An hour ago?" David clenched his teeth. If something new had been discovered, the standing orders were for him to be informed *immediately*. He stormed past his men. Since the first day, Weintraub had been testing the line between his team and David's. It looked like a lesson might be necessary.

David walked down the long tunnel leading into the massive hangar bay below the flight deck. His footsteps echoed on the nonskid surface. The hangar space ahead was a cavernous chamber, two decks high and stretching almost a third of the ship's length. Before sailing here, half of the air wing normally stowed in the hangar had been sent to Guam, leaving space for the recovered wreckage.

As David left the tunnel, he stood and surveyed the wide expanse. The chamber reeked of seawater and oil. Across the wide floor, pieces and sections of the plane were laid out in distinct quadrants. Each area was overseen by its own field expert. Overhead, in the rafters, small offices had been taken over by his men, acting as additional lookouts to spy upon the jet's remains and the personnel below.

Pausing, David observed a large section of a cracked engine nacelle being hauled up another ramp from the lower well deck.

Satisfied that all was in order, he continued through the cavernous hangar. A large circus could have performed in here. And considering the scores of investigators scurrying around the pieces of wreckage, it might as well be a circus. Clowns, all of them, David thought.

He jumped aside as an electric forklift swung a chunk of twisted wing past him, almost taking his head off. Over the past three days, the team of investigators had been shifting sections around twenty-four hours a day, as if working a gigantic jigsaw puzzle. Once the forklift had safely passed, David proceeded deeper into the NTSB base of operations. Larger pieces of wreckage towered to either side: the smashed nose of the plane, the tail fin, chunks of fuselage. Steel-ribbed gravestones to the crew and passengers.

David spotted the electronics lab, a section of the deck cordoned off by banks of computers, twisted power cables, and worktables covered with circuit boards and whorls of wiring from Air Force One. As he approached he spotted the red and orange box of the flight's data recorder. It had been splayed open and its guts torn down. Little colored flags peppered its contents; however, none of the four investigators were giving the box a second look.

Instead, the three men stood around their portly leader, Ed Weintraub, who was seated at a computer and tapping furiously.

David stepped over. "What's going on?"

Weintraub waved a hand behind him. "I think I've figured out how the recorder's data became corrupted."

David's heart jumped. He glanced at the open box. Had Gregor's tampering been discovered? "What do you mean?"

Weintraub heaved himself to his feet. "Come. I'll show you." He tugged up his pants and absentmindedly tucked in his shirt.

David could not hide his disgust. The man's skin was oily, his black hair sticking out in odd directions, his thick glasses making his eyes swim. David couldn't imagine a more distasteful bearing. Weintraub was every repugnant image brought to mind by the expression "slimy civilian."

The investigator led the way from the electronic station. "We've come upon an intriguing finding. Something that might explain the recorder's damage." He crossed over to a quadrant where sections of the fuselage lay. The pieces were laid out in rough approximation of the actual plane.

David followed. "You still haven't explained what you're talking about. And I don't appreciate being the last to know. I informed you—"

Weintraub looked at David and interrupted. "I report when I have something to report, Mr. Spangler. I needed to rule out a more plausible explanation first."

"Explanation for what?"

"For this." Weintraub crossed to the fuselage and slapped a wrench against the surface. He removed his hand, but the tool remained in place, hanging there.

David's eyes grew wide.

Weintraub tapped the plane's side. "It's magnetized." He waved a short arm to indicate the entire warehouse space. "All of it. Every bit of metal shows a magnetic signature to some degree or other. It might be the reason for the data recorder's corruption. Strong magnetic exposure."

"Could the effect be due to the electromagnet used to

haul the pieces topside? Kirkland swore it wouldn't damage anything." David's voice caught on Jack Kirkland's name. During the past three days, both men had kept their distance. In the evening's postdive debriefing, David made sure he and Jack were at opposite ends of the room.

"No. Mr. Kirkland was quite correct. The electromagnet did not cause this. As a matter of fact, I can't explain it."

"What about some weapon?" David entertained the thought that maybe the Chinese *were* actually to blame.

"Too soon to say. But I doubt it. I'd imagine the effect is due to something after the crash. I've measured the lines of polarity on adjacent sections that were fractured apart. They don't line up when I reassemble the pieces."

"What are you saying?"

Weintraub sighed, clearly exasperated.

David's hand twitched into a fist; he had to forcibly restrain himself from smashing the condescending expression from the investigator's face.

"It *means*, Commander Spangler, that the magnetization of the airplane's parts occurred *after* it had broken apart. I doubt it played a role in the crash, but it must have interfered with the flight data recorder." He pushed his glasses up again. "What I don't understand is why the cockpit voice recorder was unaffected. If the flight data recorder was corrupted, the other should have been damaged, too."

David directed the conversation away from this query. He frowned at the wrench. "If the magnetization occurred after the crash, why are you investigating it at all? Our shared orders are to bring a speedy conclusion to this investigation. To bring answers to Washington, to the world."

"I know my duty, Commander Spangler. As I said before, my initial findings are conjecture. I cannot rule out the possibility that some EM pulse or some other external force brought down Air Force One until I examine this phenomenon in detail." Weintraub removed a smudged handkerchief from a breast pocket. "Besides, I've seen the reports on CNN. It seems Washington has its own ideas. Rumblings about an attack or sabotage by the Chinese."

David feigned disinterest. He knew Nicolas Ruzickov had been using any and all bits of information to seed suspicion on the Chinese. Already in the United States public sentiment was riddled with finger-pointing. The rattling of swords would not be far behind. David cleared his throat. "I don't care what the news media is reporting. All that matters is the ultimate truth."

Weintraub wiped his nose. His eyes narrowed as he stared at David. "Is that so? Were you ever able to find out who leaked the voice recorder's transcript? It seemed many of these so-called news reports are using the transcript as fodder to support claims of an attack upon Air Force One."

David felt his cheeks growing hotter, but his voice hardened. "I don't give a shit about rumors or gossip. Our duty is to get the truth back to D.C. What the politicians do with it is their business."

Weintraub pocketed his handkerchief and plucked the wrench from the wreckage. "Then you'll have no objections if I investigate this odd phenomenon." He slapped the tool on his palm. "To discern the truth."

"Do your job and I'll do mine."

Weintraub eyed him silently for a breath, then turned away. "Then I'd best get back to work."

David watched the investigator leave, then turned back to the large chunk of wreckage. He placed his hand on its smooth surface. For a moment he wondered what really *had* happened to the great aircraft. With a shake, he dismissed this line of inquiry. It didn't matter. What mattered was how the facts were spun by Washington. Truth was of no importance.

Turning away, he left his concern behind. He had been trained well in the old school. *Obey, never question.* He crossed back through the hangar and up the ramp. Outside, the winds were kicking up. Rain pelted the flight deck, sounding like weapons' fire. David nodded to his men and hurried across to the ship's superstructure. He knew he had better let Ruzickov know of this new finding.

Passing through the hatch, he shivered against the cold

and pulled the door closed behind him. Once out of the wind, he shook the rain from his clothes and straightened to find a large form approaching.

"Commander Spangler," Admiral Houston said in greeting, stopping before him. Dressed in a nylon flight jacket, Mark Houston filled the passage. David found himself rankling at the man's air of superiority.

"Aye, sir."

"Have you heard the newest?" Houston asked. "The magnetization of the airplane's parts?"

David's thin lips sharpened to a frown. Had everyone been informed before him? He forced down his anger. "I've heard, sir," he said stiffly. "I went to check it myself."

"Has Edwin been able to formulate any explanation?"

"No, sir. He's still investigating it."

Houston nodded. "He's anxious for more parts, but another storm is blowing our way. No diving today. It looks like Jack and his crew will get the day off."

David's eyes narrowed. "Sir, speaking of Kirkland, there's something I wanted to bring to your attention."

"Yes?"

"The Navy's submersible and divers from the Deep Submergence Unit are due to arrive tomorrow. With our own men here, I see no need to keep Kirkland, a freelancer, onsite. For security purposes—"

Houston sighed, giving David a hard look. "I know of the bad blood between you two. But until the Navy's sub is tested at these depths, Jack and the *Deep Fathom* are remaining on-site. Jack is a skilled deep-sea salvager, and his expertise will not be wasted because of your past conflicts."

"Aye, sir," David said between clenched teeth, seething at the admiral's support of Kirkland.

Houston waved David out of his way. "As a matter of fact, I'm heading over to the *Deep Fathom* right now."

David watched the admiral leave, numb to the cold wind blowing through the open door. It clanged shut, but David remained standing, staring at the closed door. His limbs shook with rage.

Before he could move, booted footsteps sounded behind him.

David forced a calmer composure as he turned. To his relief, he saw it was another of his men. Omega team's electronics expert, Gregor Handel.

The man stopped. "Sir."

"What is it, Lieutenant?" David snapped at the young man.

"Sir, Director Ruzickov is on the scrambled telecom line. He wishes to speak to you ASAP."

With a nod, David strode past Handel. It must be the call he had been waiting for these past three days.

Gregor followed, in step behind him. David strode quickly through to his own room. Leaving Handel outside, he closed the door. On his desk rested a small briefcase, opened. Inside was an encoded satellite phone. A red light blinked on its console. David grabbed up the receiver. "Spangler here."

There was a short pause. The voice was filled with static. "It's Ruzickov. You have the green light to proceed to stage two."

David felt his heart beat faster. "I understand, sir."

"You know what you must do?"

"Yes, sir. No witnesses."

"There must be no mistakes. The security of our shores depends on your action these next twenty-four hours."

David had no need for this pep talk. He knew the importance of his mission. Here was a chance to finally grind the last major Communist power under the heel of American forces. "I will not fail."

"Very good, Commander Spangler. The world will be waiting for your next call." The line went dead.

David lowered the receiver back to its cradle. At last! He felt as if a heavy stone had been lifted from his shoulders. The waiting, the kowtowing, was over. He swung around to the door and opened it. Handel waited. "Get the team together," he ordered.

Handel nodded and turned sharply on a heel.

David closed the door and crossed to his bunk. Bending over, he hauled out two large cases from under his bed. One was packed with C-4 explosives, detonators, and electronic timers. The other held his newest prize. It had just arrived this morning by special courier. He rested his hand atop the case.

Distantly, thunder echoed from outside. The promised storm bore down upon them. David smiled. By nightfall his true mission would begin.

10:48 A.M., aboard the *Deep Fathom*

George Klein sat buried in the ship's library, lost in his research, oblivious to the rocking and rolling of the ocean. For the past twenty-four hours the historian had holed up here, going over old charts and stories, searching for some clue to the origin of the strange script written on the crystal pillar. Though he had achieved no success, his research had revealed something disturbing. The discovery had kept him from his bed all night.

On the teak desk, George had splayed out a large map of the Pacific. Tiny red-flagged pins speared the map, dates scrawled on each flag. They marked ships, planes, and submarines lost in the region, going back a full century: *In 1957, an Air Force KB-50 disappears near Wake Island; in 1974, Soviet "Golf II" class submarine vanishes southwest of Japan; in 1983, the British* Glomar Java Sea *is lost off Hainan Island.* So many. Hundreds and hundreds of ships. George had an old report from the Japanese Maritime Safety Agency, listing boats lost with no trace ever found.

> 1968: 521 boats
> 1970: 435 boats
> 1972: 471 boats

George stood, moving back. He studied the pins. Having sailed in these waters for years, investigating shipwrecks, he had heard of the term the "Dragon's Triangle." It extended from Japan in the north to Yap Island in the south and trailed to the eastern end of Micronesia, a triangle of catastrophe and missing ships, not unlike the region known as the Bermuda Triangle in the Atlantic Ocean. But he had never given these tales much thought until now. He'd attributed the vanishings to ordinary causes: pirate activity, wicked weather, deep-sea quakes.

But now he was not so sure. He picked up an old report from a WWII Japanese commander of a Zero fighter wing, Shiro Kawamoto. The aged commander told a curious tale, the story of the disappearance of a Kawanishi Flying Boat during World War II off the coast of Iwo Jima. Kawamoto quoted the final words of the doomed pilot over the radio: "Something is happening in the sky . . . the sky is opening up!"

He returned the report to its pile. Jack had related the details of Air Force One's transcript to him last night after it was clear the news had already been leaked to the press. The cockpit recording had struck a chord in him, sending him to his library. It had taken him an hour to dig up Kawamoto's recounting. The similarity was too striking. It took him the rest of the night to construct the model before him.

George returned to his map. Red pencil and ruler in hand, he charted the Dragon's Triangle upon the map. He worked deftly, striking the lines cleanly. Once done, he stood back again. All the tiny pins fell within the boundary of his lines, all within the infamous triangle.

The old historian sat down. He did not know the significance of his discovery, but he couldn't stop a feeling of dread from settling in his chest. Over the long night, he had read countless other stories of ships gone missing in these seas. Stories extending far into the past, to records of ancient Imperial Japan, countless centuries.

But these stories were not what disturbed him the most. They were not what kept him working all night. Instead, among the cluster of red flags, in the exact center of the marked triangle, was a single blue flag.

It marked the grave of Air Force One.

4:24 P.M., Ryukyu University, Okinawa Prefecture, Japan

At the bank of computers, Karen worked alongside Miyuki. On a tiny monitor, she watched a computer flash through various connections, winding through an Internet maze. Finally, the University of Toronto logo appeared on the active window. "You did it!" Karen said.

"Gabriel did it," Miyuki answered.

"I don't care who did it, as long as we're hooked up."

For the past day, they had been trying to get a linkup to the outside world. Blackouts, phone service interruptions, and overloaded circuits had plagued their efforts to reach networks across the Pacific, even with Gabriel's skills. But at last Gabriel had succeeded. With this Internet connection, their research into the discoveries at the Chatan ruins could continue.

"Now maybe we can get somewhere," Karen said, grabbing the computer's mouse. After learning of the crystal artifact's strange properties, she had urged Miyuki to keep quiet until she could research the language in more depth. Miyuki had not argued. Both women were too stunned—and frightened—by their discovery. They had locked the artifact up in the safe in Miyuki's office.

Karen connected to the anthropology department of the University of Toronto. She performed a quick search under the name *rongorongo* and found six websites. She worked rapidly, afraid of losing even her tenuous connection. She clicked on a web address titled "Santiago Staff." From her research, she knew this was one of the twenty-five known authentic artifacts from Rapa Nui's ancient past.

On the screen, a photograph of a length of wood appeared. Carved into its surface were rows of tiny glyphs. Below the picture was a detailed rendering of the staff's writing. Karen highlighted it. Several of the symbols looked similar to those they had found in the star chamber. "We need to compare these to the lines we photographed."

"Done," Gabriel's disembodied voice answered.

On a neighboring monitor the screen split into two halves. On the left side a copy of the Santiago Staff's glyphs scrolled. On the right the script from the star chamber rolled past. At first nothing seemed to match—they were similar but not exact—then, abruptly, the scrolling stopped. Two glyphs, now highlighted in red, shared opposite sides of the screen.

Miyuki gasped. "They look almost the same!"

Karen frowned. She was not yet convinced. "It might be a coincidence. How many different ways could there be to represent a starfish?" She spoke louder: "Gabriel, can you find any other matches?"

"I already have."

The pair of starred glyphs shrunk in size. Now each half of the computer monitor was filled with thirty glyphs, each side the mirror of the other. Human figures, odd creatures, geometric shapes—but they all matched!

"I think this is more than coincidence," Miyuki said softly.

"No kidding," Karen said.

"Adding this database to the previous," Gabriel said. *"I estimate the language constitutes some 120 main glyphs, combining to form twelve hundred to two thousand compound glyphs. With more data, I may be able to begin building a translation."*

Karen's eyes grew even wider. "I can't believe this. If Gabriel's right, the star chamber may be the Rosetta stone for this ancient language, the final key to a century-long puzzle." She returned to her monitor and computer. "Gabriel, I'm going to direct the other *rongorongo* examples to you." She returned to the main screen and began feeding in other Easter Island artifacts: the Mamari tablet, the Large and Small Washington tablet, the Oar, the Aruka Kurenga, the Santiago tablet and Small St. Petersburg tablet.

When she was done, Karen straightened, turning to Miyuki. "Toronto only has these nine artifacts. Can Gabriel search other universities' databases on his own? If we could add the glyphs from the other sixteen artifacts—"

"Then we'd have a better chance at deciphering the language." Miyuki also spoke louder: "Gabriel, can you perform a worldwide search?"

"Certainly, Professor Nakano. I will begin immediately."

Karen clutched Miyuki's wrist. "Do you have any idea what this could mean?" Excited, she answered her own question: "For centuries scholars have been attempting to translate the *rongorongo* writing. How old is the writing? Where did it come from? Who brought it to the islanders? The entire lost history of this section of the world could finally be revealed."

"Don't get your hopes too high, Karen."

"I'm not," she lied. "But either way, to discover a new source of *rongorongo* script on the opposite side of the Pacific—that alone will garner countless journal articles. It'll force historians to change their assumptions of this area. And what else is at Chatan? We've barely scratched the surface. We should—"

An alarm klaxon rang out from a wall-mounted siren.

Karen jumped at the noise. Miyuki stood up.

"What is it?" Karen asked.

"My office alarm! Someone is breaking into my office."

Karen bolted to her feet. "The crystal star!"

Miyuki grabbed her elbow. "The guards downstairs will check it out."

Karen shook out of her friend's grip and moved toward the door. Her mind spun. She *would not* lose this clue to a mystery older than mankind. She zippered down her white cotton clean suit and grabbed her pistol from its shoulder harness. Luckily, the Chatan police had not discovered her weapon after the incident at the ruins. Ever since that adventure, she did not go anywhere without it.

Miyuki followed her as far as the lab's antechamber. "Leave it to the guards," she repeated emphatically.

"The elevators aren't working. By the time they get here, the thieves could be gone. And I won't lose that artifact! It's too valuable." Trusting in her skill as a marksman, Karen

cracked open the door and peeked down the hall toward
Miyuki's office. The door lay open, its glass window shattered. Karen strained to hear anything, but the alarm was
deafening.

Taking a deep breath, she ducked out the door and crept
along the wall toward the open office. Despite her warnings,
Miyuki followed. Karen glanced at her friend, but Miyuki
waved her on.

Readying her pistol, Karen slid along the wall. She could
see a light skittering around inside the office. A flashlight.
The intruder had not been scared off by the alarm. Her heart
thundered in her ears. She swallowed hard and continued on.

At the doorway, she paused. She could hear two men arguing inside, but didn't recognize the language. There was a
loud crack of splintering wood. She squeezed the grip of her
pistol, tensed for a breath, then leaped into the entryway.

"Freeze!" she yelled.

Inside, two men glanced up at her with shocked expres-
sions. They had dark complexions, clearly South Pacific Islanders. One held a crowbar, which he'd just used to break
into Miyuki's desk. The other held a pistol. He made a move
in her direction.

Karen fired—a warning shot. Plaster puffed from the wall
behind the armed man's head. He froze.

"Drop the weapons or you're dead!" she screamed. She
did not know if the men knew English, but the single warning shot crossed all language barriers.

The thief paused, then tossed his pistol to the side, a sour
look on his dark face. The other dropped his crowbar.

Her adrenaline surging, her senses were acute. From the
corner of her eyes she saw the ramshackle condition of
Miyuki's office. In the short time, they had torn through the
filing cabinets. The drawers of the desk had been pulled and
dumped. With relief, she noted that the wall safe hidden behind Miyuki's doctoral diploma had not been discovered.

"Raise your hands," she said, motioning with her pistol.

They obeyed. Karen kept her gun raised. The building security should be arriving in the next few moments. She just
had to keep these thieves at bay.

As the men stood with their hands up, Karen noticed their bare arms. The serpent tattoo was visible even in the dim light. Recognizing the symbol, her breath caught in her chest. They were the looters from the pyramids!

Momentarily confused and shocked, she was a few seconds too slow in realizing the hidden threat. They had been attacked at the pyramids by *three* men. Only two were here. Where was the third?

To her right, Miyuki gasped. She was posted in the shadow of the door. Karen glanced her way. Miyuki was staring down the hall, past Karen's shoulder. Karen swung around.

The third thief stepped into the hall from the stairwell, a rifle at his shoulder. Clearly their lookout.

The man fired, the blast deafening.

But Karen and Miyuki were no longer there. Both women had leaped through the door into the office. The wooden door frame burst into shards behind them.

Inside, one of the men lunged for the fallen pistol. Karen fired. The man's hand blew back in a spray of blood. Moaning, he rolled away from the discarded weapon, his bloody fist clutched to his chest.

Karen darted farther into the room, giving her space to cover both men and the doorway.

The last man kept his hands raised, unmoving. It was not fear that kept him steady. Karen saw it in his eyes. His calmness was almost unnerving. He backed a step, then sidled along the wall, clearly offering no threat. He kicked his wounded companion and barked something in his foreign tongue. The bloodied man crawled across the floor, in the direction of the door.

Karen's pistol followed them. She did not shoot. Not in cold blood. If they were leaving, then let them. Hopefully, university security would capture them on the way out. But the reason for her restraint was not solely because the others were unarmed. The first man's eyes did not leave hers. In his gaze, she continued to see a calmness that belied their situation.

Then the rifleman appeared in the doorway. Before he

could swing on them, the first man knocked his companion's gun barrel aside. He eyed Karen and Miyuki, and spoke rapidly in Japanese, his accent thick. Then the trio left, the uninjured two helping their wounded companion.

Karen did not lower her pistol, even after their footsteps faded away. "What did he say?" Karen asked Miyuki.

"H-He said that we do not know what we have discovered. It was never supposed to be unearthed." Miyuki glanced at the hidden wall safe, then back at Karen. "It is a curse upon us all."

10:34 P.M., USS *Gibraltar,* Central Pacific

David Spangler led his team across the wet deck, sticking to shadows. The storms had grown worse by nightfall. Thunder boomed like distant mortar fire, while spats of lightning turned night to day for flickering seconds. Nearby, waves smashed against the flanks of the carrier, washing as high as the deck itself.

After the evening meal, the NTSB investigators had retreated to their own bunks, many seasick, abandoning the wreckage until the storm abated. Additionally, David had declared the hangar deck to be unsafe for personnel with the ship heaving to and fro, especially with all the loose pieces of wreckage. He had ordered the hangar deserted until the storm died down. Green-faced and holding their stomachs, none of the NTSB personnel had argued. Afterward, David assigned his men to guard the abandoned hangar's entry points.

With the night complete and the storm in full rage, David had chosen this moment to proceed with their plan. Sheltering for a moment in the lee of the giant superstructure, he spotted the two men guarding the entrance to the hangar ramp tunnel. One of the pair lifted a flashlight high, signaling it was all clear, then doused the light.

Diving into the sweeps of rain, David hurried forward, shielding a thick case against his chest. Behind him the other three men, laden with their own satchels, kept pace, moving with confident skill across the pitching deck.

David slid into the tunnel entrance and crouched beside the pair of guards. "All clear?"

"Yes, sir," his second-in-command reported. "The last of them left half an hour ago."

David nodded, satisfied. He turned to the others. "You know your duties. Keep up your guard. Handel and Rolfe with me."

The two men collected the equipment satchels. David kept his own case. He led them into the tunnel entrance.

It grew darker as they proceeded down. At the bottom there were no lights. Pausing, David slipped on his night vision goggles and switched on his UV lantern. The stacks of wreckage appeared out of the gloom, limned in dark purple and white. He waved the others to follow.

Striding briskly, he moved down the central corridor of the makeshift warehouse. No one spoke. David flashed his ultraviolet light along the numbered side aisles. At last he found number 22. Pausing, he cast his light around. There was no sign of anyone else here, but the boom of thunder and the rattle of rain muffled even their own footsteps. It set David's teeth on edge. When he worked, he depended on the full use of all his senses.

He searched for a full minute more, then lowered the UV light. He stood beside one of the jet's hulking General Electric engines. Except for impact damage, it was intact. He now knew where he was, and led the way to the side. His goal appeared out of the darkness: a crate marked with the designation 1-A on its side. It contained the first bit of wreckage raised to the surface.

He nodded to his men.

The pair donned surgical gloves, intending to leave no fingerprints. They worked efficiently, with minimal wasted movement. Rolfe pulled a small crowbar from his bag and loosened the crate's nails. Gregor Handel slid to his knees and primed the bomb's electronics with four cubes of C-4, enough to blow away several yards of wreckage around it.

David knelt and set down his own thick case, snapping the bindings loose.

"I'm ready, sir," Gregor said beside him.

David nodded and opened his case. It held the mission's true prize. Resting on the felt interior was a jade sculpture—the bust of a Chinese warrior.

Even through the night vision goggles, he recognized the fine work. He smiled with pride. This aspect of the plan was pure brilliance on his part. He had ordered the bust fabricated after the first day's dive on the wreck. It was an exact duplicate of the bust Jack Kirkland had rescued from the seabed. The handsome object was a fragment of the Chinese Premier's original gift, a jade replica of an ancient warrior seated on his horse. When David had first seen the fragment, he quickly modified his original strategy. It occurred to him now that he should thank Kirkland for this opportune turn of events.

He unscrewed the bust's ear, revealing a hidden compartment in the jade. He passed the bit of sculpture to his electronics expert. Working deftly, Gregor slid the bomb in place and checked all the wires and transmitters.

Nearby, Rolfe extracted the original bust from the crate's bubble packing and settled it within their own case.

David glanced at his watch. Only a minute had passed.

"I need some real light," Gregor hissed, bent over the false bust. He pulled back his night vision goggles. "This Chink electronics is crap. I need to double-check the connections."

David nodded to Rolfe. The man knelt and shone a small flashlight toward the chunk of jade. David pushed aside his own night vision goggles.

Gregor tilted his head, fingers working over the explosive unit. The timers and detonators had been stolen last week from a Chinese black market dealer; perfect to lay a false trail.

Gregor sighed in relief and held the bust toward David. "All set."

David accepted it and screwed the jade ear in place. "Let's get going," he said, standing up.

As he stepped toward the crate, a call echoed across the dark tent. *"Who's out there!"*

David and the others froze. Rolfe flicked off his flashlight. The men returned to night vision. Deeper in the tent, a new light bloomed. It lay over by the electronics bay.

"Show yourself, or I'll call Security!"

David thought quickly. He now recognized the voice. It was Edwin Weintraub, the NTSB lead investigator. He bit back a curse. The hangar was supposed to be empty. David leaned over to Rolfe. "Shut him down. Minimal harm."

Rolfe nodded and backed swiftly away, disappearing into the darkness.

Quickly, David adjusted his plans. It was what made him such a successful field commander. In the real world, few plans proceeded as planned. For a mission to succeed, a plan had to be liquid, capable of changing at a moment's notice. Like now . . .

David stood, shouting, "Quiet down, Weintraub! It's just me!"

"Commander Spangler?" The edge of panic in the man's voice died down.

"I'm just checking to make sure everything is secure before retiring. What are you doing here?"

"I was taking a nap on my cot in the back. My computer is compiling data. I'm waiting for it to finish."

"You shouldn't be out in this storm."

"Everything's insulated and surge-protected. There's no danger."

That's what you think. David knew that Rolfe should almost be in position. He raised his voice, keeping Weintraub's attention on him. "Fine! If you've got everything in hand, I'm heading out. The guards will be outside all night if you have any problems."

"Thanks! But I'll be all— Hey, who are—"

David heard a loud crash. He frowned. Rolfe was better than that. Sloppy work.

"All clear!" Rolfe called out.

"I'm sending Handel over to help you. Bring that slimy sack of shit over here."

Gregor straightened, a look of inquiry on his face, but the man knew better than to question an order. David waved him forward. Gregor quickly vanished.

As he waited, David lowered the bust to the deck and collected their tools. This unfortunate blunder could be turned to their advantage. His original plan was to set off the explosive device during the workday tomorrow. A few men would probably die, but it was a small price to pay. But now he recalibrated his plans.

Beyond the rumble of the storm, he heard the scrape of boot on deck. He turned in time to see his two men edge into aisle 22, Weintraub's slack form slung between them. His wrists and ankles were lashed with plastic straps, his mouth sealed with duct tape. The large man moaned and struggled feebly, clearly dazed by the attack.

"Bring him here and dump him."

The pair lowered their captive to the deck. "I'm sorry, sir," Rolfe apologized. "I slipped on some grease. He saw me before I could silence him."

"Poor work all around," David said harshly. "Weintraub shouldn't even be here."

"His cot was hidden behind a wall of wreckage. His computer's monitor was switched off. In the dark—"

"I don't want to hear any excuses." David turned his attention to the restrained investigator. By now Weintraub had regained full consciousness. David spotted the large lump behind his left ear. A dribble of blood marked where Rolfe had clubbed him. Weintraub stared at David, his eyes bright with hatred and anger.

"What do we do with him?" Gregor asked. "Toss him overboard. Blame the storm?"

David continued to study his prey. He watched the man's anger change to fear. "No. Drowning him will do us no good."

A flicker of hope in the man's eyes . . . and suspicion.

David reached over and pinched Weintraub's nostrils closed. "Hold him down." Rolfe pinned the man's legs; Gregor held his shoulders.

With his mouth sealed in duct tape, there was no air.

Weintraub struggled, suffocating. David held tight, speaking to the others. "We'll put his body to use. The weak spot in our plan was attempting to explain why tomorrow's explosion would spontaneously happen. Why then? What set it off? It could raise suspicions."

He nodded toward the struggling man. His color was now purplish, his eyes bulging in recognition of approaching death. David ignored his panic. "But here's our scapegoat. The poor guy was tampering with the crate and accidentally set it off."

"So we'll blow it tonight?" Gregor asked.

"Just after midnight. Afterward, we'll make sure the investigators discover the Chinese electronics. That's all the proof Washington will need. They'll come to believe the remainder of the jade sculpture had been similarly booby-trapped, that the Chinese stuffed the horse's jade ass full of C-4."

"I think he's dead, sir," Rolfe interrupted, still sitting on Weintraub's knees.

David looked down and realized Rolfe was right. Weintraub stared unblinking at the ceiling, eyes empty. David released the dead man's nose and wiped his gloved hand on his pant leg with disgust. "Free his bindings."

His men obeyed while David ripped the duct tape from Weintraub's purplish lips. Then he took the jade bust, balanced it atop the man's chest, and placed the man's hands near it. As David began to pull away, he had another idea. Fishing in a pocket, he pulled free a bit of electronic circuitry, of Chinese design, and placed it in the dead man's fingers. He closed Weintraub's hand over it. A bit of extra insurance.

Straightening, he surveyed his handiwork for a few seconds, then nodded curtly. "Let's go. I'm famished."

Gregor collected the cases. "What are we going to do with the extra C-4 and detonators?" he asked.

David smiled. "Don't worry. I have another mission for you. After tonight, tomorrow's gonna be a hectic day. Lots of chaos to conceal one more operation."

"Sir?"

"I know someone who'll appreciate that extra C-4." David pictured Jack Kirkland, wearing his shit-eating grin as he stood with an arm around his sister's shoulder. "A parting gift for an old friend."

Midnight aboard the *Deep Fathom*

In the ship's galley, Jack sat with Admiral Houston at a small table. Outside the narrow window, forked lightning streaked across the roiling skies. Due to the foul weather, the admiral had chosen to remain aboard the *Fathom*, but Jack suspected that his decision to stay was not all due to the storm.

As the ship heaved and rolled, the admiral chewed on the stubby end of his thick stogie, oblivious, and sighed out a long stretch of smoke. The old sailor was rapidly depleting Jack's Cuban cigar stock. "You really should have told us sooner about this discovery," Houston said.

Jack bowed his head. Earlier, he had played the secret recordings of the crystal spire and the strange hieroglyphics. After the close call with the giant squid, he knew he could no longer keep silent about his discoveries. "I know, but at first I didn't think it was important to the investigation."

"And you sought some way to snub your nose at the Navy."

Jack grimaced. He never could put anything past the old man.

The admiral continued, "Your discovery may explain the magnetization of the wreckage's parts. If the crystal was giving off some form of radiation, it may have affected the wreck. Weintraub will want to know about this."

Jack nodded. He had been surprised to hear about the magnetization of the plane's metal sections.

"Is there anything else you've been hiding?" Houston asked.

"No, not really."

Houston's look bore in on Jack. "Not really?"

"Just a few thoughts . . . nothing concrete."

"Like what?"

"It's not important."

Houston drilled Jack with his steely eyes. Even after twelve years, it still made Jack cringe inside. "Let me decide what's important and what isn't."

Jack felt backed into a corner. "I don't know. Don't you think it's a strange coincidence that most of the wreckage just happened to land by the pillar?"

"Strange? No doubt. But who knows how many of these spikes may lie down there on the ocean floor? Only a small fraction of the deep seabed has been investigated."

"Maybe." Jack was not convinced.

Silence descended over the pair, except for the distant rumble of thunder. Finally, Houston stretched, stubbing out his cigar. "Well, if that's all . . . It's getting late. I should get myself to bed before I totally clean out your Cuban supply. Thanks for lending me your cabin."

Jack took a deep breath. All afternoon he had been mulling over an idea he'd been afraid to verbalize. "Mark . . ."

The admiral glanced his way, eyebrows raised. It was the first time Jack had addressed him so informally. "What is it?"

"I know this is crazy, but what if . . . what if the crystal spire had something to do with bringing down Air Force One?"

"Jack, c'mon, now you're really pushing the envelope."

"Don't you think I know that? But I was the only one down there." Jack recalled when his sub's titanium arm had touched the crystal's surface. The sense of free falling, the glitches.

"What are you saying?"

Jack spoke earnestly, struggling to put what he felt into words: "I once shipped out on a nuclear sub. I bunked not far from the reactor. Though the power plant was shielded, I could still somehow sense the immense power behind the bulkhead. It was like my bones were picking up something that no machine could detect. It was like that down below. An immense power, humming along, idling."

Houston stared silently, then spoke, slowly. "I trust your

judgment, Jack. I don't doubt you felt something. If the thing could magnetize the wreckage, then it is damn strong. But to bring down a jet flying at forty or fifty thousand feet . . ." The admiral's voice died away.

"I know . . . I know what it sounds like. But I just wanted you to know what I discovered, what I felt down there. All I ask is that you keep your mind open."

Houston nodded. "I appreciate your candor, Jack. But I always keep my options open." The old man shook his head tiredly. "All I wish is that Washington would do the same. You know you're not the only one with thoughts about the crash. The new administration seems to have already made up their minds."

"What are they saying now?" Jack asked.

"Sabotage. Done by the Chinese."

Jack's brow crinkled. Over the past few days he had been too busy to follow the news. "But that's ridiculous. President Bishop was one of the staunchest advocates for negotiating a long-term relationship with China. Why would they assassinate him?"

The admiral scowled. "It's all politics. Posturing. But in response, the Chinese have already pulled their diplomats out of the U.S. and kicked ours out of their country. Just this morning I learned that the Chinese navy has been out on maneuvers. Just more posturing on their part, but it's still a dangerous game Washington is playing."

Jack suddenly felt foolish voicing his own wild conjecture. The admiral had enough on his plate. "Then I guess we need the real answer ASAP."

"No doubt. At least we'll have the Navy's own sub to aid us tomorrow. With two submersibles diving, we should be able to accelerate the pace."

Jack nodded. The sub was the newest prototype, a part of the Navy's Deep Submergence Unit, rated to the depth of fifteen thousand feet and a speed of up to forty knots. "I've read about the *Perseus*. A real Ferrari of the fleet."

"A Ferrari with teeth. It was just outfitted with an array of minitorpedoes."

Jack's eyes widened.

"It's the latest modification to the *Perseus*. Still classified info."

"Should you be telling me about it?"

Houston wayed off his concern. "You would've found out tomorrow anyway. These little submarine busters should help discourage any hostile sea life from trying to eat you again."

Jack grinned. "For once, I'm not going to object to the Navy guarding my back."

Footsteps on the stairs interrupted their discussion. Both men turned. George Klein pushed up into the galley from the lower deck. "I thought I heard voices up here," the historian said. "I was hoping you were still awake, Jack."

Jack was surprised by the professor's shabby appearance: dark circles shadowed his eyes, a scraggly gray beard covered his chin. It looked as if he had not slept in a couple days. Now that he thought about it, he hadn't seen George all day. "What is it, Professor?"

The historian lifted a rolled map in his hand. "Something I wanted to run past you. I've been researching other disappearances in this region. I think you should see this."

Jack knew George did not voice idle thoughts. The historian remained close-lipped until he was satisfied with his research. And from the condition of the man, Jack suspected he had been digging into something significant.

"What have you discovered?"

"Perhaps the underlying reason for the crash of Air Force One."

The admiral straightened and looked significantly at Jack. "It seems everyone is coming up with their own theories today."

George ignored the admiral's words and moved to the galley table. As the historian unrolled his map, Jack caught a glimpse of the Pacific Ocean and a large red-penciled triangle. Before he could get a better look, a loud boom shook through the ship.

Everyone froze.

As the sound echoed away, Jack heard Elvis barking deeper in the ship's belly.

Wincing, the professor adjusted his glasses. "That was close. That thunderclap must have been—"

Both the admiral and Jack were on their feet. "That wasn't thunder," Jack said, stepping to the door leading to the stern deck.

Outside, rain lashed the deck. The winds tried to rip the door handle from his grip. The ship rolled deeply under his feet.

Both men followed him from the galley.

Turning, Jack searched the seas. About a quarter mile away he spotted the silhouette of the USS *Gibraltar*. The ship now blazed with lights. From its deck, a small fireball rolled into the dark sky.

"What happened?" George asked, wiping at his glasses.

No one answered—but as Jack followed the fireball, he sensed that their true troubles were just beginning.

11

Exiled

Climbing the stairs of Miyuki's building, Karen was thrilled to get back to work. After yesterday's attempted theft, she and Miyuki had spent the entire day holed up with university security. Even though she had used her gun in self-defense, the authorities confiscated her weapon. With Japanese gun laws as strict as they were, it had taken Karen hours to talk her way out of the police station. Afterward, Ryukyu's president, concerned about the attack, had called to reassure the two women and promise them increased security.

Taking extra measures herself, Karen had stashed the crystal artifact in her safe deposit box at her bank in anticipation of another attempted theft.

Even now, as she climbed the building's stairs, she was accompanied by a uniformed security guard. At least the university's president had proven true to his word, she thought. At the top of the stairs she led the way to Miyuki's lab. After she knocked and identified herself, she heard the tumblers in the lock and then the door inched open.

"Are you all right, Doctor?" the guard asked in Japanese.

Miyuki nodded. She pulled the door open, allowing Karen to enter.

"We'll be fine from here," Karen said in stilted Japanese. "We'll keep the doors locked and will call down when we're ready to leave."

He nodded and turned curtly.

Karen closed the door and Miyuki locked it again. Sighing, Karen reached over and took her friend's hand. "We're safe," she said. "They won't be back. Not with the extra security around here."

"But—"

She gave Miyuki's hand a squeeze. Remembering how calm the leader of the thieves had been, and recalling how he had knocked down his companion's rifle, she said, "I don't think they truly meant us any personal harm. They just wanted the artifact."

"And are determined to get it no matter who stands in their way," Miyuki added dourly.

"Don't worry. With it locked in my safe deposit box, they'll have to defeat the Bank of Tokyo's security system to get it."

"I'm still not taking any chances." Miyuki waved Karen to the clean suits hanging on their wall. "C'mon. Gabriel has discovered something interesting."

"Really? About the language?"

"Yes, he finished compiling the other examples of the Easter Island script."

Karen hurried into her clean suit, zipping it up and standing. "Do you think he has enough information to translate it?"

"It's too soon to say. He's working on it though."

Tucking her hair into a paper bonnet as she moved toward the door, she asked, "But do you think he can do it?"

Miyuki shrugged and keyed open the door to the main lab. A whoosh of air sounded as the seal broke. "That's not what you should be asking."

Miyuki, always Japanese stoic, was seldom playful when

she talked business, so the trace of mischief in her voice intrigued Karen. "What is it?"

"You need to see this."

Clearly, Miyuki had discovered something important. "What? What is it?"

Miyuki led the way to the bank of computers. "Gabriel, could you please bring up Figure 2B on Monitor One."

"Certainly. Good morning, Dr. Grace."

"Good morning, Gabriel." By now Karen was growing accustomed to their disembodied colleague.

The two women sat down. On the monitor before them, Karen saw data scrolling, flowing so rapidly it was almost a blur, but she noted that many of the fluttering images were of the unknown hieroglyphics. Within a few seconds five glyphs were centered on the screen.

She was unimpressed. "Okay. What am I looking at? Can you translate this section, Gabriel?"

"No, Dr. Grace. With the current level of data, a decryption of this language remains impossible."

Karen frowned, disappointed. "Have you found any other examples of the *rongorongo* script?"

"I have found them all, Dr. Grace."

Karen's brows shot up. "All twenty-five? So soon?"

"Yes. I contacted 413 websites to obtain all known examples of this language. Unfortunately, three of the artifacts contained identical scripts, and one artifact contained only a single glyph. The amount of data was insufficient to complete a decryption."

Karen eyed the monitor. "So what is this? Which artifact are these glyphs from?"

"None of them."

"What?"

Miyuki interceded. "Please explain, Gabriel. Elaborate on your search parameters." Miyuki turned to Karen and added hurriedly, "He thought of this all on his own." Her face shone with excitement and pride.

Gabriel spoke. "*After searching under the term* 'Rongorongo,' *I performed a worldwide search under each individual symbol, 120 searches, to be precise. On an archaeology website at Harvard University, I discovered a matching post. It matched three of my search parameters.*" On the screen, three of the five symbols suddenly glowed red.

"What about the other two?" Karen asked, struggling to understand.

"*They do not match any known* Rongorongo *glyph.*"

"What are you saying?"

Miyuki answered, "They're new symbols. Glyphs no one's seen before."

"Th-That would mean we've discovered an undocumented artifact." She sat up straighter. "A new find!"

"The note on the Harvard website was posted two days ago."

"Can I see the posting?"

"It's right here." Miyuki slipped out a sheet. "I printed it out."

"This is unbelievable."

"I know. Gabriel was able to extend the search parameters on his own. It's true independent thinking. Unbelievable progress."

"Miyuki, I meant the new symbols." Karen rattled the paper. "This is the unbelievable part."

"In your field maybe."

Karen realized she had slighted her friend's accomplishment. "I'm sorry, Miyuki. Both you and Gabriel deserve my heartfelt appreciation."

Miyuki, mollified, pointed. "Just read it. There's more."

Karen touched her friend's wrist. "I *do* appreciate it. Really."

"Oh, I know. I just like making you admit it."

Rolling her eyes, Karen turned her attention to the e-mail post.

Subject: Inquiry about unknown Language

To Whom It May Concern:

I would appreciate any help in ascertaining the origin of the following hieroglyphic writing system. These few symbols were found etched on a piece of crystal. For further details, I would be happy to share data with anyone willing to assist my research.

Thank you in advance for your help,

George Klein, Ph.D.
Deep Fathom

----------Headers------------
Return-Path: <gklein@globalnet.net>
Received: from globalnet.net ([209.162.104.5]) by rly-ye04.mx
(v71.10) with ESMTP;
Thurs, 27 July 13:47:46-0400
X-Mailer: Microsoft Outlook Express Macintosh Edition-4.5 (0410)
From: "George Klein" <gklein@globalnet.net>
To: Arc_language@harvarduniversity.org

Karen lowered the paper. Besides the glyphs, she couldn't help but notice the reference to a second crystal. It was too much of a coincidence.

"Do we know where this came from?"

Miyuki nodded. "Gabriel ran a trace. It's from a salvage ship, the *Deep Fathom*. Right now it's located in the middle of the Pacific. Gabriel was able to track its current position by tapping into the GPS system."

"Where is it?"

"Near Wake Island. But that's not the weird part. Gabriel discovered a news article about the ship. The *Deep Fathom* is currently aiding in the deep-sea salvage of Air Force One."

"How strange . . ." Karen frowned, trying to figure out how the two items could possibly be connected. "We need to contact this George Klein."

"Gabriel is already working on it."

9:00 A.M., USS *Gibraltar*, Central Pacific

Jack sat tensely in the leather chair in the long conference room. Though the room was crowded, no one spoke. They all awaited the appearance of Admiral Houston. He was conferring with the Joint Chiefs after last night's explosion. All night long, investigators and military personnel had combed through the damage. Under sodium spotlights, a hundred men dug, shifted, and collected pieces of evidence.

The remains of the chief investigator, Edwin Weintraub, had been found and brought to the ship's infirmary. His body was badly charred and blast-burned. The initial identification was made by his wedding ring. It had been a long and somber night. With security as tight as an angry fist, Jack had been refused admission to the *Gibraltar* until this morning.

But even with the lead ship locked down, rumors had spread to the support vessels, including the *Deep Fathom*. A bomb. Hidden in the Chinese jade bust. Shards had speared everywhere, piercing the tent's tarpaulin, even embedding into the bones of Weintraub's skull and limbs. Additionally, the explosion had ignited a nearby tank of cleaning oil, creating the brilliant fireball that had blasted forth from the shaft of a cargo elevator.

Jack shivered. He had handled the jade bust himself. If the stories were true, what if it exploded while he'd been on the ocean bottom? He pushed away that stray thought.

Around him, in the room, the silence remained tense.

Everyone looked bone-tired and thunderstruck. Not even whispers were shared.

At last the door to the conference room swung open. Admiral Houston stalked into the room, flanked by his aides and trailed by David Spangler. The admiral remained standing, while the other three men took seats. Jack made eye contact with Houston, but the admiral did not acknowledge him. His face was ashen, his eyes as hard as agates.

"Gentlemen," Houston began, "first let me thank you all for your industrious efforts this past week. The tragedy last night will not minimize your significant contribution." The admiral bowed his head. "But I must now sadly announce that the remains found last night were positively identified as those of Dr. Edwin Weintraub."

A murmur spread through the crowd of NTSB personnel.

"I know all who met Dr. Weintraub held him in the highest esteem. He will be missed." The admiral's tone grew harder. "But his death was not in vain. Amidst the debris, his murderers left evidence of their cowardice. Experts—both here and in San Diego—have confirmed the origin of the electronic timer and detonator. Both were of Chinese manufacture."

A few of the NTSB men raised angry voices. The Navy and Marine personnel remained stoic, except for a lieutenant sitting near Jack who moaned a quick, "Oh, God."

The admiral lifted a hand. "It is now believed that Dr. Weintraub accidentally triggered the hidden bomb during the course of his investigation. It is conjectured that similar devices were probably planted throughout the original ten-foot-high sculpture. Such an explosion in the cargo hold is believed to have downed Air Force One."

A hush settled over the crowd.

"Back home, these findings will break with this evening's news. It cannot be kept from the American people. But once word spreads, worldwide tensions will escalate quickly, especially so soon after the Pacific tragedy. As such, I have just received word that the USS *Gibraltar* has been ordered to the Philippine Sea. En route, we will be offloading both the

NTSB personnel and the wreckage of Air Force One on the island of Guam."

New murmurs ran through the crowd.

The admiral waited for his audience to quiet down before continuing. "The Navy's salvage and research ship, the *Maggie Chouest*, along with the Navy's Deep Submergence Unit, will continue recovering the last pieces of Air Force One from the ocean floor. Once collected, they'll also be shipped to Guam. This revised mission will be overseen by the current head of security, Commander Spangler."

The admiral remained standing, silent, stone-faced, then spoke slowly. "President Nafe has promised that these terrorists will not go unpunished. Washington has already demanded that the Chinese turn over all persons involved to international authorities." Houston clenched a fist. "And let me add my personal promise. Justice will be served—whether the Chinese government cooperates or not. America will answer terrorism upon her people with swift and terrible fury."

Jack had never seen Admiral Houston so incensed. The cords of his neck stuck out, his lips were bled of color.

"That is all. If there are any further questions of detail, I refer you to my protocol officer. Thank you for your cooperation."

Jack raised a hand, unsure if his own crew would continue to play a role here. "Sir, if I might ask about the salvage op—"

The admiral cut him off angrily. "Mr. Kirkland, any such questions should be directed to Commander Spangler." Without another word, Houston swung through the door and was gone.

Jack's gaze twitched to David. A small, spiteful smirk flickered on Spangler's face before he stood. "In answer to your question, Mr. Kirkland, we thank you for your service. As this matter is now one of national security, your additional presence is no longer needed."

"But—"

"This is now a military operation. No civilians will be allowed. A two-mile cordon will be set up around the crash site. You will be expected out of the zone by 1800 hours."

Jack glowered at David, knowing this banishment was of a personal nature.

"If you are not out of the region or if you attempt to reenter, you and your crew will be arrested and your ship impounded."

This response drew murmurs from the audience.

"I have already arranged for two men to escort you from the *Gibraltar*." David lifted a hand. Two of his men stood up.

Jack's face warmed. He ground his teeth in frustration. He did not know what to say. He knew he couldn't go to the admiral, since Houston was clearly overburdened and did not need to be bothered by a petty squabble. Jack scowled at David Spangler. He had risked his life here, and was now being unceremoniously dumped out on his ear. "I have no need for an escort," he said coldly.

David signaled his men with a flip of a hand. "Make sure Mr. Kirkland leaves immediately."

Jack did not resist as he was led away. What was the use? If the government didn't want his help, so be it.

Within minutes, he found himself seated aboard a Navy launch. The pilot, a Navy seaman, revved the engine and aimed for the *Deep Fathom*, bouncing through the mild chop. With the storm front blown past, the day remained breezy but clear.

Behind Jack, Spangler's two men were seated. He had not spoken a single word to the pair of gray-uniformed men, nor did he intend to.

Jack leaned back into his seat. From the security team's lack of racial diversity, it seemed Spangler had not changed. David's sister had once confided to him that her father had been a card-carrying member of the Ku Klux Klan and often dragged David to meetings when he was a boy, beating him if he refused. Jack eyed the twin blond escorts. It seemed these childhood teachings had taken root in fertile ground.

With a bump, the seamen slid the boat near the launch

platform at the stern of the *Fathom*. "All clear," the pilot called out.

Jack stood and crossed over the boat's starboard edge. Before he could clamber onto his own ship, one of David's men grabbed his elbow. "Mr. Kirkland, Commander Spangler asked us to give you this once you boarded."

The blond man held out a small square box, the size of a jeweler's ring box. It was sealed with a small ribbon. Jack frowned at it.

"A parting gift," the man said. "With Commander Spangler's thanks."

Jack accepted the gift, and the man nodded and stepped back. Jack hopped to his own boat's platform and grabbed the ship's ladder with one hand. As he turned, the Navy boat swung away with a throaty whine of its motor. Its wake splashed over the ribbed platform, soaking Jack's boots.

Robert appeared on the main deck overhead, leaning over the stern rail. "How did it go?" he called down. "Learn anything more?"

"Yeah, gather everyone together."

Robert gave him a thumbs-up and vanished.

Jack looked down at the small black gift box. He was sure it was not a thank-you gift for his service. More likely, it was one of David's little jabs, a final insult to send him on his way. Jack had a sudden urge to fling it into the sea, but curiosity got the better of him. He fingered the ribbon, then shook his head. His day had been bad enough already—why add to it? He'd open the damned thing later. Pocketing the box in his jacket, he turned to the ladder.

Climbing up, Jack glanced over his shoulder at the *Gibraltar*. He forced down a twinge of regret. It was as if he'd been discharged all over again, cut free from a past that had been his whole life.

Surprisingly melancholy, Jack pulled himself onto the deck. Elvis came loping over to greet him. Jack knelt and gave the dog a vigorous pet, and its tail thumped in contentment. Some things never changed.

"You'd never shove me overboard, would you, boy?" he said, giving voice to his disappointment with the Navy.

Alone for the moment, Lawrence Nafe shifted in his chair, assessing the latest developments. His plan to implicate the Chinese had been proceeding like clockwork. Nicolas Ruzickov had proven a loyal friend and a skilled manipulator of the media. Earlier, Nafe had glanced over the letter his Secretary of State drafted to the Chinese Premier. It was fierce. Nafe recognized Ruzickov's fingerprints all over the letter: *no compromise . . . immediate reprisals . . . stiff sanctions . . .*

It was just short of a declaration of war. Nafe had been only too happy to sign it. As far as he was concerned, it was about time the Chinese government felt the full weight of American diplomacy . . . a diplomacy backed by the might of the world's greatest fighting force. The brief letter signaled an abrupt end to the pandering policies of Bishop's administration. A shot across the bow, so to speak.

Nafe leaned back in his chair, surveying the spread of the Oval Office. This was now *his* administration, he mused, enjoying his new status. But his short moment to himself was interrupted by a knock at his door. "Come in," he snapped.

The door was opened by his personal aide, a thin twenty-something boy whose name Nafe could not remember. "What is it?"

The youth half bowed, nervous. "Sir, the CIA director and the head of the OES are here to see you."

Nafe sat up straighter. Neither man had an appointment. "Show them in."

The boy backed out, allowing the two men inside.

Nicolas Ruzickov entered first and waved Jeb Fielding, the head of the Office of Emergency Services, toward the upholstered leather chairs to one side of the room. The older man, of bookish appearance, with rolled shoulders and an emaciated demeanor, bore an armful of papers tucked under his arm.

"Mr. President," Ruzickov said, "I thought you should see this." The CIA director gestured toward the sofas and chairs around an antique coffee table, where Fielding already sat. "If you'll join us."

With a groan, the heavyset Nafe stood and walked around his desk. "It's late, Nicolas. Can't this wait? I have my nationwide address first thing in the morning and I don't want to look too tired. The American people will need a strong face in the morning as the news of Air Force One sinks in."

Ruzickov bowed his head slightly, remaining officious. "I understand, Mr. President, and I implore your forgiveness. But this matter may have a bearing on tomorrow's address."

Nafe settled onto the sofa in the informal seating arrangement. Ruzickov and Fielding were in the chairs, the OES chief with his pile of papers . . . maps, Nafe realized.

"What is all this?" Nafe asked, leaning forward, as Fielding unfolded a map on the coffee table.

Ruzickov answered, "Late news."

"Hmm?"

"As you know, the OES has been investigating the series of quakes from eight days ago. Given the devastation on the West Coast, detailed information was slow to dribble out."

Nafe nodded impatiently. He had publicly addressed the whole "national disaster" bit last week. It was no longer his concern. He knew that in another few days he was due to tour the region, to shake hands at various homeless shelters and attend memorial services. He was even scheduled to cast a wreath off the coast of Alaska to mourn the thousands of deaths associated with the sinking of the Aleutian Islands. He was ready for the trip. He had his suits picked out and had posed before a mirror with his Armani jacket over his shoulder, his sleeves rolled up to the elbows. It was a solid down-to-earth look, a President ready to help out his people.

Ruzickov drew Nafe's attention to the map now open on the table. "With data flowing again from scientific stations on the West Coast, Jeb's office has been compiling the information and seismic readings, trying to explain the natural catastrophe."

Nafe looked up. "Do we know what triggered it?"

"No, not exactly, but maybe Jeb had better explain from here." Ruzickov nodded for Fielding to speak.

The older man was clearly nervous. He wiped a handkerchief over his forehead and cleared his throat. "Thank you for your time, Mr. President."

"Yes, yes . . . what have you learned?"

Fielding smoothed the map on the table. It depicted the Pacific Ocean, a topographic map of the sea floor, continental shelf, and coastlines. Drawn over it were a series of concentric circles. The outer circle, the largest, brushed across the western coast of the United States and arced around to the islands of Japan. The inner circles grew progressively smaller. Little red crosses dotted the coastlines and islands caught within these narrowing rings, marking disaster sites. Fielding ran his fingers along the concentric circles. "Our office has been able to map out the vectors of tectonic force during the series of quakes."

Nafe wrinkled his brow. He hated to admit ignorance, but Ruzickov picked up on his confusion and said to Fielding, "Start at the beginning."

Fielding bobbed his head. "Of course . . . I'm sorry . . ." He licked his lips. "We've known from the start that the eclipse-day quakes all occurred along the edge of the Pacific tectonic plate." He marked out the rough margins of the outermost ring on his map.

Nafe's brow remained wrinkled.

"Maybe I'd better elaborate further," Ruzickov said, putting Fielding on hold. "As I'm sure you know, Mr. President, the Earth's surface is actually a hard shell over a molten core, a fractured shell, actually, like a hardboiled egg struck on a table. Each shell piece or 'tectonic plate' floats atop this liquid core and is constantly in motion, one grinding against another, sometimes sinking under to form trenches, or conversely, riding up to form mountains. It is at these friction points between plates that seismic activity is highest."

"I know all this," Nafe said irritably, feigning insult.

Ruzickov pointed to the map. "There's one big plate under the Pacific Ocean. The quakes and volcanic activity eight days ago all occurred along the margins or fault lines of that plate." The CIA director pointed at some of the islands in the center of the map. "Additional catastrophes to coastlines and islands were the result of tidal wave activity generated by quakes under the sea."

Nafe sat up, too tired to feign interest any longer. "Fine. I understand. So why this late night science lesson?"

"Jeb, why don't you finish from here?"

Fielding nodded. "For the past week, we've been trying to find out what triggered so many points along the Pacific plate's edge to go active at the same time, what triggered this catalytic reaction."

"And?" Nafe said.

Fielding pointed to each concentric ring drawn on the map, starting at the outermost and ticking down each smaller ring. "By triangulating data from hundreds of geologic stations, we've been able to trace the direction of intensity, zeroing in on the true epicenter of this entire series of quakes."

"You mean all these quakes may have originated from a single bigger event somewhere else?"

"Exactly. It's called plate harmonics. A strong enough force striking a tectonic plate could send shockwaves radiating out, causing the plate's rim to blow out with activity."

"Like a pebble dropped into a still pond," Ruzickov added. "Generating waves on the shorelines."

Nafe's brows rose. "Do we know what this 'pebble' might be?"

"No," Fielding said, "but we do know *where* the pebble struck." The head of OES continued to draw his fingertip down the map until he reached the centermost circle, a tiny red ring. He tapped his finger. "It was right here."

Leaning closer, Nafe studied the map. It was only empty ocean. "What's the significance?"

Ruzickov answered, "That circle is where Air Force One crashed."

Nafe gasped. "Are you saying the crash of Air Force One caused this? That Bishop's jet was this pebble we've been talking about?"

"No, certainly not," Fielding said. "The quakes started hours before Air Force One crashed. In fact, it was the quakes in Guam that required the President's evacuation. But either way, a plane crash would not yield a fraction of the force necessary to trigger a harmonic wave across the Pacific plate. Instead we're talking about a force equal to a trillion megaton explosion."

Nafe settled back onto the sofa. "Are you saying, then, that such an event occurred down there?" He nodded toward the tiny red circle.

Fielding slowly nodded back.

Ruzickov spoke into the silence. "Jeb, that's all we'll need for now. We'll talk in the morning."

Fielding reached for the map.

"Leave it," Ruzickov said.

The man reluctantly pulled back his hand. He gathered up his other papers and stood. "Thank you, Mr. President."

Nafe lifted a hand, dismissing him.

As Fielding moved off, Ruzickov said, "And, Jeb, your confidence in this matter would be appreciated. This stays between us for now."

"Of course, sir," Fielding replied, then left the room.

When he was gone, Nafe spoke. "So what do you think, Nick?"

Ruzickov pointed to the map. "I think this discovery may be the most important find of this century. Something happened out there. Something that might be related to the crash of Air Force One." The CIA director stared Nafe full in the face. "That's why I wanted you to hear about this tonight, before the official announcement tomorrow, before we commit ourselves fully to our current plan of blaming the Chinese."

Nafe shook his head. "I'm not changing our position. Not at this late stage of the game." He scowled at the concentric rings. "All this is just . . . just science. Not politics."

"I agree," Ruzickov said with a firm nod. "You're in

charge. It is ultimately your decision. I wanted you to be fully informed."

Nafe felt a surge of self-pride at the CIA director's support. "Good. But Nick, what about all this other information? Can we keep it buried?"

"Jeb's my man. He won't talk unless I tell him to."

"Good, then tomorrow's announcement will go along as planned." Nafe leaned into the sofa, relieved that nothing would upset his schedule. "Now what did you mean about this being the discovery of the century?"

Ruzickov remained silent for a few moments, studying the map. "I've been keeping abreast on all reports from the crash site. Did you know that all the wreckage's parts are magnetized?"

"No, but what does that matter?"

"The chief investigator, the deceased Edwin Weintraub, theorized that the parts were exposed to a strong magnetic force shortly after settling to the ocean's bottom. I also read reports that the salvage operation's submersible experienced some strange effects while down there . . . something associated with the discovery of a new crystalline formation."

"I still don't understand the significance."

Ruzickov looked up. "Whatever is down there was strong enough to shake the entire Pacific plate. As Jeb said, a force equal to a trillion megatons. What if we could harness that power? Discover its secret? A supreme new energy source. Could you imagine that firepower at our fingertips? It could free us of the Arab's stranglehold on our oil supply . . . power weapons and ships to dwarf any other military. There would be no end to the possibilities."

"Sounds pretty far-fetched to me. How can you harness a onetime event at the bottom of the ocean?"

"I'm not sure yet, but what would happen if some other foreign nation were to get hold of this power? Jeb is not the only scientist in the world. In the months to come, someone else might devise a similar map and go to investigate. Those are international waters out there. We couldn't stop them."

Nafe swallowed. "What are you proposing?"

"Currently, we are uniquely situated to explore this site without raising suspicion or outside interest. We're just recovering our lost President's ship. It's the perfect cover. We've got men and ships on-site already. Commander Spangler has it cordoned off. Under this cover, we could send down a research team."

Nafe watched as Ruzickov's eyes lit up. "So you've already thought about this?"

"And I've developed a tentative plan," he said with a grim smile. "Off the coast of Hawaii, a deep-sea project, jointly run by the National Science Foundation and a consortium of Canadian private industries, has been under way for the past decade. They have developed and constructed a self-contained deep-sea research lab . . . equipped with its own submersible and ROV robots. It could be on-site and manned in four days. The two missions—recovering the last pieces of Air Force One and our clandestine research—should merge together smoothly. No one would suspect."

"Then what's the first step?"

"I just need your okay."

Nafe nodded. "If there is something down there, we can't risk it falling into foreign hands. You have the go-ahead to proceed."

Ruzickov collected the map and stood. "I'll contact Commander Spangler immediately and begin the operation."

Nafe pushed to his feet. "But, Nick, after we set things in motion tomorrow, no one must know about this. No one."

"Don't worry, Mr. President. Commander Spangler will lock everything down tight. He has never failed me."

Nafe swung around his desk and settled into the executive chair once again. "He had better not."

Jack and the *Deep Fathom*'s crew sat around the table in the ship's wet lab. The marine laboratory was one of the roomiest spaces on the small ship, a convenient meeting hall—if not the most homey. There were only hard metal stools on which to sit, and lining the cabin's shelves were hundreds of clear jars of marine-life samples, preserved in brine or formaldehyde. The rows of dead animals seemed to stare down upon the assembled crew.

"I'm still not buying this explanation," George said heatedly. "I've wired into the news reports all day long, heard the so-called experts spouting on CNN, CNBC, and the BBC. I'm not believing a word of it."

Jack sighed. Earlier, he had related to his crew the findings announced at the briefing and their new orders: *vacate the area*. It took the entire afternoon to restow their gear, secure the *Nautilus*, and get under steam. By evening they had long cleared the crash zone, and only empty sea surrounded them.

"The crash is no longer our concern," Jack said, exasperated.

The meeting was not going along as he'd expected. He had called this evening's session to congratulate everyone for their help and to concoct a plan. With the treasure ship *Kochi Maru* sunk into a deep-sea volcano, the *Fathom* would need a new target. The two gold bars dredged up from the dive a week ago had been shipped to Wake Island, and from there to Kendall McMillan's bank in San Diego. The small treasure barely covered their expenses in the year-long search for the *Kochi Maru*. The salvage fee for their assistance with the Navy would buy them a bit of latitude, but not much. They would still need to renegotiate a loan.

McMillan, the bank's accountant, sat at the far end of the table, still looking green around the gills from yesterday's storms. Whatever was decided here, the bank would make the final decision, deciding whether or not to finance their next venture. McMillan sat with a pen in hand, doodling in the margins of his legal pad. The crew, still angry at being so rudely booted out, had yet to make any progress.

Jack tried to refocus the discussion. "We need to put this matter behind us and consider what to do from here."

George scowled. "Listen, Jack, before the explosion last night, I wanted to show you something. I still want to get this off my chest."

Jack recalled the historian's interrupted midnight talk with Admiral Houston. "Okay, but this is the last time we discuss this matter. Then on to real business."

"Agreed." George reached down and retrieved a rolled map from beside his chair. With a flick of his wrists, he unrolled its length across the table. The map held a view of the entire Pacific basin. A large red triangle had been penciled on its surface, with tiny X's marked within its boundaries.

Lisa stood up to get a wider view. "What are you showing us?"

George tapped the map. "The Dragon's Triangle."

"The what?" she asked.

George ran a finger along the boundaries of the penciled triangle. "It goes by other names. The Japanese call it, 'Mano Umi,' the Devil's Sea. Disappearances in this region go back centuries." He sat down and tapped each of the tiny X's, describing the tragedy of a lost ship, submarine, or plane.

Lisa whistled. "It's like the Bermuda Triangle."

"Exactly," George said, and continued his litany, ending at last with the story of a WWII Japanese pilot and the man's final, fateful words before his plane disappeared. " 'The sky is opening up!' That was his last radioed message. Now, I find that a remarkable coincidence. Air Force One crashes into the center of the Dragon's Triangle, and the final words from its pilot are the same as the vanished Japanese pilot from half a century ago."

"Amazing," Lisa agreed.

Robert just stared, his boyish eyes wide.

Charlie leaned in closer, running a finger along longitude and latitude numbers. His brows were deeply furrowed.

George looked up at Jack. "How do you explain that?"

"I saw the explosion site from the bomb," Jack said. "*That* was no weird phenomenon. That was plain murder."

George made a scoffing noise. "But what of your own findings down below? The crystal spire, the strange hieroglyphics, the odd emanations. On top of all this, most of the wreckage of the President's plane just happens to settle at this site. If a midair explosion had truly happened, the debris field would be much wider."

Jack sat silently. In George's words, he heard his own argument with the admiral last night. He, too, had been convinced that something powerful lay down there. Something with the strength to knock a plane from the sky. He studied the map. The number of coincidences kept piling up, too high to ignore. "But the bomb in the jade bust, the electronic circuitry . . . ?"

"What if it was staged?" George asked. "A frame-up. Washington had already been implicating the Chinese *before* the explosion."

Jack frowned.

Charlie spoke up, his Jamaican accent thick. "I don't know, *mon*. I think ol' George might be on to something."

"What do you mean?"

"I, too, have heard of this Dragon's Triangle. I just never made the connection until now."

"Great, another convert," Kendall McMillan mumbled from the far side of the table.

Jack ignored the accountant. He turned to the ship's geologist. "What do you know of the region?"

As answer, Charlie nudged Robert. "Would you please grab the globe from the library?"

"Sure." Robert took off.

Charlie nodded to the map. "Do any of you know the term 'agonic lines'?"

Everyone shook their heads.

"It is one of the many theories for explaining the disappearances here. Agonic lines are distinct regions where the

Earth's magnetic field is a bit off kilter. Compass readings are slightly out of sync with the rest of the world. The principal agonic line of the Eastern Hemisphere passes through the center of this Dragon's Triangle." Charlie looked around the table. "Do any of you know where the *Western* Hemisphere's main agonic line passes through?"

Again a general shaking of heads.

"The Bermuda Triangle," Charlie answered, letting the fact sink in.

"But what causes these magnetic disturbances in the first place?" Lisa asked. "These agonal lines?"

"Agonic," Charlie corrected. "No one knows for sure. Some blame it on increased seismic activity in the regions. During earthquakes, strong magnetic fluxes are generated. But in general, magnetism, including the earth's magnetic field, is still poorly understood. Its properties, energies, and dynamics are still being researched. Most scientists accept that the Earth's magnetic field is generated by the flow of the planet's molten core around its solid nickel-iron center. But many irregularities still remain. Like the fluidity of this field."

"Fluidity?" George interrupted. "What do you mean?"

Charlie realized that in his excitement he'd spoken too fast. "From a geological standpoint," he went on, speaking more slowly, "man has only been here for a flicker. During such a small scope in time, the Earth's magnetic field seems fixed. The North Pole is up and the South Pole is down. But even over this short course, the poles have wobbled. The true position of magnetic north constantly bobbles around a bit. But this is only a minor fluctuation. Over the course of Earth's entire geologic history, not only have these poles shifted dramatically, but they have *reversed* several times."

"Reversed?" Lisa asked.

Charlie nodded. "North became south, and south became north. Such events are not fully understood yet."

Jack scratched his head. "What does this have to do with anything?"

"Hell if I know. Like I said, I find it intriguing. Didn't you say that Air Force One's wreckage was magnetized? Doesn't this fact add to the list of coincidences? And what about your own compass problems down there?"

Jack shook his head. After the passing of a couple days, he was not so sure what he had experienced down there.

"And what about those strange time lapses?" Lisa asked. "I've been struggling to find out why the *Nautilus*'s clock was always messed up when the submersible neared that crystal thing, but I could never find anything wrong afterward."

George sat up straighter. "Of course! Why didn't I make that connection, too?" He began sifting through his pile of papers. "Time lapses! Here's a report from a pilot, Arthur Godfrey. Back in 1962 he flew an old prop plane to Guam. His craft traveled the 340 miles in one hour. Two hundred miles farther than his plane could have traveled in an hour." George lifted his nose from his papers. "On landing, Mr. Godfrey could not explain his early arrival, nor why his clocks read differently from the airport's."

Lisa glanced at Jack. "That sounds damn familiar."

"I have other examples," the historian said excitedly. "Modern planes crossing the Pacific but inexplicably arriving hours earlier than their ETAs. I have the details down below." George stood. "I'm going to go fetch them."

"This is ludicrous," Jack said, but he had a hard time mustering much strength behind his words. He recalled his own forty-minute time gap.

"It may not be that strange," Charlie said as the historian slipped past. "It has been theorized that strong enough electromagnetic fields could possibly affect time, similar to a black hole's gravity."

As the historian left the room, he almost collided with Robert. The marine biologist stepped aside for the old professor, then entered. He bore a beachball-sized globe in his hands.

"Ah!" Charlie said. "Now let me show you the really bizarre part. Something I remember reading in a university research paper."

Robert passed the geologist the blue globe.

Charlie held it up and pointed a finger at the Pacific. "Here is the center of the Dragon's Triangle. If you drove an arrow from this point through the center of the world and out the other side, do you know where it would come out?"

No one answered.

Charlie flipped the globe around and jabbed a finger on it. "The center of the Bermuda Triangle."

Lisa gasped.

Charlie continued, "It's almost as if these two diametrically opposed triangles mark another axis of the Earth, poles never studied or understood before."

Jack stood up and took the globe from Charlie. He set it on the table. "C'mon. All of this is interesting, but it's not going to pay the rent, folks."

"I agree with Mr. Kirkland," McMillan said sourly. "If I knew this was going to turn into an episode of *Unsolved Mysteries*, I could've been in bed."

Jack rested his palm on the globe. "I think we need to turn this conversation over to more than theories and ancient myths. Set aside conjecture for now. This is a business I'm trying to run."

George reentered the room then. He wore a blanched expression and held a single sheet in his hand. "I just received this e-mail." He held up the paper. "From an anthropology professor in Okinawa. She claims to have discovered more of the strange hieroglyphic writing . . . etched on the wall of a secret chamber in some newly discovered ruins."

Jack groaned. He could not seem to squelch this line of discussion.

"But that's not the most amazing thing." George looked around the room. "She discovered a *crystal*, too. She has it!"

Charlie sat straighter, abandoning his interest in the map. "A crystal? What does she say about it?"

"Nothing much. She's vague, but hints that it bears some odd properties. She refuses to give out further information . . . not unless we meet with her."

Jack found everyone's eyes turning in his direction. "None of you are going to let this go, are you? Strange crystals, ancient writing, magnetic fluxes . . . listen to you!"

Except for the bank's accountant, Jack saw a wall of determination. He threw his hands in the air and sank to his stool. "Fine . . . whether the Navy wants our help or not, whether we go broke or not, you all want to continue investigating what's down there?"

"Sounds good to me," Charlie said.

"Yep," Lisa added.

"How could we walk away?" Robert asked.

"I agree," George said.

Only Kendall McMillan shook his head. "The bank is not going to like this."

Jack stared at his crew, then sighed. He rested his head in his hands. "Okay, George, how soon can you book me a flight to Okinawa?"

12

A Line in the Sand

Wrapped in a leather flight jacket, David Spangler stood at the bow of the Navy's salvage ship, the *Maggie Chouest*. It was an ugly ship, painted bright red and festooned with antennas, booms, and satellite dishes. A two-hundred-foot homely bitch, David thought. Manned by a crew of thirty, the salvage ship was the temporary home of the Navy's Deep Submergence Unit and the unit's newest rescue vessel, the submersible *Perseus*. Currently, the large sub still rested in the ship's dry dock at the stern, awaiting its first deployment later this day.

Alone at the bow, David sucked a long draw from his cigarette. Morning was still hours away, but he knew any attempt at sleep would fail him this night. Two hours ago he had gotten off the scrambled line with his boss, Nicolas Ruzickov. They had talked at length concerning David's revised assignment.

His primary goal of implicating the Chinese in the crash of Air Force One had been accomplished. With the country still struggling to recover from the disaster on the West Coast, and with paranoia sky high across the country, the public was ready to accept any explanation. It was an easy sell. David had received the thanks of a grateful President. In fact, Lawrence Nafe would be making a formal announcement in only a couple more hours, confronting the Chinese aloud, drawing a line in the sand between their two countries.

But now David had a new assignment: to oversee a clandestine research project into an unknown power source. Something to do with the quakes from nine days ago.

He did not understand half the details Ruzickov related, but it was not important. All he had to do was maintain a blanket over the site. To the world abroad, the activity here had to look like the continuing salvage ops.

Staring out at the dark seas, David exhaled slowly, a circle of smoke curling up from his lips. Half a day ago the USS *Gibraltar* had left with the setting sun, steaming toward the Philippine Sea. Without the giant ship here, the seas seemed empty. Besides the *Maggie Chouest*, only three other ships still circled the region—destroyers with enough firepower to maintain their privacy.

Behind David a hatch clanged closed.

"Sir."

David glanced over a shoulder. "What is it, Mr. Rolfe?"

"Sir, I just wanted to let you know that the research site in Hawaii has been locked down. They're dismantling the sea lab for shipment."

"Any problems?"

"No, sir. The head of the project has been informed and signed a confidentiality agreement. The only concession was to let him oversee the research here. Our scientific liaison at Los Alamos vouched for the man. And the CIA director signed off on it."

David nodded, wearing a grim smile. It seemed Ruzickov was getting as little sleep as he. "When are they due to be under way?"

"Less than two days."

Two days. Ruzickov was moving fast. Good. David studied the sea.

Later today he planned to dive in the Navy's submersible, to give the *Perseus* its first trial run here. He had watched the video recordings from Kirkland's other dives, but David wanted to see the crash site for himself. Once this mission was under way, Omega team would oversee topside, while he would remain below at the sea lab.

"Sir, the . . . um, other objective . . . Are we to continue . . . ?"

David took a drag on his cigarette. "Yes. There'll be no change. If anything, we now have a stronger mandate to proceed. No outsider must know what lies below. Those are the standing orders."

"Yes, sir."

"Are we still tracking the *Deep Fathom*?"

"Of course, sir. But when do you expect to proceed with—"

"I'll let you know. We can't move too soon. I want him well away from here before we proceed." David flicked the dying butt of his cigarette into the sea, angered that his moment of peace had been shattered by the intrusion.

After waiting for over a decade, he told himself, he could be patient a bit longer. Three days, he decided. No more.

13

Trade Secrets

Just after midnight, a knock interrupted Lawrence Nafe's meeting with a trio of Democratic senators, three stubborn holdouts on his West Coast disaster-relief bill. The bill would be voted on in the morning, and his entire staff was working through the night to ensure they had the votes needed to pass. The door to the Oval Office opened and his personal aide stepped inside.

Nafe had finally learned the boy's name. "What is it, Marcus?"

"Sir, Mr. Wellington is here to—"

His Chief of Staff pushed past the young man. "Excuse the interruption, Mr. President, but I have an urgent matter to bring to your attention."

Nafe noticed the hard set to the man's eyes and lips. William Wellington, from a rich Georgian family, usually exuded a gentile charm. Something was wrong. Nafe stood. "Thank you, gentlemen. That'll be all."

The senator from Arizona opened his mouth as if to complain, but Nafe stared him down. If Jacobson wanted his support in next year's election for the Arizona seat, he had better tow the line. On this bill, he would brook no defectors in his own party's ranks. The man closed his mouth. The others mumbled their thanks and departed with his aide.

Nafe turned his attention to his Chief of Staff. "What is it, Bill?"

Wellington spoke formally, strained. "Mr. President, you're needed in the Situation Room."

"What's happened?"

"The Chinese, sir. Their air and naval forces have made a strike against Taiwan."

Nafe almost fell back into his chair. "What? When? It's the goddamn middle of the night."

"It's midday in the Far East. They struck just before noon Taiwan time."

Nafe was stunned. He had not thought the Chinese would be so bold. Nicolas Ruzickov had assured him that the Chinese Premier would bow to Washington's accusations, paving the way to garner stiffer concessions from the People's Republic. Nafe wanted answers for this mistake. "Where's Nick Ruzickov?"

"In the Situation Room. The National Security Council and Cabinet are already gathering." William Wellington backed toward the door. "Sir, we must get going. An immediate response will be necessary."

Nafe nodded and headed toward the door. The Joint Chiefs had better have a contingency plan in place. With the Chief of Staff at his side, he strode through the West Wing, trailed by his Secret Service men. In short order, Nafe pushed angrily into the White House's inner sanctum.

The agitation and noise in the Situation Room quieted at his entrance.

Around the long table, a score of uniformed men and women stood at his arrival: the Chairman of the Joint Chiefs, the Secretary of the Navy, the U.S. Army Chief of Staff, the Commandant of the Marine Corps, and other military heads. Nafe's own Cabinet members stood to either side of the table.

On the far side of the room a wall-sized monitor displayed a complicated map of the Philippine Sea. Forces were highlighted in blues, reds, and yellows.

Scowling, Nafe crossed to the head of the table. He would make sure the U.S. answered this display of Chinese aggression. There would be no diplomacy. If necessary, he would wipe the Chinese navy from the seas.

He sat down. Those members who had seats returned to their own chairs. The others remained standing.

"So where are we?" Nafe asked.

No one spoke. No one would even meet his gaze.

"I want answers and a plan for an aggressive response," Nafe said angrily.

Nicolas Ruzickov stood. "Mr. President, it's too late."

"What do you mean?"

"The fighting is already over. Taiwan conceded."

Nafe struggled to understand. "How could that be? Are you saying during the time it took me to cross from the Oval Office, the Chinese have taken Taiwan?"

Ruzickov bowed his head. "With their island in shambles from the recent quakes, the Taiwanese could offer no resistance. Before we could respond, their government had agreed to rescind their independence, accepting Chinese hegemony in exchange for both aid and an end to hostilities. Chinese forces have already landed. Taiwan is once again a Chinese province."

Nafe was too stunned to speak. It had happened so fast.

The Secretary of Defense spoke up. "We can't just accept this. We have forces on the island . . . in the area."

The Chief of Naval Operations answered, "We cannot act without a request from the Taiwanese government. And we won't get it. We've been in touch with their embassy. They do not want to be caught between our two warring forces, fearing in their current state that it would lead to the annihilation of their island. In fact, we've just received word that their government has demanded that our forces evacuate their waters."

Nafe felt the heat rising in his face. Less than two weeks in office, and he was losing Taiwan to the Chinese. He clenched his fists. "I do not accept this. I will not see the spread of communism while I'm in charge."

"Sir—" Ruzickov cautioned.

Nafe slammed his fist against the table. "It's time to stop coddling China. It will stop here. Now."

"Sir, what do you propose?"

"With the cowardly assassination of President Bishop and this newest aggression, I see no other choice." Nafe stared down the heads of the United States fighting forces. "I will demand a declaration of war from Congress."

2:40 P.M., Naha City, Okinawa Prefecture, Japan

Forgetting how much he hated airline travel—the stale air, the cramped seats, the crying children—Jack was glad when the jet's tires finally touched down and he was freed from the belly of this beast. Though, in truth, his annoyance did not entirely arise from the usual discomforts of flight, but from his memory of Air Force One's crash. The flight here had been in the same class of jet, a Boeing 747. Jack had spent much of the journey staring out the window, studying every wing seam, bolt, and flap.

But after three days since making the decision to travel here, he had finally reached Okinawa. The journey had taken so long because the closest airport was on Kwajalein Atoll, a day's sail in the *Deep Fathom*. And once there, he had been forced to fly standby, killing another half day waiting for a seat to open up. But at least the journey was finally over.

Free of the plane now, Jack crossed through the concourse to the customs area. His only luggage, a single backpack, was hooked over his shoulders. He stepped up to the Japanese customs agent and slapped down his passport. The officer gestured him to open his bag.

As Jack obeyed, the man studied his passport and spoke to him in English. "Welcome to Okinawa, Mr. Kirkland. If you'll step over to the right."

Jack turned and saw a second agent carrying a metal-detecting wand.

The first man spoke as he sifted through Jack's backpack, picking through his underwear and toiletries. "Extra security," the officer explained, "because of China's attack."

Jack nodded. Over the plane's intercom, the pilot had described the short skirmish and Taiwan's concession. The strong were always eating the weak.

Jack stepped over to the second agent, who waved a metal detector over his legs and up his body. The detector buzzed at his wrist. He pulled back his sleeve to expose his watch. The officer continued his sweep. The detector sang out again as it passed over his heart. The officer looked up at him.

Frowning, Jack patted his jacket. There was a small bulge in the inner pocket. He opened his jacket and reached inside, remembering David Spangler's parting gift as he pulled out a tiny, ribbon-wrapped box. With all the commotion, he'd forgotten about it.

"You'll have to open that," the first agent said.

Jack nodded and moved back to the customs table. He tugged the ribbon free. *Leave it to David to cause trouble from half a world away.* He popped open the tiny ring box.

Inside, resting on its velvet-lined interior, lay a small piece of circuitry. A couple of blue wires stuck out of it.

"What is that?" the agent asked, tweezing it between his fingers.

Jack had no idea, but he knew some explanation was needed. He thought fast. "It . . . It's for a repair job. An expensive and critical component. I'm a computer consultant."

"So you gift-wrapped it?" the man asked, studying the tiny piece of electronics, searching for some threat.

"It's a joke between—" He struggled to remember the name of the computer scientist helping the anthropologist. "—Professor Nakano and myself."

The customs officer nodded. "I've heard of her. The university's computer expert. Smart woman. Nobel Prize winner." He replaced the circuit, snapped the ring box closed, and passed it back. "She taught my nephew."

Jack shoved the box into his backpack.

Behind him, a loud Portuguese family aimed for the customs station. A large woman was arguing with her husband. Both dragged gigantic suitcases.

The agent glanced at them and sighed in exasperation. "You're free to go." He waved Jack off.

Jack zipped his bag and proceeded through the gates into the main terminal. The airport was in a tumult, with masses of travelers leaving. Clearly, the Chinese attack had made everyone nervous. Taiwan was too close for comfort, just south of the Ryukyu chain of islands, of which Okinawa was a part.

Jack's eyes drifted over the crowd. The terminal was so busy he failed to notice the woman trying to get his attention until she called out his name.

"Mr. Kirkland!"

Jack stumbled to a stop, glancing to his left.

The woman hurried over. She had been waiting at the customs gate. She stopped and held out her hand. "I'm Karen Grace."

Jack blinked stupidly at her for a second. "The . . . the professor?" He had not expected her to be so young.

She smiled. "I know you told us you would call once you were settled in your hotel, but . . . well . . ." A blush brightened her cheeks. "Miyuki hacked into the airport's computers and downloaded your itinerary. I figured you could stay at my apartment rather than a hotel. It'll make things easier." She began to stammer, clearly realizing she might be stepping over a line. "That is . . . if you'd like."

Jack rescued her from further embarrassment. "Thanks. I appreciate the offer. I hate hotels."

"Good . . . good . . . We'll get a taxi."

She turned and led the way. Jack watched her. For just a moment as the woman had rushed up to him, Jennifer's memory had flashed before him. Not that the two women looked anything alike. Except for the blond hair, the professor bore no resemblance to Jennifer. Karen was taller, her hair cropped shorter, her eyes green. She carried herself differently, too. Striding sternly, no sway in her step.

Still, Jack recognized a similar energy coming from this

professor. She practically glowed with it, a light that shone past the superficial differences.

"So you're that astronaut," Karen said when he caught up to her. "I remember the news stories. The hero. God, I'd love to go up there sometime."

"I can't say I enjoyed it much."

Karen stumbled to a stop. "Oh, God, I'm sorry. The accident. You lost friends up there. What was I thinking?"

"It's ancient history," he mumbled, wanting to end the conversation.

She stared up at him with an apologetic grin. "I'm sorry."

Jack turned the conversation in another direction as they moved off again. "So you're American?"

"Canadian actually. A visiting professor. I have an apartment near the university . . . faculty housing."

"Sounds good. After I clean up, I'd like to get to work as soon as possible."

"Of course."

Exiting the terminal, Karen pushed forward through the throng. At the curb, she raised a hand to hail a cab. One zipped to a stop at the curb. Stepping forward, she pulled open the door. "C'mon. I want to get to the bank before it closes."

Jack ducked inside the small car as Karen spoke rapidly to the driver in Japanese. Then she slid in next to him. "If you want to work this afternoon, I'll need to collect something from my safe deposit box first."

"What's that?"

"The crystal."

"You have it at the bank?"

As the taxi wove into highway traffic, aiming for the city, she looked at him, studying him. In her eyes, Jack saw her weighing something in her mind. Finally, she said, "You don't have any tattoos, do you?"

"Why?"

She just stared, waiting for him to answer.

"Okay, I do. I *was* with the SEALs."

"Could I see them?"

"Not unless you want me to moon the driver."

She blushed again.

Jack fought down a grin. He was growing to like this reaction.

"Um, that won't be necessary," she mumbled. "How about snake tattoos? Any of those?"

"No. Why?"

She chewed her lower lip, then spoke. "We've had some trouble with a group trying to steal the crystal artifact. They bear these snake tattoos on their forearms. That's why I insisted on meeting you in person. We need to be cautious."

Jack pushed back his jacket's sleeves, baring his forearms. "No snakes. Anywhere. I swear."

She grinned at him, settling back into her seat. "I believe you."

After a short drive, they exited the highway. Signs for the university were written in both Japanese and English.

Karen leaned forward and again spoke to the driver, who bobbed his head. She pointed at the next corner, to a large Bank of Tokyo sign. The taxi squealed to a halt. "I'll be right back." She hopped out.

Jack sat in the steaming heat. With the car stopped, there was not even a breeze through the window to move the air. His thoughts drifted back to the professor. She smelled vaguely of jasmine. Her scent remained in the cab. He could not help smiling. Perhaps this trip wasn't such a bad idea.

Then Karen was climbing into the cab again. "Got it. Here." She handed him a small leather satchel.

He took it—and almost dropped it. Its weight caught him by surprise.

"Heavy, isn't it?"

"This is the crystal?"

"See for yourself."

Jack fingered loose the leather straps and tugged the satchel open. At the bottom lay a crystal star, smaller than his outstretched hand. Even in the shadowed light of the cab, he appreciated its brilliance. He also recognized the distinct appearance: translucent crystal veined with azure and ruby whorls. "It's the same."

"What?"

He reached in and pulled out the crystal. "I'd swear this is the same type of crystal that I found at the crash site."

"The crystal obelisk with the inscription on it?"

"Exactly." Jack held the artifact up to the direct sunlight. Its facets burst with brilliance.

"Notice anything odd about it?"

"What do you mean?"

"You're holding it up with one hand."

"Yeah, so."

Karen pulled out a black handkerchief and tossed it over the crystal. Jack's arm dropped. It was as if the handkerchief weighed ten pounds. "What the hell?"

"The crystal's weight is dependant upon light exposure. The stronger the light, the less it weighs."

Jack whisked off the bit of cloth, exposing the crystal again. It *was* lighter. "My God!"

Karen took the crystal and lowered it back into her satchel.

"My geologist would sell his soul to see this."

"We've already arranged to have it studied. Next Monday, in fact, when the university's geology staff returns. I'll pass the data on to your friend."

Jack knew this would hardly satisfy Charlie. He wished he had collected a sample of the crystal pillar himself.

"Now it's your turn," Karen said. "You said you would bring a copy of the obelisk's inscription."

He patted his own bag. "I have it."

"May I see?"

Shrugging, Jack bent over and fished through his backpack for his notebook. Pulling it free, he handed it to her.

Karen opened the book. The first page was covered with the tiny hieroglyphics. A small gasp escaped her throat. *"Rongorongo."*

"Excuse me?"

Karen flipped through the remainder of the notebook. There were forty pages of glyphs. The book trembled in her fingers as she mumbled, "There has never been a discovery of this length before."

"Discovery of what?"

She closed the book and gave him a quick lesson on the history of the etchings found on Easter Island. "Over the centuries," she finished, "no one has been able to translate them. This may hold the final clue."

"I hope it helps," Jack said lamely as his mind spun. If the language was from Easter Island, what was it doing inscribed on a crystal spire six hundred meters underwater? He struggled to incorporate this newest bit of information. Could this have anything to do with the crash of Air Force One?

Before flying here, he had not mentioned to Karen his own agenda in meeting with her—to tie the strange crystal to the downing of Air Force One. It seemed too far-fetched to admit to a stranger. "Do you think you'll be able to translate what's on the pillar?"

Karen clutched the notebook in her lap. She stared out the window, lost in her own thoughts. "I don't know."

Within a few minutes they reached her apartment: a second-floor town house, two bedrooms, neat and wonderfully cool. Karen apologized for the drab furnishings, all beige and browns. "It came prefurnished."

But Jack noted small personal touches. On a mantel rested a collection of stone statues and fetishes from Micronesia. In a corner were four carefully tended bonsai plants. And stuck on the apartment's refrigerator were scores of pictures—family, friends, old vacation photos—affixed by an equally colorful assortment of kitchen magnets.

Jack followed Karen toward the bedroom area. As his host passed the decorated refrigerator, all the magnets suddenly clattered to the floor, the pictures fluttering after them.

Startled, Karen jumped away.

Jack glanced from the refrigerator to Karen. She stood with the satchel clutched to her chest. "It think it's the crystal. It's demonstrated strange magnetic effects before."

As proof, he waved her away. When she moved off a few steps, he collected one of the magnets and put it back on the refrigerator. It stuck again.

"That is so weird," Karen said. "No wonder the looters thought the crystal was cursed."

Jack frowned. "Cursed?"

She matched his frown with a nod to the single magnet. "It seems both of us have been holding back a little. Let's get you settled and then head over to the lab. We have much to discuss."

Jack slowly nodded.

He showered, shaved, and changed into a pair of loose khakis and a light short-sleeve shirt. He repacked his backpack: camera, notebooks, pens, cellular phone. He felt worlds better as he left Karen's apartment. It was only a short walk to the university.

"I already called Miyuki," Karen said. "She's waiting for us at her lab."

Jack nudged his pack higher on his shoulder. "You mean Professor Nakano?"

Karen nodded. "She has a program to decrypt the language."

As they walked an awkward silence descended. Jack sought to break it. "So tell me where you found the crystal."

Karen sighed. "That's a long story." But she gave Jack a quick sketch: the risen pyramids, the ambush, the escape through an underwater passage.

As the story unfolded, Jack's respect for the two women grew. "And these looters were the same ones who broke into Professor Nakano's office?"

Karen nodded.

"How could they possibly know about the crystal within the pyramid?"

"I'm not sure they did. They just know we found *something*. Something they think is cursed."

Jack thought about the crash of Air Force One, wondering if these men's warning might hold a kernel of truth. "Definitely strange," he mumbled.

"Here we are," Karen pointed to a building just ahead. She led the way. Inside, she flashed her credentials, and a guard escorted them to the elevators.

"The lifts are working again?" she asked as the doors opened.

The guard nodded. He joined them in the small space.

Karen caught Jack's inquisitive look at their escort. "Precautions because of the break-in last week."

The elevator ascended swiftly. When the doors opened, Jack found a small Japanese woman waiting for them, pacing anxiously.

Stepping forward, Karen introduced them. Miyuki bowed slightly but offered no hand. Jack nodded in greeting. Asian customs involved little physical contact. "Professor Nakano, thank you for your help."

"Please call me Miyuki," she said shyly.

"Let's go," Karen said as the guard returned to the elevator. "I want to enter Jack's data as soon as possible." Karen hurried forward, waving for Jack and Miyuki to follow.

Jack leaned over to Miyuki. "Is she always like this?"

Miyuki rolled her eyes. "Always," she said with an exaggerated sigh.

Once at the office, Miyuki stepped forward and keyed open the lock. Karen was first through the door. "Miyuki maintains a clean room for her computers," she explained as Jack entered. She pointed to a row of starched coveralls hanging on the wall. "You'll need to wear one of those."

"I don't know if I have a suit that'll fit him," Miyuki said. She sifted through the coveralls. "This might do." She passed him a large suit.

Jack took it and placed his backpack on a bench by the wall.

Karen was already zipping into her own coverall. "Jack, while you dress, may I show Miyuki your notebook?"

He nodded and nudged his pack in her direction, then applied himself to forcing his large frame into the tight suit.

"Miyuki, come see this." She tugged free his notebook. As she did, something tumbled from his backpack and rolled across the floor.

Miyuki bent to pick it up.

As Jack struggled to work both shoulders into the coveralls, he saw that Miyuki held David Spangler's gift box, and an idea dawned on him. "Open it," he said to Miyuki. "I could use your expert opinion."

She pulled back the lid. Her eyes narrowed as she peered at its contents.

"What do you think it is?" Jack asked.

Miyuki leaned closer. "It's an inexpensive switching circuit." She closed the box with a snap. "Worthless really."

Jack frowned. What was David's scam here? The circuitry must contain some veiled insult, but what?

Miyuki handed the box back to Karen. "It's just an obsolete Chinese design."

Her words struck Jack in the stomach. He suddenly felt ill. *"Chinese?* Are you sure?"

She nodded.

Jack's mind fought for any other explanation. His first suspicion couldn't possibly be true. But he remembered George's question a few days back: *What if the explosion had been staged? A frame-up?* Jack ran various scenarios through his mind, but only one rang true: Spangler had faked the explosion.

"That bastard!" he spat out. Even the little "gift" was David's way of rubbing his nose in this fact, knowing he couldn't do a thing about it. Washington had wanted this explanation for the tragedy, and David had handed it to them. No one would listen to anything contradictory.

Bile rose in Jack's throat. *The stupendous gall of the murderous bastard!* And how far up did this treachery go? he wondered. Was it just a frame job, or had David played a role in the jet's downing, too? Jack swore under his breath and clenched his fists, sharpening his resolve. He would discover the truth behind the crash—or die trying!

"What's wrong?" Karen asked.

Jack finally noticed the two women gaping at him. He sat down, his legs suddenly weak as his anger faded. "It seems I also have a long story to share."

"About what?" Karen sat down next to him.

"About the crash of Air Force One."

6:30 P.M., Central Pacific

On his belly in the submersible, David Spangler ascended through the depths of the sea, rising in a slow spiral toward the surface. Over the past three days the Navy's new prototype sub, the *Perseus*, had been functioning far better than the estimates from the drawing board.

David lay sprawled on his stomach within the sub's inner shell, a torpedo-shaped chamber molded of two-inch-thick Lexan glass. Except for the clear nose cone, where his head and shoulders protruded, the rest of the Lexan cubicle was encased in the sub's outer shell, a top-secret ceramic composite that was lighter and stronger than titanium. Within this outer shell were housed all the ship's mechanical, electrical, and propulsion systems. This dual shell system was designed for safety. In case of emergency, the entire outer shell could be jettisoned with manual pyrotechnics, freeing the inner Lexan pod to rise to the surface under its own buoyancy.

"Perseus," a voice said in his ear, "we have you locked in. If you'd like to switch to autopilot, we'll guide you into the docking bay."

David answered the topside technician, "I'll take her in myself." This was his sixth dive in the *Perseus*, and he felt comfortable enough with her controls now to do this manually. With his thumb, he flicked a switch, and a heads-up display appeared superimposed over the nose cone's glass. His trajectory to the bay of the Navy's salvage ship, the *Maggie Chouest*, was delineated in red. It was simply a matter of guiding his sub along the designated approach, not unlike a flight simulator.

"I'm hooked into the tracking computer," he radioed. "I'll be at the bay in three minutes."

"Aye, sir. See you topside."

Slowing the thrusters, David eased the sub upward. Around him, as he neared the surface, the dark waters began to lighten. As he aligned his sub he could not escape the sensation of true flight. On his belly, it was as if he and the ship were one. The sub's hand controls were as responsive as his own thoughts. The telescoping wings to either side were like the fins of a creature born to the sea, twisting and tucking to guide the vessel.

But this was no creature of the sea. Under its belly a pair of titanium manipulator arms were folded and stored, capable of crushing granite, and atop the sub, protruding like a shark's dorsal fin, stood a stacked array of minitorpedoes, on a pivoting dolly for ease of targeting. Though small, each missile was tipped with a powerful warhead, able to pierce an armored submarine. They were nicknamed "sub-busters" by the *Perseus*'s support team, the Navy's Deep Submergence Unit. The weapons gave the tiny rescue sub an extra advantage in hostile waters.

David ran a finger over the torpedoes' activation control. Earlier that day he had been informed of the loss of Taiwan to the Chinese. The news had kept him agitated all day. How had they lost the island to the goddamn Communists? It was an embarrassment and a black eye to all of America. If only he could have taken part in the fighting . . .

The technician came on the line. "Sir, one of your men is here. He says it's urgent he speak with you."

"Put him on."

A short pause, then Rolfe's voice came over the radio. "Sorry to disturb you, sir, but you told us to let you know if there were . . . um, any change in your secondary objective."

David frowned. *Secondary objective?* He had been so focused on the timetable here and on the growing drums of war that he had momentarily forgotten about Jack Kirkland. "What is it?"

"The target has vacated the zone."

David bit back a long curse. Kirkland had gone missing. He knew any further details and explanations could not be discussed over an open radio. "I'll be topside in two minutes. Meet me in my cabin and brief me then."

"Yes, sir."

Grimacing, David shoved aside his concerns about Kirkland. Right now he had work to finish. He swept the sub around on a wingtip, aligning its trajectory into the proper approach. He checked the sub's clock. He had been underwater for almost six hours. After he surfaced, the *Perseus* would be checked over and reoutfitted for the day's third dive. An alternate Navy pilot would take the submersible down to the work site on the seabed floor. Then, in another seven hours, it would be David's shift all over again.

But the two pilots were not the only ones with tough schedules. Since the arrival of the research team and barges from Maui, the entire crew had been working around the clock. Aided by the researcher's submersible and robots, the sea base's support framework had already been bolted to the bottom. Starting this afternoon, the three-tiered living units and labs would be sunk to the bottom and assembled. Barring any mishaps, David expected the entire base to be established within the next forty-eight hours and manned soon afterward.

He had been ordered to get this base up in four days, and he would not disappoint, even if it meant cracking the whip. In fact, earlier in the day, when the research team's leader, a geophysicist named Ferdinand Cortez, objected to the strenuous pace, David encouraged him to call Washington. It had given David great pleasure to see the Mexican browbeaten by Nicolas Ruzickov over the satellite phone. Even from a step away David had heard Ruzickov screaming at the scientist. Afterward, though tensions remained acute, no one questioned his orders nor his schedule again.

He was in sole control of this operation, and he would not let anyone or anything delay its completion—not the embarrassing loss of Taiwan, nor the mysterious disappearance of Jack Kirkland. He would not fail.

Ahead, out of the gloom, the submerged docking bay appeared. David angled the sub with deft skill, gliding her skids onto the submerged platform. He settled the sub between the self-locking clamps. As he released the controls, the sub's wings retracted and two C-clamps snugged against the vessel's ceramic sides. "Locked and loaded," he called topside.

"Locked and loaded," the technician acknowledged. "Pulling you up."

Through the *Perseus*'s hydrophones, David heard the whine of the hydraulics as the captured submersible was drawn to the surface. Around him the seas grew brighter until, at last, he surfaced. Saltwater sluiced over the nose cone and small waves crashed against the sub's side, but the vessel did not move. And after a few seconds even the waves were no threat. The *Perseus* and its pilot were hauled up out of the ocean and craned onto the stern deck of the *Maggie Chouest*.

As soon as the platform settled to the deck, the sub's five-man maintenance crew swarmed over the vessel. The nose cone's O-ring was unscrewed and the glass bubble dropped open. David slid like a beaching seal onto the deck. One of the crewmen offered him a hand. After six hours on his belly in the cramped space, his limbs were untrustworthy.

Once on his feet, David unzipped his wet suit and stretched the kinks from his muscles. Behind him the maintenance crew was already at work: checking seals, blowing the carbon dioxide scavengers, piping fresh oxygen into the two flank tanks. They reminded David of an Indy 500 pit crew. Fast, efficient, and coordinated.

David turned his back on them and found Cortez aiming his way across the deck. Groaning, David straightened. Right now all he wanted was a hot shower and his bunk. He did not want to deal with the geophysicist. He set his face to a hard scowl as the man stopped before him. "What is it, Professor?"

From the dark circles under his eyes, the man had slept little. Even his clothes, khakis and a flannel shirt, were wrinkled and worn. "A request, Commander."

"What?"

"On this next dive, I was wondering if Lieutenant Brentley could take a few moments and scout closer to the crystalline formation. From the video feed of the previous dives, we've spotted some scratches on its surface. They appear too regular to be natural. We think its some form of writing."

David shook his head. "Any such investigation will have

to wait. My first priority is to get that base built and manned. After that, you and your scientists can begin your own investigation."

"But it would only take a few—"

"My orders stand, *Professor*." David spat out the last word as if it were an insult. "Stay clear of the crystal until the station is built. That pillar radiates a strong magnetic signature, creating glitches and communication problems. I will not risk the *Perseus* just to satisfy your curiosity."

"Yes, Commander."

Though the researcher backed down, David spotted the contempt in the man's eyes. He did not care. The Mexican was under his command. He would do what he was told.

Across the deck, near the aft hatch, one of David's subordinates was on guard. He stalked up to the man. "Where's Lieutenant Rolfe?"

"In your cabin, sir."

David nodded and ducked through the hatch. He climbed two flights up to the ship's flag deck. He had commandeered this level's cabins for his men. Ahead he saw his room's door was ajar. Another of his men patrolled the passageway. He nodded and pushed into his cabin.

Inside, Rolfe stood up.

David closed the door and began stripping off his wet suit. "So what happened to Kirkland? Did you lose his ship?"

"No, sir." Rolfe cleared his throat. "We've been monitoring the location of the *Deep Fathom* continually. It still circles the Kwajalein Atoll."

"So then what went wrong?"

"Earlier this morning, Lieutenant Jeffreys got suspicious about why the ship was remaining in the area for so long. So he did a little checking and found Jack Kirkland's name on a Quantas passenger list leaving the atoll."

David kicked out of his wet suit and stood naked. "Dammit! When did he leave?"

"Two days ago. From the itinerary, it appears he traveled to Okinawa."

David scowled. What was the bastard doing in Okinawa? He stalked to his cabin's bathroom and twisted on the shower nozzle. "Do we know exactly where he went?"

"No, sir. He had reservations at the local Sheraton, but he never showed up. However, he did book a round-trip ticket. He's due back in two days."

David's face darkened. *Two more days.* He had been looking forward to completing this little side objective much sooner. Still, he was impressed by his own team's resourcefulness. Kirkland would not escape him. As busy as he was here, he could wait out another two days.

"Very good, Mr. Rolfe. But I want to know as soon as we have confirmation that Kirkland's back on his boat."

"Yes, sir."

David tested the shower. The small bathroom was filling with steam.

"Sir, we have another problem." The lieutenant's voice was pained.

"What is it?"

"I don't know if we have two days to wait. According to Handel, the transmitting signal has been deteriorating. He estimates a day or two until we lose contact."

David swung around, angry. "I told Handel to make sure the bomb remained functioning for at least two weeks."

"He knows, sir. He believes one of the bomb's electrical circuits may be faulty. He says that Chink crap is not reliable."

David stood there, almost shaking in frustration. Refusing to admit defeat, he pondered other options and angles. He knew no plan was as foolproof as on paper. Improvisation was the key to a mission's final success. As he thought about it, a new strategy formed. "Fine. Then if Kirkland's not back in time, we blow his ship anyway."

"Sir?"

"Destroying his boat and killing his crew will be only our first steps in bringing Kirkland down." As David stood in the steamy bathroom, he warmed to his new plan.

Slowly torturing Jack Kirkland did have its appeal.

"Anyone for dinner?" Karen asked, stretching her neck. Her eyes were blurry from studying the computer screens. "I can't take any more of this."

To her left, the tall American sat crouched over his terminal. He seemed not to have heard her. "Gabriel, let's move on to symbols Forty A and B."

"Certainly, Mr. Kirkland."

On the far side of the American, Miyuki remained lost in her own work, busily scanning in the final few pages from the notebook. Processing the data had turned out to be a slow and tedious chore. It had become necessary for the computer to compare each glyph to the set already catalogued.

Karen glanced at Jack's workstation. Two figures appeared on his screen: one from his notebook and one from their own collection of glyphs.

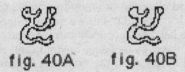

fig. 40A   fig. 40B

The American's notebook contained only a handwritten copy of the pillar's inscription, drawn by the historian aboard his boat. This led to a certain level of ambiguity at times. Like now. Were the two figures the same glyph, Karen wondered, or were the subtle differences just minor discrepancies on the part of the transcriber?

During this process, Gabriel had learned to compare over two hundred loci sites on each corresponding glyph. As long as there was at least a ninety percent match, it was decided that the two symbols were the same. A match ranking less than fifty percent was considered unique enough to be classified as a new symbol. This resulted in a gray zone between fifty and ninety. And so far, there were three hundred paired symbols falling into this category. Each of these required visual inspection by the trio of humans.

"Figures Forty A and Forty B," Gabriel explained, *"are a match at fifty-two percent. Will we classify A as the same or different from B?"*

Jack leaned closer to the screen. "It's like that old children's puzzle. What's different between these two pictures?"

Miyuki piped in as she finished the last scan and leaned back, "The first figure has an eye drawn on it, the other doesn't."

Jack nodded. "And the first figure is holding up two balls, the other only one." He glanced at Karen.

Again she was struck at what a brilliant blue the man's eyes were. They had to be contact lenses. No one had eyes *that* blue. "The rest looks the same," she said, clearing her throat.

Jack asked, "So what's the verdict, folks? Are they different enough from one another to be two separate symbols?"

Karen shifted closer to the monitor, brushing her shoulder against Jack's. He did not move away. Instead he bowed his head beside hers, both concentrating on the screen. "I'm gonna dismiss the eyes as being insignificant," Karen said. "But not the differences in the number of items in the figure's raised hand. I think this discrepancy is significant enough to be unique. Over the past few days, we've discovered other symbols with counting icons built into them: the number of legs on a starfish, the number of fish in a pelican's mouth. I think this is one of those counting icons. Though similar to one another, they are ultimately unique."

Jack nodded, satisfied with her answer. "Gabriel, please classify Figure Forty A and Figure Forty B as separate icons."

"Done. Shall we proceed to Figures 41A and 41B?"

Karen groaned. "I don't know about the both of you, but I'm starved and my eyes are aching. How about a couple hours rest break?"

"I guess I could use a little dinner myself," Jack said. "All

I've eaten for the past twenty-four hours has been airplane food."

As Jack stretched, Karen tried not to notice the breadth of his shoulders or the way his neck muscles corded up. "I know a restaurant only a few blocks away. They serve the best Thai food around."

"Sounds good. The spicier the better."

"It's tongue-blistering. Guaranteed."

"Just the way I like it."

Standing, Miyuki shooed them. "You two go on by yourselves. There's something I'd like to try with Gabriel."

"Are you sure?" Karen asked.

Miyuki nodded, but her eyes traveled up the tall man as he stood. Once Jack's back was fully turned, she winked at Karen. "I'm sure," she said to Karen with a small smile.

Karen blushed. Was her attraction to Jack so obvious? She scolded Miyuki with a consternated expression, but this only widened her friend's smile.

"Besides, I just had Thai food," Miyuki said louder. "But I know how many months it's been for you."

The double meaning was not lost on Karen. Her blush darkened. She glared at her friend as Jack called from the doorway, "Is there anything you'd like us to bring back for you, Miyuki?"

"Oh, I'm fine. I'm not the hungry one here, but you'd better get something into Karen right away."

"Will do!" Then he was out the door.

Karen playfully swatted at Miyuki. "You are so wicked."

"And you are so smitten. Go on. Make a move. I already checked him out. No ring, not even a girlfriend. And I think he sort of likes you, too."

"He does not. He never even looked twice at me."

Miyuki rolled her eyes. "Not when you would notice. It was like watching two teenagers, both of you sizing each up when the other's back was turned."

"He was *not* checking me out."

Miyuki shrugged and turned back to her computer.

Karen touched her shoulder. "Was he really?"

"Like a lovesick puppy. Now go on. Give that puppy's belly a rub and leave me alone for a few hours."

"We're only going to dinner."

"Uh-huh."

"We're both professionals, colleagues in this matter."

"Uh-huh."

"He's only going to be here for a couple more days."

"Uh-huh."

Karen grew frustrated and stormed away. "It's only dinner!" she called back to Miyuki.

As she exited, Miyuki's answer followed her. "Uh-huh."

10:02 P.M., Ryukyu University, Okinawa Prefecture, Japan

As they walked back from the Lucky Thai Restaurant, Jack bellowed out a laugh that had the smaller Japanese pedestrians glancing in his direction. Embarrassed, he leaned closer to Karen. "You've got to be kidding! You told the president of the British Anthropology Society to pull his head out of his ass?"

Karen shrugged. "He ticked me off. Him and his stick-in-the-mud ideas. What does he know about the South Pacific? My great-grandfather had traveled South Pacific islands for decades before that man was in diapers. What right did that pompous ass have in claiming my ancestor was a crackpot?"

"Oh, and I'll bet your response set him straight. He must think your entire family is nuts. No wonder you had to come all the way to Japan to teach."

Karen glared up at him, but Jack could tell her anger was feigned. "I wasn't exactly expelled from Canada's shores. I chose to come here for my own research. Colonel Churchward, my mother's grandfather, may have jumped to some ridiculous conclusions about a lost continent in the middle of the Pacific, but I came out here to prove that much of the accepted historical dogma of this region is wrong. And with what we both have been uncovering here, I'm beginning to think my ancestor's claims may not have been so off base."

"A lost continent?" he scoffed.

"C'mon, Jack, think about it. Off the coast of Chatan an ancient city rises from the sea. And if Gabriel's translation of the star chamber's calendar is correct, it dates the construction around twelve thousand years ago. During that era, the seas were about three hundred feet lower than they are now. Who knows how many other landmasses and cities might be hidden in these waters? And what of your own pillar? Are you saying this lost race could dive to the ocean bottom and carve letters on a crystal pyramid?"

"I don't know what I'm saying. But after all you've shown me today, I'm learning to see things with a more open mind."

Karen nodded, as if satisfied. "You really should see the ancient city and pyramids. That would help convince you."

"To be honest, I wouldn't mind a trip out there."

"If we have time, I'll take you. It's only a couple hours by boat."

"I . . . I'd like that. It's a date."

A long awkward moment arose between them. They continued in silence through the university's grounds. The scent of lavender and hibiscus colored the garden paths, but all Jack could smell was Karen's jasmine perfume. What was so captivating about this woman? Back on the *Deep Fathom*, Lisa had twice the physical attributes. Still, there was something exciting about Karen's passion and boldness.

During dinner, Jack discovered Karen was also her own woman. Her wit was as sharp as a knife blade, while her eyes shone with constant mischief. Her crooked smile both mocked and enchanted. Over dessert he had stopped seeing Jennifer and saw only Karen . . . and he wasn't disappointed.

"We're almost to the computer building," Karen said quietly, breaking the silence.

Was there a trace of regret in her voice? Jack knew he felt it in his own heart. He longed to spend more than a few snatched hours with her in private. He found his steps inadvertently slowing.

She matched his pace. At the bottom of the stairs to the

building, she stopped and turned to him. "Thanks for dinner.
I had a nice time."

"It's the least I could do for your putting me up for the
night."

They stood too close together, but neither moved.

"We should see if Miyuki has discovered anything new,"
Karen said, half raising an arm to point toward the building.
She climbed the first step.

Her face was now even with his. Their eyes met and held
each other for a heartbeat longer than necessary. Jack leaned
closer to her. It was foolish, inappropriate, juvenile . . . but
he could not stop. He was not sure if she shared any of his
feelings, so he moved slowly. If she pulled away, he would
have his answer.

But she maintained his gaze. Only her lids lowered im-
perceptibly.

He began to reach his arms around her when a voice
barked from the doorway. The pair were speared by a flashlight's beam.

Karen coughed in surprise and backed up a step, retreating.

The man called out to them in Japanese.

Half turning into the flashlight's glare, Karen answered in
the same language.

As the light was turned aside, Jack saw it was one of the
security men from the building. "What did he want?" he
asked as the guard swung away.

Karen turned to him. "Miyuki warned him to watch out
for us. She has news." Karen led the way up the steps. Her
voice grew excited, drowning away the passion from a moment ago. "Let's go!"

Jack followed, both disappointed and relieved. It was
ridiculous to start anything with this woman, especially
since he was leaving in two days. Not that he had any rule
against one-night stands. Though his heart was guarded, he
had physical needs like any other man, and seldom had
problems finding a willing partner during port calls. But in
this case he knew any brief dalliance with Karen would
hardly satisfy him. In fact, it would make matters worse.

He climbed the steps and passed through the doorway. Maybe for all concerned, he thought, it was best to leave their passions at the bottom of the stairs.

Across the lobby, Karen waved to him from beside the elevator bay. He stretched his stride to reach her just as the doors opened. With the guard escorting them, neither one spoke. Each stood in a cocoon of privacy.

When the doors whooshed open, they hurried down the hall. As they neared the door to the lab, it cracked open and Miyuki gestured them to hurry, saying, "It worked! Come see! I have all the glyphs catalogued."

"All of them?" Karen said.

Jack understood her surprise. It had taken them hours to reach number forty in a list of discrepancies that numbered over three hundred. How had the computer scientist accomplished so much in so little time?

Miyuki didn't respond. Instead, when they had accompanied her into the lab and to her computer station, she pointed to the screen. Symbols were flashing past. "Gabriel is rechecking his data," Miyuki said. "It will take another hour to double-check everything for accuracy, then he'll try decoding the various inscriptions."

Karen just stood there shaking her head. "How? How did you do it?"

"As I mentioned before, Gabriel is an artificial intelligence program. He can learn from experience. While you were at dinner I had him study the first forty pairs of glyphs and incorporate why the three of us rejected or accepted various symbols as unique or not, then apply those parameters to the remaining couple hundred." Grinning, Miyuki said, "He was able to do it! He *learned* from our examples!"

"But he's a computer," Karen said. Jack noticed how she whispered these words as if somehow afraid of hurting Gabriel's feelings. "How can we trust that his decisions were correct?"

Instead of her words dampening Miyuki's glee, she grew more excited. "Because after completing this exercise, he's been able to expand his rudimentary understanding of these people's lunar calendar and dating system."

"What do you mean?" Karen asked, still skeptical. "What has he learned?"

"Buried in the text are hidden references to a specific site in the Pacific."

"What site? I don't understand."

"I'll let Gabriel explain, because frankly even I have trouble understanding it." Miyuki glanced to the side, speaking to their invisible partner. "Gabriel, please explain your calculations."

"Yes, Professor Nakano. From the celestial map and my understanding of their lunar calendar, I discovered a reference to a specific location, triangulated by the position of the moon, the sun, and the north star in the text."

Jack was stunned by this revelation. "And you're able to do this even though you can't translate the language yet?"

"It's all astronomy and mathematics," Miyuki explained. "Numbers and the movement of the stars are really a cosmic language. Such information is the easiest to translate since it is a relative constant across cultures. In fact, when archaeologists first attempted to decipher the hieroglyphics of ancient Egypt, the first thing they understood were the Egyptians' mathematics and celestial designations." Miyuki pointed to the scrolling glyphs. "The same is true here."

"So what did you find?" Karen asked, impatient.

"In the pyramid's inscription," Miyuki said, "there are two references. Each mentions the same site in the Pacific. Gabriel, bring up the map on the second monitor, and highlight the location for us."

A map of the Pacific appeared on the small screen. Jack had a flash of déjà vu. It reminded him of a similar discussion aboard his own ship, when George had related the mysteries of the Dragon's Triangle. Jack assumed the mysterious site from the inscription was going to be the location of the crystal pillar—but instead a small red blinking dot bloomed farther south on the map, just north of the equator.

"Gabriel, zoom in on the location. Three hundred times normal."

The map swelled, sweeping deep into the South Pacific.

Islands, once so tiny they could not be seen, grew in size until names could be read: Satawal, Chuuk, Pulusuk, Mortlock. They were all islands of Micronesia. The red dot was positioned at the southeastern tip of one of them.

It was Pohnpei, the capital of the Federated States of Micronesia.

Karen sat up straighter. "Gabriel, can you pinpoint the location in any finer detail?"

Though Jack had known Karen less than a day, he sensed that she was on to something.

The other islands of Micronesia faded off the screen as the outline of Pohnpei filled the monitor. Individual villages and towns grew clearer. The blinking red marker hovered near the island's southeast coastline.

Jack leaned toward the screen. He could just make out a name written beside the red marker. "What does that say?"

Karen remained stiff in her seat. She was hardly looking at the screen. "It's Nan Madol."

Jack glanced over at her. "A village?"

"Ruins," she answered. "One of the most spectacular set of megalithic ruins in all the South Pacific. The site covers eleven square miles of coastline, an engineering marvel of canals and basalt buildings." She turned toward him. "To this day no one knows for sure who built them."

Jack sat back and nodded to the neighboring screen, where the glyphs continued to scroll. "Maybe now we do."

"I have to know more!" Karen said, grabbing Miyuki's sleeve.

The computer scientist frowned. "I'm sorry. That's all I have. After Gabriel double-checks his own work, it'll still take at least a day to begin any significant decoding. With these new additions, the total number of individual glyphs is now over five hundred, and the list of compound glyphs has grown into the range of ten thousand. This is no easy language."

"How long do you think it'll take?" Karen asked, breathless.

"Try me late tomorrow afternoon," Miyuki said. "I might—and I repeat *might*—have something then."

"A whole day," Karen groaned. "What am I going to do for a whole day?"

Jack knew the anthropologist needed something on which to focus her energy. "How about your promise to me?"

Karen's brows bunched up, not understanding.

"The ancient city off the coast of Chatan. You promised to tour me through there."

She brightened, but not for the reason Jack had hoped. "You're right. If the ruins of Nan Madol are referenced, some other clues may still be hidden out at Chatan. It's worth investigating again."

"And this time out, you'll have better company than me," Miyuki added. "A strong man to guard your back."

Karen looked at Jack, as if finally seeing him again. "Oh."

In her green eyes, Jack recognized her burning passion for this newest mystery. He searched for something more—but came up empty.

He smiled weakly. So much for romance.

14

On the Run

David Spangler glided his submersible in a slow dive around the steel support base of the deep-sea research station. Each of the frame's four alloy legs were solidly bolted to the seabed floor with ten-foot-long metal spikes. None of the stout legs even budged when the first section of the four-ton research station settled atop the landing base.

"Looking good from up here," a topside technician radioed to him. "How's it looking down there?"

David continued his survey. The laboratory had the appearance of a twenty-meter-wide white doughnut sitting on a raised platter. He dove underneath the section, craning his neck to make sure the piece was properly seated, then keyed his transmitter. "All clear. Perfect landing. I'll unhook the winches and lines." David goosed his thrusters and swung around, aiming for the four thick cables that had been used to lower and guide the laboratory section into place.

"No need. We're getting good video from the ROVs,

Commander. Our team has practiced this a thousand times. All we need you to do is monitor from there."

On the seabed floor, David watched as a pair of boxy robots slowly lurched forward, churning up silt behind them. The pair, named Huey and Duey, were remotely operated by the topside technicians. They set about the task of latching the first section to its support base.

Over the next day, the team would lower the other two sections, secure them together, one atop the other, and then evacuate the water from the drowned labs. The plan was to pressurize the facility to one atmosphere, exactly matching the surface pressure, thus allowing the scientists to journey up and down in their own submersible without the need to decompress.

So far, everything was proceeding smoothly. David had to give some credit to the Mexican leader of the research team. With a fire lit under his ass, Cortez ran a tight ship himself. As such, perhaps the scientist deserved a bone tossed in his direction. Since yesterday, Cortez had not stopped nagging him for a closer peek at the crystal pillar. Perhaps it was time to oblige him a little.

After giving the developing station one final pass, David circled out in a widening spiral. About fifty yards away rested the graveyard of Air Force One, many of its parts still strewn across the seabed floor. In the distance giant flat-topped seamounts shadowed the site, while surrounding it all lay the twisted forest of lava pillars. David could not imagine a more inhospitable place on Earth.

He pushed the throttles on his sub and swept toward the wreckage site. In the center, the strange crystal obelisk thrust up from the seabed floor. He gave it a wide berth in the *Perseus*, still nervous about getting too close to the giant structure that had demonstrated such odd properties during Kirkland's dives. Even from ten yards away he could appreciate its size. The top of the spire disappeared into the inky gloom far overhead.

Hovering in place, David guided his lights along its length. Its faceted surface seemed to absorb his lamplight and cast it back tenfold. Undoubtedly a marvel—and if his boss was correct, also potentially one of the world's most powerful energy sources.

With care, David maintained his distance. Using the touchpad on his video monitor, he zoomed in on the crystalline surface. Tiny scratches focused into row after row of small figures and geometric shapes, etched and shining silver. His eyes grew wide. It was writing!

"Goddamn you, Kirkland!" he mumbled.

"What was that, sir?"

"Nothing. Continue securing the station!" David thumbed off the transmitter. He needed to think. Jack Kirkland had not mentioned writing on the crystal in any of his reports, and David knew he'd been close enough to see this. He couldn't have missed it. The silver symbols practically glowed on the crystalline surface. So why hadn't he reported it? What was he up to? David gripped the throttles tightly. What else was Jack Kirkland keeping secret? Every instinct in him screamed with suspicion.

On his touchpad, he activated his private encrypted line to the surface. He had it implemented after running into problems communicating directly with his team through an open channel.

It was answered immediately by his second-in-command. "What is it, sir?"

"Rolfe, we may have a problem. I need access to all communication into and out of the *Deep Fathom* since it first arrived here."

"Sir, we didn't tap the ship's communication system."

"I know that. But it's a goddamn boat. Any telephone communication would've passed through a traceable satellite system. We may not know *what* he said, but I want to know *who* he said it to."

"Yes, sir, I'll put Jeffreys on it right away."

"I'm coming topside immediately. I want some answers by the time I'm on deck."

"Aye, Commander."

David switched channels and hailed the sub's technician.

He repeated his plan to surface earlier than scheduled. "Get Brentley suited up," he finished brusquely. "The lieutenant can finish babysitting the robots down here."

Without waiting for an assent, David flicked off the radio and blew the ballast on his sub. He shoved both throttles forward. The *Perseus* shot upward, its thrusters whining as they were fully engaged.

What was Kirkland up to?

9:42 A.M., off the coast of Yonaguni Island

With the sun hovering above the eastern horizon, Jack stood behind the wheel of the sleek nineteen-foot Boston Whaler. "I'll be damned," he muttered as he cut the motor and glided around the headlands of Yonaguni Island.

Ahead, the small coastal city of Chatan lay nestled along the shore, a ramshackle village of cheap hotels and seaside restaurants. But it was not the town that captured Jack's attention. It was the pair of terraced pyramids towering above the waves offshore.

"Amazing, isn't it?" Karen said.

Beyond the pyramids, more of the ancient city appeared: basalt columns, roofless homes, sharp-edged obelisks, worn statues. The city spread toward the horizon, fading into the morning mists.

" 'Amazing' hardly describes this sight," Jack said. "You told me what to expect, but to see it . . ." His voice dwindled away in awe. Finally, he settled back into the pilot's seat and throttled up. "It was worth the hassle getting here."

"I told you it was." Karen remained standing as the boat sped toward the city, her hair blowing back, her cheeks rosy in the wind as the boat bounced through the chop. Her figure was framed in sea spray.

Jack studied his companion from the corner of his eye. At the port of Naha, he had spent an aggravating hour scrounging up this boat. With the island's U.S. military bases at full alert because of the Chinese, sea traffic had been congested and chaotic. Jack was forced to pay an outrageous rental fee for the day use of his boat. Luckily, they took his American Express. Still, as he watched Karen, he knew the trip was *definitely* worth the hassles.

As they neared the first pyramid, Jack cut the engine and slowed the boat into a gentle glide.

Karen settled into her own seat. "Once you see this city, how can you *not* believe that a prehistoric people once lived among these islands?" She waved her arm to encompass the spread of ruins. "This is not the work of early Polynesians. Another people, an older people, built this, along with the many other megalithic ruins dotting the Pacific: the canal city of Nan Madol, the lattes stones of the Mariannas, the colossal Burden of Tonga."

"If these ancient people were so skilled, what happened to them?"

Karen grew thoughtful, eyes glazed. "I don't know. Some great cataclysm. My great-grandfather believed, from studying Mayan tablets, that a larger continent once existed in the middle of the Pacific. He called it Mu . . . after the Hawaiian name for this lost continent."

"Your great-grandfather?"

"Colonel Churchward." She smiled back at him. "He was considered . . . well, eccentric in most respectable scientific circles."

"Ah . . ." Jack rolled his eyes.

Karen scowled good-naturedly at him. "Regardless of my ancestor's eccentricities, myths of the lost continent persist throughout the Pacific Islands. The Indians of Central and South America named these lost people the *viracocha*. In the Maldive Islands, they are the Redin, their word for 'ancient people.' Even the Polynesians speak of 'Wakea,' an ancient teacher, who arrived in a mighty ship with massive sails and oarsmen. Across the Pacific, there are just too many stories to dismiss it out of hand. And now here we have another clue. A sunken city rising again."

"But this is just *one* city, not a whole continent."

Karen shook her head. "Twelve thousand years ago these seas were about three hundred feet shallower. Many regions now underwater would have been dry land back then."

"Still, that doesn't explain the disappearance of a whole continent. We'd know about its presence, even if it was under three hundred feet of water."

"That's just it. I don't think the continent's disappearance was due *only* to a change in the water table. Look at this city. An earthquake shoved this section of coastline up, while in Alaska the entire Aleutian chain of islands sinks. There are hundreds of other such stories. Islands sinking or rising."

"So you think some great cataclysm broke up this continent and sank it."

"Exactly. Around the same time, twelve thousand years ago, we know a great disaster occurred, a time of major worldwide climatic changes. It happened suddenly. Mastodons were found frozen on their feet with grass in their bellies. Flowers were found frozen in mid-bloom. One of the theories was that a massive volcano or series of volcanoes erupted, casting enough smoke and ash into the upper atmosphere that it caused dramatic climatic shifts. If such an extreme seismic event truly happened, perhaps the quakes were bad enough to break up and sink this lost continent."

As Jack listened, he remembered the crystal column six hundred meters under the sea. Could this have once been dry land? he wondered. A part of Karen's lost continent? He pondered her theories. They seemed far-fetched. But still . . .

Karen glanced at him, blushing. "Sorry, I didn't mean to bend your ear like that. But I've been buried in books and historical texts all week. It helps to voice some of my theories aloud."

"Well, there's no doubt you've been doing your homework."

"I'm just following up on my great-grandfather's research." She turned her attention forward. "He may have been crazy. But if we can decode the language here, I believe we'll have our answer—one way or the other."

Jack heard the frustration in her voice. He wanted to reach out to her, to reassure her. But he kept his hands on the boat's wheel. The best way to assist her was to help solve this mystery.

As he glided up to and between the two pyramids, he put

Karen's theories together in his mind: a lost continent sunk during an ancient cataclysm, an ancient seafaring race who demonstrated mysterious powers, and at the center of it, a crystal unlike anything seen before. As much as he tried to dismiss it all, he sensed that Karen was on the right track. Still, a critical question remained unanswered: How did any of this explain the downing of Air Force One?

He had no answer himself— but he knew this intriguing woman was closer than any of them to solving it. For now, he would follow her lead.

A whining roar cut above the rumble of their boat's engine. It drew their attention around. Low in the sky, a military jet sped toward them. Jack recognized its silhouette as it shot past and screamed south—an F-14 Tomcat—from one of Okinawa's military bases.

Frowning, Karen followed the path of the plane. "This war is gonna get ugly," she said.

11:45 A.M., aboard the *Maggie Chouest*, Central Pacific

David stormed into his cabin. Two men jumped to their feet at his arrival: Ken Rolfe, his second-in-command, and Hank Jeffreys, the team's communications officer. In the center of the cabin, the table was covered with various communication tools: two satellite phones, a GPS monitor, and a pair of IBM laptops trailing both modem cables and T-lines.

"What have you learned?" David demanded.

Rolfe visibly swallowed. "Sir, we've traced all telephone communication from the *Deep Fathom*." From the clustered worktable, he found a sheet of paper and looked at it, saying, "Calls were sent to First Credit Bank of San Diego . . . a private residence in the suburbs of Philadelphia . . . an apartment building in Kingston, Jamaica . . . a Qantas Airline office on Kwajalein Atoll, and—" Rolfe looked up at David. "—several calls to Ryukyu University on Okinawa."

David held out his hand for the list.

Rolfe passed it to him. "We have it correlated by date and time."

"Very good." David scanned the list to the bottom. *Ryukyu University*. A woman's name was listed with the connection: Karen J. Grace, Ph.D. "Do we know who this woman is?"

Rolfe nodded. "We connected to the university's Internet site and downloaded a fact sheet on Dr. Grace. She's an associate professor of anthropology, visiting from Vancouver."

"What's her connection to Kirkland?"

Rolfe flicked a nervous glance at Jeffreys. "We've been working on that, sir. We noticed the first communication between the *Deep Fathom* and the university was the day after the ship sailed from here."

"Any idea why Kirkland was calling this woman?"

"Actually, that's what we were just working on when you arrived. It seems it was not the *Deep Fathom* that made the initial contact call, but the other way around. She called him."

David frowned, lowering the sheet of paper. "She called him?"

"Yes, sir. We found it suspicious, too. So Lieutenant Jeffreys spent the last half hour gaining access to all e-mail coming and going from the ship. It took a bit of time to convince their ISP to allow us access." Rolfe swung one of the laptop computers around so its screen faced David. "We downloaded the e-mail. There were five exchanges between the two parties."

David leaned his palms on the table and bent nearer the computer.

Rolfe continued, "All the mail dealt with some cryptic language."

David slammed his fist against the table. "I knew it. The bastard *did* discover the inscription!"

Reaching over, Rolfe clicked on one of the e-mails. The page opened up on the screen. "Here's a bit of the language. It seems the naval historian aboard the *Deep Fathom* had blanketed the Internet news boards, inquiring about the origins of this language."

On the screen, David stared at the five tiny icons included

in the e-mail. He recognized their similarity to what he had seen below. "And this professor from Okinawa responded to the inquiry?"

"Yes, sir. She answered, saying she had more examples of the language and wanted to meet."

"So Kirkland went out there. The bastard is investigating this lead."

"That's not all, sir."

David turned from the computer screen. "What else?"

"You'd better read her response yourself." Rolfe clicked open a second piece of mail.

David leaned over and read the message. As he scanned the e-mail it was clear the woman knew more than she was willing to divulge. But one item caught his eye. She hinted at the discovery of a crystal that exhibited unusual properties. He straightened up. "Goddamn it! She must have some of our crystal."

"That's what we thought, too."

"If she has some of it, our mission here is compromised. No one was supposed to know of the crystal deposit. If Kirkland goes blabbing about it and they have a sample of the crystal . . ." David's voice trailed off. This was bad. He waved his men away. "Clear out. I need to talk to Ruzickov."

"Aye, sir." Both men quickly left the cabin.

Alone, David crossed to his bunk and pulled out his personal scrambled phone. It was late evening in Washington, but he knew this information was too vital to sit on overnight. He opened a channel and keyed in the number for the head of the CIA. With the escalating tensions between the U.S. and China, he suspected that the director would still be in his office. He was not wrong.

"Ruzickov here."

"Sir, it's Commander Spangler."

"I know who it is," the director snapped at him. Even over the encrypted line, David could hear the exhaustion in the man's voice. "What do you want? I have a war about to erupt out here."

"Yes, sir. I've been following the reports."

Nicolas Ruzickov sighed. "It's worse than in any reports.

The Chinese know of the President's intention to seek a declaration of war. It's chaos out there. The Chinese navy has already secured a blockade around Taiwan—from Batan Island to the south and swinging full around the Taiwanese coastline."

David gripped the phone's receiver tighter. "And our forces?"

"The USS *John C. Stennis* is already in the region, just awaiting word from us. But with tensions so high out there, the whole mess could explode before Washington officially responds. As you can imagine, I'm up to my neck with problems. So your call had better be important enough to interrupt me."

"I think it is, sir. The security of this site may be compromised." David related the discovery of the communication between Kirkland's ship and university on Okinawa. "If other parties gain wind of the crystal's properties, we could lose our edge here."

Ruzickov's voice lost its exasperated tone. "You were right to bring this to my attention." David was impressed by the man's ability to switch gears so smoothly from one crisis to the next. The CIA director quickly put together a game plan. "It seems this professor knows more than we do. I want you to fetch her, convince her to join our team. But more importantly, her crystal sample must be confiscated. This is a black priority."

"Yes, sir. I understand." *Black priority* were the code words to unleash Omega team with lethal force. There was no higher designation for a mission.

"Do you truly understand, Commander? If the tensions out East turn to war, we may need a secret weapon, the equivalent of the atomic bomb during World War Two. We cannot let this discovery fall into foreign hands. And with Okinawa only a stone's throw from the battlelines being drawn out there, I don't want that crystal sample anywhere near there."

"Don't worry, sir. I will see to it personally."

"Do so." It sounded like Ruzickov was about to sign off.

David spoke quickly. "What about Jack Kirkland?"

Ruzickov sighed. "I told you this is a *black* priority mission. No word must leak out about what we're doing. Silence him however you must."

David smiled grimly. "I'm already on it, sir."

"Don't fail me, Commander." The phone line went dead.

David slowly lowered the receiver and clicked its case closed. He sat for a moment with his palm resting atop the case. *Black priority.* His blood thrilled with those two words. He savored them for a moment, then stood up.

He crossed to the cabin door, opened it and barked an order to his man in the hall: "Fetch Lieutenant Handel. Tell him to bring the detonation transmitter."

With a nod, the man hurried away.

David closed the door and leaned his back against it. He would bring a whole shitload of hurt down upon Kirkland's head, he thought. And he knew where to strike first—at the man's heart and soul.

At the *Deep Fathom.*

5:45 P.M., aboard the *Deep Fathom*, east of the Kwajalein Atoll

It was Charlie Mollier's turn to prepare dinner. Behind him the galley door to the stern deck was open. But no breeze blew in to relieve the moist heat. The day had started out humid and grew worse as the sun climbed into the sky. In the galley, with both of the stove's burners going, the heat was stifling.

Charlie, though, whistled in tune to the reggae music of Bob Marley on the tape deck beside the sink. Wearing only a pair of baggy swim shorts that reached his knees, he swayed slightly as he stirred his homemade gungo pea and coconut soup, a family recipe. The spicy steam stung his nostrils. He smiled widely. "Nothin' like hot food on a hot day."

Reaching behind him, he tapped the blender. Its grinding roar drowned out the reggae music. "And margaritas, of course. Lots of margaritas!"

Ladle in hand, he spun around in sync with the chaotic melody of kitchen noises. With Jack gone, the entire ship had relaxed, enjoying the temporary reprieve. And Charlie was in an especially good mood. The moist heat, the tropical islands dotting the horizons . . . it was as if he were back home in the Caribbean. Bending over, he checked the oven. The fruity scent of his jerked chicken rolled out as he cracked the door open.

"Perfect," he said contentedly.

Bent over, he felt something goose him from behind. He snapped upward with a squawk of surprise. Swinging around, he found Elvis staring up at him. The German shepherd nosed Charlie again, a small whine rising from his throat.

"Come begging, my ol' *mon*? You smell ol' Charlie's cookin' and think to sneak a little mouthful?" He grinned at the large dog and grabbed a chicken wing from the countertop. "Don't go telling Jack, now. You know how he hates you begging. I'm not supposed to encourage you."

He held out the treat. Elvis sniffed at it, then backed up a step and gazed toward the open galley door.

Charlie frowned. "What's wrong, my ol' *mon*? Don't like my cookin'?"

Elvis backed toward the doorway and barked at Charlie.

"What's the matter with you?"

Lisa appeared in the doorway. "Now he's bothering you," she said with a concerned look. Lisa was dressed in a bikini. She'd been sunbathing on the aft deck. "He woke me up when I dozed off and wouldn't leave me alone until I shoved him away."

Charlie turned off the noisy blender. "Must be missin' Jack. The captain's never left the ship for longer than a day before."

"I guess."

From the ladder to the lower deck, Robert climbed into the galley. "Is dinner ready? I can smell your cooking all the way down in the bilge."

Charlie waved him off with an exaggerated scowl. "Your nose could smell bacon cooking from over the horizon." It was an ongoing joke. The young marine biologist had the most remarkable metabolic rate. He ate four times his body weight every day but remained as skinny as a bamboo pole.

"So is lunch ready?" Robert asked, hungrily eyeing the stove.

"Almost."

Robert glanced at Lisa, kneeling by Jack's dog. "Is something wrong with Elvis?"

Charlie shrugged. "Missing the boss, we think."

"He was pestering me all day. It wasn't until I hid in the cargo hold that he left me alone."

Lisa stood. "He's been bothering all of us . . . and I don't think it's all because of Jack being gone. I think it's something more."

As if understanding her, Elvis barked and wagged his tail. He edged through the galley door, then stopped and looked back at them.

"What is it?" Lisa asked. She stepped toward Elvis, and the dog moved another few steps away, stopping again, egging her to follow him. Lisa turned to Charlie and Robert. "He wants something."

Charlie rolled his eyes. "Maybe Timmy's stuck down in a well."

The trio moved after the dog. As if realizing his message had been understood, Elvis moved quickly, leading the group up the stairs to the bridge.

"Where's he going?" Robert asked.

Elvis scratched on the door. Lisa opened it for him, and the dog dashed toward the small hatch to the communications room.

Lisa glanced at the others with a frown, then opened the hatch door.

"Must be after a rat," Charlie said. "When he was a pup, he was always hunting them down. Better than any cat."

Inside the small space, Elvis had his nose pressed against a door to a lower drawer. Lisa pulled it open. Charlie crowded next to her. The drawer was full of fax paper and old receipts.

"I don't see anything," Lisa said.

"Maybe he wants you to fax a note to Jack," Robert joked.

Elvis nudged between Charlie and Lisa. He began pawing at the drawer, whining in the back of his throat. His digging became more vigorous.

"Okay, ol' *mon*. Let me help you." Charlie shouldered the dog aside and pulled free the drawer. He set it on the floor.

But Elvis ignored the drawer and had his nose pointed into the empty space in the cabinet. Charlie knelt on hands and knees and peered inside, but it was too dark. "Pass me a flashlight."

Robert grabbed one from the bridge and tossed it to Lisa, who passed it to Charlie.

With his cheek close to the deck, Charlie probed the light into the dark space. "If there's a rat in here . . ." he warned. Then the light reflected off something hidden in the dead space beneath the drawer's steel runners. "Oh, shit . . ."

"What is it?" Lisa asked.

Charlie swore under his breath. Leaning closer, he ran his light over the array of electronics perched atop a nest of tiny gray cubes. Red LED lights blinked at him. "I think I've found Elvis's rat."

7:50 P.M., ruins off the coast of Yonaguni

Karen sipped from her water bottle as they rested inside a roofless building among the Chatan ruins. "Stories of a lost continent in the Pacific aren't limited just to the islands," she continued, snugging her water bottle into her pack. "During the period of the Chinese Warring States, ancient stories describe a huge land mass in the Pacific, named Peng Jia. A place supposedly inhabited by a people who could fly and who lived forever."

"Uh-huh," her companion responded.

Karen looked at Jack, who leaned out one of the windows. He soaked his handkerchief with cold seawater, then sat on the windowsill, draping the wet cloth over his sweaty face. They had been clambering among these ruins all day, going from one site to another, stopping only for a cold lunch of bread and cheese. So far their search had proved fruitless. They had found a handful of barnacle-encrusted pieces of pottery and broken bits of statuary, but no further evidence of writing or crystals. Just rock and more rock. The ravages of sea, sand, and currents had erased everything but the basalt bones of this ancient city.

"Tired?" she asked, realizing her litany of stories were probably falling on deaf ears by now. She sat down on the wide sill beside him. "Sorry to take up your whole day. Maybe it would be best if we headed back." She checked her watch. "Hopefully, Miyuki has made some headway on the translations."

Jack pulled the wet handkerchief from his face and smiled. "There's nothing to apologize for. You've opened my eyes on a past I never knew existed out here. I've traveled these seas in search of treasures for over a decade, but never heard a tenth of these stories."

"Thanks for listening."

Jack stood. "But you're right. We should be heading back."

Karen glanced out the window. Dusk was falling. Long shadows crept across the waters. She nodded.

Jack helped her stand, his grip firm on her hand. They crossed over to the building's entrance where their motorboat was docked. Jack worked the rope loose, while Karen tossed her backpack into the stern.

Rope in hand, Jack suddenly froze. "Did you hear—" Then he was flying across the small room, tackling her to the hard floor. "Stay down."

She heard it, too. A high-pitched whistle that was growing louder. She lifted her head. "What is it?"

"Rockets," he hissed, straddling her.

"What—"

Then the world exploded with a crashing roar. Jack rolled off her and peeked out the window. Karen joined him. Off to the south she saw a billow of smoke and bits of rock climb high into the sky. As they watched, another explosion blew apart one of the basalt statues far to the west. A stone hand flew across the setting sun.

"What's happening?" Karen asked, cringing.

Overhead, a military jet streaked south. United States markings. Twin streams of fire bloomed as a pair of missiles were launched from the jet's underbelly, screaming across the darkening sky. Other jets shot past, one winging low across the islands, trailing smoke.

Jack pulled Karen back down. "Something tells me the blockade around Taiwan just exploded." Together, they crawled to a window. The southern horizon glowed as if a new sun were rising. "We'd better get clear of here."

Another explosion erupted nearby, quickly followed by another. Karen's ears rang with the echoing roars as she scrambled to her feet. Out the window the twilight sky was streaked with ribbons of smoke. They moved back to the door.

"Damn it," Jack muttered. Their motorboat, untethered a moment ago, had drifted several yards away. He shrugged out of his own pack and kicked off a boot. "I'll fetch it."

Karen grabbed his elbow as he teetered on one foot. Another telltale whistle pierced their ears, much louder this time. Jack's eyes were huge as he glanced at her. Together, they leaped away from the doorway and rolled behind sheltering walls.

Karen screamed as the blast shook the walls and dust showered her. The roar of the detonation seemed endless. Jack scuttled to her side. His lips moved but she could not make out his words. A huge boulder landed in the next room, crashing down. As the echoes faded, she could finally hear Jack's words.

". . . okay. It was a near hit, but we're safe."

She nodded, her eyes blurry with tears.

He helped her up. This time she remained in the shelter of his arms. They returned to the door.

Jack kicked off his other boot. "I'll just grab the boat, and we'll get our asses out of the line of fire."

Karen groaned as they reached the threshold. "Oh, no."

His grip tightened on her.

The squat building across the canal was a blasted ruin.
Smoke was so thick it was hard to see clearly. The force of
the explosion had blown the boat right back to their doorway. They could easily clamber back in. But the boat was
quickly filling with water. Huge rocks had pelted it, punch-
ing holes through its hull. Gas leaked in a slow spray from
its ruptured outboard tank.

"Now what?" Karen asked.

Jack shook his head.

More explosions erupted—but farther south. Jack pulled
Karen to his side. "Sit down."

They sank to the stone floor, leaning against the wall.
Each explosion trembled the stones. Karen found herself
leaning less on the wall and more on Jack's arm.

For a half hour they listened. Beyond the window, full
night descended. The whistle of rocket fire and dull rumblings continued, but now far to the south.

Jack finally spoke. "I think maybe they're done with us.
Just retaliatory strikes. Harassing fire meant to intimidate. I
think we'll be okay. We'll hole up here tonight. In the morning I'll swim to Chatan and get help."

Karen shivered with his words. "The Chinese—"

"I think they'll leave us alone now." Jack got up and
crossed to the doorway. "I'll keep watch."

Karen stood and joined him. She kept near his shoulder.
With the night already cold, she could feel the heat radiating
from Jack's body and leaned closer.

The dark sky was foggy with smoke. A jet sped past to
the west. Karen followed its course with worry. Movement
closer at hand caught her eye. Glancing to the sea beyond
the ruins, she spotted a brief glint of starlight on metal.
"What's that?" she asked, squinting.

"What?"

She pointed.

Jack squinted, then fished her binoculars out of her pack.
He stared through them for a few seconds and scowled.
"Great . . ."

"What is it?"

"Conning tower. Chinese sub. Now I know why they were bombarding the ruins. Covering fire as it crept beyond the blockade. I spotted some type of special forces team loading into a pontoon."

"Why? What are they doing?"

"Probably being sent in for surveillance and sabotage." He lowered the binoculars. "How good a swimmer are you?"

Cold terror trickled through her veins. "I was on the university's intramural swim team. But that was ten years ago."

"Good enough. We're getting out of here."

Off in the distance, silent explosions bloomed in fiery flowers.

"We'll be okay," he promised.

Through the rumbling explosions, Karen heard a sound much closer. A scuff of rock. She swung around and was startled to see a dark stranger standing in the doorway. "Jack!"

He spun, moving like a lion.

The man leveled a pistol at him.

Even in the gloom, Karen recognized the tattoo on the man's forearm: a coiled snake with ruby eyes.

5:55 A.M., Washington, D.C.

A knock on the door woke Lawrence Nafe. He pushed to one elbow. "What is it?" he asked blearily. He glanced to the clock on the nightstand. It was not even six.

The door swung partly open. "Sir?"

He recognized the voice and felt a twinge of misgiving. "Nicolas?" The CIA director had never called upon him in his bedroom. "What's gone wrong?"

Nicolas Ruzickov entered the room, pausing at the threshold. "I'm sorry to disturb you and the First Lady, but—"

Nafe rubbed his eyes. "Melanie is still down in Virginia

for the dedication of some damned statue. What do you want?"

Ruzickov closed the door firmly behind him. "The Chinese have attacked Okinawa."

"What?" Nafe sat up and switched on a lamp. In the light, he saw that the director was wearing the same suit as the night before.

Ruzickov moved farther into the room. "We've just received word of skirmishes between their forces and ours along the Ryukyu Island chain."

"Who shot first?"

"All our reports claim the Chinese . . ."

"And what are the Chinese saying?"

"That we attempted to break their blockade of Taiwan, and they were defending."

"Great, just great . . . and which is true?"

"Sir?"

"Between us and these four walls, who pulled the first trigger?"

Ruzickov glanced at a chair. Nafe waved him into it. The CIA director sat down with a long sigh. "Does it matter? The Chinese know of our intention to push for a formal declaration of war. If they mean to hold the region, Okinawa is the closer and more significant threat. They've been bombarding the island with missile fire."

"And the damage?"

"A few strikes. Uninhabited areas. So far, our new Patriot missiles are doing a satisfactory job of protecting the island."

Nafe eyed his CIA director. "What are we going to do?"

"The Joint Chiefs have already convened in the Situation Room, awaiting your order."

Nafe got out of bed and paced the room. "With this newest aggression directed against our forces in the Pacific—" He stared pointedly at Ruzickov. "Unprovoked, of course . . ."

"That is the way all newscasts will report it."

He nodded. "Then we should have little political opposition to a formal declaration of war."

"No, sir."

Nafe stopped before the mantel of the cold fireplace. "I'll address the Joint Chiefs, but I want Congress fully behind this declaration. I don't want another Vietnam."

Ruzickov stood. "I'll make sure all is in order."

Nafe clenched a fist. "If need be, we'll bring this war to Beijing. It's about time we instilled the fear of God into the Chinese people."

"That's all they respond to, sir. Strength. We cannot show weakness."

Nafe scowled. "And neither will we show them mercy."

8:14 P.M., ruins off the coast of Yonaguni

Crouched, Jack eyed the snub end of the pistol pointed at his chest. In a fraction of a second he quickly calculated the odds of disarming their assailant. He would have to take a bullet—there was no way around it—but he could still tackle the smaller man and probably knock the gun away. But what then? Depending on where he was hit, could he keep the man down long enough for Karen to grab the weapon? And what if there were others?

"He's the leader of the group that attacked us before," Karen whispered beside him, hands half raised.

Recalling Karen's stories, Jack leaned closer to her. "I can take him out . . . but be ready."

"How can I help?"

He was surprised by Karen's resolve. This woman was no wilting flower. "A distraction—"

Before any plan could be set in motion, the man acted first. "Come wit' me," he whispered in stilted English. "We must leave here. Danger." He lowered his gun and holstered it at his waist.

Jack straightened from his half crouch, suspicious. He looked with confusion toward Karen, who wore a matching expression. "Do we trust this guy?" he asked.

She shrugged. "He didn't shoot us."

The man disappeared through the low doorway into the

roofless building's rear chamber. Jack glanced behind him. Distant explosions continued to echo across the water. Through the window, the glow of fires dotted the southern horizon.

Karen nodded toward the grim view. "It's not like we have a lot of choices here. Maybe we should go."

Jack joined her. "Yeah, but did you ever hear the expression, 'Out of the frying pan, into the fire'?"

She waved him through the doorway. "Then by all means, you go first."

Jack ducked through the low door and found the stranger standing by another window, his back to them.

Beyond the window, a small dark boat floated in the lapping waters. As Jack moved nearer, he recognized it as a sampan, one of the ubiquitous fishing vessels of the eastern seas. Made of wood, it was short and narrow-beamed, with its stern half covered in a frame of bamboo and tattered tarpaulin. Two other men were aboard the sampan. One held the mooring line and kept glancing nervously to the south.

"Chinese come," the leader said, indicating that Jack should board the vessel. "We take you to Okinawa."

Karen joined Jack and gave him a gentle nudge. "We could always jump overboard if there's trouble."

Gathering his pack in one hand, Jack climbed over the stone sill. The man with the mooring line offered him a hand of support, but Jack ignored it. Instead, he dropped to the boat and eyed the men. Dark-skinned and short, they were clearly South Pacific islanders, but he could not place where exactly. He noticed that both men wore holstered weapons.

With a moan of complaint, Karen landed beside him. She grabbed his elbow as the boat shifted under her weight. He steadied her, but she kept her grip on him. "Okay, now what?"

Behind them a few terse words were passed between the leader and his men before he climbed in to join them. Once aboard, he waved for Karen and Jack to follow him under the overhang.

The other two men used long paddles to push away and propel them between the buildings. Jack now understood how he had been ambushed. The sampan moved silently through the waters, its dark wood matching the sea.

As they glided, Jack searched for the Chinese submarine. It was gone—as was the pontoon full of armed men. They could be anywhere.

For close to twenty minutes, the sampan slowly drifted among the ruins, moving skillfully through the dark. No one spoke. Distant thunder warned of the war to the south. At last, two large structures towered to either side.

The Chatan pyramids.

From his spot under the overhang, Jack allowed himself a sigh of relief. They were almost free of the ruins.

Rifle fire suddenly tore through the tarpaulin fabric. Bullets chewed into the old wooden sides of the boat. Jack pulled Karen to the floor, shielding her. The leader yelled orders.

A motor at the stern suddenly roared. Jack felt the bow end lift as the prop dug into the water. The sampan lurched forward.

A small explosion blew not far from the stern. A column of water flumed up. Grenade.

Hurry, he urged silently. Rifle fire continued to pepper the boat.

The leader, busy with the rudder, leaned toward Jack. He held out his pistol, offering it. Jack hesitated, then took it. The man pointed to the bow.

Jack crawled forward.

"Jack?" Karen warned.

"Stay down. I'll be right back."

Jack inched his way toward the other two men, who crouched with pistols in hand. When he reached them, he silently pantomimed that they should wait for his signal.

Free of the shelter, there was a light breeze. Jack listened as rifle fire pelted the starboard rail over his head, digging away chunks of teak. He waited for a pause in the attack.

When it happened, he jerked up, firing blindly in the direction of the rifle blasts. The other two followed suit. Jack fired for a count of five, then ducked down. Again the other two men followed his lead.

Covering his head, the next barrage was less riotous. Most shots whizzed by harmlessly. By now the sampan had gained sufficient speed to race and bounce away. Jack stayed down. When they were past the range of the rifles, the men tentatively stood.

Jack rolled to his feet and slipped under the overhang. He found Karen sitting up, eyes worried. "You okay?" he asked.

She nodded.

The leader met Jack's gaze. They stared at each other quietly for a moment, then Jack handed the pistol back. The man took the weapon, slipped it back into its holster, and waved them to a worn teak bench.

Karen sat down, but Jack remained standing. He wanted answers. "Who are you?" he asked.

"I am Mwahu, son of Waupau."

"Why did you help us?"

This earned a scowl from the man. "Elders say we must. To punish us. We failed our great ancestor."

"Failed to do what?" Jack jerked a thumb in Karen's direction. "Failed to kill her and her friend last week?"

"Jack . . ." Karen cautioned him under her breath.

Mwahu leaned on the rudder, glancing away. "We want to hurt no one. Only to protect. It is our duty."

"I don't understand," Karen said softly. "Protect who?"

The man remained silent.

"Who?" Jack repeated.

He raised his eyes to the roof. "Protect the world. Oldest teachings say that none must disturb the stone villages, or a curse will come to destroy us all." He glanced back toward the fires near the horizon. "Already the curse comes."

Jack leaned toward Karen. "Do you recognize any of his mumbo jumbo?"

She shook her head but kept her eyes on the leader. "Mwahu, tell me more about these teachings. Whose are they?"

"The words of our great ancestor, Horon-ko, were written long ago. Only elders read it."

"Elders of which island? Where is your home?"

"No island home." He cast an arm to encompass the open seas. "Here is our home."

"The ocean?"

He frowned and turned his back on Karen. "No."

"Mwahu—"

"I no speak no more of it. The elders tell me to help you. I help you."

Jack interrupted. "Why did they tell you to?"

The islander fingered the coiled serpent tattoo. "Elder Rau-ren says you cannot put poison back into snake's fang once it bites." He lowered his arm, signaling the end to this discussion. "Killing the snake, no good. Only help can save you."

"In other words," Karen whispered to Jack, "the cat's out of the bag. The wrong can't be undone."

"What wrong?" Jack asked.

"Something about us taking the crystal out of the pyramid."

He frowned. "Everything keeps coming back to the crystal."

"If his elders have some ancient text that warns about these ruins, it must have come from the same era in which they were built." Karen stood up, excited. "Mwahu, can you read any of the ancient writings?"

He glanced at her. "Some. My father was an elder. He teach me before he die."

Karen shuffled in her pack for pen and paper. Moving closer to Mwahu, she held the paper to the deck and scrawled a crude rendition of a few of the symbols. He leaned over, one hand still on the long wooden rudder.

"Can you read any of this?" she asked.

As he stared at it, his breathing became harder and his eyes widened. Then, abruptly, he ripped it from the deck, crumpled it and tossed it into the sea. "It is forbidden!" he said between clenched teeth.

Karen backed away from his vehemence and sat down. "It must be the same language," she said to Jack. "But clearly there's some taboo about putting it to paper."

"Maybe it's their attempt to maintain the language's secrecy."

She was thoughtful for a moment. "You're probably right, but I've never heard of any island sect like this. Why the mystery? What were his ancestors warning against?"

Jack shook his head. "Who knows?"

"Perhaps there might be an answer in the inscriptions. If we could get Mwahu to help us, it might accelerate our work."

"That is, if you can trust anything this man says."

Karen sighed. "He seems sincere enough. And he clearly believes what he said."

"Just because he believes it doesn't make it true."

"I suppose. Still, it's a place to begin." She leaned back, her eyes glazing as she stared out at the sea.

Sighing, he leaned back, too, but ignored the view and kept a wary watch on the three men aboard the boat. They might claim to want to help, but considering Karen and Miyuki's encounters with them, he knew they could be dangerous.

The rest of the journey was made in silence. Soon the lights of Naha's harbor could be seen ahead. Even from a mile out, it was apparent that the island was in turmoil. The U.S. base on the south side of the harbor was lit up like Times Square. Planes of all sizes circled the island, while the waters ahead were thick with military vessels.

Jack and Karen moved to the bow. She pointed. One of the government buildings was now a cratered and smoking ruin.

"Rocket strike," Jack commented.

Karen's eyes widened. "Miyuki . . ."

He took her hand in his. "I'm sure she's fine. The university is inland, away from the most likely targets. Besides, she has thirty-nine U.S. military bases protecting her."

Karen did not look convinced.

En route to the island, their own boat was stopped twice and searched before it was allowed to proceed. Jack was glad to see the trio's weapons taken from them during the first search. He had tried to urge Karen to abandon these islanders and board the military cutter, but she refused. "Mwahu might hold the only key to this language," she'd mumbled. "I can't lose him."

So they remained on the sampan as it glided through the harbor to the marina. They moored and climbed onto the docks. A Japanese officer checked their papers. Jack was surprised to see the Pacific islanders produce tattered and weathered passports.

When the officer handed back all their papers, he spoke to them in English. "You picked a poor time to go sightseeing. We've had a flood of refugees from the south. We're trying to divert as many to the north as possible. Otherwise, all other civilians are being evacuated via the international airport."

"You're evacuating the entire island?" Jack asked.

"Or relocating them into bunkers. As many as we can. We don't expect fighting to reach our shores, but we're taking no chances. Another rocket barrage could occur at any time. I suggest you collect your personal belongings and report to the airport."

Karen nodded. "Ryukyu University . . . ?"

"It's already cleared out." The man waved them down the dock as more makeshift crafts drifted in. "Good luck."

Jack led Karen and Mwahu toward the shore and the city. Mwahu's two men remained with the sampan. Karen moved up next to Jack. "What if Miyuki is already gone?" she asked.

"She'll be there. I can't imagine her leaving her lab unless they dragged her out kicking and screaming."

She smiled at that. Without thinking, Jack put his arm around her. Karen leaned in to him, tucking herself against his side.

No words were spoken. With Mwahu following, they moved on through the earthquake-ravaged city to where a bus still serviced the university area. It was a short ride to Ryukyu, and a quiet walk to the computer facility.

Once at the steps, Karen pointed toward the fifth floor. There were no lights on. Then they discovered that the door to the building was locked and the lobby dark. "Hello!" she called out, knocking.

A guard appeared around a corner, his flashlight's beam washing across the three of them and settling on Karen.

"Professor Grace," he said with clear relief. He climbed the stairs, passing Mwahu with a suspicious glance. With a jangle of keys, he moved to the door. "Professor Nakano refused to leave until you returned."

"Is she in her lab?"

"No, she's in my office. We've locked down all the upper floors."

He opened the door and led them into the lobby, guiding them with his flashlight through the dark interior. From under a door ahead, light glowed. The guard knocked, then pushed the door open.

Miyuki was sitting at a desk, the thick briefcase open before her containing a portable computer. At the sight of them, she burst to her feet. "Thank God you're okay!"

"We're fine," Karen said, hugging her reassuringly. "What about you?"

"Shaken up. Lots of fireworks."

Karen noticed the portable computer. "What are you doing?" she asked.

"I couldn't risk losing all our work. So I diverted Gabriel into moving all our research off site and backed up everything onto this computer, just in case. I also revamped the portable unit to accommodate Gabriel." Miyuki reached out and touched a key.

A familiar disembodied voice arose from the tiny speakers. *"Good evening, Professor Nakano. I will continue troubleshooting our connections and interfaces to make certain all is in order."*

"Thank you, Gabriel."

Behind Jack, the South Pacific islander pushed into the room, glancing with suspicion toward the computer. Miyuki noticed him and jerked back.

Karen put a hand on her shoulder, steadying her. "It's okay," she said. "I'll explain it all later."

Keeping a watch on the tattooed stranger, Miyuki snapped the computer case closed. She unhooked the cables and wound them up. "We need to leave."

"I heard about the evacuation. Do you have the crystal?"

Miyuki frowned at her, then tilted her head toward Mwahu.

"It *really* is okay," she said. "He's here to help us now."

Miyuki hardly looked convinced. Jack moved beside her. "And if it helps, he's alone and unarmed."

She studied Jack for a breath, then seemed to sag. "The star's in my luggage." She nodded toward a wheeled suitcase behind the desk. "I also went to your flat and collected everything I could see that you might want . . . including Jack's stuff." She pointed to a second suitcase.

"We could've done it ourselves," Karen said.

"Not if you want to catch a flight off this island. My cousin pilots a small private jet, a charter service. He's agreed to get us out, but we have to leave—" She glanced at her watch. "—in thirty minutes."

Jack frowned. Everything was moving too fast. "Where to? Tokyo?"

Miyuki bit her lip. "No. I thought it best if we leave the area entirely."

"Then where?" Karen asked.

"I asked him to take us to Pohnpei Island." Miyuki looked from one of them to the other. "I thought if we had to go somewhere, why not follow the one clue in the transcription? To the ruins at Nan Madol."

Karen laughed. "Fantastic. I knew you were an adventurer at heart."

"It's not a bad plan," Jack said. "We can search for additional clues without being in the middle of a war zone. But I'll need to contact my ship first, let them know the change in plans."

"Oh God, in all the craziness, I forgot. Just before I left Karen's apartment, I received a call from your boat. A Charles Molder."

"Charlie Mollier?"

"Right. He seemed anxious to speak to you."

"When did he call?"

"About half an hour ago."

"Is there a working phone around here?"

Miyuki nodded. "The line I was using for the computer should still be okay." She hooked up a small desk phone and passed him the receiver.

He crouched over the desk and tapped in the *Deep Fathom*'s satellite number. A short burst of static briefly turned into Charlie's voice.

"Jack? Is that you?"

"Yeah, what's up? All hell's breaking loose out here and I'm heading to Pohnpei."

"In Micronesia?"

"Yeah, it's too long a story. You still near Kwajalein?"

"Yeah, but—"

"It's not that far from Pohnpei. Can you meet us there?"

"Yeah, but—"

"Good. I'll keep you post—"

"Goddamn it, Jack!" Charlie burst in. "Listen to me."

"What?" Jack realized he hadn't asked Charlie why he'd called.

"We've got a bomb on board here."

It took Jack a few moments to understand. "A bomb?"

"A goddamn bomb. As in big fucking explosion."

"How . . . ? Who . . . ?"

"It was planted in the radio room."

"Get rid of it!"

"Oh jeez, *mon*, why didn't I think of that? I may not know much about explosive devices, but this baby looks booby-trapped and has an electronic receiver. I ain't touching it."

As his shock bled away, Jack suspected that David Spangler was the culprit behind the bomb. He remembered the little gift of Chinese electronics. "Spangler," he hissed.

"What?"

"One of Spangler's men must have planted it." In the back of his mind he wondered if this act of sabotage was simply revenge on David's part, or if David had suspected that he was on to something. "Listen, Charlie, I don't know

what you're still doing on the *Fathom*, but get everyone off
and alert the authorities."

"Already working on that. We've got the launch outfitted.
Everyone is loaded up, except Robert and I. You almost
missed us."

"Get your asses out of there! Why did you even bother to
call?"

"We were hoping you could talk us through defusing it?"

"Are you insane?"

"Hell, it's the *Fathom* we're talking about, Jack."

Jack gripped the receiver tightly. "Listen to me—"

"Just a sec . . ."

Jack heard Charlie call out, then heard another voice,
faintly in the background. It was Robert. *"The light . . . it's
blinking more rapidly."*

Oh, God! Jack yelled into the phone. "Charlie! Get out of
there!"

The receiver suddenly squelched with static, standing his
small hairs on end—then the phone went ominously dead.
"Charlie!" He clicked the receiver again and again. A dial
tone returned. Savagely, he tapped in the code for the *Deep
Fathom* again. "Goddamn it!"

Karen stood behind him. "Jack? What's wrong?"

He didn't answer. He listened as the satellite connection
fed through, but all he got as an answer was a screech of
white noise. Then nothing again. He lowered the phone. He
was numb all over, fearing the worst. He prayed it was just
the connection frizzing out. But in his heart he knew he was
wrong. He had heard the panic in Robert's voice.

"Jack?" Karen placed a hand on his shoulder.

He slowly lowered the receiver into its cradle. "I . . . I
think someone just blew up my ship."

10:55 P.M., aboard the *Maggie Chouest*, Central Pacific

"It's done," Gregor Handel said. "I'm reading nothing from
the *Deep Fathom*. Not even a mayday. She's tits up, sir."

"Perfect." David lowered the headset from his ears. Earlier, Rolfe had succeeded in breaking the *Fathom*'s Globalstar code, allowing them to tap into the transmitted call. Using the headphones, David had eavesdropped on the final phone conversation between Jack and his ship. He placed the headset on the table. "What could be better?" he said. "Jack knew it was me. He heard his fucking ship explode. And he knows his crew was still on board."

Rolfe spoke from his station. "I've got the port authority of Kwajalein. Do you want me to send a helicopter to confirm?"

"Wait about an hour. Ideally, we don't want any survivors."

Handel made a scoffing noise. "With that much C-4, almost a pound, there's a kill zone of a good hundred yards. Nothing could've survived."

David's grin grew wider. "Well done, men." He reached under the table and pulled out a bottle of Dom Pérignon. He raised the bottle. "To the perfect execution of this mission."

"Execution is right," Rolfe said with a smirk of satisfaction.

David stood and twisted the cork free of the bottle. It popped and shot across the cabin. As the champagne frothed over the neck, he lifted the bottle high. "And this is only the first step in bringing Kirkland down."

15

Pohnpei

Karen sat in the spacious cabin of the private Learjet as it taxied across the tarmac of Pohnpei's airport. Outside, a fine misty rain drizzled down, muting the views of the jungle-draped peaks of the South Pacific island. As the plane turned, the island's most prominent feature came into view: Sokehs Rock, a towering volcanic plug overlooking Kolonia harbor, nicknamed the "Diamond Head of Micronesia."

"It's beautiful," Miyuki said beside her, leaning closer. Her friend, clearly exhausted, had slept most of the way, only awakening as the plane began to land.

Karen, however, had not been able to sleep. Neither had Jack. She stared across the cabin. He still sat stiff in his seat, barely noticing the passing scenery. Mwahu sat slumped beside him, snoring.

Earlier, after boarding the plane, Jack had spent a few frantic hours trying to discover the fate of his ship. By the time he reached someone in authority who would listen, he was informed that a search helicopter had already been sent out to investigate. So they were forced to wait. Jack had paced up and down the cabin, clenching and unclenching his fists. When the report finally came in, it was not good.

Lit by a burning pool of oil, the debris from the ship had been easy to spot.

After the news, Jack had not spoken a word. He'd crossed to the cabin's bar, poured himself a couple fingers of whiskey, downed it, and repeated it two more times until Karen coaxed him back to his seat. And there he had sat, just staring, unblinking. At first she had tried to engage him in conversation, but his only response was cold and savage: "I'm going to kill that bastard." So she returned to her seat, watching the world pass beneath her.

It had been a monotonous journey until they reached their destination. Before landing, the jet circled the island. Pohnpei was roughly thirteen miles across, encircled by a protective ring of coral reefs, creating an island of lagoons and mangrove swamps. Inland, its mountainous interior was all rain forests, streams, waterfalls, and steep cliffs.

Studying the circular island from above, Karen had hoped to spot Pohnpei's other well-known feature—the seaside ruins of Nan Madol—but the mists had been too thick on the southeast side of the island.

Miyuki settled back in her seat as the jet taxied toward the terminal. She nodded toward Jack. "Is he going to be okay?"

"It'll take time, I think." Karen knew Jack bore a lot of guilt. It was etched in the lines on his face and the hollowness in his eyes.

As the plane rolled to a stop, Miyuki unbuckled her seat belt. "Let's get him moving. Try to get his mind off what happened."

Karen nodded, though she doubted it would help. Jack's brooding went beyond simple distraction.

Across the cabin, Mwahu stretched. "We here?"

"Yes," Karen said, freeing herself from her seat. Jack had still not moved.

Fresh sunlight entered as the aft door cracked open. Karen crossed the cabin as Mwahu and Miyuki moved toward the exit. She sat down and touched Jack's arm. "Are you all right?"

He remained silent for a few moments, then spoke, his voice numb: "It was all my fault . . . again. First the *Atlantis*, now the *Fathom*."

"It wasn't your fault."

He didn't seem to hear her. "I should never have left. If I'd been there, I could've defused the bomb."

"And maybe you would've been killed with them. Then this Spangler fellow would have truly won. If what you say is right—that he planted the bomb amidst the wreckage aboard the *Gibraltar*—then you're the only one who knows the truth. All hope of exposing him would be lost if you were killed."

"What does the truth matter? It's not worth this cost." Jack finally looked directly at her.

Karen was shocked at the pain in those blue eyes. She had an urge to pull him to her chest, to envelope him, to hold him until the pain went away, but knew any true solace could not come from her. He would have to find his own way past this tragedy. "If you want justice for your friends," she said softly but firmly, "you're gonna have to win it. You're not gonna get it by killing Spangler."

Rage flickered through his pain. "Then how?"

She faced his anger and matched it. "By exposing the goddamn bastard, Jack. That's how you'll win!" She touched his knee. "And I'll help you. You're not alone in this, Jack. You have to understand that."

He closed his eyes, sighed, and after a few moments opened them again. The pain was still there, but it was not all-consuming anymore. She saw a glimmer of the Jack she had met in the Okinawa airport. "Maybe you're right," he said. "There's too much at stake. David needs to be brought down, but the only way to do it is to discover the truth about Air Force One. I won't let him win."

"We'll do it together."

Jack nodded, almost reluctantly.

Karen sensed a critical moment had passed between

them. . . . that the ex-SEAL seldom allowed anyone to share his grief or his guilt.

Turning in his seat, Jack took her hand from his knee and raised it to his lips. The brief touch on her skin sent an electric thrill through her. "Thank you," he whispered.

Shocked at the sudden intimacy, Karen could not move.

Jack lowered her hand. In his eyes, she saw a twinge of bewilderment, as if the impulsive act had surprised him as much as it had her.

Miyuki called from the doorway with a wave, "We need to go."

The two stared at each other for a silent moment.

"Let's go," Karen finally said. "We have a lot to plan."

8:23 A.M., *Maggie Chouest*, Central Pacific

David stood near the stern of the research vessel. Behind him the last of his team's gear was being loaded into the helicopter. The journey to Pohnpei Island would take seven hours. With Ruzickov's help, the U.S. embassy on the island had been alerted and expected his arrival.

"Commander Spangler."

David swung around. He had been so lost in his own plans that he hadn't heard the approach of the paunchy Mexican leader of the research group. "What is it, Cortez?"

"You asked that I inform you when we were ready to evacuate the water from Neptune base."

David cleared his throat. "Of course. Are you prepared?"

"Yes, sir. If you'll join us in the command center, you can oversee the process."

David gestured the man to lead. Cortez crossed to the ship's superstructure and wound toward the main monitoring station on the second level. The ex-wardroom was now a jumble of computers, monitors, and other equipment. Four other scientists were crowded into the small room but they made space for David, moving out of his way with nervous glances.

Cortez motioned David to join him before a console of monitors. He tapped two of the screens. "Here we have feeds from the two ROV robots. As you can see, Neptune is ready for the second stage."

David studied the assembled base. It was a stack of three doughnuts, one atop the other, sitting on a four-legged frame. Power cables and other lines wound from its top shell toward the surface. He watched as one of the robots positioned another of the site's "lamp poles." Each illumination pole was six meters, surmounted by a sealed halogen spotlight. Twelve in all, the poles were positioned around the base. The dark seabed had become a well-lit parking lot.

In the bright lights, David watched the *Perseus*, piloted by Lieutenant Brentley, slowly circle the large sea base. Now assembled, the structure contained almost four thousand square feet of living space.

Cortez sat down at the console. "Watch the three center monitors; I'm going to bring up the inner cameras. One for each level of the complex."

Murky images appeared on the screens, watery views of dim rooms. Little detail could be discerned. The only light filtered through tiny portholes along the curved walls.

"What am I looking at?" David asked.

Cortez tapped the first monitor. "The lowest level is solely for docking the submersibles. The middle level houses the labs; the top level, living quarters." He glanced over his shoulder at David. "We chose this arrangement so, in case of emergency, the top level could be freed manually and rise to the surface on its own. There are multiple redundant safety features built throughout the complex."

David sighed, not bothering to hide his exasperation. "Fine. Are you ready to drain the complex or not?"

"Certainly. We've triple-checked everything."

"Then let's get this done. I'm due to leave within the hour." Off to the side, David caught the relieved smile pass between the two technicians. It seemed his team's absence would not be missed.

"We were just awaiting your arrival." Cortez busied himself at one of the computers. He spoke into a microphone.

"*Perseus*, this is Topside. Clear for blowout. I repeat, clear for blowout."

On one of the monitors the torpedo-shaped submersible banked sharply and glided away from the sea base. Lieutenant Brentley's voice scratched from a set of speakers. "Roger that. Clearing out."

"Here we go," Cortez said. He tapped a series of buttons on his keyboard. "Level 1 . . . *blowing*. Level 2 . . . *blowing*. Level 3 . . . *blowing*."

On the screens the view of the deep-sea station vanished in an explosion of bubbles, the visibility obscured by the roiling waters.

"Look." Cortez pointed to the center monitors.

The interior views were clearing as the water lines dropped below the level of the camera lenses. Within a few minutes the water drained away, leaving the rooms wet but habitable. Interior lights flickered, then blazed.

"Bringing the pressure down to one atmosphere," Cortez said. "Checking hull integrity." He smiled up at David. "Green lights all around, Commander. Neptune is ready for company."

David clapped the Mexican on the shoulder. As much as he hated to admit it, the man knew his job. "Good work, Cortez."

"We can take it from here, Commander." The research leader stood up from his console. "I know you've been ordered away for a few days, but there's no need to worry. My team won't let you down."

"It had better not," David said as he turned to leave, but he could not give his statement much heat. Cortez ran a tight ship.

Leaving the command center, David climbed down to the deck. As soon as he pushed out of the air-conditioned superstructure and into the heat, he was met by his second-in-command.

Rolfe was dressed in a black flight jacket. "We're loaded and ready, sir," he said. "Jeffreys just heard from our contacts on Pohnpei. Jack Kirkland and the woman landed an hour ago. They're under surveillance as we speak."

"Good." Everything was going well. First the base, now this. It was as if Kirkland were trying to make his job easier, David thought. To extract the scientist and her crystal from the growing war zone around Okinawa would have been complicated. But out in the backwaters of Micronesia, on an island sympathetic to American concerns, it shouldn't be a problem. Everything was falling into perfect place.

"Sir, Jeffreys also reports that the woman has been making inquiries about hiring a boat to take them all to some ruins on the southeast side of the island."

David nodded. Overnight he had studied topographic maps of Pohnpei. He knew the island's entire terrain by heart. "When are they planning to go out there?"

"Late afternoon."

David thought a moment and nodded. There should just be enough time. "Get me Jeffreys. I want a boat arranged." He zipped up his jacket. "We're going to prepare a little welcome for Mr. Kirkland and his friends."

4:34 P.M., Pohnpei Island, Madolenihmw Municipality

Jack's headache still pounded behind his eyes. And the bumpy ride along the jungle road in an old rusted Jeep Cherokee wasn't helping. Karen sat behind the wheel, squinting through the grimy window for landmarks.

"Are you sure you know where you're going?" Miyuki asked from the rear seat. A particularly large bump sent the small woman flying for the roof. She swore at Karen in her native language.

"This is the right way," Mwahu said, also in the backseat. "Bridge to Temwen Island is not far."

"So you've been to Nan Madol before?" Karen asked, trying to glean more information from the man.

"Sacred place. I visit with father three times."

Karen glanced at Jack, as if to stress the coincidence.

Jack rubbed his temples, trying to grind away the headache. After landing, he had finally slept a bit, but the pain of the last twenty-four hours could not be alleviated with a nap.

While he'd slept, Karen had hired a car and arranged for a boat to explore the ruins of Nan Madol. Because the best time to explore was at high tide, they were leaving late in the day, when boats could traverse the meter-deep canals. Otherwise, at low tide, it meant slogging through the ruins in knee-deep water and mud.

Clearing his throat, Jack sought some way to distract himself from the pounding in his skull. "Karen, you never did tell me the full story of Nan Madol. What's so special about this place?"

"There are many stories and myths surrounding this island," she replied, "but the story of Nan Madol's origin is the most intriguing. According to the myth, two demigods, Olhosihpa and Olhosohpa, came to the island in a great ship from some lost land. With magical powers they transported the gigantic basalt logs across the island and helped the natives build the canal city. Some say the stone logs flew through the air."

Jack shook his head. "Yeah, right."

Karen shrugged. "Of course, who knows the truth for sure? But mysteries remain. Some of the stones weigh up to fifty tons. The entire complex of Nan Madol is composed of 250 million tons of crystalline basalt. How did it all get there?"

Jack shrugged. "On large rafts. Bamboo is great building material, and there's plenty of it on the island." He nodded to the rain forest out the windows.

Karen shook her head. "Back in 1995, researchers tried to float a one-ton basalt log using every sort of raft imaginable. They failed. The best they could manage was a stone that weighed a couple hundred pounds. So how did these unsophisticated natives move rocks weighing *fifty tons*? And once at the site, how did they lift and stack them forty feet in the air?"

Jack's brow crinkled. As much as he hated to admit it, the mystery was intriguing. How *had* it been done?

Karen continued, "I have no idea what the real answer is, but I find the myth of the demigods interesting. Another story of a magical people from a lost continent."

Jack settled back in his seat. "So how old are these ruins?"

"Hmm . . . that's another bit of controversy. Nine hundred years is the current estimate, based on carbon dating on fire pits done by the Smithsonian Institute in the sixties. But others have argued for an older date."

"Why?"

"Carbon-dating of the fire pits only proves that it was *occupied* during this time, not that the place was built then. In the early seventies an archaeologist from Honolulu, using newer techniques, came up with a date over two thousand years old." Karen shrugged. "So who can say for sure?"

From the backseat Miyuki shifted forward and pointed between them. "Look."

Karen slowed the Cherokee as raw sunlight appeared ahead. It was the end of the forest road.

"Finally," Jack murmured.

The view opened before them as they swung out of the forest. A wide bay lay ahead, sparkling in the late afternoon sunlight. In the middle of the bay towered a steep mountainous island, fringed by swamps. From the height of the jungle road, a coral reef could be seen in the shallows circling the small island, mottling the blue waters in hues of rose and jade.

Karen pointed. "Nan Madol is on the far side of Temwen Island. Facing the open ocean."

Turning, she guided the Jeep down the steep grade toward a long, two-lane steel bridge that spanned the strait between coast and island. They descended into shadows as the sun, setting toward the western horizon, disappeared behind the mountainous peaks of Pohnpei. Then they were trundling across the bridge, passing over coral atolls and deep blue waters.

Karen played tour guide. "The harbors around here are fraught with submerged sections of other ruins: columns, walls, stone roads, even a small sunken castle. Back during

World War Two, Japanese divers reported discovering caskets made of pure platinum down there."

"Platinum? Here?"

"Yep. The divers brought up quite a bit of it. Platinum became one of the island's major exports during the Japanese occupation."

Jack eyed the water. "Strange."

"In fact, just recently a large megalithic discovery was made in the deep waters off the east coast of Nahkapw Island." She pointed to a speck of an island just visible near the southern horizon. "A submerged stone village named Kahnihnw Namkhet. For decades natives told stories about it, but it was only in the last five years that divers rediscovered it."

With a kidney-jarring bump the Jeep left the bridge and turned onto the coastal road that circled the small island. Karen accelerated. Soon they wound out of the shadows and into the sunlight of the southern coastline.

Ahead and below, the ruins of Nan Madol appeared.

Jack lowered his map, stunned by the sight. Spreading far out into the shallow sea from the coastline were a hundred man-made islets. The buildings and fortifications were all composed of basalt columns and slabs, constructed similar to American-style log cabins. Framing the entire site was a gigantic sea wall, also of basalt.

"Amazing," he said. "I can see now why the place is called the Venice of the Pacific." The ancient city spread over ten square miles, with canals intersecting and connecting the entire community. Mangrove trees and ferns grew thickly throughout it. Looking down, the stones of the city sparked in the sunlight, reflecting off the quartz crystals in the basalt.

"It's been compared to the building of the Great Wall of China," Karen said. "They built the entire city atop the coral reef, carving deeper channels and canals out of the reef itself. There's also an extensive tunnel system connecting the various islets. It was lucky the eclipse-day quakes weren't too bad out here. It would've been a great tragedy to lose this historic site."

Jack stared, struck by its breadth and size. "It's so large."

Karen nodded and guided their vehicle down the last few switchbacks toward the city's edge. "That's another mystery. Why *is* it so big? To support such a city would require a populace ten times larger than currently living on the island and a land area thirty times as big."

"Further evidence of your lost continent?"

"Perhaps." She turned into a parking lot before the entrance to the ruins, parked under the shade of a large mangrove tree and switched off the engine. Then she turned her attention to Mwahu, in the backseat. "You said before this place was sacred to your people. Before we go further, I want to know why."

Mwahu stared out the open window, silent for a long time, then spoke slowly, as if it pained him. "It is the last home of our ancient teacher, Horon-ko. He came here to die."

"When was this? How long ago?"

Mwahu turned to face Karen and Jack. "Long, long ago."

"But why did he come *here*?" Karen asked.

"Because his own home was gone."

"His own home?"

Mwahu again seemed reluctant to answer. His voice became a whisper. "He came from Katua Peidi."

Karen gasped at his answer.

"What?" Jack said to her, puzzled.

"According to myth," she explained, "Katua Peidi was the name of the original homeland of the magical brothers who had helped build Nan Madol."

Jack frowned. "He thinks his teacher was one of these Katuans?"

"So it would seem." She turned her attention back to the rear seat. "What did Horon-ko teach your ancestors?"

"He teach many things. Mostly he teach us to guard the old places. He tell us where they are. Word pass from father to son. Forbidden to speak. He say none must open the heart of old places." He stared hard at Karen.

She ignored his accusing eyes and sat pondering. "A secret sect assigned to guard the Pacific's countless megalithic ruins . . . by the last survivor of some lost continent." She swung one more time on Mwahu. "You say Horon-ko died here."

He nodded.

"Is he buried here?"

He nodded again and turned toward the watery ruins of Nan Madol. "I will take you. But we must leave before night."

"Why?" Jack asked.

Karen answered instead. "A superstition about the ruins. If someone stays among the ruins overnight, it is said he will die."

"Great," Miyuki mumbled from the backseat, eyeing the low sun.

"It's only myth," Karen said.

All their eyes swung to Mwahu. The man slowly shook his head.

5:45 P.M., Neptune base, Central Pacific

Ferdinand Cortez rode as passenger aboard the researchers' two-man submersible, the *Argus*. The pilot, seated ahead in his own acrylic dome, signaled a thumbs-up as he guided the vessel under the sea base and up into the entry dock on the station's underside. The docking hatch sealed under them and the seawater was pumped out.

Ferdinand watched the waterline recede down his dome. The whole docking procedure took less than five minutes. He smiled at his success. After his wife died, he'd devoted all his energies to the Neptune project. It had been a goal he and his wife had shared.

A functioning deep-sea research station.

"We did it, Maria," he whispered to the station. "We finally did it."

As the central computer calibrated the air pressure in the docking bay, a green light flashed on the wall, indicating it was safe to depart the *Argus*. Ferdinand unscrewed the dome's seal using a motorized winch. The seal broke with the barest hiss of pressure differentials. Ferdinand smiled. Perfect.

He pushed back the dome and climbed out of the sub, hauling his bag with him. The pilot remained in his forward dome. He had another four research members to ferry down to the deep-sea station.

Free of the sub, Ferdinand breathed deeply. The air tasted stale, but that couldn't be helped. No amount of conditioning would freshen it.

Waving a thanks to the pilot, he crossed to the door and unscrewed its three latches. Beyond the door, he found John Conrad wearing a wide shit-eating grin.

"We're here," his friend and colleague said. "We're on the goddamn bottom of the ocean."

Ferdinand smiled and clapped him on the shoulder. "Then how about a tour?" he asked—not that he needed one. The Neptune had been based on his own design specs. He knew every inch of the base, every circuit, every switch.

John took his bag and slung it over his shoulder. "C'mon. Everyone's waiting." He led the way to the ladder up to the second tier of the station. As John climbed, electronic sensors marked his presence and opened the hatch overhead. It was all automated. Once both men clambered up to Level 2, the hatch self-sealed. Another safety feature. Each of the tiers were sealed from one another unless a crew member was on the ladder. The hatches could also be cranked shut and locked in case of power failure or a system malfunction.

Stepping from the ladder, Ferdinand surveyed his domain. Level 2 contained a circular series of labs: marine biology, geology, climatology, physiology, even archaeology. The base's tiny hospital ward also shared a wedge of this floor's space. The tier above this, Level 3, housed the living quarters, galley, tiny recreation room, and unisex bathroom.

Ferdinand could not wipe the smile from his face. The Neptune was finally up and functioning. As he passed through the labs, other scientists called to him, congratulating him. He acknowledged the well-wishes and continued to his own wedge: the geophysics laboratory.

John accompanied him. "Can't stop working, can you?"

"How can I? Especially with that pissant Spangler gone. He's been hobbling my work ever since we first arrived here. This may be my only chance to be free of the asshole, and I'm going to take advantage of it."

Ferdinand settled onto a fixed stool before a smooth metal console. He hit a button, and like a rolltop desk, the airtight seals on his station wheeled open to reveal a bank of computers, monitors, and tools. "Is the *Perseus* over by the crystal pillar?" he asked.

"Yep. Lieutenant Brentley has been waiting for an hour, and he's growing a bit impatient. We had to argue against him collecting your sample on his own."

"Good, good . . . I should oversee the sampling. We can't risk damage to the pillar."

"Brentley's audio is on Channel 4. Video feed on Channel 3."

Ferdinand called up the proper channels on his central monitor. "*Perseus*, this is Neptune. Do you read?"

Lieutenant Brentley answered. "Aye, Neptune, read you loud and clear. Just cooling my thrusters."

Ferdinand adjusted the monitor to pick up the video feed from the Deep Submergence Unit's sub. He was surprised at the clarity of the image. The sub faced the crystal pillar from a distance of ten yards away. Its faceted surface filled the screen. Across its smooth planes the silver etchings were plainly evident. "Have you recorded the entire pillar?"

"Aye, completed and recorded. Just waiting to collect the sample."

Ferdinand heard the exasperation in the man's voice. "I appreciate your patience, Lieutenant. We're ready to proceed. Try to collect a sample without marring any of the writing."

"Aye, sir. I've studied the pillar. There's no writing near the top. Should I attempt a sampling there?"

"Yes. Very good."

On the screen, Ferdinand watched the *Perseus* circle the forty-meter length of crystal, climbing toward its apex. Once there, the image focused on the faceted top of the obelisk. "I'll try to nip a bit off the very tip." The pilot's voice crackled with static as the vessel edged toward the pillar.

"Be careful."

As they watched, the video feed began to flicker with static, too. The sub floated toward the pillar, slower and slower. It was almost as if the video feed were playing in slow motion. As the sub neared its goal, a titanium arm reached cautiously outward.

"Careful," Ferdinand warned. "We don't know how fragile that thing is."

A few jumbled words answered, frosted with static: ". . . odd . . . trembling . . . can't hear . . ."

John touched Ferdinand's shoulder. "The crystal's emissions must be messing with the sub's communications. Remember the reports from the salvage ship's sub."

Ferdinand nodded, worrying that perhaps he should've waited until Spangler had returned. If the Navy's sub were damaged . . .

The titanium claw reached for the pillar, intending to pinch the tip off the crystal. It was agonizingly slow.

"The first deep-sea circumcision," John mumbled.

Ferdinand ignored his friend's attempt at humor and held his breath.

The pincer closed on the faceted point. Brentley's voice suddenly came through the speakers, crystal clear again. "I think I've—"

The video image froze. Both John and Ferdinand glanced in puzzlement at each other. Frowning, Ferdinand tapped the screen. For a brief moment he thought he saw the submersible vanish then flicker back.

Abruptly, the video image resumed. "—got it!" Brentley finished. On the screen, the sub retreated from the pillar, its titanium arm held up high, a chunk of crystal in its grip.

"He did it!" Ferdinand said.

"To hell with the glitches!" John blurted out happily.

A cheer arose from the crew—but broke off as a fierce rattling began to shake through the base.

A wary hush descended. Ferdinand held his breath.

The rattling grew into a savage shaking. Doors rattled. Shelved containers tumbled.

"Sea quake!" John yelled.

Cries rose from the various science stations. The video connection to the *Perseus* disappeared as the monitor's screen shattered into a spiderweb of cracks.

John stumbled to one of the porthole windows. "If any of the seals break—"

Ferdinand knew the threat. At a depth of six hundred meters, the pressures outside were close to half a ton per square inch. Any rupture would lead to immediate implosion.

Emergency klaxons bellowed; red warning lights flared.

Ferdinand yelled in a firm tone of command. "Retreat to Level 3! Prepare to evacuate!"

One of the marine biologists ran toward them, almost colliding with John. "The interlevel hatches have sealed themselves. I can't override on manual."

Ferdinand swore. In case of flooding, the safety systems automatically locked down and isolated each tier—but the manual override should have worked. He stood up on the bucking floor as the main lights flickered out. Everything became red-tinged in the glow of the emergency lights.

"Oh, God!" John said. His face was still pressed to the porthole.

Ferdinand stumbled to a neighboring port. "What is it?" It took him a moment to comprehend what he was seeing. The neighboring forest of lava pillars shook and vibrated as if a mighty wind were blowing through it. Distantly, bright fiery glows marked opening magma fissures. But neither sight was what had triggered John's outburst.

In the direction of the pillar, a jagged crack split the seabed floor. As Ferdinand watched, the rift widened, and in vicious zigzags it raced toward the Neptune.

"No . . ."

There was no time to evacuate.

Other scientists took up positions at other portholes. A heavy silence settled. From somewhere across the way, a whispered prayer began to echo.

Ferdinand could do nothing as his lifelong dream was about to end. His fate was in the hands of God. He closed his eyes and pressed his forehead against the cold glass. How many had he killed down here? As fear and guilt clutched him, it took him a moment to realize the rumbling roar had begun to recede. The temblors underfoot calmed.

Ferdinand lifted his face.

John was staring back at him, wearing a frightened smile. "Is . . . is it over?"

Ferdinand glanced out the porthole. The jagged fissure had reached within a yard of Neptune's steel legs.

The quake shook with one last fierce rumble, then died away.

"That was too close," John said.

Ferdinand nodded.

Over the radio, a squelch of static erupted. "Neptune, this is *Perseus*. Is everyone okay in there?"

Ferdinand stumbled to the transmitter, relieved that Brentley had safely weathered the quake. "All clear, *Perseus*. Just shaken up."

"Glad to hear it! I'll pass the news topside."

"Thank you, *Perseus*."

Ferdinand slumped in his seat. He turned to John. "Let's hope that doesn't happen again."

John nodded. "Oh, yeah. I don't have enough clean pairs of underwear."

Ferdinand smiled weakly. He willed his heart to stop pounding. That had been too damn close.

6:22 P.M., Nan Madol, Southeast of Pohnpei Island

"Kaselehlie!" The small dark-skinned boatman greeted Karen in native Pohnpeian, smiling broadly. He was bare-chested and wore loose shorts that hung to his knobby

knees. Behind him, the ruins of Nan Madol spread in a series of man-made islets toward the open sea. *"Ia iromw?"*

"We're fine," Karen answered, bowing her head slightly. *"Menlau.* Thank you. I called earlier today about a day rental of one of your rowboats."

The man nodded vigorously. "The scientists. Yes, I have better than a rowboat." He turned and led them down a short stone quay of black basalt to a pair of long canoes. "Much better. Smaller. Travel the canals better. Faster." He motioned with a hand, sweeping it back and forth.

Karen eyed the worn fiberglass canoes dubiously. They hardly looked seaworthy enough even for the shallow canals. "I guess these will be fine."

The boatman's smile widened. "I have map. Two American dollars."

Karen shook her head. "I have my own. Thank you."

"I act as guide. Seven American dollars an hour. I show you all the sights. Tell you stories."

"I think we can manage on our own. Besides, we have our own guide." She nodded toward Mwahu.

The boatman looked crestfallen and waved them toward the canoes.

"Menlau," she said, passing down the quay, leading the others.

Jack kept pace with her and mumbled, "A real capitalist, that guy."

At the two canoes, Miyuki joined them. She studied the sun low on the horizon. "Let's get going. We don't have that much daylight left."

Karen sighed. She knew her friend still fretted over Mwahu's earlier warning. "Miyuki, you're supposed to be a computer scientist. Since when do you believe in ghosts?"

"Looking at this place, I'm beginning to waver." Overhead, a pair of fruit bats swept past. Distantly, the calls of birds sounded lonely and lost. "It's so creepy here."

Karen nudged one of the boats. "Well, you're right about one thing. We should get going. Why don't you and Mwahu take this one? Jack and I will take the other."

Miyuki nodded and climbed into the canoe as Mwahu held it steady. Then the islander clambered skillfully in afterward.

"Are you sure you can lead us to the grave of your ancient teacher?" Karen asked Mwahu.

He bobbed his head.

Satisfied, Karen turned to the other canoe. Jack already sat in the stern. She carefully stepped into the canoe's bow end and picked up a paddle. "Everyone ready?"

There was a general sound of assent.

"Let's go!"

Karen dug in her paddle, and the canoe slid smoothly from the dock. Ahead, Miyuki and Mwahu led the way, paddling under the basalt entry gate of the ruins. Past the gate, the breadth and scope of the site opened before them. High palaces, low tombs, great halls, miniature castles, simple homes. All framed by watery canals. Mangrove trees and thick vines were draped throughout, creating a maze of water, stone, and overgrown vegetation.

Karen paddled silently, while Jack guided the canoe with considerable skill. He cut the boat around a narrow corner. They were traveling through what was known as the "central city" of Nan Madol. The canals here were less than a meter wide, the basalt islets tightly packed around them. Jack continued to follow Mwahu's zigzagging course.

"You're good at this," Karen said as Jack swung the canoe smoothly under a bridge of vines and lilting white flowers. "SEAL training?"

Jack laughed. "No. It's a skill learned from years of float trips down the rivers and creeks of Tennessee. It's like riding a bike. You never forget."

Facing forward, Karen hid her smile. It was good to hear Jack laugh. She settled back as they paddled slowly toward the heart of the ruins, crisscrossing from canals dark with deep shadows to sunlit channels. Some paths were so choked with overhanging ferns and mangrove boughs that she wished they had a machete. Yet at all times the stacks of basalt logs surrounded them, prismatic crystals glowing in the late afternoon sunlight. Walls towered up to thirty feet, only broken by the occasional window or doorway.

Finally, the canals widened. To the right, an especially huge basalt island appeared, a great structure built upon it. Its walled fortifications towered forty feet, a monstrous construction of logs and gigantic boulders.

"Nan Dowas," Karen said, pointing at it. "The city's central castle." They glided along the fern-choked coastline of the wide island. Doorways opened into the structure, some intact, some collapsed.

"It's huge," Jack said.

They passed another entrance guarded by a large basalt boulder. Nodding toward the structure Karen explained, "It's one of the entrances to the subterranean tunnel network. The passages here have never been fully explored and are considered feats of engineering. In fact, further west, there's an islet named Darong with a man-made lake atop it. At the bottom of the lake is a sea tunnel that leads to the reef's edge. It allows fish to travel into the artificial lake, maintaining its stock."

"Impressive." Jack dug in his paddle and turned the canoe away from the castle as Mwahu led them to a more open section of the city. They floated over coral reefs rich with anemones and colorful fish.

From here the imposing sea wall of basalt pillars and slabs came into view. Taller monoliths dotted its lengths, silent stone sentinels staring out to sea. Periodically, narrow spaces opened: gates to the ocean beyond.

After a few minutes of gliding along the walls, they cut back into the maze of islets. Soon Karen found herself drifting down a narrow canal, the walls festooned with tiny pink and blue blossoms, scented not unlike honeysuckles. She inhaled deeply.

A slap drew her attention around. "Bees," Jack warned.

Karen smiled. "Leave them alone and they'll leave you alone." She felt something crawling on her arm and jumped—then realized it was Jack tickling her with a long blade of dry grass. "Funny," she scolded him.

He tossed the blade away with a look of total innocence.

Karen faced forward, paddle across her knees. At least Jack seemed to be coming out of his funk.

Behind her, he spoke up, more serious. "Do you have any idea where this guy is taking us?"

She fished out her map and spread it on her lap. She eyed the islets around her, then bent over the map. "Hmm . . ."

"What?"

"I can guess where he's leading us. There's a sacred place near here." She looked up as they rounded a tall promontory.

Ahead appeared a huge island, even larger than Nan Dowas. But instead of a single castle, the artificial island held a sprawling complex of buildings and crumbled walls.

Mwahu aimed his canoe toward its shore.

"Pahn Kadira," Karen said, naming the place. "The 'Forbidden City' of Nan Madol."

Mwahu glided into the island's shadow and beached at a low spot. He waved them over.

"Why forbidden?" Jack asked.

"No one can say. It's a term passed from generation to generation."

Jack guided them toward the bank, pulling alongside the other canoe. "It seems we're about to find out."

Jack held the boat steady while Karen climbed ashore. As she joined Miyuki and Mwahu, Jack roped the canoes to the bole of a lone mangrove.

"This way," Mwahu said softly. His gaze flickered across the deep shadows as he led them along a thin trail through a dense accumulation of ferns to an arched entry.

Beyond the gate, a wide stone plaza opened. Grasses and flowers sprouted between the cracks. To the left, the remains of an ancient fortification lay toppled. To the right stood low-roofed buildings with narrow doorways and small windows. Ahead, splitting the plaza in half, was a thin carved channel, an artificial creek forded by a wide bridge.

"It is so hot," Miyuki said. She wiped her face with a handkerchief, then pulled out a small umbrella. Pohnpei was known for its frequent showers, but today the sky had remained cloudless. Miyuki opened her umbrella and sheltered in its shadow.

As a group, they crossed the long plaza.

Karen would have liked to explore the surrounding sites, but Mwahu continued on single-mindedly, looking neither right nor left. He led them across the bridge and toward a tall building on the far side. It rose ninety feet above the plaza, with two low wings sprouting off from the central keep.

Karen stepped up next to Mwahu. "Is this the tomb of Horon-ko?"

Mwahu did not answer. He made a vague motion to remain silent. Reaching the wide entrance to the central keep, he paused and bowed his head, his lips moving silently.

Karen and the others waited.

Finished with his prayer, Mwahu took a deep breath and led them inside, with Karen right behind him.

The entrance hall was dark and refreshingly cool. As Karen entered she was struck by how clean the air smelled. No mustiness, just a hint of salt and dampness. The short passage led into a cavernous chamber. Their footsteps on the stone floor echoed off the heights. She fumbled through her pack and removed a penlight. The thin beam pierced the darkness, splashing across the featureless walls and roof.

Basalt and more basalt. No crystals, no indication of any writing.

Mwahu frowned hard at her, then continued to lead them on.

Jack whistled. "This place is massive. You described it, but to see this construction firsthand . . . It must've taken thousands and thousands of people to build this single building, even aided by a pair of the magical brothers."

Too awed to speak herself, Karen nodded.

They left the huge hall and entered another low passage. The press of stone overhead seemed to weigh down upon Karen's head. She wasn't prone to claustrophobia, but there was a certain heaviness about the place that couldn't be ignored. The passage turned sharply and sunlight flared ahead.

Mwahu led them into a rear courtyard. Karen stepped back into the brilliance of the sunlight—and the heat. Miyuki shook open her umbrella again.

Around the space, the once-tall walls lay toppled. Lengths of cracked basalt logs were tumbled amid boulders and smaller rocks. Still, the solemnity of the yard was not diminished. Though no longer inside the keep, Karen still felt the weight of centuries there.

Adding to this effect was the courtyard's central altar: a massive hewn block of prismatic basalt. At four meters in length and a meter high, she guessed that it weighed several tons. They were all drawn to it as it glowed and sparked in the last rays of the afternoon sun. None of them could keep their hands from touching its surface.

Mwahu dropped to his knees.

Karen noted that the spot where he knelt was worn into the rock. How many generations of his people had made the pilgrimage here? she wondered, moving beside him. "Is this the gravestone of your ancient teacher?" she asked.

He nodded, head bowed.

Jack circled the great block. "I don't seen any writing. No clues."

Mwahu stood and indicated that Karen should give respect and kneel. She nodded, not wanting to offend, dropped her pack and knelt. Mwahu pointed toward the stone.

She stared, not sure if she was supposed to bow, recite a prayer, or perform some other act of respect. As she looked at where Mwahu pointed, however, she had her answer. "Holy shit."

"What is it?" Jack said. Miyuki stepped to her other side.

"Come see." Karen stood and returned to the stone. She brushed the block's surface with the palm of her hand. It was no optical illusion. "I'm not surprised you missed it. You can only see it if you're kneeling."

"See what?"

She tugged Jack down by an arm so he could look across the stone's surface. She traced a finger. "There."

Jack's jaw dropped. "A star!"

"Carved so thinly, or simply worn faint by time, that the only way to see it is from an extreme angle."

He straightened. "But what does it mean?"

Miyuki took a peek, too, then answered from under her umbrella, "It's like back at the pyramid. We need the crystal."

Karen nodded and tugged open her pack.

Jack still looked confused. "What are you talking about?"

Karen hadn't told him about how she'd used the crystal star, and now she tugged out a black cloth bag and shook it out. Behind her, Mwahu gasped with awe. She crossed to the stone as the others gathered around her, carefully placing the artifact atop the thin carving. It was an exact match. She held her breath, not knowing what to expect. Nothing happened.

Disappointed, Karen stepped back. "The crystal star must act as a key, but how?"

Miyuki, leaning over the stone, said, "Remember back at the pyramid—darkness was the final key."

Karen slowly nodded. It had taken perfect *darkness* for the crystal star to function as the key to release them from the heart of the Chatan pyramid.

"So what do we do?" Jack asked. "Wait until nightfall?"

Miyuki looked sick at this suggestion.

"I don't know. . . ." Karen studied the stone. Something didn't sit right with her. Then it struck her. She recalled the symmetry and balance of the Chatan pyramids. The yin and the yang. "Of course!"

"What?" Jack moved to her side.

"It's not darkness we need!" She waved Miyuki away from the stone. Her friend's umbrella had been casting a shadow over the crystal. As Miyuki stepped back, raw sunlight bathed the crystal. The star burst with radiant brilliance. "It's *light*!"

A loud crack sounded from the stone. The others moved back a few steps but Karen stood her ground.

A hidden seam appeared around the solid block. It outlined a four-inch-thick lid resting squarely atop the stone block.

Karen stepped forward.

"Be careful," Jack warned.

She touched the block's lid and pushed. The slab of basalt shifted, moving as easily as if it were Styrofoam. "It hardly weighs a thing!"

Jack moved beside her, his gaze fixed on the crystal star. He shadowed his hand over it. "Try pushing now."

She did. The lid wouldn't budge.

Jack removed his hand, exposing the crystal to sunlight again, and using a single finger, he moved the slab of stone to the side. "The star has somehow extended its weight-altering properties to the basalt."

Karen was stunned. "Amazing. This must be how the magical ancients 'floated' the stones in the past."

"It looks downright magical enough to me, that's for damn sure."

Miyuki, beside them, pointed into the block's interior.

Karen leaned over as Jack pushed the stone lid back farther.

Inside the altar there was a carved alcove, lined by a shiny metal. Karen touched it. "Platinum."

Jack nodded. "Like your story. The platinum coffins the Japanese divers discovered underwater during World War Two."

Karen nodded. "But *this* coffin isn't empty."

Resting inside were the bones of a human skeleton.

Mwahu spoke at Karen's shoulder, a whisper. "Horon-ko."

Karen studied the remains. Clinging to the bones were a few scraps of dusty cloth, but what had captured her eye was a book, bound in platinum, clutched in the bony grip of the coffin's occupant.

Carefully, she reached inside.

"No!" Mwahu cried.

Karen could not resist. She gripped the book and lifted it.

Disturbed, the bones of the fingers fell away to dust. Then, like toppling dominoes, the degradation of the bones spread. The rib cage collapsed, the femurs and pelvis disintegrated, the skull caved in. Soon the form was no longer recognizable.

"Ashes to ashes," Jack mumbled.

Karen held the platinum book in her fingers, stunned by her thoughtless act of desecration.

Mwahu began to weep behind her. "Doomed," he moaned.

As if hearing him, the first bullet struck the basalt altar, stinging Karen's face with a spray of rocky shards.

6:45 P.M., USS *Gibraltar*, Philippine Sea

Admiral Mark Houston climbed the five levels to the bridge of the USS *Gibraltar*. They were under full steam from Guam, where two days ago they had offloaded the civilian NTSB team along with the crated wreckage of Air Force One. In Guam, the *Gibraltar* had also reacquired its normal complement of aircraft—forty-two helicopters, both Sea Knights and Cobras, and five Harrier II fighter/bombers—along with its usual complement of LCAC amphibious landing craft. All to land the ship's Marine detachment safely on Okinawa and bolster the island's defense.

Reports coming from the region were growing worse by the hour. Apparently, the Chinese naval and air forces were merciless in their determination not to surrender Taiwan.

Passing through a cipher-locked hatch, Houston shook his head. *It's folly. Let the Chinese have the damn island.* He had read the intelligence reports on the agreement signed between the leaders in Taipei and Beijing. It was not all that different from China's assumption of control in Hong Kong and Macau. It would be business as usual. As they did in Hong Kong, the Chinese had no intention of weakening Taiwan's economic base.

Still, he could understand the administration's position. President Bishop had been murdered. Whether the upper levels in Beijing knew of the plot or not, the crime could not go unanswered.

Upon hearing of the escalating conflict, Houston had offered his services to remain on board and proceed to the beleaguered front. Calmer heads were needed out there. He was to oversee the situation and report his recommendations to the Joint Chiefs.

He climbed the last ladder, his knees protesting, and entered the bridge of the *Gibraltar*. The navigational equipment, map table, and communication station were all manned and busy.

"Admiral on the bridge!" an ensign called out.

All eyes turned in his direction. He waved them back to their duties. A groggy-eyed Captain Brenning pushed from his day cabin into the main bridge. He looked like he'd had less than an hour's sleep in the past three days. "Sir, how can I help you?"

"I apologize for disturbing you. Just coming topside to stretch my legs. How are things faring?"

"Fine, sir. We're thirty-six hours out and ready."

"Very good."

The C.O. nodded aft. "Sir, the Marine commander is over in debark control. I can let him know you're here."

"No need." Houston stared out the green-tinted windows of the bridge. Rain sluiced across the glass. All day long a thin rain had been falling and a misty haze obscured the horizon. Having been holed up in his cabin since morning, conferring with Washington, he had primarily come up here to see the sun. He had thought a climb up to the bridge would do him some good, cheer him up. But instead he felt a heaviness grow in his chest. How many would die these next few days?

At the communication station, a lieutenant pulled headphones from his ears and turned to his captain. "Sir, I have an encrypted call from the Pentagon. They're asking for Admiral Houston."

Captain Brenning nodded to his day cabin. "Admiral, if you'd like, you could take the call in my cabin."

Houston shook his head. "That's no longer my place, Captain. I'll take it out here." He crossed and picked up a handset. "Admiral Houston here."

As he listened, the cold of the island's superstructure crept into his bones. He could not believe what he was hearing, but he had no choice. "Yes. I understand." He handed the receiver back to the lieutenant.

The others must have sensed his dismay. The bridge grew quiet.

"Sir?" Captain Brenning stepped toward him.

Houston blinked a few times, stunned. "Maybe I'll take you up on your offer to borrow your day cabin." He turned and walked toward the door, indicating that Brenning should follow.

Once inside, he closed the door and turned to the C.O. "John, I've just received new orders and a new objective."

"Where do they want us to go?"

"Taiwan."

The captain blanched.

"Word has come down from the Hill," Houston finished. "We're officially at war with China."

16

Cat and Mouse

"Get down!" Jack yelled. He pulled Karen to her knees. Bullets sprayed the courtyard. Jack quickly assessed the situation as the four of them took shelter behind the basalt crypt. *Rifle fire. From two locations.* He tried to spot the snipers along the walls, but the suppressing gunfire was too intense.

He studied the others. Blood dribbled down Karen's cheek. "Are you okay?" he asked.

Eyes wide, she nodded, then touched her cheek. "Rock shards." The momentary shock faded from her eyes. She crammed the crypt's platinum book into her pack.

Jack, suspicious, eyed Mwahu. "Do you know anything about this?"

The islander shook his head vigorously.

Jack leaned back against the stone. He thought quickly. None of them had been shot. Why? They had been sitting ducks. They should not have survived the surprise assault. Beyond the stone, the rifle fire faded. "They're pinning us down here," he said aloud. "They want something from us or they would've killed us by now."

"What do they want?" Miyuki asked angrily.

"The crystal," Karen said. "That's what everyone seems to want."

Jack nodded. He crept to the edge of the crypt. The crystal star still rested atop the block's lid. "It's just out of reach. I'm going to need a distraction in case I'm wrong." He looked back over his shoulder. "Miyuki . . ."

The professor nodded as Jack told her his plan, then slid to the opposite end of the basalt coffin.

"On my count," Jack whispered. "One . . . Two . . . *three!*"

Miyuki shoved her umbrella into the air, opening it and waving it about.

Rifle fire blasted, ripping and shredding the umbrella's cloth. Miyuki gasped, cringing, but held tight.

Jack listened. Both guns were firing. Good. He burst from his end of the crypt, grabbed the crystal star, and dove back into cover. Hunching, he clutched the artifact to his chest.

"You're bleeding," Karen said.

Jack glanced down. A trail of red dribbled across the crystal. He hadn't felt the bullet that grazed the edge of his hand. The snipers were damn fast, he realized. He had better not underestimate them. "I'm okay. It's just a scratch."

Karen crawled to his side and wrapped his hand in her handkerchief, tugging it tight.

"Ow!" he said.

"Oh, quit complaining, you baby."

Even in their predicament, Jack couldn't help but grin.

The rifle fire again quieted as the targets remained hidden.

"What now?" Miyuki asked.

"They're holding us here. Which means others are on the way."

Mwahu moved nearer. "I know a secret way out of Forbidden City. But we must get back there." He pointed toward the dark hall into the central keep.

Jack stared, biting his lower lip, thinking. It was only ten yards away—but it might as well have been a hundred. They would be exposed to the snipers for too long. "Too risky."

Karen grabbed her pack and tugged a side pouch open. "I have an idea." She pulled out a package of Trident gum.

"Good," Jack said. "I was worried about my dental hygiene right now."

She smirked at him. "Put the crystal down." When Jack complied, she flipped the star over and unwrapped a piece of gum. She popped it in her mouth, chewed it for a couple seconds, then stuck the wad on the back of the crystal.

"What are you—"

She nodded toward the lid, and Jack understood. "Let me help you." He grabbed a few pieces of gum and chewed them vigorously.

Miyuki stared at them as if they'd gone crazy.

Jack smeared a sticky chunk of gum on the crystal's underside, then held it up.

Karen eyed the star. "That should be enough gum."

"Do I have to return the star to the exact spot?" he asked.

"I don't know. Just make sure it's in the sunlight."

Jack grabbed the crystal star, gummy side up. Taking a deep breath, he reached up and slapped the crystal down upon the nearest edge of the stone lid. He pressed hard, twisting it to ensure the gum stuck well. He yanked his hand back as gunfire spat again, sparking off the stone. He checked his hand, then held it toward Karen. "Look, Ma, no cavities."

"Very funny. Test the lid."

From the safety of the shelter, Jack reached out to the underside of the lid's protruding edge. He pushed up on it. Rock scraped on rock as the lid rose an inch. "Light as a feather."

"Then let's get our asses out of here."

Jack slid the lid to their side of the crypt, then stood, tilting the top between him and the snipers, like a stone shield. Bullets rang off the rock.

"Oof!" Jack felt the impacts all the way to his shoulders,

but the shield held. Backing up, he dragged the makeshift shield off the crypt, tilting the lid vertically so the others could crouch in its shadow. "Okay, time to vamoose."

Shuffling backward, he kept them all covered. Only his fingers were exposed on the far side. He prayed the riflemen were not good enough shots to take off one of his fingers.

"Keep the crystal in the light," Karen urged. "We're almost there."

Rifle fire continued to pelt the stone lid. Jack's hands began to slip, jarred by the force of the continued rifle blasts.

"Almost . . ." Karen said.

Jack stepped into darkness. He took another step and the stone lid's weight suddenly returned. Caught off guard, he couldn't hold it. "Back!" he yelled as it came toppling toward him.

From behind, someone grabbed his belt and yanked him clear. He stumbled and fell hard on his rear end. The lid crashed to the ground, barely missing his toes. Jack hoisted himself up to a crouch. Karen had also fallen to her knees. She dusted off her hands, standing up.

"Thanks," he said.

"Grab the crystal." She motioned to the cracked lid.

Jack snatched the star, peeling it off the basalt. He passed it to Karen, who shoved it in her pack. Rifle blasts continued to abrade the hall's entrance, but the group was far enough down the passage to be out of the direct line of fire. "Keep moving. It won't be safe much longer."

"This way," Mwahu hissed from farther down the tunnel. "Hurry. Someone comes."

Jack and Karen joined the other two at the edge of the cavernous central chamber. Across the room, Jack spotted a shaft of light flaring from the opposite hall. They were cut off from the exit.

"This way," Mwahu whispered, slinking along the wall to the left.

In the deep gloom, the group slid close to the walls. Jack reached behind and took Miyuki's hand. The professor's fingers shook in his grip. He squeezed reassuringly. Together they followed Mwahu to a corner of the large chamber. By now hushed voices echoed from the opposite hall. No words could be made out, but from the angry tone, Jack suspected that the snipers' failure to hold the captives had been radioed. The light quickly grew.

Hurry, he silently urged Mwahu.

A flashlight's beam speared across the chamber as someone entered.

Jack pushed Miyuki behind him.

A hiss drew Jack's attention around. In the deep shadows, he barely saw Mwahu crouched beside a thin crevice in the wall. It was no higher than Jack's knee and narrower than his shoulders. Karen was already crawling inside, pack shoved in front of her. Mwahu stared with fear toward the men stepping into the chamber.

Jack was sure they would be caught.

He pushed Miyuki toward the opening, and, without any hesitation, her small form vanished down the tunnel's throat. Jack indicated Mwahu should go next. He was the only one who knew where the tunnel led.

The islander dove into the hole.

Behind Jack a new light bloomed. Crouching, he spun around. It came from the hall leading to the courtyard. Shadowy figures entered. *The snipers*. The two parties signaled each other with their lights. Jack saw one of the beams flash in his direction.

He dropped to the floor, flattening himself. The light passed over where he had been standing. It did not pause.

Crawling on hands and knees, he slithered across the floor and into the crevice. It was a tight fit. Holding his breath, he crooked his shoulders and shoved himself inside. Crouching lower on his elbows and scrabbling with his fingers, he worked deeper into the chute, sure at any moment that lights would flare up around him. But finally he pulled his feet fully into the tunnel. He paused, suppressing a sigh of relief, he stared ahead—and saw nothing. The tunnel was pitch-black. The only evidence of the others was the occasional furtive scuffling.

Squeezing his large form along the chute, Jack listened for the noises as he followed the turns and twists of the tunnel. He scraped his shoulders and tore his fingernails on the rough surface as he went. In the dark, blind, his exertions seemed compounded. How long was this tunnel?

Finally, he was able to make out the dim form of Mwahu crawling a few yards ahead and he heard echoed whispers.

"I see the end," Miyuki said distantly.

Jack prayed they remained cautious. He increased his pace, scraping his elbows and knees. Soon he, too, saw the end of the passage. A square of bright sunlight. "Careful," he whispered ahead.

Jack watched the professor slide from the tunnel—and vanish. The others followed. He crawled after them, reached the tunnel's exit and peered out. Below, the others were crouched in a meter-wide channel of stagnant water, waist-deep. He realized then where they were, recalled the thin artificial creek bisecting the plaza. Head hanging out, he surveyed the situation. The stone bridge lay twenty yards away. He listened for voices and heard none.

Jack wormed out of the chute and lowered himself into the creek. After the exertion, the water felt wonderfully cool, but the saltwater stung his cuts and abrasions.

Karen nodded to the tunnel. "Drainage system," she said softly.

He nodded. Nothing like crawling through a sewage pipe. He eyed Mwahu, silently asking the islander where to go next.

Before Mwahu could direct them, however, a loud voice cracked across the open plaza behind them. "Kirkland! If you want the others to live, show yourself!"

Jack froze. He knew that strident voice. *Spangler*. His fists clenched.

Karen touched his shoulder and shook her head. She pointed to Mwahu, who was half swimming down the artificial creek away from them.

Miyuki followed. Karen went next. Jack unclenched his fists. He knew it was not the time to confront David. Not yet.

Not when others were in harm's way. Lowering himself into the water, he silently glided after the others.

He heard the tromp of boots on stone . . . coming their way. He hissed at the others, pointing a thumb up.

Mwahu ducked under the bridge and twisted around. He motioned the others to join him. Jack and the two women were soon at his side. The bridge was so low that only their heads were above water.

The tread of boots, now running, aimed right for their hiding place. Two men.

Jack bit his lip. With the sun so low, the channel was thick with shadows. Under the bridge it was even darker. Still, if they thought to flash a light . . .

The pair hit the bridge and stopped. Their shadows could be seen on the far wall of the canal.

"Any sign?" Spangler asked harshly.

"No, sir. We're still combing the building. They won't get away. With the island under surveillance, they won't be able to leave here without being spotted."

"Good."

"Sir, I'm getting a report from Rolfe over the radio." A pause, then the man's voice grew more excited. "He found a tunnel!"

"Goddamn it! Why didn't someone spot this earlier? C'mon. Have Rolfe ready with the grenades."

"Yes, sir." The echo of boot steps retreated from the bridge and headed back toward the large structure.

Jack did not wait. He thumbed for Mwahu to continue.

One after the other the group swam toward the distant fortifications. No one breathed. All of them clung to the deepest shadows of the channel. As they neared the wall, Jack spotted where the creek ended. He saw no way forward.

Mwahu waited for them to gather. Once Jack was near enough, the islander made a diving motion with his hand. Then, to demonstrate, he sank under the water and vanished.

Karen whispered to Jack, "The creek must connect to the canals, or the channel would have dried out." But she eyed the wall of stacked basalt logs with concern.

"You can do it," he said.

Karen nodded, unhooking her backpack so it was loose in her hands. "I'll go next." Taking a deep breath, she ducked under the stagnant water. With a kick, she vanished into the underwater tunnel.

Miyuki looked too frightened to move. Jack slid beside her. "We'll go together."

She nodded, swallowing hard. "I'm not the strongest swimmer." But she held out her hand, her eyes determined. He took it.

"On three," he said.

"On three," she repeated.

Jack counted it off, and they both dove under. He found the passage easily. It was quite large. Kicking off the nearby creek wall, he led Miyuki through the tunnel. It was no longer than two yards. Light filtered ahead.

Jack popped out and found himself in one of the surrounding canals. Miyuki surfaced beside him, wiping back her wet hair. The group was hidden in an overhang of ferns.

Jack heard a vague whining. The noise grew as he listened. "Shit."

"What?" Karen asked.

"How long can everyone hold their breath?"

Karen shrugged. "As long as we need to."

The whining was now a high-pitched screaming. It came from just around the corner.

"What is—" Karen started to ask.

"Take each other's hands," Jack said. "Duck underwater until I signal you."

They obeyed, and their heads vanished. Holding his breath, Jack sank until only his eyes were above the water. Peering between the fern fronds, he watched a sleek black jet ski turn the corner with a roar. It angled down the canal toward them, sweeping back and forth, lightly bumping the walls to either side. Jack pressed himself against the stones.

Half standing, the driver glided his jet ski along the passage. He studied the walled island, slowing as he puttered past Jack's hiding spot. The man, in a black wet suit with his mask pushed up on his forehead, wore a pair of mirrored sunglasses.

Keep going, asshole. Jack knew the others could not hold their breath forever. In the reflection of the man's sunglasses, Jack spotted his own face hidden by leaves. His skin, pale, seemed to shine in the shadows. He should have smeared his face with mud, he thought. But it was too late now.

The jet ski inched past him, its fiberglass edge almost grazing his cheek as it swept by him. The man remained unaware of his presence. As he drifted away, Jack recognized the automatic weapon strapped to the man's back. A Heckler & Koch MP5A3 assault weapon. The SEALs' weapon of choice.

He kept an eye on the gunman until he disappeared around the corner, then pulled the others up. They gasped for air.

Jack strained to listen. Another whine arose from across the ruins. A second jet ski! He surmised there were two guards, circling in tandem around the island. He had maybe three minutes to come up with a plan.

"We need to get out of here," he said. "Now."

Mwahu pointed toward an islet fifty yards down the waterway. "More tunnels. Go over to shore." But he seemed unsure of himself.

"Are you certain?"

Mwahu stared Jack down, then shrugged.

Jack sighed. "You make a very good point." The group had no other choice. They'd have to take their chances. "Move fast, folks. We've got more company coming."

The sound of the second jet ski grew louder.

Mwahu led the way. Here, the water was deeper. They were forced to swim. Jack cringed at the amount of splashing. If the second guard should turn the corner now, they would be spotted easily.

Positioned at the rear, Jack kept glancing over his shoulder. The whining began to roar, echoing off the walls. "Faster," he urged the others.

The splashing worsened, but their progress only improved

slightly. Jack realized they would not make it. Ahead, he
spotted a narrow side channel jutting from the main canal.
"Turn in there!"

With a kick, Mwahu led them into the tight alley.

Jack swam after them into the cramped space. Bare walls
surrounded them on either side—and the canal dead-ended
only a couple yards away. They were boxed in. Jack swung
around. "We'll have to hold our breath again."

Resigned nods answered him.

Jack judged their waning strength, knowing they were all
growing cold and exhausted. The rising scream of the jet ski
drew his attention around. "He's coming." He knew he could
not risk even peeking out. He listened, trying to time it,
grabbed Karen's hand and raised his other arm.

The noise drilled his ears. He held his breath, waiting,
tense. Then he lowered his arm, and the others sucked air
and dove. Again Jack lowered his face to eye level with the
water.

The jet ski roared up to the opening of the side channel,
but the driver, a clone of the other, maintained a watch on
the larger island across the canal. Standing, the man had a
hand pressed to an ear, listening to his radio, reporting in.
His words were muffled by the jet ski's engine.

Jack willed him to continue past.

As if hearing his silent plea, the man swung around. Jack
just barely managed to duck underwater in time. From under
the surface he stared up. He could see the man's watery
image, saw him pause, floating the jet ski in place.

Jack felt Karen tug on his hand. She and the others were
running out of air. He squeezed her hand, then released his
grip and slipped away from her side. Karen tried to grab the
back of his shirt, but he knocked her hand aside.

Overhead, the jet ski turned in their direction. Jack saw
the man reach for his rifle. Exhaling slowly, Jack sank
deeper. He slid out of the side channel, scuttling under the
starboard edge of the ski. He hated to abandon the others,
but he needed a moment's distraction.

Crouching down on the bottom of the canal, he positioned his feet and squinted up. *C'mon*, he urged the others. Then he heard a frantic kicking as one of his group ran out of air and was forced to surface.

Jack did not wait. He shoved with all the strength in his legs and shot out of the water.

The driver, still facing the channel, had his weapon pointed in the wrong direction. He noticed Jack's attack a moment too late.

Jack knocked him off the jet ski's seat. The man grabbed the handlebars and twisted around, but by then Jack's elbow had smashed him in the face, crushing his nose, driving the bone into his brain. Instant death.

Jack did not pause. His old instincts arose. He relieved the guard of his rifle and radio headpiece, then shoved the man into the canal.

As he swung back into the jet ski's seat he found Karen staring up in shock from the canal.

"Kill or be killed," he grumbled, then gunned the jet ski. "C'mon."

Karen held out a hand, and Jack pulled her into the seat behind him. There was not enough room for the other two.

"Grab the edge of the jet ski," he instructed them. "I'll drag you both."

Miyuki and Mwahu swam to either side, fingers clutching for handholds.

"Ready?"

"Y-Yes," Miyuki said, shivering.

Jack edged the ski forward. Over the noise of his own watercraft he heard the growing roar of the other jet ski. He increased his pace, but a squeal of protest from Miyuki forced him to throttle down. The professor gagged out a mouthful of seawater.

"Sorry," he said, twisting around and watching for the other guard. Jack clutched the handles in a tight grip. "We can't outrun them like this."

Karen nodded down the canal. "What about Mwahu's tunnel?"

They should have just enough time, Jack thought, and slowly throttled up. "Hold your breath."

Gliding the jet ski, he headed toward the islet Mwahu had pointed out. Once abreast of it, he ducked the ski into another side canal and parked it out of sight.

"Is this the place?" Karen asked Mwahu.

Half drowned, the islander indicated the rear side of the islet's single squat building.

Shouldering the rifle, Jack hopped to shore and helped the others up onto the weed-choked island. He quickly led them around the building, where he stumbled to a stop. "Goddamn it!" The entrance to the building was blocked by a large basalt boulder. He sagged and turned. "Is this your entrance to the tunnels?"

Mwahu crossed and placed a hand on the boulder. He looked near tears. Answer enough.

Karen joined the islander. "We can move it," she said, wiggling out of her wet pack. "It's basalt. We have the crystal."

Jack looked at the boulder. It was deep in shadows as the sun hovered at the horizon. "We need sunlight."

Karen passed him the crystal. "I'll get it for you." She removed a plastic compact from her pack, opened it and broke off the mirror. Stepping back to the corner, she aimed the mirror toward the sun and deflected a beam toward the boulder so a spot of sunlight danced on the boulder's surface.

Jack smiled. "It's worth a try."

He crossed to the boulder and slapped on the star, still sticky with gum. It failed to adhere to the uneven surface, but he found he could hold it in place and push with his shoulder. He nodded to Karen.

It took her a few tries to hit the star with the reflected sunlight. Jack pushed each time the star burst with radiance. The boulder, much more massive than the crypt's lid, was still heavy. Jack dug in his heels, straining against the rock, fighting it. Mwahu joined him and pushed, too. Slowly, the boulder shifted.

"I don't hear the other jet ski," Miyuki said.

Jack paused. She was right. Silence lay over the ruins. "He must have discovered the body. He's probably reporting in." He hunkered down again. "C'mon, we're running out of time."

Karen tilted her mirror. The star flashed brilliantly. Jack and Mwahu groaned, against it. The boulder rolled a full foot. The gap opened enough for a small person to crawl inside.

"That'll have to do," Karen said. "We can squeeze." She passed Jack her pack and crouched down, slithering into the space. Once through, she called back. "Mwahu was right. There is a tunnel. It leads steeply down from here."

Jack waved for Miyuki and Mwahu to follow. The pair quickly squeezed inside, into the stone building, while Jack backed to the far side of the boulder. The stone's far edge, now pushed beyond the shelter of the building, was bathed in sunlight.

"Now you," Karen called out to him. "Jack?"

He hooked Karen's pack to his own shoulder and placed the crystal star against the sunlit edge of the boulder.

"Jack?"

The crystal glowed brightly. Jack crouched down and shoved against the boulder, legs straining. The large stone rolled back into the shadows. Then he straightened and walked back around. Without sunlight, the boulder was now impossible to move any farther.

"What are you doing?" Karen asked from the other side. The crack was no wider than the palm of his hand. Her face was pressed to the gap.

"We can't leave the way open," he said. "They'll find the jet ski and quickly discover the opening. They'll hunt us in the tunnels."

"But—"

The roar of a jet ski echoed over the water. First one, then another, then another.

"They're coming," Jack said, standing. "I'll try and lead them away." He stepped back and tucked the crystal into the pack on his shoulder. "But if they catch me, I'll have what they want—the crystal. Either way, they should leave you all alone."

"Jack . . ." Karen wiggled a hand through the crack.

Jack knelt and took her hand. "Try to get to someone in authority."

Karen nodded, eyes moist. "I will."

Jack turned her hand and gently pressed his lips to her palm. "I'll see you soon."

She closed her hand, savoring his kiss. "You'd better."

Jack pushed back up. There was nothing else to say. He hitched Karen's pack higher on his shoulder and hurried to the lone watercraft. The screams of the other jet skis echoed across the ruins.

Jack settled into the jet ski's seat, hooked the radio headset in place and strapped the assault weapon over his shoulder. Ready, he gunned the jet ski, adding its voice to the chorus of others. Opening the throttle, he shot forward.

Across Nan Madol the sun was sinking below the horizon. As darkness descended, Jack remembered Mwahu's earlier warning.

An old superstition.

Death lay among the ruins at night.

8:45 P.M.

David Spangler stood atop the stone roof of the central keep, one of the tallest points in Nan Madol. He had a comprehensive view of the entire megalithic city. Using a night vision scope, he watched the chase begin. He saw Jack's jet ski suddenly burst from out of hiding behind one of the islets.

"He's in quadrant four," David radioed his men. "Circle the area and keep him contained." On his command, the other three jet skis swung around, circling toward the designated region. He listened to the chatter over the radio as his team closed the noose.

David allowed himself a hard smile. Darkness was

Omega team's ally. While Jack stumbled around blindly, his own men, equipped with goggles and UV lanterns, moved with skill and certainty. He watched the trap tighten. He would end this tonight.

He touched his microphone. "Jeffreys, check out the island where Jack was hiding. Make sure he hasn't left anyone behind." David knew it was not above Jack to play hero, leading his team on a wild goose chase while the real prize lay hidden.

Below, he heard a jet ski throttle up. He had held Omega team's last jet ski in reserve, for emergencies and backup. Now, the jet ski roared away, angling toward the tiny islet.

Sighing, David returned his attention to the chase. When they first arrived, he had ordered his men to capture Kirkland and the others alive. But the man was proving more of an adversary than he'd imagined. As a consequence, he adjusted his estimation of Kirkland and upgraded his order to "Kill on sight."

Still, he found it frustrating. His team had been outwitted. He'd spent many hours planning the day's mission. He had commandeered a local police cutter and the six jet skis. "Drug runners" was the official explanation. He had stationed the boat outside the reef and awaited the arrival of Jack and the others. Once they were there, he had watched them paddle around the ruins and finally beach their canoes. From that point it was a simple matter to jet-ski into the ruins through the sea gates and sneak onto the island silently. He had then ordered the area cordoned off, while he and his extraction team hunted Jack's group.

Even now David was not entirely certain how Jack and the others had escaped his trap. Rolfe and Handel had sketched a story of Jack using some sort of stone shield to flee into hiding. Then he apparently disappeared down some secret tunnels, where Kirkland killed one of his men as he escaped. It was a sorry excuse all around, and he would demand a full debriefing on his men's failure once this was over.

From his vantage point, David watched as Jack's jet ski was encircled within an especially cramped section of the ruins. All exits from the area were blocked by his men. Jack was trapped. He would not escape a second time.

"Get him!" David ordered. "Shoot to kill!" Gleefully, he watched his men close in. If he couldn't be there personally, this was the next best thing—watching Jack hunted down like a dog and shot.

"I see him!" one of the men shouted over the radio. The jet ski in the background made it difficult to hear.

Rifle fire rang out, the sound echoing over the ruins. Off to the left a flurry of birds took flight from their nests, frightened by the blast. But David's scope remained fixed on the glowing mote of Jack and his jet ski.

The spot flared brightly, stinging his eyes like a camera flash. Swearing, David shoved away the night vision goggles and blinked away the glare. He stared across the ruins.

Noises of victory sounded over his radio. David clenched a fist of satisfaction. Across the dark islands a bonfire burned high into the sky, reflecting off the waters.

The radio squelched, and Rolfe's voice whispered in his ear, "We got him, sir. Blew his ass out of the water. The target's eliminated."

9:05 P.M.

Down in the tunnels, Karen heard the gunshot. She cringed, then heard an even more ominous sound: a muffled explosion. The noise thundered through the tunnel system, echoing and reverberating from everywhere. Sound traveled strangely through the low passages. Even their own echoing footsteps sounded more like a score of people tromping throughout the tunnels. It made her edgy . . . as if they weren't alone.

And now the gunshot and explosion.

Karen held a fist at her throat, praying Jack was okay.

Ahead, Mwahu crouched in the low passage. He held her small penlight. It was their only source of light.

"Keep going," Miyuki said, voice trembling. "There's nothing we can do to help Jack."

Mwahu nodded. Karen followed them.

The tunnels had been carved out of the coral itself. The walls and roof were coarse, and they had to be careful not to brush against it. Only the floor was smooth, worn by centuries of feet and the occasional flood of water. In fact, several of the passages still held trapped pools of water, chilly and oily with algae.

"Not much further," Mwahu promised.

Karen hoped so. Rather than safe, she felt helpless and trapped down here. It seemed with each step she took, she was abandoning Jack to the murderous scum back there. If only her pistol had not been confiscated back in Japan . . .

Mwahu turned a corner and gestured to her and Miyuki. "Come see!"

They quickly joined the islander. Beyond the turn in the tunnel, an opening lay directly ahead. Though the sun had set, the early evening was still brighter than the dark tunnels. Together, they hurried toward the exit.

Karen was a moment too slow to realize the danger. "Wait!"

Miyuki and Mwahu were already outside.

Karen stumbled after them. She pointed at Mwahu's light. "Turn it off!"

Mwahu gaped at his light as if it were a poisonous snake and dropped it.

Diving down, Karen retrieved the penlight and flicked it off. Straightening, she surveyed their surroundings. They had exited a squat basalt building, not far from the shore of Temwen Island. In fact, the stone quay where they had rented their canoes lay less than fifty meters away.

She looked down at the extinguished light. Had it been spotted? Had they just thwarted Jack's attempt to draw the others away?

The answer came soon enough. Karen heard the whine of a jet ski escalate. Someone was coming to investigate. She eyed the distance between them and the coastal gate. The assassins, alerted now, would know where her group was heading—where else could they go?

She closed her eyes and made a decision, then flicked on the light.

"What are you doing?" Miyuki said.

"They know we'll try for the exit. But if I run the other way with the flashlight"—Karen pointed in the opposite direction—"they'll have to follow."

"Karen . . . ?"

She reached out and clutched her friend's arm. "Go. I dragged you into all this. I'll get you out."

"I don't care."

"Well, I do." She stared Miyuki down as the noise of the jet ski grew louder. "Go!"

Karen backed away, lifting her penlight high. She hopped into the canal. This close to the shore, the waters were shallow, only chest-deep. She slogged and swam away from the coastal gate. Behind her, she heard splashes as Miyuki and Mwahu jumped into the canal and made for the exit.

Alone, Karen swam through the murky water, trying to put as much distance as possible between her and the others. She soon lost sight of the exit. Only shadowy walls surrounded her.

But she was not completely alone.

She heard the growl of the jet ski as it roared toward her.

9:27 P.M.

David rode behind Jeffreys on the jet ski. He clenched his teeth in a silent curse. Kirkland had tried to play him the fool.

Shortly after the explosion, Lieutenant Jeffreys had reported in. David had almost forgotten he had sent the man to reconnoiter Kirkland's original hiding spot. The lieutenant reported no sign of anyone else.

This news had puzzled David. Where had Kirkland stashed the others? His primary assignment, after all, had been to kidnap the Canadian anthropologist and retrieve her crystal sample. Suspicious about their absence, he had ordered Jeffreys to come and get him. Together they would search the surrounding islets. The others had to be somewhere.

It was only pure luck that he caught the brief clue to the others' whereabouts. Donning his night vision goggles for the search, he caught the flare of brightness off by the coast, about a quarter mile away, and knew what it meant. He had read of the subterranean passages here.

While Jack had distracted him, the others had almost burrowed their way out of his trap. But Kirkland had failed, David thought with satisfaction. His sacrifice had achieved nothing.

Now, as he and Jeffreys raced through the ruins on the jet ski, David unhitched his rifle. The target was within reach. For a brief moment the light flicked out, but now it had returned.

"It's moving away from the exit," Jeffreys yelled to him.

"I see that. Keep following it. They must be trying to make for another tunnel. We have to catch them before they disappear."

Jeffreys nodded, swinging the ski around, following the trajectory of their target. They whipped back and forth through the maze of islets. David kept a firm grip around the lieutenant's waist, his rifle resting on his shoulder. As they swept around tight turns, waves broke against the canal walls, buffeting David with the spray. He ignored the dousing and urged Jeffreys to faster speeds.

Jeffreys called out, "Just ahead!" He spun around the next corner, tilting the ski savagely.

"Run 'em down if you have to!" David yelled.

Jeffreys raced down a channel and sped around another corner. The wash of the jet ski swept forward as he dug in. The source of the light lay just ahead.

David stood as Jeffreys throttled down. "Fuck!"

The tiny penlight was jammed in the crook of a mangrove branch. He searched around him. No one was here. He had been tricked . . . *again*.

His radio buzzed in his ear. It was Rolfe. "Sir, we've found no sign of Kirkland's body."

Suspicion and mistrust rode high in David's mind, especially after this newest ruse. "Who shot him?"

"Sir?"

"Who the fuck got on the radio and yelled that he saw Kirkland and *shot* him!"

David listened to the radio silence. No one answered.

"Did any of you actually fire your damn rifles?"

Again silence.

It dawned on David that his murdered teammate had not only been missing his rifle, but his radio headpiece, too. *Shit.* Jack had staged his own death, eavesdropping over the radio and masquerading as one of his men. "Fuck!" He touched his microphone and screamed, *"Find that bastard!"*

"What is it?" Jeffreys asked, cutting off the throttle.

"It's Kirkland! He's escaped!"

As David collapsed to his seat, he heard a small splash echo from nearby. He froze, silencing Jeffreys with a hand signal.

Someone else was there.

10:22 P.M.

On the other side of the ruins, Jack slowly surfaced. Stripped to his boxers, he silently shoved his rifle under a heavy fern at the shoreline and strained for sounds of pursuit. It was difficult to hear well. His head still rang with the jet ski's explosion. He'd been too close—but had little choice. He had to make sure the fuel tank was hit squarely by his single shot.

But the strength of the explosion had caught him by surprise, throwing him backward, singeing his eyebrows, knocking off his radio headpiece. Dazed, he'd been forced to dive quickly and swim under the jet skis of the swarming ops team. He swam until his lungs burned, then surfaced. As he'd hoped, the others had pulled off their night vision eyewear, the flames too bright for their equipment.

The misdirection had allowed him time to escape deeper into the ruins. As stealthily as possible, he had hurried, having no idea how long his ruse would last. He searched for some way out of the ruins. His plan was to reach the coastal mangrove swamps of Temwen Island. But he knew he had wasted valuable time, and only succeeded in getting himself lost in the dark.

A quarter mile away, hearing the jet skis rev and whine, he concluded that his pursuers had realized his ruse. He listened for a few moments. They were spreading out. Search pattern. The hunt had started again.

So far he had kept in the water as much as possible, staying hidden, trying to keep his body heat from revealing the fact that he still lived. But now he knew such subtlety was useless. He needed to find a way out of here—and quickly. The mangrove swamps were his only hope. The jet skis would be useless among the mud and dense roots.

But first to get there . . .

Heaving his tired body up onto the islet, Jack sprawled on his belly before crawling to his feet. A steep slope led up from there. A difficult but not impossible climb. He needed to reach higher ground to get his bearings, even if it meant exposing himself for a few seconds.

He retrieved his rifle and shouldered the pack.

Stifling a groan, he pushed up the slope, discovering it was steeper than he'd estimated. He scrabbled through clinging brush and terraces of basalt. His fingers slipped and his knees, already raw, were savagely scraped. His limbs, leaden and weak, shook with exhaustion, but at last he dragged himself onto the summit.

Staying on hands and knees, he surveyed his position. In the darkness, he had not thought freedom was so close, but under the starlight, he watched small waves pound against the artificial breakwater just thirty yards away.

Open sea lay beyond.

Out in the deeper waters, Jack spotted a small cutter, painted white with a blue light atop a tall pole. A coastal police vehicle. Its running lights were ablaze. A small figure stood on the bow deck. A tiny glint indicated the man was spying with binoculars, most likely equipped with night vi-

sion capability. Jack knew this was no friendly ship. Probably Spangler's means of transportation.

Now that he was at the summit for the first time, Jack noticed the body of water on top. It was roughly square and
looked like a small lake, and for some reason he felt drawn
to it. In fact, the dark body of water was ringed by a narrow
beach of sand and finely crushed coral, and Jack's hands and
knees sank into soft sand.

A grenade hit the far side of the islet, exploding and casting dirt and shredded ferns high into the air. Jack flattened
himself, his ears ringing from the concussion. As the blast
subsided, he heard the telltale sound of jet skis converging
on his spot, then spotted the tiny figure on the police ship.
The figure was frantically pointing toward him.

Another grenade sailed through the air, bounced across
the stony summit of the island, and rolled over the edge, exploding in the canal. Water geysered up in a wide funnel.
Someone was targeting the islet with a grenade launcher.

On his belly, Jack shimmied toward the summit's edge.
He needed to reach the canals. He'd been lucky twice, and
knew the odds were running thin. Peering over, he spotted
two jet skis racing his way, another arcing to circle around
the back. He was about to be surrounded. Then rifle fire
spattered against the stones, missing his head by no more
than a foot. He pulled back, but not before he spotted his adversary.

The sniper was perched atop a low building about three
islets away.

As Jack rolled away, another grenade whistled through
the air, exploding in the sand and water of the summit lake.
Shrapnel tore through the air.

Damn it!

Jack unhooked his weapon and remained prone on the
stone, offering no target to the sniper. He positioned the rifle
and crawled forward, keeping an eye focused through the
scope. As the squat building on the far side appeared in his
sights, he froze, hoping his submersion in the seawater had
not damaged the rifle. He waited, exhaling slowly, steadying

his gun. Spotting a flicker of movement, he fired a volley of shots, then rolled away. On his back, clutching the rifle to his chest, he didn't know if he had nailed his target, but either way, it would make the sniper more cautious. And now, at least, he knew that his gun would fire.

Across the channel, something heavy hit the water with a loud splash. A voice called out from one of the jet skis, "Handel's down! Get that shithead!"

Jack rolled back to his stomach and crawled to the far side of the islet. He would have to take his chances and leap. The canals here were only six feet deep, but the enemy was closing in too fast. He had no choice.

Reaching the edge, he prepared to jump, then spotted a jet ski directly under him. In all the commotion, he hadn't heard it come up.

He dove away as rifle fire peppered the edge. His right ear flared with pain, but he ignored it and rolled deeper, reaching the sandy slope of the summit lake. Listening, he heard the other jet skis closing in. Blood ran down his neck. He positioned his rifle, knowing he was doomed, and edged farther back, keeping his barrel forward. His feet and ankles now dangled into the water of the lake. He had nowhere else to go. His only consolation was that Karen and the others had escaped.

As he waited for the full assault, tiny fish nibbled at his toes, drawn by the blood of his abraded feet. He kicked them away.

Then he remembered the story Karen had told him about the construction of Darong Island. A sea tunnel connected the lake to the sea beyond the reef, she'd said, allowing fish to enter. He looked back; the breakwater lay only thirty yards away. A tough swim, but not impossible.

He heard the scuffle of stone.

Of the two risks, he knew which was the less dicey.

He dropped his rifle and, tugging the backpack over both shoulders, slid into the lake. Its bottom fell away steeply. He tread water for a few breaths, taking deep lungfuls of air. Usually, he could hold his breath for up to five minutes, but this was going to be a long dark swim.

With a final deep breath, he dove down into the depths. The fresh wound in his ear burned in the saltwater, but at least the pain kept him focused.

His hands reached the silty bottom. Curling around, he searched the edges of the artificial lake, struggling to find the sea tunnel opening. He swam first along the section facing the breakwater, believing this the most likely place. It quickly proved true: his arm disappeared down the throat of a stone tunnel.

Fixing its location in his mind, he rose to the surface and refreshed his lungs with rapid, deep inhalations. As he readied himself, he listened. It sounded like the jet skis were leaving. But the sounds echoed strangely around the lake. He couldn't be sure, especially with so many. Then closer, he heard whispers, arguing, and the rattle of loose rocks, the word "bomb." That was enough for him.

He dove with a clean scissor kick and reached the entrance to the tunnel. Not pausing, he ducked into the coral-encrusted hole and pulled and propelled himself down the chute, using hands and toes. There was nothing to see. Scooting blindly, his legs and arms were scraped and cut by the sharp coral. But he no longer felt the pain. He pushed past it, concentrating on one thing—moving forward.

As he wiggled and kicked, his lungs began to ache.

He ignored this pain, too.

Reaching forward, his hand touched stone. A moment of panic clutched him. He frantically reached out with both palms. A wall of stone blocked his way forward. He struggled, gasping out a bit of air, before he forced himself to calm down. Panic was a diver's worst enemy.

He searched the walls on either side and realized the way opened to the right. It was simply a blind turn in the tunnel. He reached it and pulled himself around the corner.

Though relieved, he was also concerned. How long and torturous was this tunnel? Darong Island lay only thirty yards from the edge of the reef, but if the passage twisted and turned, how long did he really have to swim?

By now he was running out of air. The hours of exertion

were taking their toll. His limbs demanded more oxygen. Small specks of light began to dance across his vision. Ghost lights of oxygen deprivation.

Jack increased his pace, refusing to let panic rule him. He moved quickly but methodically. The passage made two more turns.

His lungs began to spasm. He knew that eventually reflexes would quickly kick in and make him gasp. But blind, with no idea how far he had yet to traverse, he had no choice but to squeeze past his animal instincts.

Jack's head began to pound. Lights swirled in multicolor spectrums.

Knowing he was close to drowning, he slowly exhaled a bit of air from his lungs. This gave his body a false sense that he was about to breathe. His lungs relaxed. The trick bought him a bit more time.

He kicked onward, periodically blowing out a bit more air.

But eventually this last ruse failed him. His lungs were almost empty. His body screamed for oxygen.

Jack strained to see, searching for some clue to how far he had to travel. But darkness lay all around him. There was no sign of an end to the tunnel.

He knew he was lost.

His arms scrabbled but he had no strength. His fingers dug at the rock.

Then a flicker of light appeared far ahead. Was it real? Or was he hallucinating, close to death?

Either way, he forced his leaden limbs to move.

He heard a muffled explosion behind him, the noise reverberating through his bones. He glanced over his shoulder just as the shock wave struck him. He was shoved roughly by a surge of water, tumbled in the tide, bumping along the walls. Water surged up his nose. With the last of his air, he choked it back out. Blindly, he pawed around him. It took him a second to realize walls no longer surrounded him.

He was out of the tunnel!

Jack crawled toward the surface. Air, all he needed was one breath.

He stared up and saw starlight . . . and a moon!

Kicking, writhing, he fought upward. His fingers broke the surface just as his lungs gave out and spasmed, sucking saltwater through his nose and mouth. He choked and gasped. His body wracked as it sought to expel the water.

Then his hair was grabbed and his head pulled out of the water. Into air, into light. Jack looked up. The moon had come down to the sea. A circle so bright. He twisted around . . . or was flung around.

"Get that light out of his face!"

Voices surrounded him. Familiar voices. The voices of the dead.

He saw a dark visage bent over him. It was an old friend, come to take him away. He reached numbly up as darkness again swept over him. In his head, he whispered his friend's name: *Charlie* . . .

11:05 P.M.

"Is he going to be okay?" Lisa asked.

Charlie hauled Jack's limp body into the pontoon boat. "You're the doctor, you tell me." He rolled Jack over, pulled off the water-logged backpack, and pumped a wash of salt-water from his drowned chest. Jack coughed and vomited out more.

"He's breathing, at least." Lisa bent over Jack's form. "But we need to get him back to the *Deep Fathom*. He'll need oxygen."

The motor revved as Robert, at the stern, gunned the engine and spun the launch toward the waiting ship. The *Fathom* lay not far across the bay. Two other police cutters patrolled back and forth along the edge of the ruins.

Earlier, Charlie had spent half the evening trying to convince the local authorities to aid him in his search for Jack and the others. No one had listened, insisting he wait until

morning. Then a frantic call had come in from Professor
Nakano, relating an attack upon their party at Nan Madol.
Now motivated, the police had converged on the location,
arriving with the *Fathom* to find the place already deserted.

Apparently, Spangler's assault team had been tipped off,
for just as they entered the bay, a large blast blew apart one
of Nan Madol's tiny islets. Already in the *Fathom*'s launch,
Charlie had aimed for the site, knowing there must be a reason for the explosion.

As they neared the reef's edge, Robert spotted a bubbling
surge. He aimed for it just as a pale hand broke the surface.
Then the fingers sank back down. It would have been easy to
miss.

The sea gods must have been watching over their captain,
he thought afterward.

In the boat, Jack groaned and struggled to right himself.
His eyelids fluttered but he did not regain consciousness.
Charlie leaned down to his ear and whispered, "Rest, *mon*.
We got you. You're safe."

His words seemed to sink in. Jack's limbs relaxed.

"His color's looking better," Lisa said, but she herself
was as pale as a ghost, bloodless with fear and worry.

If they had arrived even a minute later . . .

Robert spoke up from the rear. He had a radio pressed to
his ear. "The police say they'll search the ruins until sunup."
He lowered the radio. "But it looks like the ops team got
clean away."

"Damn those bastards," Charlie swore. "If I ever get my
bloody hands on them . . ."

11:34 P.M.

David stormed down the narrow stairs of the small commandeered police cutter. His team's escape had been too damn
close. Over the radio, he received word of the police at the
same time his assault team found Jack.

Pressed for time, David had ordered explosive charges set

around the islet, then ordered all of them to evacuate to the
boat. For a black ops mission, exposure or capture was
worse than death. Working efficiently, they left no trail behind. Gathering their dead, they quickly vanished into the
maze of atolls and islands. All told, it took less than five
minutes to evacuate the site.

Even so, it had been a close call. Running without his
lights, David had watched the first police cutter, its sirens
blaring, enter the bay just as he slipped away. The explosion
helped cover their escape, distracting the arriving ships.

Still, never in his career had he come so close to capture.

Scowling, David reached the lower level of the ship and
crossed to a steel door. He tapped in the electronic code and
shoved into the small cell beyond. Though he had lost two
good men on this mission, the sortie hadn't been a total failure. Inside the cell, the Canadian anthropologist was tied,
spread-eagled, to the bed. She struggled against her bonds as
he entered. Gagged, her eyes grew large at the sight of him.

"Give it up. You can't escape." He slipped his diving
knife from its thigh sheath and crossed toward her.

Instead of crying or struggling further, she just glared at
him.

Sitting on the edge of the bed, he reached out with the
knife and cut her gag. She spit out the wad of cloth. "You
bastard!"

David fingered the edge of his blade. "We're gonna have
a little chat, Professor Grace. Let's hope I don't have to free
your tongue with this blade." He spotted a trickle of blood
running from her hairline down her neck, reached out and
pressed his thumb against the lump there.

She winced.

It was the spot where he had bludgeoned her with the butt
of his rifle after discovering her hiding place. Her ruse with
the penlight had come close to working. He dug his thumb
into the tender spot, eliciting a sharp cry from her. "Now are
you done with your little tricks?"

She spat at him, the spittle striking his cheek.

He let it dribble down, not bothering to wipe it away.

"Just so we both understand each other." He grabbed her between the legs. She was still damp from the swim through the canals. He squeezed her, hard.

She gasped, her eyes growing wide, and tried to squirm from his touch. "Get away from me, you goddamn bastard."

He held her tight. "Though my bosses may want you alive to pick your brain, that doesn't mean we can't hurt you in ways you never imagined. So let's start again. Where's the crystal you mentioned in your e-mail to Kirkland?"

"I don't know what you're talking about."

"Wrong answer," he said with a hard smile.

A knock on the door drew him around from his play. He saw Rolfe standing at the threshold, still in his wet suit, half unzipped. The man eyed their prisoner, then his gaze returned to David.

"Sir, Jeffreys has continued to monitor the police bands. Some . . . um, startling news has come through." Rolfe nodded to the prisoner. "Perhaps outside . . ."

The woman spoke from the bed. "Jack's alive, isn't he?"

David struck her with the heel of his hand. "Mind your manners, bitch."

Rolfe nervously shifted his feet. "She's right, sir. They've dragged Kirkland from the ocean. He's hurt but alive."

David felt a surge of heat. "Goddamn it! Can't that man stay dead?"

"That's not all."

"What?"

"He . . . he's aboard the *Deep Fathom*."

David was too stunned to speak.

Rolfe explained, "I don't know how, but his ship is here."

Closing his eyes, rage swelled through David. At every turn, Kirkland had thwarted him. He swung to the bound woman. Kirkland had risked his own life so she could escape. Why? He studied her. He sensed an edge here, a way of turning this to his advantage.

David stood up and pointed back at their prisoner. "Haul her ass on deck."

Jack woke slowly. It took him several breaths to realize where he was. The teak paneling, the chest of drawers, the captain's table and hutch. It was his own cabin aboard the *Deep Fathom*. It made no sense.

"Well, look who's up," a voice said.

He turned his head, noticing for the first time the oxygen mask strapped to his face. Tubes led to a portable tank. He lifted a hand to brush it away.

"Leave it."

Jack focused on his bedside companion. "Lisa?" Beyond her, he saw Charlie Mollier standing over her shoulder. At the sound of his master's voice, Elvis lifted his head from the floor and rested it on the bedside.

"Who did you expect?" Lisa straightened his pillow. "Do you feel strong enough to sit up?"

Jack's mind fumbled, trying to recall his situation. He remembered the chase through the ruins of Nan Madol, the struggle through the underwater tunnel, but . . . "You're all dead." He coughed thickly as he pushed up, then groaned loudly.

"Careful." Lisa helped him sit up, cushioning his back with pillows.

"Ow." Every inch of him ached. He lifted his arms and saw an IV line trailing to a bag of saline. His arms were smeared with salve and bandages.

"*We're* supposed to be dead?" Charlie said with a toothy smile. "*Mon*, you're the lucky one to be alive."

He coughed again. It felt as if someone had scoured his lungs with a Brillo pad. "But the bomb . . . ?"

Charlie sat on the edge of his bed. "Oh, about that, sorry, but we needed to make everyone think we were sunk. The bomb is down in my lab, locked away."

Jack shook his head, then regretted it, grimacing at the pain. "What the hell happened?" he barked with irritation.

Charlie related the events. The crew had found the bomb, and Robert recognized the trigger as a radio receiver. With Lisa's skill at electronics, it was a simple matter to remove the receiver. But they knew whoever had set it would not be satisfied unless the ship blew up. So they placed a call to Jack and warned him about the bomb, knowing that if someone were eavesdropping, they would probably trigger the device. "Which they did," Charlie explained. "When we saw the detached receiver blink, we knew the signal to blow the bomb was being sent, so we staged our own deaths. Dumped a bunch of oil and fuel, threw in some deck chairs and floaters, then lit the whole mess on fire."

Jack's eyes had grown wide by now.

"From there, we just hightailed it here to Pohnpei. Of course, we had to run silent. No communication of any sort or we'd blow the ruse."

"But . . . but . . ." Jack felt his old anger returning, fueling his strength. He pushed off his oxygen mask and glowered at the two of them. "Do you have any idea how worried I was?"

Charlie looked innocently at him. "So what are you saying . . . you'd rather we all blew up?"

Jack stared at Charlie's hurt expression, then burst out laughing. He held his sides against the pain. "Of course not." He glanced up at them; his eyes began to tear up. "You have no idea what it means to see you all here. . . ."

Lisa reached over and gave him a quick hug. "Just rest. You've had a rough day."

Jack suddenly remembered. "But what about Spangler? And the others?"

Charlie looked to Lisa, then back at Jack. "Spangler's long gone. But I've been in contact with Professor Nakano. She was hoping you knew what had happened to Dr. Grace. They've been unable to find her."

Jack felt a sick lump in his gut. "What does she mean? I left Karen with her."

Charlie shook her head. "The police are still questioning Professor Nakano on one of their boats. She asked if she could join us here. I said it would be okay."

Jack nodded, but his mind spun. *Where was Karen? What had happened?*

Running footsteps sounded in the hall. Robert burst into

the room and eyed the others. "Thank God you're awake, Jack."

"What is it?"

"A radio call." He was out of breath. "From David Spangler. He wants to speak to you."

Jack swung his legs off the bed, moving Elvis aside. He motioned Lisa to the IV. "Unhook me."

Lisa paused.

"Do it. I'm fine now. I've survived worse."

Lisa peeled back the surgical tape and slid out the catheter, covering the site with a small Band-Aid. She glanced at Charlie with concern.

Jack stood, wobbling on his feet. Charlie reached out to steady him, but Jack waved him away. "C'mon. Let's see what this bastard wants now."

As a group, they climbed up to the pilothouse. Jack grabbed the mike to the VHF radio. "Kirkland here."

Spangler's voice crackled from the radio. "Jack, glad to hear you're up and about. Rumor is you got pretty shook up."

"And fuck you, too. What do you want?"

"It seems you have something I want, and I have something you want."

"What are you talking about?"

A new voice came on the line. "Jack?"

He clutched the phone tighter. "Karen! Are you okay?"

Spangler answered. "She's enjoying our company. Now let's talk business. I have no need for this woman. All I want is that bit of crystal."

Jack switched off the transmitter and looked at Lisa. "My pack?"

"It's down in your cabin."

Jack returned to the radio. "What are you proposing?"

"An even exchange. The crystal for the woman. Then we all part friends and forget this ever happened."

Right, Jack thought. He trusted David about as far as he could throw him. But he had little choice. "When?"

"Just so no one tries to pull any stunts, let's say dawn tomorrow. At sea. In the light of day."

"Fine, but I pick the location." A tentative plan began to gel.

"Agreed . . . but if I see a single police vehicle, the woman gets cut up into bite-sized pieces and fed to the sharks."

"Understood. Then we'll meet at dawn off the eastern coast of Nahkapw Island." Jack spelled the name out. "Do you know where that is?"

"I can find it. I'll see you there." The radio went dead.

Jack rehooked the mike.

"You know it's a trap," Charlie said.

Jack slumped into the pilot's seat. "Oh, yeah, no doubt about it."

17

Change of Course

Half an hour before sunrise, Jack swam through dark water. He checked the glowing dial on his dive watch. So far he was on schedule. He had left the stern deck of the *Deep Fathom* ten minutes ago. Outfitted in a Body Glove neoprene wet suit, fins, tanks, and buoyancy compensator, he had long ago worked out of his aches and pains. He swam steadily, kicking his fins slowly but deeply, sweeping rapidly along the seabed. He swerved cleanly around another stone column that loomed out of the darkness. Equipped with Robert's night-dive gear—a small ultraviolet flashlight strapped to each wrist and a night vision mask—he had no difficulty seeing.

He glanced at his compass, maintaining his pace toward where Spangler's police cutter floated. An hour before dawn, both men's ships had arrived on the eastern coast of Nahkapw Island. Each party maintained a cautious half nautical mile between them, awaiting dawn.

But Jack was already in the water before his ship had

even come to a stop. His plan required speed, stealth, and the cover of predawn. Earlier he had been faxed the layout of the Pohnpeian police cutter and the code to the cipher lock of this particular ship's brig. If Karen was held anywhere, it was there. Or so he hoped.

Another stone column appeared, then another. Jack slowed. Ahead, walls and crumbled buildings appeared, all thickly coated with coral and waving fronds of kelp. Jack lifted his wrist lights. More structures and facades stretched into the distance.

Here was the sunken stone village of Kahnihnw Namkhet.

Karen had described the place yesterday on the way to Nan Madol. It was the reason he had chosen this spot. The police cutters were outfitted with sonar, and Jack needed as much cover as possible to swim up on Spangler's ship undetected.

He dove along the bottom, sticking close to the columns, walls, and buildings. He wanted to cast as little sonar signature as possible. As he approached within an eighth of a mile of his target, he began winding in a circuitous path, attempting to keep stone walls between him and the ship.

Overhead, he saw the cutter's searchlights basking over the waters. Through his night vision mask, the place was lit up like a Christmas tree.

He continued even more cautiously, pausing and waiting in alcoves and behind piles of tumbled stone.

Finally, he found himself directly under the keel of the ship. It floated thirty-five feet above. He checked his watch. He was now a few minutes behind schedule. The sun would soon be up.

Emptying his buoyancy compensator, Jack settled to the sea bottom, forty feet under the cutter's keel. He hid in the shadow of a thick-walled fortification. Wriggling, he wormed out of his tanks, kicked off his fins, and dropped his weights. He kept a bite on the air regulator as he did, taking a few good breaths for the swim up. Bent over, he unstrapped the second, smaller reserve tank from his hip. The thermos-size pony tank was for Karen. He placed it beside his own gear. All was in order.

Straightening, he patted his belt and double-checked that the two waterproof plastic bags were still in place. Satisfied, he switched off his UV lights. Darkness closed around him.

Ready, Jack spit out the regulator and shot toward the surface, kicking to aim for the stern. As he raced upward, he slowly exhaled, compensating for the change in pressure. He was rising too fast for safety, but could not risk being exposed for too long.

Within a few seconds his palm touched the smooth underside of the hull. He worked toward the rear, careful of the idling prop. In the shadow of the stern, he surfaced and pushed back his mask. He had painted his face and hands with engine grease to limit any reflection.

He spotted one of Spangler's men leaning on the rail. A cigarette hung from his lips. Jack listened. He heard no others, but couldn't take any chances. Sliding to the starboard side, he pulled out a mirror attached to a telescoping pole from his belt and extended it toward the rail. In the mirror's reflection, he surveyed the stern deck. There was only the single guard. Good, he thought. With the cutter's bow pointing toward the *Fathom*, they had posted little security at the rear. He twisted the pole, searched the ship's forward section and spotted movement. Two men. Maybe more.

Jack quickly lowered and secured the mirror, then sidled back to the stern ladder. He tested it with a hand. The safety ladder was permanent, secured with bolts, so it shouldn't rattle.

From his belt, he removed one of the clear plastic bags. His hand settled around the grip of the pistol inside. Raising it above the water, he poked his finger through the thin plastic to rest a finger on the trigger. The safety was already off. He waited for an opportunity.

As he did, his eyes flicked to his watch. The eastern horizon was already beginning to glow with the approach of dawn. *C'mon, damn you . . .*

Overhead, the guard flicked his cigarette into the sea. The

glowing butt arced over Jack's head and hit the water with a sizzle. Yawning, the guard turned and leaned his back against the rail. Fishing in a pocket, the man pulled out a pack of Winstons. He tapped it, trying to free one of the cigarettes.

One-handed, Jack pulled himself up on the ladder, planted his feet—then pointed his gun and fired. He covered the dull sound of the pistol's silencer with an inconspicuous cough. Gore splattered the white deck. Jack reached out and grabbed the man's body as it fell. Using the man's dead weight for leverage, he clambered over the rail, then lowered the limp body to the deck.

In a crouch, he ran to the cutter's external reserve fuel tank, freed the second plastic bag and pressed a red button. Swallowing hard, he checked his watch, then tucked the package beside the steel barrel.

He twisted around and darted to the door leading to the lower deck stairs. Gun pointed forward, he peeked around the open door. No one was there. Swinging it wide, he raced down the dimly lit stairs to the lower deck. At the end of the passageway lay a stainless steel door with a single tiny window.

Jack entered the passage cautiously. Crates and rolls of tarpaulin were stored in the lower passage, creating potential hiding places. He continued carefully, gun pointed ahead of him, searching corners and blind spots. No one was about. Reaching the far door, he glanced through the tiny window and bit back a sigh of relief. Karen was tied to the thin bed inside.

Jack quickly tapped in the code to the electronic cipher lock and heard the telltale click of the lock releasing. He grabbed the door and yanked it open. Taking no chances, he rolled into the room, ready for an ambush. He spun, weapon ready. No guards.

Karen struggled in her bonds, eyes wide with surprise. "Jack!" As he stepped toward her, Jack realized that it was not surprise in her voice—but fear.

He heard a rustling behind him, from the doorway, and turned around. In the hall, David stood with a gun pointing at his chest. The crumpled tarpaulin he'd been hiding under was now a cape about his shoulders.

"Drop your weapon, Kirkland."

Jack hesitated, then lowered his weapon and placed it on the floor.

David shrugged off the tarpaulin. "Kick your gun here."

Hands raised, scowling, Jack did as he'd been ordered.

"You are so predictable, Jack. Always the hero." David moved into the room. "With the right bait, I knew I could lure you here. But I must say you haven't lost your training. You got past my own men without alerting any of them." He lifted the pistol. "Luckily, I trust no one but myself."

"You never were a team player, Spangler. That's why I was promoted over you." As his opponent's face reddened with anger, Jack spoke more slowly. "That's what's really got a corn cob up your ass about me, isn't it? It's not your sister. It's not Jennifer's death. You couldn't stand a commoner like me beating a purebred Aryan stud like yourself, could you?"

David took an angry step toward him, leveling the gun at his head. "Don't ever speak Jennifer's name again."

Jack risked a glance at his watch. *Fifteen seconds*. He had to keep David angry and close. "Quit the act, Spangler. Your sister and I had long talks about you. I know about you and your father."

Sputtering, David pointed the gun. His face was almost purple. "What did she tell you . . . whatever it was, it was all lies. He never touched me."

Jack crinkled his brow. Long ago, Jennifer had mentioned that David had been physically abused by his father. But had it gone further? Jack lowered his voice conspiratorially. "That's not the way I heard it."

David stepped nearer. "Shut the fuck up!"

Five seconds . . .

Jack braced his legs. His hands formed fists.

Spittle flew from David's lips in rage. "He never touched me!"

One . . .

Jack swung a fist as the explosion roared through the

ship. The deck bucked underfoot. His fist glanced off
David's jaw, knocking him aside.

The pistol went off, a wild shot. The bullet dug into the
wall behind Jack. He spun and kicked the gun from David's
hand. It went flying across the floor.

David lunged. Jack instinctively dodged to the side, and
as he swung back around realized the mistake. His reflexes
had betrayed him. David might have been an asshole, but he
was a keen killer. He landed near Jack's discarded pistol,
which had been his intent, and David rolled toward the
weapon.

Karen yelled from the bed, "Run, Jack!"

He froze. "He'll kill you—"

"No! His superiors want me alive! Go!"

Jack paused. David reached to the gun.

"Run!" Karen screamed.

Swearing, Jack darted through the door, slamming it behind him. Ahead, smoke filled the hall. Flames danced at the
top of the stairs. Jack tore into a neighboring cabin. The
bomb, primed with a small bit of C-4 from David's own
bomb, had been meant as a distraction so he and Karen
could escape.

Jack crossed the cabin and tugged down the folded emergency ladder. Cinching down his diving mask, he mounted
the ladder and twisted the release to the aft deck's hatch.

An alarm sounded.

Flinging back the small door, he dove out. He rolled
across the deck and to his feet. Men were running with
buckets and hoses. One stopped and blocked his escape,
mouth open in surprise.

As the man dropped his bucket and reached to a holstered
pistol, Jack ran at him, elbowing him across his Adam's
apple. The guard fell back, gagging. His way clear, Jack
dove over the starboard rail.

Holding his mask, he struck the water, then kicked and
dug his way toward the bottom. He flipped on his ultraviolet
wrist lights just as bullets began to ping and zing through the
water around him. He ignored the threat and searched for
where he'd stored his equipment.

He quickly found it. Hidden in the shadow of the crumbling wall, Jack took a quick drag from the pony tank's regulator, then tossed it aside. Karen would not be needing it. He looked up.

The cutter remained topside, but it wouldn't be there for long. The exploding fuel tank was the signal for Charlie to call in the police. The original plan was for he and Karen to hide down here until the police chased them off.

As he fit his feet into his fins, Jack spotted movement from the corner of his eye. He twisted around, glancing up.

Small metallic objects, no bigger than soda cans, were sinking into the water around him. A dozen, maybe more. As he watched, one of them struck a tall column fifteen yards away. The explosion threw Jack to the sand, slamming the air from his lungs. His ears flared with pain. Bits of rock pelted him. Blind for a moment, he rolled across the sea floor.

As his vision snapped back, he spotted a dozen other charges falling around him. Another trap. He had less than five seconds until the area was blown to fragments.

Grabbing his buoyancy vest and attached air tank, he twisted the vest around and jammed his arms in the wrong way. The tank, instead of on his back, lay upside down on his chest. Swinging with his hips, he jammed the tank against a nearby stone wall and the valve snapped off. Compressed oxygen exploded out.

The tank, now a rocket, jetted away.

Hugging the tank tight to his chest, Jack rode it away from the cascade of depth charges. Fighting for control, his back slammed into the side of one of the submerged ruins. A rib snapped with a jolt of fire. He bit his lips against the pain and twisted his arms more snugly in the tangled buoyancy vest. Using his fins and legs, he roughly guided his trajectory through the maze of columns and walls, shooting like a pinball through an underwater arcade game.

As he rode, the explosions blasted behind him. He felt each charge as if kicked by a mule. A large chunk of basalt flew past him and bounced across the sand.

In seconds Jack's flight slowed as the air evacuated from the tank. He swam and kicked to put additional distance be-

tween him and the depth charges. Finally, he could not ignore the fire in his lungs. He dumped the expired tank and
pushed for the surface.

The upper waters were no longer midnight blue, but a
deep aqua. The sun was rising.

He paddled toward the weak light and sucked air as his
head broke the surface. His broken rib complained with each
breath, but the relief of fresh air overwhelmed the ache. He
swung around.

The morning was misty, heavy with the promise of rain.
Seventy yards away, the seas still roiled around the police
cutter. It looked as if the ship floated on a boiling pan of
water. As he watched, one last explosion blew to the surface,
casting a geyser of water high into the air.

In the distance, the multiple sirens of police vessels
whined. Closer, the diesel motor of Spangler's cutter began
to roar. Its bow end surged up as the ship took flight. Wakes
churned and the boat swept away.

Jack watched, helpless, hurt. As he tread in place, a sense
of defeat washed over him.

He had survived, but he'd lost Karen. And no matter what
she argued, her life was on a short fuse. Once her usefulness
ended, she would be eliminated.

Off near the coast, the cutter raced away, moving faster,
disappearing around the headlands of Nahkapw Island.

As he stared, hopeless, a light rain began to fall, pebbling
the seas around him. Then he rolled onto his stomach and
began the long swim back to the *Deep Fathom*.

8:46 A.M., off the coast of Pingelap Atoll

Three hours after Jack's escape, David stood in the pilothouse of the sleek cutter. Rain sluiced and beat against the
window. The storm was worsening, but he did not care. The
cover of rain and mist had allowed them to escape once
again. Hidden by the heavy morning fog, they had traveled
over fifty miles, putting as much distance as possible between them and Pohnpei Island.

Off to the north, he could see the small atoll of Pingelap. His men were busily offloading their equipment into the cutter's launch. After they finished and collected their prisoner, they would scuttle the ship and travel to the nearby empty beach. An evac helicopter was already on its way to collect them.

Over the scrambled radio, David listened as Nicolas Ruzickov continued to chastise him. Not only had the mission almost been a total failure, it had been a sloppy one, implicating the U.S. government. The American embassy on Pohnpei was already spinning the events like a whirling top, extolling the local authorities and spouting assurances that they would root out the culprits involved. The ambassador had vigorously denied any knowledge of David's men or what they were doing at Nan Madol. Funds were already being wired into the private accounts of critical Pohnpeian officials. David knew there was no problem or embarrassment that couldn't be made to disappear by throwing enough cash at it. By tomorrow, all evidence of U.S. involvement would be muddied away.

Ruzickov finished his tirade. "I have enough problems with the war. I don't need to be cleaning up your messes, Commander."

"Yes, sir, but Jack Kirkland—"

"Your report stated that you eliminated him."

"We believe so." David remembered the seas erupting around the ship, bobbling and rocking the vessel. There was no way Jack could have survived, he thought, but his eyes narrowed. He could not be sure. The bastard had more lives than a damn cat. "But his crew, sir. We believe they still possess the crystal."

"That objective no longer matters. The researchers managed to collect their own sample. They're experimenting with it as we speak, and so far the initial results are intriguing. But more importantly, Cortez believes translating the inscription on the obelisk may accelerate his research. So forget the fragment of crystal. Your mission's top priority is to bring the anthropologist to Neptune base."

David clenched his fist. "Yes, sir."

"After you accomplish this, you'll help the Navy's team extract the crystal pillar and return it to the States. Only then will you be allowed to tie up these loose ends." Anger ran clear in the former Marine's voice.

Heat rose to David's face. Never before had he been reprimanded by the CIA director. Three dead, one severely injured. The mission would be a black mark on his record.

"Did you hear me, Commander Spangler?"

David had stopped listening, too filled with anger and shame. "Yes, sir. We'll evacuate the professor to the sea base immediately."

A long sigh followed. "Commander, the conditions out East are worsening as we speak. A major sea battle is raging around Taiwan. Okinawa is under repeated missile attacks. And in Washington there is already talk of a nuclear response." Ruzickov paused to let the significance sink in. "So you understand the importance of your efforts. If there is any way to utilize the power hidden in that crystal, it must be discovered as soon as possible. Every means must be utilized to accomplish this end. Private wars and vendettas have no place here."

David closed his eyes. "I understand. I won't fail you again."

"Prove it, Commander. Bring that woman to the Neptune."

"We're already on our way."

"Very good." The line went dead.

David held the receiver a moment. *Fuck you*, he added silently, then slammed down the phone.

In the distance, a *whump-whump* echoed over the waters. Their evac helicopter was early. David cinched up his jacket and pushed out the door into the rainstorm. He crossed to Rolfe.

The lieutenant commander turned at his approach.

"Get the woman up here," David ordered him.

"I think she's still unconscious."

"Then carry her. We're leaving now." David watched as his second-in-command swung away. He placed his fists on his hips. Maybe he had been too rough on the woman, he thought, recalling how after losing Kirkland, he had vented his frustration on her. But he would no longer tolerate failures—not from himself, not from his men, not from her.

Rolfe reappeared, climbing from the doorway with their captive slung over a shoulder.

The rain seemed to revive the woman a bit. She stirred, raising her face. Her left eye was bruised and blood dribbled from her nose and split lip. She coughed thickly.

David turned away, satisfied she would live.

No, I wasn't too rough.

3:22 P.M., USS *Gibraltar*, Luzon Strait

The strip of water between Taiwan and the Philippines was tight with ships, many with guns blazing. Admiral Houston watched the fighting through the green-tinted windows of the bridge. Overhead, the sky was choked with smoke, turning day to a gloomy twilight. That morning the *Gibraltar* had joined the battle group of the USS *John C. Stennis*, consisting of the massive Nimitz-class aircraft carrier, its air wing and destroyer squadron.

Just as the *Gibraltar* arrived, an attack by the Chinese air force began. Jets roared across the skies, bombarding the ships below with missile fire. In response, Sea Sparrow anti-aircraft missiles blasted skyward. A handful of jets exploded, tumbling in fiery streams into the ocean—but the true battle was only beginning. The Chinese navy, over the horizon, had soon joined the conflict, bombarding the region with rocket barrages.

All day, the sea war had raged.

Off to the south, a destroyer, the USS *Jefferson City*, lay burning. An evacuation was under way. ASW helicopters from the *Gibraltar* were already in the air, rising like hornets to aid in the defense of their section of the sea.

To Houston's side, Captain Brenning shouted orders to his bridge crew.

Houston stared out over the smoke and chaos. Both sides were chewing each other apart. And for what?

An alarm sounded. The Phalanx Close-in Weapons System at the front end of the island's superstructure swung its 20mm Gatling guns and began firing, chugging out fifty rounds a second. Off on the starboard side an incoming missile, a sea-skimmer, blew apart about two thousand yards away.

Orders were screamed.

Rocket fragments rained down upon the *Gibraltar*, pounding and peppering the ship's Kevlar armor panels. The ship bore the assault with minimal damage.

"Sir!" One of the lieutenants pointed. Two of the ASW helicopters, pelted by the missile shards, tumbled into the sea. At the same time, the Phalanx CIWS defensive guns near the fantail sponson rattled as more missiles bore down on the beleaguered ship. Mortars were launched by the SLQ-32, throwing up a cloud of chaff against the attack.

The *Gibraltar* echoed and rattled with frag impacts.

Captain Brenning said, "Admiral, we must retreat. The zone is too hot for the helicopters."

Houston clenched his fists, but he nodded. "Order the flight deck cleared." As his command was relayed, Houston turned toward the *Jefferson*, bearing silent witness to the death of so many sailors. He watched as the fires worsened. Tiny lifeboats fled the sinking giant.

Then a huge explosion blew near the ship's stern and a fireball rolled over the ship. Lifeboats, too near, were thrown through the air. The great ship's bow rose ominously, its stern sinking. In seconds the *Jefferson* slipped deeper and deeper. Houston refused to look away.

"Sir!" a lieutenant yelled from the radar station. "I have multiple vampires vectoring in from the north. Thirty missile signatures across the board."

Captain Brenning responded, screaming orders.

Houston continued to watch the *Jefferson* sink. He knew the limits to the *Gibraltar*'s defense systems and made a silent prayer for his crew as the first explosion blew out the fantail section of his ship.

6:32 P.M., en route to Neptune base

Karen sat in the Sea Stallion helicopter. Through the windows, she watched dully as the ocean passed beneath her. Her face ached, and she could not completely swallow away the taste of blood. The beating from this morning had left her weak and sick. She had already vomited twice.

Across from her, Spangler lay slumped in his seat, eyes closed, lightly snoring. Three of his men took up the other seats, strapped in. One of them, Spangler's second-in-command, stared at her. She glared back at him. He looked away, but not before she spotted the flicker of shame on his face.

She returned her attention to the sea, thinking, plotting. They might hurt her physically, but she would not give up fighting. As long as she lived, she would strive for a way to thwart Spangler and his team.

As she stared at the passing water, she leaned against the cool window. Even with all the horror of the past day, one worry remained foremost in her mind—*Jack*. Bound to the cell's bed, she had heard the muffled explosions, felt the ship rock.

She closed her eyes, remembering the pain in his eyes as he swung through the door and left her behind. Was he alive? She made a silent promise to herself. She would survive, if only to answer that question.

7:08 P.M., *Deep Fathom*, off the northern coast of Pohnpei Island

Jack stood at the head of the worktable in Robert's wet lab. His crew were seated around its length, including two newcomers to the *Fathom*: Miyuki and Mwahu. The pair had boarded a few hours ago.

The police had questioned all of them, but it was clear where the blame lay. They were released. The chief of police seemed more interested in seeing them gone from the area, than in getting to the bottom of the night's attack and kidnapping. Jack suspected an unseen hand urging the whole matter to be brushed under the rug.

Rogue pirates was the final lame answer. The chief of police promised to continue the search for the missing anthropologist, but Jack knew it was a line of bullshit. As soon as they left, the matter would fade away.

"So what do we do from here?" Charlie asked.

With a wince of complaint from his wrapped rib cage, Jack lifted the backpack at his feet. It was Karen's bag. He dumped its contents on the worktable. The crystal star rattled on the tabletop. Beside it dropped the platinum-bound book recovered from the crypt.

"We need answers," he stated fiercely. He slid the book toward Miyuki. "First, we need this translated."

Miyuki opened it. Jack knew what lay inside. Earlier, he had studied it himself. Its pages were thin sheaves of platinum, crudely etched with more of the hieroglyphic writing. "Gabriel and I will get to work on it immediately."

Mwahu leaned over the book as Miyuki closed it. He touched the single symbol drawn into its top cover. A triangle within a circle. "*Khamwau*," he said. "I know this mark. My father teach. It means 'danger.'"

"That's a real surprise," Kendall McMillan said sarcastically. Eyes turned in the accountant's direction. Jack had offered to leave the nervous man on Pohnpei, but he had refused, stating, "With the cover-up going on here, I wouldn't stand a rat's ass of a chance getting off this island alive." So he had stayed on the *Fathom*.

Returning his attention to the book, Jack said, "Mwahu, since you know some of the ancient language, maybe you could help Miyuki with its translation."

Next, Jack passed the crystal star toward Charlie. "I need you to research its properties and abilities."

The geologist smiled, eyeing the artifact greedily.

"George . . ." Jack turned to the gray-haired historian. "I want you to continue researching the lost ships of this Dragon's Triangle. See if you can spot any other patterns."

He nodded. "I'm working on a few theories already."

Kendall McMillan frowned, speaking up again. "How is

any of this going to pull our asses out of the fire? Why don't we just lay low? Keep running."

"Because we'd never stop running. They'd never stop hunting us. The only way out is to discover the true reason for the crash of Air Force One." Jack leaned on his fists. "That answer lies at the heart of it all. I just know it!"

Lisa spoke up from the other end of the table. "But Kendall's right. What are we going to do in the meantime? Where are we going to go?"

"Back to where we started. Back to the crash site."

Lisa frowned. "But why? It's heavily guarded by the military. We won't have a chance of getting near there."

Jack's voice grew tight. "Because if David is heading anywhere, it's there."

18

Dark Matters

Lawrence Nafe listened to the late night reports from each of his Joint Chiefs. The news was grim. The Chinese naval and air forces were holding U.S. forces at bay.

The Secretary of the Navy stood at the foot of the table. "Following the earthquakes, military bases up and down the West Coast are still struggling to dig out of the rubble, hampering an ability to sustain a prolonged conflict across the Pacific. A second aircraft carrier, the USS *Abraham Lincoln*, and its battle group are en route from the Indian Ocean. But it's still three days out."

"So what are you saying?" Nafe asked, exhausted and irritable.

Hank Riley, Commandant of the Marine Corps, answered, "We're fighting this battle with one hand tied behind our back, sir. Our supply lines across the Pacific are weak at best. After the tidal waves, Honolulu is still under three feet of water. Its air bases—"

"I've already heard from the Air Force Chief of Staff," Nafe said sourly. "I need answers, alternatives . . ."

General Hickman, Chairman of the Joint Chiefs, stood. "We do have one option left to consider."

"And what is that?"

"As has been mentioned already, we're fighting this battle with one fist tied behind our backs. We can change that."

Nafe sat up straighter. This was what he came to hear—answers, not problems. "What do you propose?"

"A limited nuclear response."

A hush fell over the Situation Room. Nafe's hands gripped his knees. He had already discussed such an option with Nicolas Ruzickov earlier in the day. Nafe tried to keep the excitement out of his voice. "Have you formulated a plan?"

The general nodded. "We break the blockade decisively. A balls-out response. Military targets only."

Nafe's eyes narrowed. "Go on."

"From two Ohio-class subs off the coast of the Philippines, we strike three critical zones with Trident Two missiles." The general pointed out the targets on the highlighted map. "It'll break the back of the blockade. The Chinese will be forced to retreat. But more importantly, they'll get the message how serious we are to protect our interests in the region."

Nafe flicked a look toward Nicolas Ruzickov. A similar scenario had been proffered by the CIA director. It was clear his influence and string-pulling had reached all the way to the Joint Chiefs. Nafe assumed a look of somber thoughtfulness, playing the concerned patrician. "A nuclear response." He shook his head. "It's a sorry day that the Chinese have driven us to."

"Yes, sir," the general agreed, bowing his head.

Nafe sighed, sagging as if defeated. "But tragically, I see no other choice. Proceed immediately." After an appropriately long pause, he dragged himself to his feet. "And may God forgive us all." He turned and strode to the room's exit, flanked by his Secret Service.

Once out the door, Nicolas Ruzickov was not long in catching up with him in the hall, matching his stride.

Nafe allowed a slim smile to shine for a moment. "Well done, Nick. Well done indeed."

11:15 A.M., *Deep Fathom*, Central Pacific

Lisa spotted Jack by the bow rail, staring at the horizon. Overhead, the skies were slate-gray, with thin scudding clouds and a perpetual haze that even the noon sun had failed to burn away. Jack stood in his customary red trunks, a loose shirt open in front.

Elvis sat by his side, leaning against Jack's leg. Lisa could not help but smile at the loyalty and affection in the simple gesture. One of Jack's hands lightly ruffled the fur behind the dog's ear.

Lisa crossed to him, compelled by the need to get something off her chest. "Jack . . ."

He turned toward her and winced, fingering the Ace bandage wrap around his chest. "What?"

She moved to his side, put her hands on the rail. The solitary moment gone, Elvis loped to a sunny spot on the deck and sprawled out.

Lisa stared out at sea, silent for a moment, then spoke. "Jack, why are we doing this?"

"What do you mean?"

She turned to him, leaning a hip against the rail. "We've got the crystal. Miyuki says she's close to a translation. Why don't we just keep a low profile until we have answers, then send the entire story out to the *New York Times*?"

Jack gripped the rail with fists. "If we did that, Jennifer would be dead before the first paper hit the stands."

Silently, Lisa stared at him, searching his face to see if he recognized his slip of the tongue. He just kept staring off to sea. "Jennifer?"

"What?"

"You just said *Jennifer* would be as good as dead."

Jack finally looked at her, his face a mask of hurt and confusion. "You know what I meant," he mumbled, waving off any significance.

Lisa grabbed his hand. "She's not Jennifer."

"I know that," Jack snapped.

Lisa kept him from turning away. "Talk to me, Jack."

He sighed, but his shoulders remained tight. "Karen's in this danger because of me. I . . . I ran off, leaving her with that madman."

"And you explained why. Karen was right. Staying would have only gotten you both killed. If she's as strong as you say she is, she'll survive."

"Only as long as she's useful to that bastard." He twisted away. "I have to try to rescue her. I can't just keep running away."

Lisa touched his shoulder lightly. "Jack, for as long as I've known you, you've been running away. From Jennifer, the shuttle accident, your past. What's stopping you now? What does this woman mean to you?"

"I . . . I don't know." Jack sagged, head hanging over the rail, studying the waves. Finally, he looked at Lisa again. "But I'd like the chance to find out."

She slipped an arm around his waist. "That's all I wanted to hear." She leaned her head on his shoulder, swallowed back the twinge of sadness and the ache in her heart. Jack had finally opened himself, if only a crack, to a woman . . . and it wasn't her.

He put his arm around her shoulders and pulled her close, seeming to sense her sorrow. "I'm sorry."

"I'm not, Jack. But Christ, you've picked a hell of a time to fall in love."

He returned her smile and kissed her forehead. They stood in each other's arms until Mwahu called from an open doorway. "Miyuki says come!"

Jack slipped from beside her. "She's translated the language?"

Mwahu nodded vigorously. "Come!"

Lisa followed Jack as he strode after the dark-skinned islander. Belowdecks, Miyuki had set up a computer station atop Robert's long worktable. The work space was crowded with printouts, scribbled notes, and coffee mugs.

Miyuki looked up from a sheaf of papers with a worried expression.

"You've succeeded?" Jack asked.

She nodded, straightening her papers. "Gabriel succeeded. But Mwahu's help was critical. With his ability to apply context to a score of symbols, Gabriel was able to compile the entire vocabulary. He's translated everything—the crypt's book, the pillar's inscription, even the writing in the Chatan pyramids."

"Great! What have you learned?"

She frowned. "The obelisk inscription appears to be mostly prayers, asking the gods for a good harvest, fertility, that sort of thing." She teased out one page and read. " 'May the sun shine on the empty fields and make them fertile . . . may the bellies of our women grow heavy with children as plentiful as the fish of the sea.' "

"Not much use," Jack concurred.

"But the other writings are more interesting. They both describe the same thing—an ancient cataclysm."

Jack picked up the book from the table. "Karen suggested something like that. A lost continent sunk during a great disaster."

"She was right."

He raised the platinum book. "What does this say?"

Miyuki looked grim. "It appears to be the diary of Horon-ko."

"Our most ancient teacher," Mwahu interjected.

Miyuki nodded. "It recounts how his people, a seafaring tribe, once fished and traveled throughout the Pacific, some ten to twelve thousand years ago. Though they were fairly nomadic, their homeland was a large continent in the middle of the Pacific. They lived in small coastal villages and seaside towns. Then one day a hunter returned from a journey to the inner continent with 'a piece of the sun's magic.' A magical stone that shone and glowed. Horon-ko spoke at length of how the gift granted his people the ability to make stones fly."

"The crystal!" Jack said.

"Exactly. They excavated other crystals . . . all at the same location deep in the interior of their continent. They carved tools and worship fetishes."

"What does it say about the crystal's properties?"

Lisa interrupted. "Maybe Charlie ought to listen to this."

Jack nodded. "Gather everyone. They all should hear this."

It took less than five minutes to reconvene in Robert's lab. Once everyone was settled, Lisa motioned to Miyuki. "Go on."

With a nod, Miyuki quickly repeated the story, then continued anew. "These crystals changed Horon-ko's people. They were able to build great cities and temples throughout many lands. As they spread, their society constructed elaborate mines, searching for more crystals. Then, one day, they found a rich vein of crystal buried in the heart of a hilltop. Over the course of fifteen years, they excavated the entire hill away, exposing the crystal spire."

"The pillar!" Jack exclaimed.

"So it would appear. They worshiped the spire, believing it a blessing from their gods. It became a great pilgrimage spot. In fact, Horon-ko was one of the priests of the pillar."

"And this great cataclysm?"

"That's the strange part," Miyuki replied, turning to her computer system. "Gabriel, could you read the translation starting from section twenty?"

"Certainly, Professor Nakano," the computer responded from the tiny speakers. " '*There came a time of bad omens. Strange lights were seen in the north. Ribbons of light, like waves of the sea, rode the night skies. The grounds trembled. The people came to the god pillar to pray for help. Sacrifices were made. But on that last day, the moon came and ate the sun. The goddess of night walked the land.*' "

"An eclipse," Charlie mumbled.

Gabriel continued, " *'The god pillar, angry at the moon, blazed brightly. The ground shook. Mountains fell, seas rose. Fires opened in the ground, swallowing villages. But the gods did not forsake us. A god of light stepped from the pillar and ordered us to build great ships. To gather our flocks and people. The god spoke of a terrible time of darkness, when the seas would rise up and swallow our land. In our great ships, we must travel the drowning seas. So we gathered our seeds and our animals. We built a great ship.'* "

"Like Noah's ark and the flood," Lisa whispered.

Gabriel continued his recitation, " *'The god spoke true. A great darkness filled the skies. For many moons the sun was gone. Fiery pits blazed, openings to the lower world. Killing smoke filled the air. It grew hot. The seas rose and took our lands. In great boats we traveled to the Land of Big Ice, far to the south. And once there—'* "

Miyuki cut him off. "Thank you, Gabriel. That's enough." She stood. "The remainder of the book relates how the survivors kept their civilization's history alive. They traveled all around the world, finding other races of man to whom to pass on their stories and teachings, until eventually they were spread so thin that their civilization ceased to exist. Only Horon-ko and a handful of others returned to the grave of their homeland to die. He warned those that remained to beware the old places and avoid trespassing lest the angry gods reawaken." Miyuki sighed. "It is there the tale ends."

Jack glanced around the room. "So what do you all think?"

No one spoke.

Jack eyed George. "Does this help with your research into the Dragon's Triangle?"

"I'm not sure." The old historian had remained quiet during the discourse, smoking a pipe. He cleared his throat. "Earlier today I came up with intriguing statistics concerning the lost ships of the region. But I'm not sure what they mean."

"What did you find out?"

"Let me show you." He rifled through his pockets, searching one then another. Finally, he yanked out a folded computer printout. "I plotted the number of recorded disappearances for each year, going back a hundred years." He unfolded the paper.

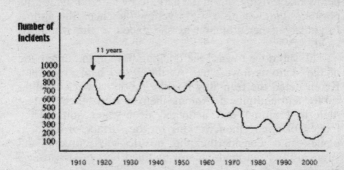

"As you can see, there's a pattern." He tapped the paper. "The number of incidences peak and trough very regularly. The numbers grow to a certain peak then taper back off. The size of the peak varies, but not the frequency. There's a distinct clustering every eleven years."

Bent over the sheet, Charlie let out a murmur of surprise. Heads turned in the geologist's direction.

"Is this significant?" Lisa asked.

"I'm not sure. I need to follow up on a few things." Charlie turned to George. "Can I borrow this?"

George shrugged. "It's all in my computer."

"What're you thinking?" Jack pressed.

Charlie shook his head, lost in thought. "Not yet." He excused himself and crossed to his own lab, closing the door behind him.

They all stared after him until Lisa said, "So, Jack, now it's your turn. What about Karen? What's this rescue plan of yours?"

11:45 A.M., Neptune base

The submersible glided toward the deep-sea research station. From the rear passenger compartment of the two-man sub, Karen stared in awe. After twenty minutes of sinking through an ever-deepening gloom, the base had appeared below like a rising sun in the dark, lit by external lamps, its portholes aglow with a warm yellow radiance. She almost forgot about her situation as she gaped at the wondrous sight.

The sub dove toward the docking bay on the underside of the station's lowest tier. As the vessel banked around, Karen noted the trundling boxlike robots at work hauling cables and equipment. Among them moved other figures: men in armored and helmeted deep-water suits. They looked like spacemen working on the surface of an alien planet—and considering the hostile environment and strangely twisted landscape of tumbled lava pillars, it *was* another world.

A lantern fish, attracted by their movement, drew nearer the sub. Karen stared back through the five inches of glass, two strangers from different lands ogling each other. Then, with a flick of its tail, it vanished back into the gloom.

From the forward compartment she heard the muffled voice of the sub's pilot attending to the docking procedure, confirming and rechecking the station's status.

An okay must have been given because the sub and its two occupants were rising through a garage-door-size hatch and into the docking bay. In short order the hatch was sealed and the water pumped out. Soon afterward, Karen was helped out of the sub's cramped compartment.

She stretched a kink from her back. The pilot, Lieutenant Rolfe, ordered her to hold out her arms and then undid her handcuffs.

It was the first time since her capture that she was unfettered. Rubbing her wrists, she gazed around and understood why she was granted this new freedom. Where could she go? There was no better maximum-security prison in the world. Escape was unthinkable.

A door opened near the rear of the bay. A man in his early sixties, gray-haired and stocky, stormed inside to join them. He strode up to the lieutenant. "What is the meaning of this? There was no reason to bring her down here. The professor could have aided us just as well topside. The risks to her—"

"Those were my orders, Dr. Cortez," Rolfe said curtly. "The prisoner is your responsibility from here."

Cortez moved to block the lieutenant, then thought better of it. "And what about these new orders? Your commander can't be serious."

"You've read the reports." The lieutenant climbed back into the pilot's seat. "I'll be returning next with Commander Spangler. Take up your objections with him."

Cortez's attention shifted to Karen, his brows furrowing as he took in the condition of her face. "What the hell happened to her?" He reached a tentative hand toward her puffy eye, but she shied from him. Cortez swung on the lieutenant. "Answer me, goddamn it!"

The lieutenant avoided eye contact. "Take it up with Commander Spangler," he repeated, from the sub's pilot compartment.

The researcher's face darkened. "C'mon," he said brusquely to Karen. "I'll have Dr. O'Bannon take a look at you."

"I'm fine," she said as she followed him toward the exit. Earlier, she had been given a couple of aspirin and a shot of antibiotics. She was sore but not incapacitated.

Once through the hatch, Cortez led her to the upper deck ladders. He gave her a running tour of the facility as he guided her up. Karen listened intently, impressed by her surroundings. She was two thousand feet underwater. It was hard to believe.

She climbed the ladder up to the second tier, where men and women bustled around minilabs. Heads turned in her direction as she stepped forward. Whispers were shared. She knew what a sight she must look.

". . . and the level up from here is the living quarters.

Tight but with all the conveniences of home." He tried a weak smile.

Karen nodded, feeling out of place, eyes staring at her.

Cortez sighed. "I'm sorry, Professor Grace," he said. "This is hardly the most opportune way for colleagues to meet and—"

"Colleagues?" She frowned at him. "I'm a *prisoner*, Professor Cortez."

Her words wounded him. "That was none of our doing. I assure you. Commander Spangler has full control and authority over these facilities. With the nation at war, we have little say. Our research here has been labeled a matter of national security. Liberties have been taken in the name of protecting our nation's shores."

"It's not my nation. I'm Canadian."

Cortez frowned, not seeming to see the significance. "The best way to keep further . . . um—" He frowned at her bruised face. "—abuses of power from occurring is to cooperate. To work from within. After this is over, I'm sure the government will have a place for you."

Bullshit, Karen thought. She knew where her place would be: six feet under, shot as a spy. But she saw no need to burst this man's bubble. "So what have you learned down here?" she asked, changing the subject.

He brightened. "Quite a lot. We managed to harvest a small sample of the crystal. After a cursory study, it has displayed the most surprising properties."

Karen nodded, remaining silent about her own knowledge.

"But with the newest directives from Washington, any further research has been put on hold."

"New directives?"

"With the war so close, Washington now considers the site too vulnerable. Just yesterday we were ordered to extract the crystal pillar and ship it back to the United States for further study. But now even that order's been changed."

"What do you mean?"

"Initial assays of the sediment and seabed show the spire

is but a single pinnacle of a larger sample. Much larger. At the moment, we've not even been able to determine the deposit's true depth and extent. So far the damned thing has defied standard scanning methods. All we know is that it's massive. Once word reached Washington of our newest discovery, our orders were revised." His eyes narrowed with worry. "Rather than just the pillar, we've been ordered to harvest the entire deposit if possible."

"How are you going to do that?"

He waved her to one of the portholes. She peered out.

In the distance she could just make out a tall spire beyond the lights. Jack's pillar! Around the area, more of the armor-suited deep-sea workers labored. "Who are those men?"

"The Navy's demolitions experts. They plan to use explosives to blast a hole into the core of the deposit, then mine the load from there."

Karen stared in shock. "When do they begin?"

"Tomorrow."

She turned. "But the obelisk . . . the writing . . ."

He looked stricken, too. "I know. I've been trying to urge caution. This whole region is geologically unstable. We've had daily temblors and even one serious quake two days ago. But no one will listen to me. That's why— regardless of the circumstances of your arrival—I'm glad to have you here with us. If we knew what was written on the obelisk, it might stay the government's hand longer, buy us some time for our own research."

Karen balked at helping her captors, but the thought of the ancient artifact's destruction disturbed her even more. She stepped away from the porthole. "What if I can point you in the right direction about the inscription?"

His eyebrows rose with interest.

She lowered her voice. "But we'll need to trust each other."

He slowly nodded.

Karen said, "I'll need a computer and your current research into the language."

He waved for her to follow him and kept his voice low.
"Rick is our team's archaeologist. He's still topside, but I
can have him transmit the data to an empty workstation."

"Good. Let's get to work."

As Cortez led her to an unoccupied cubicle, Karen calculated, planned. As much as it bothered her to deceive the
man, she had no choice. "If you can get me an open Internet
line," she said, "I'll show you what I've learned."

6:45 P.M., *Deep Fathom*, Central Pacific

Jack knocked on Charlie's door. No one had heard from the
geologist all day except George Klein, and afterward the historian locked himself into the ship's small library. The two
were clearly working on something, but Jack was losing his
patience.

"Who is it?" Charlie called out, his voice hoarse.

"It's Jack. Open up."

A shuffle of noises, then the door cracked open. "What?"

Without invitation, Jack pushed inside. What he found
startled him. Charlie's usually tidy lab was in a shambles.
The worktable along one wall was covered in equipment and
gadgets. In the center of the mess, the crystal star was
clamped in a stainless steel vise. Charlie's computer displayed inexplicable graphs and tables. Jack had to step over
piles of journals and scientific magazines. Specific articles
were ripped and hung on the bare wall.

It was as if a hurricane had struck there. And Charlie
looked no better. His eyes were red-rimmed, his lips
chapped. His clothes—baggy shorts and a shirt—were
stained with ink, oil, and grease. It was hot and humid in the
room, and sweat soaked his armpits and lower back.

Jack noticed that the room's single fan had been un-
plugged to make outlet room for Charlie's equipment. Jack
yanked a cord, shoved in the fan's plug and switched it to
high.

"Christ, Charlie, what are you doing in here?"

The geologist ran a hand through his hair. "Research. What do you think?" He kicked aside some of the scattered magazines and pulled up a chair, sitting on its edge.

"Have you even slept since I gave you that thing?"

"How could I? It's amazing. Nothing like this substance has ever been discovered. I'm sure of it. I've hit it with every test I can manage here: the mass spectrometer, the proton magnetometer, X-ray diffraction. But it defies everything. At this point I couldn't tell you its atomic weight, its valence, its specific gravity—nothing! I can't even get the friggin' thing to melt." He tapped his mini-oven. "And this thing heats to a temperature of seven hundred degrees."

"So you don't know what it is?" Jack leaned against the worktable.

"I . . . I have my theories." Charlie bit his lip. "But you have to understand. My research is still preliminary. A lot is still speculative."

Jack nodded. "I trust your hunches."

Charlie scanned the lab. "Where to begin . . . ?"

"How about at the beginning?"

"Well, first there was the Big Bang—"

Jack held up a hand. "Not that far back."

"The story *goes* that far back."

Jack's eyebrows rose.

"I'd better take you through it a step at a time. After I heard your description of the crystal's effect on basalt, it got me thinking. I tried to repeat the effect on other rocks. Granite, obsidian, sandstone. No luck. Only basalt."

"Why basalt?"

"That's just what I wondered. Basalt is actually hardened magma. Not only is it abundant in prismatic crystals, but it's rich in iron, too. So rich, in fact, it's capable of being magnetic."

"Really?"

"You remember the strange magnetization of Air Force One's metal parts. The same thing happens to basalt when it comes in close contact with the energized crystal. When powered, the crystal is able to emit a strange magnetizing energy."

"So how does this magnetization make the mass of the rock change?"

"The mass doesn't change. Only its *weight*."

"You lost me."

Charlie frowned. "You've been in space."

"So?"

"In space you're weightless, right?"

"Yeah."

"But you still had *mass*, didn't you? It is *gravity* that gives mass its weight. The more gravity, the more something weighs."

"Okay, I get that."

"Well, the converse is true. The less gravity, the less something weighs."

Jack began to catch on. "So the crystal is not changing the mass of an object, it's changing gravity's effect on it."

"Exactly. Making the magnetic basalt weigh less."

"But how?"

Charlie rolled a chunk of basalt toward Jack. He caught it. "Do you even know what gravity is?"

"Sure, it's . . . well, it's . . . okay, you smartass, what is it?"

"According to Einstein's Unified Field Theory, gravity is merely a frequency."

"Like a radio station?"

"Pretty much. The frequency of Earth's gravity has been determined to be 10^{12} hertz, somewhere between shortwave radio and infrared radiation. If you could get an object to resonate at this frequency, it would lose its weight."

"And the crystal can do this?"

"Yes. The crystal emits this energy. It magnetizes the basalt's iron content, which triggers the crystalline structure to resonate. Vibrating at a frequency equal to gravity, the rock loses its weight."

"And you learned all this overnight?"

"Actually, I learned it within the first hour of experimenting with the crystal. That was the easy part. But understanding the energy radiating from the crystal—*that* was the hard part." Charlie grinned tiredly at him.

"You've figured it out?"

"I have my theory."

"Oh, out with it already. Tell me."

"It's dark energy."

Jack sighed, sensing another lecture. "And what's dark energy?"

"It's a force conjectured by a cosmologist, Michael Turner, in an article in the *Physical Review Letters.*" Charlie nodded to one of the pages taped to the wall. "After the Big Bang, the universe blew outward, spreading in all directions. And it's still expanding. But from the newest studies of the movement of distant galaxies and the brightness of supernovas, it is now accepted that the rate of expansion is accelerating."

"I don't understand."

"The universe is expanding faster and faster. To explain this phenomenon, a new force had to be coined—'dark energy.' A strange force that keeps the universe expanding by *repelling gravity.*"

"And you think this energy given off by the crystal may be dark energy."

"It's a theory I'm working to prove. But it's a theory that could possibly explain the crystal's *substance*, too. Dark energy is tied to another theoretical bit of physics—dark *matter.*"

Jack rolled his eyes.

Charlie chuckled. "What do you see when you look up at the night sky?"

"Stars?"

"Exactly, *mon*, what astronomers call *luminous* matter. Stuff we can see. Stuff that lights up the sky. But there is not enough of the observable stuff to explain the motion of galaxies or the current expansion of the universe. According to calculations of physicists, for every gram of luminous matter there must be nine grams of matter we can't see. Invisible matter."

"Dark matter."

"Exactly." Charlie nodded, his gaze flicking to the crystal. "We know a lot of the missing matter is just run-of-the-mill stuff: black holes, dark planets, brown dwarves, and other material our telescopes just haven't been able to detect. But with ninety percent of the universe's matter still missing, most physicists suspect the true source of dark matter will be something totally unexpected."

"Like our crystal that emits dark energy?"

"Why not? The crystal acts as a perfect superconductor, absorbing energy so completely that most methods for scanning for its presence would fail."

"So astronomers have been looking the wrong way all along. Rather than in the night sky, they should have been looking under their own feet."

The geologist shrugged.

Jack finally understood Charlie's drive. If he was right, the answer to the fundamental mysteries of the universe's origin lay in this room—not to mention a source of amazing power. A power never seen before. Jack pictured the massive crystal on the seabed floor. What could the world do with such an energy source?

George appeared in the open doorway behind him, shuffling papers. "Charlie, you should . . . oh, Jack, you're here." George looked disheveled and out of sorts.

"Were you able to find out what I asked?" Charlie asked.

George nodded, a glint of fear in his eyes.

Jack turned to Charlie. "What's going on?"

Charlie nodded to George. "His graph. The fact that every eleven years the number of ships missing in the area spiked. It got me thinking. It looked familiar, especially the dates. I rechecked George's data. His graph follows almost exactly the cycle of sunspot activity. Every *eleven* years the sun enters a period of increased magnetic storms. Sunspots and solar flares reach peaks of activity. These peaks coincided with the years when the most vessels vanished in the region."

"And you knew this solar cycle off the top of your head?"

"Not exactly. I was already researching this angle. Remember on the day of the Pacificwide quakes, there was an eclipse coinciding with a major solar storm. I wondered if there might be some correlation."

"You think the solar storms triggered the quakes—and the pillar had something to do with it?"

"Think about the platinum book. Even back then, the writer reports seeing strange lights in the northern skies before the big quake. The aurora borealis. It grows more brilliantly and expands far south during a solar storm. The ancients were experiencing a peak of solar activity prior to the disaster."

Jack shook his head. "This is all too much."

"Then let me put it all together for you. You remember our talk about the Dragon's Triangle a few days back?"

Jack nodded.

"And do you remember me telling you how it is exactly opposite the infamous Bermuda Triangle? How the two create some type of axis through the planet that causes disturbances in the magnetic lines of the Earth? Well, now I think I have an explanation. I would wager there are two massive deposits of this 'dark matter' crystal—one under the Dragon's Triangle and one under the Bermuda Triangle. The two poles have been acting like the positive and negative ends of a battery, creating a massive electromagnetic field. I believe it is this field that drives the Earth's magma to flow."

Jack tried to wrap his mind around this concept. "The Earth's battery? Are you serious?"

"I'm beginning to think so. And if I'm right, those ancients made a horrible mistake by digging free a sliver of this battery and exposing it to direct sunlight. They made it vulnerable to the big solar storm. A lightning rod, if you will. The crystal took the solar radiation, converted it into dark energy, and whipped up the Earth's magma core, creating the tectonic explosion that destroyed the continent."

"And you're suggesting something like that happened *here* two weeks ago?"

"A watered-down version of it, yes. Remember in the past the pillar was on dry land. Today it's insulated by six hundred meters of water. The depths served to shield it from the strongest of the storm's energy. It would've taken a significant solar event to trigger the recent quakes."

George lifted his hand to speak, but Jack interrupted, afraid to lose his train of thought. "How does all this tie into the President's plane?"

"If it was passing over the site when the crystal was radiating, the dark energy could have damaged the jet's systems. I've noted strange fluxes myself when experimenting with the crystal: magnetic spikes, EM surges, even tiny fluctuations in time, not unlike your own short lapses in the sub. I bet these bursts of energy have been messing with vessels in the area for centuries."

"If what you say is true . . ."

Charlie shrugged. "I don't purport to be an expert on dark energy . . . at least not yet. But can you imagine the devastation here millennia ago? Quakes that tore apart continents. Massive volcanic eruptions. Ash clouds that circled the world. Floods."

Jack remembered words in the ancient text: *the time of darkness*. The insulating layer of ash would have created a greenhouse effect, melting the ice caps and drowning their ravaged lands.

"We got off easy," Charlie said. "Can you imagine living during that time?"

"We may have to," George said sharply, his face stern.

Jack and Charlie turned to him.

George held up a sheet of paper. "I contacted the Marshall Space Flight Center. I confirmed what you wanted, Charlie. On July twenty-first, four days before the quakes, the Yohkoh satellite recorded a massive CME on the sun's surface."

"CME?" Jack asked.

"Coronal mass ejection," Charlie translated. "Like a super solar flare. They can hurl billions of tons of ionized gas from the sun's surface. It takes four days for the explosion to hit the Earth, creating a geomagnetic storm. To support my theory, I postulated that such a violent event would have been necessary for the submerged pillar to react so severely."

George sighed. "They also confirmed that the epicenter for the Pacific quakes has been calculated to be where the pillar lies. At the spot where Air Force One crashed."

Charlie lit up. "I was right. Not bad for a couple days' work."

Jack turned to George. The historian held a second piece of paper, at which he was glancing nervously. "You have more news, don't you?"

George swallowed. "After I contacted the Space Center, they forwarded the latest pictures from the Japanese satellite. Another coronal mass ejection occurred just three days ago. It was the biggest ever recorded." George stared at them. "A hundred times larger than the last one."

"Oh, shit," Charlie said, his grin fading away. "When does NASA expect its energy wave to hit us?"

"Tomorrow afternoon."

"Damn . . ."

"What?" Jack asked. "What's gonna happen then?"

Charlie looked over at him. "We're not talking quakes and tidal waves this time. We're talking the end of the world."

7:02 P.M.

Miyuki sat at the worktable in the marine biology lab. In the background she heard the muffled voices of Jack and a pair of his crew talking animatedly in the geology suite. Around her a thousand eyes watched from the clear plastic specimen jars lining the shelves and cabinets. It made it hard to concentrate.

Shaking her head against these distractions, Miyuki continued her own line of research. Earlier she had Gabriel do a global search through all the *rongorongo* examples gleaned from Easter Island to see if there were any other references to the pillar or the ancient disaster. She had little luck. A few scant allusions, but nothing significant. Now she was rereading through the passages in the platinum diary.

At her elbow, the briefcase-mounted computer chimed. Gabriel's voice came through the tiny speakers. He had been assigned to work out a linguistic equivalent to the language, using phonetics supplied by Mwahu. Miyuki looked up from her sheets.

"I'm sorry to disturb you, Professor Nakano."

"What is it, Gabriel?"

"I have an incoming call from Dr. Grace. Would you care to take it?"

Miyuki almost fell out of her chair. "Karen . . . ?" She slid in front of the computer. "Gabriel, patch in the call!"

Above the flat monitor, the one-inch video camera blinked on. On the screen, a cascade of pixels slowly formed a jerky image of her friend. Miyuki leaned near the microphone. "Karen! Where are you?"

Karen's computer image flittered. "I don't have much time. I was able to contact Gabriel with your coded address for him on the Internet. He was able to encrypt this video line, but I can't trust that someone won't catch on."

"Where are you?"

"At some undersea research base near Jack's obelisk. Is he there?"

Miyuki nodded. She leaned back. "Jack! Come quick!"

The captain of the *Fathom* poked his head out of the geology lab, his face worried. "What is it?"

Miyuki stood up and pointed to the screen. "It's Karen!"

His eyes widened. He fell out the door of the geology lab and stumbled around the table. "What do you—" Then he came in view of the computer's screen. He rushed forward, leaning close. "Karen, is that you?"

7:05 P.M., Neptune base

Karen watched Jack's face form in the small square in the lower right-hand side of her computer monitor. He was alive! Tears welled in her eyes.

"Karen, where are you?"

She coughed to clear her throat, then briefly summarized the past twenty-four hours: her capture, the trip by helicopter, the imprisonment in the sea base. Afterward, she continued, "I tossed a bone the researchers' way and told them about the *rongorongo* connection. It's a useless lead without the additional examples we discovered, but they don't know that. By feigning cooperation, they've given me a little latitude." She looked over her shoulder when a spat of laughter echoed down the curving length of the tier. "The others are up at dinner or working in private. I don't know how long I can keep this line open without arousing suspicion."

"I'll find a way to get you out of there," Jack said. "Trust me."

Karen leaned closer to the screen. "I wanted you to know. They're planning to blow up the obelisk sometime tomorrow afternoon. They've probed the area and seem to believe there's a larger deposit under it. The tip of the proverbial iceberg."

On the monitor, Jack glanced to the side. "You were right, Charlie!"

"Of course I was," someone said off screen.

Karen frowned. "What do you mean? What do you know?"

She listened as Jack sketchily recounted what they had learned from the platinum book and Charlie's theories. Karen sat frozen as the story unfolded: ancient disasters, dark matter, solar storms. She listened with her mouth hanging open as Jack told her of the coming danger.

"Oh my God!" she said. "When is this storm supposed to strike?"

"Just after noon tomorrow."

A new face appeared on the screen. Jack made the intro-
duction. "This is Charlie Mollier, the ship's geologist."

"So what do we do?" Karen asked. Sweat trickled down
her back. She was sure she would be caught any moment.

"Tell me about the explosives and intent of the demolition squad," Charlie said.

Karen explained the Navy's plan to blast into the core of
the crystal's main vein.

Jack spoke up. "Maybe that'd be good. At least the pillar
won't be poking out any longer."

"No," Charlie said, "if they succeed, it'll make matters
worse. They'll be laying open the very heart of the deposit,
increasing, not lessening, the area of exposure to the solar
storm. The only way to protect against this disaster is to bury
the pillar or cleanly clip it off, separating it from the main
deposit."

"In other words, knock down the lightning rod," Jack
said.

Karen checked her watch. If the geologist was right, they
had only seventeen hours. "What if we specifically target the
crystal pillar with the explosives?"

"Still dangerous," Charlie mumbled. "Even if you could
arrange it, the kinetic energy of the blast could be absorbed
into the main deposit." He shook his head. "It's risky. The
strength of an explosion sufficient to crack a pillar of that
immense size could trigger the very disaster we're trying to
avoid."

The video phone line went silent as parties pondered the
hopelessness of their situation.

"We need more help," Charlie mumbled.

Karen chewed on this idea. "I could try enlisting the aid
of the head researcher here. Dr. Cortez. He's cautioned the
Navy against blasting the crystal, and I don't think he's a big
fan of Spangler's, either."

"I don't know," Jack said. "I'm suspicious of anyone
working alongside that bastard."

"But he's a geophysicist," Karen argued. "Renowned in
his field."

"And I could truly use some expert help," Charlie agreed.

Jack frowned and looked directly into the camera. "But can we trust him, Karen?"

She sat quiet for a long moment, then sighed. "I think so. But I'll need your data. I'll need to convince him."

Jack turned to Charlie. "Can you download your research?"

He nodded and disappeared.

Miyuki spoke from off screen. "I'll compile all the translations, and prepare Gabriel to transmit everything."

"Great," Jack replied. He turned back to the camera, and Karen thought he seemed to stare right into her heart. "How are *you* doing?" he asked softly.

"Considering the fact that I'm imprisoned a mile under the sea and the world's gonna end tomorrow, I'm not too bad."

"Did they rough you up?"

She remembered her black eye, fingering its sore edges. "No, I fell onto a doorknob . . . a few times in a row."

"I'm sorry, Karen. I shouldn't have gotten you involved in all this."

She sat straighter. "Don't take the guilt for this, Jack. I'd rather be where I am now than back at the university, oblivious to all this. If there's a way to stop what's gonna happen, I'd rather be here on the front lines."

Miyuki spoke from off screen. "I've got all the data collected. But to send it, I'll need this video line to upload the information."

Jack nodded. "You hear that?"

"Y-Yes," Karen fought to keep her voice from breaking. She hated the thought of losing contact with her friends.

"Gabriel will keep monitoring this channel afterward," Miyuki said. "Use his code if you want to speak to us."

Jack leaned nearer, his face filling the little screen. "Be careful, Karen. David is an ass, but he's no fool."

"I know."

They stared at one another for an extra breath. Jack kissed his fingers and pressed them against the screen. "I'll get you out of there."

Before she could answer, the phone line switched off and

the video square vanished. Replacing it was a colored bar, filling slowly with the incoming data stream. She directed the information to a DVD recorder. Alone, she waited for the file to be transmitted.

A voice spoke off to the side. "What are you doing?"

Karen turned. David was climbing up from the lower deck. He was supposed to be out in the *Perseus,* overseeing the demolition team. He must have returned early.

Barefoot and in a wet suit, he stepped from the ladder and moved toward her. "I told Cortez to keep someone with you at all times. What are you doing here unattended?"

She fixed a bland expression on her face. Out of the corner of her eye she watched the colored bar fill slowly. "I gave Cortez what you wanted. The key to the ancient script. They're researching it and didn't want my help."

He moved to her side.

Karen twisted around, blocking the view of the data bar with her elbow.

He glanced at the screen, then back at her. His eyes narrowed. "If you're not needed, you should be confined to your quarters." He grabbed her by the shoulder. "Come with me."

He yanked her to her feet. She dared not even glance back at the screen, lest it draw his attention. "Why confine me?" she asked boldly, stepping in front of him, blocking his view. "Where am I going to go?"

David scowled. "Because those were my orders. No one goes against them. Not even Cortez."

"To hell with—"

The back of his hand struck her face, hard, knocking her to the side. Caught by surprise, Karen gasped and almost fell to one knee. She grabbed her chair to keep upright.

"No one questions my orders," he said thickly. Rubbing the back of his hand, his eyes flicked to the computer monitor.

Karen winced. *Oh, God* . . . She turned to the screen.

It was mercifully empty. The transmission had been completed.

She straightened with relief.

David glanced along the curved row of labs, clearly suspicious, looking for some evidence of a foul plan. She saw his nostrils flaring, scenting the air like a bloodhound, before he whipped back toward her.

Karen inadvertently shied away.

He leaned near her. "I can smell Kirkland on you, bitch. I don't know what you're up to, but I'll find out."

A cold chill slithered up her back.

He snatched her by the elbow, fingers digging hard. "Now let's find the others. It's time they were taught a thing or two about military protocol."

As she was pulled away she glanced at the empty workstation. Hidden on a little silver disk over there were the answers to everything—ancient mysteries, the origin of the universe, even the fate of the world. She had to find a way to place it in the hands of someone who could help. *But how?*

8:12 P.M., *Deep Fathom*

Jack sat on a stool in the geology lab. Charlie worked at his computer, reviewing his data. Both were searching for answers. Jack struggled to think, but Karen's face, bruised and scared, kept appearing in his head, distracting him. He closed his eyes. "How 'bout if we tried short-circuiting the damn thing?"

"What?" Charlie asked.

"You said the deposit acts like some electromagnetic battery. What if we, I don't know, *overloaded* it or something."

Charlie turned from his computer, frowning tiredly. "That would only accelerate—" The geologist's frown deepened. Jack could practically see the calculations running in the man's head.

"Do you think it might work?"

His eyes focused back on Jack. "No, not at all. But you've given me an idea." He stood, crossed to the worktable and scrounged through his gadgetry. In a few moments Charlie had a spare marine battery hooked to a meter.

"What are you doing?" Jack asked.

"Running a little experiment." He lifted the battery's leads and connected them to the steel clamps holding the crystal star. He put on one of Robert's night vision masks. "Can you hit the lights?"

Jack slid off his stool and flicked the switch. In the dark cabin, he heard Charlie shuffling around. Then he heard a tiny snap of electricity. A blue arc zapped between the battery's leads, painfully bright in the dark. The crystal artifact lit up like a real star.

The radiant light fractured into a spectrum of colors. Jack remembered a similar sight—when the electromagnet used to haul up sections of Air Force One had brushed too near the pillar. The spire had glowed with the same brightness.

As he watched, the star grew brighter and brighter. He raised a hand to shield his eyes. Charlie was bent over the star, flicking his gaze between it and the meter. One hand turned a dial. The hum of the battery grew louder.

"Charlie—"

"Hush." He twisted the dial more.

The star began to rise from the table, floating a few inches off the surface. Its light was almost too intense. An electric tingling swept through the air. The small hairs began to dance on Jack's arms, and the fillings in his teeth began to ache in his jaw. It was like being back in the sub.

His eyes were drawn to a wall clock, hanging above the experiment. The second hand was running in the wrong direction.

"Amazing," Charlie mumbled, still bent over the floating star.

Then a loud *crack* exploded in the small space. Darkness fell over the room. Jack heard the crystal star drop back to the tabletop with a clatter.

"Get the lights," Charlie ordered.

Jack rubbed the tingling from his arms, then flipped the switch. "What were you doing?"

Using tongs, Charlie picked up the star. The steel clamps holding it glowed hot. "Hmm . . . interesting . . ."

"What?"

The geologist tilted the star for Jack to see. Within the clamps, the crystal had cracked in half.

"What does it mean?" Jack asked.

Charlie looked up. "I'm not sure yet."

8:56 P.M., Neptune base

Karen tried not to cry. She sat on a narrow cot in a cabin no larger than a half bath. What was she going to do? David had gathered the entire crew of the station in the dining room. He spent fifteen minutes browbeating them all. One of the scientists made the mistake of asking a simple question. For his impudence, David shattered his nose with a sudden blow. The room had grown deathly silent afterward. David had proven his point. He was the master here. After his demonstration, he stormed out with Karen in tow.

She soon found herself locked in this cabin. It all seemed impossible, hopeless. Over the past two days, she had hardly slept at all. She was sore, exhausted, and drained.

She rested her face in her hands. She couldn't do this alone.

As a sob welled up from deep inside, a soft knock sounded on her door. "Dr. Grace?"

She sat up, wary. "Who is it?"

"It's Dr. Cortez. May I come in?"

Karen almost choked with relief. "Of course."

She stood as she heard the key in the lock. The older scientist slipped in and closed the door behind him. "I'm sorry to disturb you so late."

"No, it's okay. I can use the company." She allowed the relief to ring in her voice.

"He's one scary bastard, isn't he? I should never have left you alone down there. I wasn't thinking. I was too excited about your discovery of the connection to the Rapa Nui script."

Karen sat down. She waved him to the sole stool. "It wasn't your fault."

"Well, after this is over, I'm filing a formal complaint."

She nodded, allowing him the fantasy that it would have any impact. Spangler was operating under the guise of the highest office in the nation. He could act with full impunity.

Cortez continued, "I came here to see if you could help us. We're still having trouble deciphering these glyphs."

Karen swallowed. If there was to be any hope, it was time to start trusting someone else. No more games. "Dr. Cortez, I haven't been totally honest."

"What do you mean?"

"I possess the *full* translation. Not only of the pillar's inscription, but additional texts written at the time of the obelisk's discovery."

Cortez sat stunned, silent, then tried to talk. "I don't . . . how could . . . but when . . . ?"

"I have information I must get to someone in authority," Karen said. "Someone out of Spangler's chain of command."

"Information about what?"

"About the end of the world."

Cortez frowned, looking doubtful.

Karen stood. "I know how it must sound. But get me to the workstation on Level 2, and I'll get you proof."

Still, he hesitated.

Karen stared him down. "After tonight's demonstration, who are you willing to trust more, Spangler or me?"

Cortez bowed his head for a moment, then pushed off his stool. "That's no contest. C'mon, the commander is bunked out in his cabin, but his second-in-command is patrolling. Stick to my side. As long as you're with me, we should be okay." He opened the door.

Karen followed him out. Though there was no ban on her being free under supervision, it still felt like a prison break. Both crept silently through the living quarters, peeking around corners, holding their breath. No one was around.

They got to the ladder heading down to the lab level, and Cortez went first. He signaled the all clear for her to follow. As she climbed, the interlevel hatch sealed with a snug hiss.

Silently, they worked around the ring of labs to the tiny station assigned to her.

"What now?" Cortez asked, glancing about the deserted space.

Karen pointed Cortez to the chair, while she remained standing. "I have the data on a disk." Reaching past him, she punched the keyboard, calling up the information.

Data scrolled across the screen. She helped guide the researcher through the information, pointing out the text of the platinum book and where it was found. She gave him a shortened version of her own exploits and Jack's.

After a bit, Cortez waved her silent. He leaned closer, his fingers flying over the keyboard, calling up screen after screen of data. Much of it was too technical for Karen, but Cortez was drinking it up. "This Charles Mollier is an amazing scientist. What he's discovered about the crystal in such a short time—it's astounding! But it corroborates much of my own early testing." He continued reading through the streaming text and graphs.

As he did so, Karen watched his face slowly change from amazement to horror. Once done, he sat back and took off his glasses. "I knew we should have proceeded with more caution. It's madness to be fooling with a power of this magnitude."

She crouched beside him. "Will you help get this to somebody who will listen? We have only fifteen hours until the solar storm strikes."

"Yes, of course. I have friends at Los Alamos and at the Lawrence Berkeley National Laboratory. There are ways to circumvent the normal government channels."

Karen felt a surge of hope.

Cortez rubbed his eyes. "Is there any more data?"

"I'm not sure. That's all they sent me. But I can find out."

"How?"

She typed in Gabriel's code on the computer keyboard. Almost immediately, a voice came over the speakers. *"How may I help you, Dr. Grace?"*

"Who is that?" Cortez asked.

"No one . . . really." Karen directed her attention back to the computer. "Gabriel, I need to contact the *Deep Fathom*."

"Of course. Right away."

The connection whirred through to the distant ship, and a small video window bloomed in the screen's corner. Miyuki's face flickered into existence. "Karen?"

"I have Dr. Cortez with me. He's willing to help."

Miyuki vanished from the camera's view for a few moments, then Jack and Charlie appeared. Introductions were quickly made.

"Do either of you have any recommendations?" Cortez asked. "I can get the information to the right people, but what then? From the data, I can only assume we must find a way to block the solar storm's bombardment from reaching the main deposit. That leaves few options."

Jack nodded. "We've been discussing it. The easiest method is to shield the pillar. Bury it, seal it in a lead box, something like that. But I don't know if either is feasible in the narrow time frame. If this can't be done, then we take our chances and adjust the explosives to a specific focused charge, aimed at cracking the pillar from its base."

Cortez frowned. "But the kinetic energy from the blast—"

"We know, but like I said, it's our *second* option. And it's better than doing nothing because there's only one option after that."

"And what might that be?"

"We kiss our asses good-bye."

Cortez's face grew grim.

Charlie spoke into the silence. "I'll keep working with the crystal, see if I can come up with anything else." But he didn't sound hopeful.

Jack continued, "That leaves only one other obstacle—Spangler. I can't risk leaving Karen over there any longer than necessary. Once word reaches David that you're going behind his back, her life won't be worth a plug nickel. We need to make sure she's out of there before Spangler finds out what we're doing."

Cortez frowned. "That'll be difficult. Tomorrow morning

they're evacuating the station as a safety precaution before they blow the explosives. I already checked on the departure schedule. Karen and I are the last to leave, along with Spangler."

Karen moved in front of the camera. "And after today's incident, I doubt Spangler will let me out of his sight tomorrow."

"Then it looks like we'll need your help again, Professor Cortez. My ship is a half day out from your perimeter. Once close enough, I'll dive down in my own submersible. From there, we'll need to coordinate sneaking Karen out from under that man's nose."

"I'll do my best. I'll show Dr. Grace everything I know about the Neptune, and we'll come up with some sort of game plan."

Jack nodded. "I'll contact you when I'm en route."

Somewhere behind Karen, a hatch clanged shut. Both she and Cortez jumped. "Someone's coming," Karen hissed. She faced the screen. "We have to sign off."

Jack stared back at her. "I'll see you tomorrow."

Karen touched the screen as the line went dead.

Cortez slipped out the DVD disk and pocketed it. "I'll get on the wire as soon as I settle you back in your room. By morning it will be a whole new day. We'll get through this— both you and the world."

Karen grinned, finding a twinge of hope. She remembered Jack's last words: *I'll see you tomorrow*. She meant to hold him to that promise.

10:55 P.M.

"You were right, sir," Rolfe said, pulling off his radio headpiece.

Huddled in his cabin, David yanked off his own headphones. The two, with topside assistance from Jeffreys, had eavesdropped on the covert transmission to Kirkland's ship. David threw his radio headpiece across the room.

"The bastard's still alive. The next time I see Kirkland, I'm going to shove a grenade up his ass. Make sure he stays dead."

"Yes, sir. What are your orders?"

David leaned back in the chair and folded his fingers across his stomach. He had heard only the last portion of the conversation. Jeffreys, the team's communication expert, had kept a close ear to the wire and knew when the connection was made, but the damn thing had been cleverly encrypted. By the time Jeffreys decoded it, the conversation was ending. Still, David had heard enough. The group was planning to sabotage the site and free the woman.

"Sir?"

David cleared his throat, arranging a plan in his head. "We keep quiet. Let them think they've won."

"Then when do we act?"

"Once we know Kirkland's on his way here. Away from his ship. Isolated." He sat up. "Then we end it. You take his ship, jam all communication, and leave Jack to me. As long as I have the woman, he'll come to us."

Rolfe nodded. "Very good, sir. But what about Cortez?"

David grinned, unfolding his hands. "It seems we still have a bit of housecleaning to do tonight."

11:14 P.M.

Grumbling, Cortez climbed down the ladder to the docking level.

The lowest tier was divided into three sections: the large docking bay; the pump room, with its quad of six-hundred-pound hydraulic ram pumps; and a small control room with neighboring storage facilities, called "garages." The DSU's armored suits were currently stored here.

Cortez crossed to the control panel. The board was automated. Push one button and the whole docking procedure would run smoothly. The bay would pressurize to match the outside water. Once done, the doors would open, allowing a sub egress or ingress; then the doors would close again.

Or so the blueprints suggested.

After dropping Karen off in her cabin, he had been informed by one of his technicians that there was a problem with the docking board. He thought about leaving it to one of the technicians, but no one knew the Neptune's systems as well as he did. And with a call out already to his friend at Los Alamos, he was full of nervous energy.

Crouching by the control panel, Cortez slipped out a tool kit and quickly had the board open. The problem was easy enough to discover. One of the pumps had burned out a fuse. A minor problem. The docking bay could still function with the three remaining pumps, but it would slow things down.

Cursing the nuisance, Cortez made sure his toolbox held the proper fuses and entered the empty bay. The two subs—the *Perseus* and the *Argus*—were currently topside. In preparation for tomorrow's evacuation of the sea base, both subs were being dry-docked and examined. Empty, the bay looked like a large warehouse, the walls lined by thick water pipes.

Toolbox in hand, he crossed toward the far side. It was a simple repair.

As he walked, he sensed that he wasn't alone. Some primitive intuition of danger tingled his nerves. He slowed and turned, saw movement outside the bay door, a twitch of shadows.

His heart thundered in his chest. "Who's there?"

He studied the door and the tiny observation window over the control station. No one answered. No one moved. Maybe it had been his imagination.

Slowly, he turned and continued walking toward the screw plate on the far side of the room. Already on edge, his nerves jangled warnings. His ears were keen to the smallest noises. All he heard was his own footsteps.

As he neared the far wall, a loud clang rang across the bay. He gasped with shock. With his heart now in his throat, he swung around. The bay's hatch was closed. He watched the latches wheel tight.

"Hey!" he hollered. "I'm in here!"

He dropped the toolbox, pushed up his glasses and hurried across the bay. What if he got locked down here all night? The others were counting on him.

Halfway across, he heard a high-pitched hissing from overhead. He looked up in horror. He knew every inch of this place, every sound and wheeze of the great station. "Oh, God . . . no!"

The docking procedure had been engaged. The room was pressurizing.

He ran toward the door. He had to let someone know he was in here. Then movement caught his eye. Through the observation window, a head came into view. Cortez knew that face and its twisted, condescending smirk.

Spangler.

This was no accident. Cortez stumbled to a stop. Already, the pressure grew in his ears. Unchecked, it would build to match the outside depths—over a thousand pounds per square inch.

Cortez spun. Spangler must have been the one who had damaged the pump's fuse—a trap to lure him down here. His only hope was to disable the remaining pumps' engines. If he could remove the other three fuses . . .

He crossed toward the far wall and the abandoned toolbox. As he did, the pressure climbed in the room. It was getting hard to breathe. His vision narrowed. Gasping, he struggled onward.

Pain exploded in his head as his eardrums ruptured. He cried out, his hands flailing up, knocking his eyeglasses off. Blood ran down his neck.

And still the pressure built.

Stumbling, his vision dimmed; lights danced at the edges. Falling to his knees, he fought for breath. He collapsed to one hand, then another, as the pressure crushed him. Unable to breathe, he rolled to his side and fell. On his back, he was blind now, his eyes forced too deep into their bony sockets.

His fingers scrabbled at the floor, begging for mercy.

The large weight on his chest continued to grow. A flood of fire pained him as his ribs began to break, collapsing, ripping lungs that could no longer expand. And still the weight grew.

He quit struggling, releasing control. His wife, Maria, had given her life to the Neptune project before she died. It was somehow fitting that it should take his life, too.

Maria . . . honey . . . I love you.

Then at last, as if sighing out a final breath, his consciousness fled and darkness took him.

11:20 P.M.

Through the observation window, David stared out at the sprawled and broken body of the former research leader. He watched the man's skull implode under the pressure, brain matter splattering out. As a diver, he had always known such a danger was faced by all who challenged the depths. But to witness it firsthand . . .

David turned away, swallowing back a twinge of queasiness. Horrible.

Rolfe stood by the control board. "Sir?"

"Flush this toilet."

His second-in-command obeyed, flooding the bay.

19

Man o' War

Admiral Houston stood on the stern deck of the destroyer, the USS *Hickman*. Dawn had yet to rise, but to the south, fires raged, lighting the entire horizon.

He had never seen the ocean burn.

The nuclear strikes had been clean and decisive, destroying missile and air support installations along the blockade's front. Batan, Senkaku Shoto, Lu wan: unknown to most of the world, these tiny outlying islands would soon become synonymous with Nagasaki and Hiroshima.

Already, American forces were moving in to shatter the remaining blockade.

But not the *Hickman*. It was limping with the wounded back to the refuge of Okinawa. His right arm in a cast, Houston was counted among the injured. He had survived the sinking of the *Gibraltar*, escaping the ship just before the rain of missiles had torn her apart. Many had not. The dead and missing numbered in the thousands, including the C.O. of the ship and much of his command staff.

As he stood, he silently spoke their names . . . those he knew. There were so many more he did not.

"Sir, you shouldn't be out here," a lieutenant said softly at his side. The young Hispanic officer had been assigned as his aide. "We're all supposed to be belowdecks."

"Don't worry. We're far enough away by now."

"The Captain—"

"Lieutenant," he warned sternly.

"Yes, sir." The young man fell silent, stepping back.

Houston felt a chill morning breeze slip through his loose flight jacket. With his arm in a sling, he couldn't zip the jacket fully. He shivered against the cold. They would be reaching Naha on Okinawa within the hour, just as the sun rose. From there he was scheduled to ship back to the States.

Slowly, the fiery devastation sank beyond the horizon, becoming a fading glow. Dull booms occasionally echoed over the waters.

Houston finally turned his back. "I'm ready to go below," he said tiredly.

The lieutenant nodded, offering an arm of support just as a klaxon blared. Both men froze. Radar warning. Incoming missile.

Then Houston heard it. A whistling roar.

The lieutenant grabbed his good arm, meaning to drag the admiral to the closest hatch.

He shook off the grip. "It's heading away."

As proof, the fiery trail arced high across the night sky, aiming north over the ship.

"An M-11," Houston noted, moving to the starboard rail with the lieutenant in tow.

As they followed its course, another missile joined the flaming display . . . then another. The new rockets rose from the west, from China. Though coming from different directions, Houston could guess their target. Okinawa lay directly ahead. "Oh, God . . ."

"What is it?"

To the northeast new fireworks joined the show. A dozen thin flames streaked upward into the night, on intercept courses. The bevy of Patriot II missiles whistled skyward, like bottle rockets on the Fourth of July.

One of the Chinese missiles was struck a glancing blow. Its fiery arc became a tumbling fall, flaming out and disappearing. But the other two continued their course, vanishing over the dark horizon.

"What's happening?" the lieutenant asked.

Houston just stared.

At first there was no sound. Just a flash of light, as if the sun itself had exploded beyond the horizon.

The lieutenant backed away.

A low sound flowed over the water, like thunder under the sea. At the horizon, the brilliant light coalesced down upon itself, forming a pair of glowing clouds, sitting at the edge of the world. Slowly, too slowly, they rolled skyward, pushed up atop fiery stalks. Brilliant hues glowed from the hearts of the caldrons: fiery oranges, magentas, dark roses.

Houston closed his eyes.

The blast wave, even from so far off, struck the *Hickman* like a hammer, burning Houston from the deck before even a last prayer could be uttered.

6:04 A.M., *Nautilus*

Dressed in an insulated dry suit, Jack climbed into the *Nautilus* as it bobbed in the small waves behind the stern of his ship. He wiggled himself down into the pilot's seat and began running through one last systems check.

He knew it probably wasn't necessary, and the press of time weighed upon him, but he used the routine to settle himself. He would not fail. He must not fail.

All night long, as the *Deep Fathom* continued to steam toward the site where Air Force One had crashed, his crew had labored at readying the sub for the long trek: charging the main batteries, topping off the oxygen tanks, changing the filters to the carbon dioxide scrubbers, lubricating the thruster assemblies. With a fresh wax and polish, it could've passed for new.

But it was all necessary. Today, Jack was about to take the *Nautilus* on its longest trip yet.

An hour ago the *Fathom* had dropped anchor on the lee side of a small island, no bigger than a baseball field. It lay some twenty nautical miles from the crash site. Jack's plan was to sneak the sub in as close as possible, then coordinate with Dr. Cortez and Karen on a plan to free her from the sea base. It would take impeccable timing.

Jack gave a thumbs-up to Robert, who lowered the acrylic dome and used a portable power drill to screw the O-rings tight. This was normally Charlie's job, but he had been holed up in his lab all night, working with the crystal.

Robert patted the side of the sub, the usual two-thump signal that it was okay to dive. Jack nodded to the marine biologist. Robert laid a palm atop the dome, silently wishing him good luck, then dove off the sub.

Jack glanced back. His entire crew had gathered along the stern rail. Even Elvis stood by Lisa's side, the old dog's tail slowly wagging.

He saluted them all, then hit a button, sucking ballast water into the empty tanks on either side. The submersible slowly sank. As the waterline rose over the dome, he felt a twinge of misgiving. He dismissed it as the usual predive jitters, but in his heart he knew that this time it was more.

In six hours the mother of all solar storms was going to strike the Earth— and if he and the others failed, it wouldn't matter if Karen were rescued or not.

Jack let the sub sink under its own weight. He could have descended faster under thruster power, but he had to reserve his batteries. Around him the water turned a midnight-blue as he aimed for the fifty meter mark. Once there, he gave the thrusters the tiniest juice to push the *Nautilus* into a gentle glide, aiming away from the tiny island and out into open sea.

Slowly, the sub sank into twilight . . . *one hundred meters* . . . then full night . . . 150.

Jack kept the ship's xenon lamps switched off, preserving the batteries, guiding himself through the black waters with the computer alone. The region had been mapped by sonar when the *Fathom* first arrived and the information loaded into the sub's navigation. He would switch to active sonar once he was near the bottom. He had also ordered radio silence between himself and the ship, maintaining as much stealth as possible.

Two hundred meters . . . small pinpoints of light began to appear. Bioluminescent plankton and other tiny multicelled bits of life.

Jack enjoyed the display. Even here, life found a way to survive. The sight gave him a flicker of hope.

Four hundred meters. He finally switched on the sub's sonar for the final approach to the seabed. Where he was headed, it was too dangerous to fly blind. He watched both the analog depth meter and the sonar readings. With the deftest touches he manipulated the foot pedals to make tiny course corrections.

He watched the numbers climb. *Five hundred meters*. Finally, he thumbed the switch, and twin spears of light shot forward, penetrating the gloom, illuminating the landscape below.

Jack pushed a pedal and tilted the sub on its side, surveying the terrain below him. It was as perfect as he had hoped, the seabed maze of deep canyons. The section of broken landscape beneath him led all the way to the crash site. The plan was for him to use the sheltering cover to mask his approach, similar to the way he had used the sunken ruins to sneak up on David's cutter. However, this time he hoped the end result would improve. Before, he had come back empty-handed.

As the depth gauge approached the six hundred meter mark, Jack angled the sub into a wide canyon between two ridges. He slowed his speed, balancing out his ballast to neutral buoyancy.

Ready, he engaged the thrusters and began the long winding journey.

The walls to either side were covered with clams and mussels, anemones and deep-sea coral. Lobsters and crabs worked around the boulders, waving and clacking claws at the stranger in their midst. Other life fled from his lights:

schools of silver-bellied fish darted in unison and vanished in a blink, bloodred octopi swept away in panicked clouds of murky ink, and winged black skates shuffled deeper into the silt.

Momentarily awed by the marine life around him, Jack continued gliding along the canyon. Over the next hour, using his sonar and compass, he navigated the maze as best he could, wending a zigzag path.

Circling around a seamount, he dove into a long narrow canyon. It was perfect. Side channels and offshoots branched away, but ahead was a straight shot to his target.

He checked his watch. *Four hours till noon.* He was cutting it close. Gunning the thrusters, he shot into the channel. It was this sudden burst of speed that saved his life as the rock wall to his right suddenly exploded.

Caught from behind, the sub's stern catapulted upward, flipping the *Nautilus* end over end and slamming it into the far cliff.

Jack gasped, his head cracking against the dome. The *Nautilus* scraped down the rockface, rolling. A sickening metallic scrunch sounded as something tore away from the sub's undercarriage. One of the xenon lamps burst with an audible pop, casting shards of thick glass.

He fought to keep his seat, praying for the inner shell of titanium and bulletproof acrylic to maintain its integrity. Even a single seam rupture at these depths would implode the sub in a nanosecond, crushing the life from him.

Working the foot pedals, he righted the sub. His visibility was zero as he hovered in a cloud of silt and sand. Through his hydrophones, a hollow tumble of rock sounded behind him. Looking over his shoulder, he could just make out a collapsed wall of boulders.

He craned his neck up. Beyond the top of the seamounts the silt cloud was clearing as swifter currents swept it away.

Overhead, he spotted his attacker.

Another sub circled like a shark. Cigar-shaped with stubby wings, it prowled along, hunting. He knew this vessel.

The *Perseus*—the Navy's newest submersible, as deadly

as she was sleek. The admiral had shown him the specs on the night of the sabotage. She was twice the vessel the *Nautilus* was: quicker, able to dive deeper, more maneuverable. But worst of all—she had teeth.

Jack spotted the dorsal fin of this titanium Great White.

A stacked array of minitorpedoes.

With a twitch, Jack flicked off the remaining lamp of his sub. Darkness collapsed over him. Through the murk above, a weak beam of light sought him out, circling and circling overhead.

The hungry predator hunted its trapped prey.

8:02 A.M., *Deep Fathom*

Charlie paced the small confines of his lab, mumbling to himself. "The idea could work. . . ." He had run the calculations over and over again, and tested the crystal several more times.

Still, he remained unconvinced. Theory was one thing. Before he was ready to commit to his plan, he wanted to consult with Dr. Cortez at the sea base. But time was running out, and Charlie had no way of checking in with the geophysicist. They were dependent on the sea base calling there.

Leaning back over the computer, he tapped a button, and a three-dimensional globe of the Earth appeared on the monitor. A hundred small X's orbited the planet. They moved slowly in a complex ballet. Off to the left a radiating wavefront of tiny lines edged minutely toward the center of the screen, toward Earth. It marked the front edge of the solar storm blowing their way. Charlie checked the upper right-hand corner, where a little clock was counting down the time until collision with the upper atmosphere.

Four hours.

The dance of X's around the globe were based on real-time data from the Marshall Space Flight Center, monitoring the incoming wavefront and extrapolating how it might affect the satellites in orbit.

Charlie placed his finger on one of the small X's.

A knock on his door interrupted him. Lisa said, "Charlie, we have a call from Karen."

Charlie straightened with relief. "Thank God! It's about bloody time, *mon*!" He popped the disk of his latest data from the computer's zip drive and dashed out the door.

He found Lisa and Miyuki gathered in front of the professor's portable supercomputer. He immediately sensed the tension in the room. Neither woman looked happy.

"What's wrong?" he asked Lisa, coming around the table.

On the screen, Karen had heard him and answered, "I was calling to see if you had heard from Dr. Cortez."

Charlie bent in front of the camera. "What do you mean? Why not ask him yourself?"

"Because this morning I'd heard he'd gone topside during the night, and I've heard no word since. I had hoped he contacted you."

"No. Not a word." Charlie assimilated the information. "I don't like this. With Dr. Cortez AWOL, maybe we'd better rethink things on our own. Just in case. Jack's already left in the sub. I'll patch you to the *Nautilus* so you two can coordinate on getting your ass out of there."

Karen's image flickered. "Maybe we'd better. The last scientists are due to leave in an hour, leaving me alone with David's second-in-command. If there's gonna be a rescue, it'll have to be soon. But what about the pillar? What are we going to do if we don't hear from Dr. Cortez?"

"Pray we do. Pray he's been too damn busy making arrangements to save the world to bother updating us." But even Charlie knew that such a prayer was unlikely to be answered. "Listen, Karen, I've been working on something, something we might try. Let's all keep in close contact from here."

"I'll try, but it'll be difficult. Lieutenant Rolfe is below assisting in the launch of the next sub. I feigned an urgent need to go to the bathroom to make this call." She checked her watch. "And I'm running out of time. I should be getting back down there."

"Then let me patch you through to Jack." Charlie turned to Miyuki.

The professor hit a button and spoke aloud. "Gabriel, can you patch this line to the *Nautilus*."

A pause. *"I am afraid I cannot comply. There appears to be some sort of interference."*

Karen's brows knit with worry, then her image flickered, giving way to static, which ate the rest of the transmission.

"Gabriel, get her back!" Charlie ordered.

"I am afraid I cannot comply. There appears to be some sort of interference."

Before Charlie could ask for clarification, the sound of someone running down the stairs drew his attention.

Robert's voice came over the tiny intercom speakers, "We've got—"

"Company," Kendall McMillan finished as he burst into the room. "Two ships, military, circling around from both sides of the island."

They all moved toward the stairs except Miyuki, who remained at her computer, her fingers flying over the keyboard. "I'm not abandoning Karen," she called to him. "I'll keep trying to reach her, let her know what's happening."

Charlie nodded. "Do your best. But if we're boarded, hide that computer. It may be all that stands between us and the end of the world."

He climbed to the stern deck of the *Fathom* and watched a long ship sweep around the southern coast of their little islet.

An air horn blared from its deck, followed by a message. *"Prepare to be boarded! Any resistance will be met with deadly force!"*

McMillan stared. "What are we going to do?"

"We have no choice," Charlie said. "Not this time. We surrender."

8:14 A.M., Neptune base

Karen tried typing in Gabriel's address again. Still no answer. Checking her watch, she pushed out of her seat. She could delay no longer without risking suspicion. She frowned one last time at the computer. The abrupt end to her conversation with the *Deep Fathom* threatened to send her into a panic.

Crossing to Level 2's ladder, she climbed down, her mind still on the communication glitch. As she reached a leg down to the next rung, her ankle was grabbed and yanked.

She squawked and fell from the ladder.

Rolfe caught her, clamping her upper arm. "What took you so long?"

Karen swallowed, avoiding his accusing stare. She forced a tremor into her voice; not all of it was feigned. "It . . . it's . . ."

"It's what?"

She glared at him. "It's my time of the month, if you must know!"

Rolfe's face grew a shade more ruddy. It seemed even these tough SEAL-trained assassins did not care to know about such fine womanly details. "Okay then, but stick by my side. We're just about to launch the last shuttle to the surface."

Karen did not like the sound of that. *Last shuttle . . .* What about her?

Rolfe led her to the docking bay's control station. He gazed through the window, then spoke into the thin-poled mike. "All set, *Argus*?"

Karen peeked through the window. The pilot and the last two scientists, both crammed into the rear passenger compartment, were locked into the sub.

"Systems green. Ready for launch," the pilot radioed.

"Pressurizing." Rolfe poked a large blue button, initiating the docking bay system.

Karen watched. As soon as the pressures equalized, the outlet pipes opened and water poured into the bay, quickly

swallowing up the sub. She studied it all intently. Without
Dr. Cortez here, she might need to do this herself.

All morning long she had dogged Rolfe's steps, learning
by quiet observation how the base operated. It was all user-
friendly, thanks mostly to this compact control station. A
bank of four monitors showed external views from all
around the station. An additional two monitors for the ROV
robots rested above a pair of joysticks. The remainder of the
panel was devoted to the docking bay itself.

She watched the seawater level rise past the tiny porthole
observation window. As the bay filled, a glint of metal
caught her eye. Something small floated loose in the docking space. She dismissed it as some mislaid tool and returned her focus to the sub. Across the bay, the pilot tested
the sub's thrusters, floating up from the deck.

But again the glint drew her eye. It was the same object,
whirling past the tiny window now.

Leaning closer, Karen recognized the bit of flotsam.

A pair of eyeglasses. Its lenses broken, its frame twisted
and bent.

She covered a gasp with a hand over her mouth.

8:15 A.M., *Nautilus*

Hidden in a cloud of silt, Jack edged his sub along the base
of the cliff, clinging under a lip of rock to diminish his sonar
shadow to the sub above. He feathered his pedals with the
lightest touches, trying to move no faster than the current.
He dared not move any quicker, lest he raise a wake trail in
the cloud and reveal his position. Overhead, the glow of the
Perseus's spotlight swept past in a crisscrossing pattern,
searching, waiting for the silt to settle.

Jack knew he had to be gone before that happened.

Still, he forced himself to maintain a snail's pace, flying
the sub blind, no lights, guided by sonar alone. He edged
forward. His goal: a side canyon up ahead. He had no idea
where it led or if it was a blind alley, but knew he had to be
out of the main channel before the cloud dissipated.

Then a voice blared from his radio earpiece. "I know you're down there, Kirkland. You can't hide forever."

Spangler . . . great . . . no surprise there.

Jack remained silent, playing dead.

"I have your woman trapped at the sea base, and your ship impounded. Show yourself and I'll let the others live."

Jack resisted the urge to laugh. *Sure you will.*

The silence stretched. David's voice returned again, growing more angry. "Would you like me to teach Professor Grace a few lessons in your absence? Perhaps hear her screams as Lieutenant Rolfe rapes her?"

Jack clenched his hands into fists but remained silent. Revealing himself would hurt Karen more than it would help. His best chance lay in stealth.

Ahead, a side canyon finally opened on the right. Jack guided the *Nautilus* into the narrow cut. He juiced the thrusters. Sonar feed began to fill the computer navigation screen. He sighed in relief. The side canyon was not a dead end. It wound far, branching and dividing.

Anxious, he moved more swiftly. He raced along the deep crack. Walls flashed past. He needed time and distance to shake the bastard.

"Where you going, Jack?" Lights flared behind him.

Jumping, Jack craned around. *Damn it . . .*

The *Perseus* swept down into the slot canyon after him, diving with murderous intent.

Staring behind him, Jack realized his error. A dusty spray of silt trailed behind the sub's tail, coughed up from the seabed floor by his passage. A clear trail. A stupid mistake.

Giving up any pretense of hiding, he speared on his lamplight and floored the pedals. The *Nautilus* shot up, corkscrewing out of the canyon.

As he spun, a minitorpedo zipped past the sub's dome, narrowly missing his vessel. To the left, a brief explosion flared as the torpedo struck a seamount, its thunder echoing through his hydrophones.

Jack tilted his sub into a steep dive, riding the shockwave, and dropped into a neighboring canyon. Flattening out, the bottom of his sub scraped through the silt, casting up a cloud.

What had betrayed him a moment ago could save him now. He thumbed off his lamp and coasted without thrusters, vanishing into the widening cloud of sand and silt.

He heard David over the radio, swearing. In David's anxiousness to pursue him, he had forgotten his radio line was still open. Jack did not correct this mistake. He eavesdropped. "Goddamn you, Kirkland. I'll see you die before this day is out."

Jack grinned. *Keep trying, asshole.* He raced down the chute, gliding around an outcropping. A sonar warning chimed. The canyon ended in a flat cliff face only twenty yards away.

"Oh, shit . . ." He flung the thrusters in reverse, earning a high-pitched whine of protest, and flung the nose of the sub straight up. But it wasn't enough to halt his momentum. The bottom of the *Nautilus* struck the wall hard.

Jarred forward, the belts of his harness dug into his shoulders. He forced himself back and worked the thrusters, climbing straight up the wall.

A new warning rang from his computer. His batteries were running low.

"Great . . . just great . . ."

Clearing the wall, Jack leveled out and sped along the mount's summit. He prayed his power lasted long enough. Sensing movement on his left, he turned and was blinded by a shaft of light.

The *Perseus* flew out of a nearby canyon, straight at him.

Rather than being rammed broadside, Jack rolled the sub, taking the collision on his undercarriage. The *Nautilus* jolted violently. Struck at the stern, Jack's sub spun. He struggled to right himself, to no avail. The sub struck the seamount, burying its nose in the thick silt.

Sweating, ears ringing, he fought the thrusters to tug himself out.

With a groan of stressed metal, the *Nautilus* popped free. As he swung his sub upright, he peripherally saw the

Perseus swinging in a tight loop, its torpedo array swiveling in his direction.

Time to go!

He slammed the foot pedals. Thrusters whined. The sub rumbled and tremored but refused to move. His front thruster assembly was jammed with sand. "C'mon, c'mon . . ."

He slammed the sub into reverse, blowing clear the choked props.

The *Perseus* sped closer, determined not to miss this time. "Ready to die, Kirkland?"

Free of debris, Jack goosed his thrusters. With no time to escape, he aimed straight for his adversary, playing a risky game of chicken, trusting in David's cowardice. An explosion too close would threaten David's own sub.

He floored the foot pedals and streaked forward.

Rather than shying, the *Perseus* remained on course.

Jack flicked on his xenon lamp. Light lanced out to stab the other sub, blinding its pilot.

At the last moment Spangler angled away.

Jack flashed under the enemy sub. He caught a quick glimpse of David sprawled on his belly in his cigar-shaped glass pod. Then the *Perseus* was gone.

Watching it retreat, Jack spotted the torpedo array spinning to track him as the *Perseus* fled. A finger of fire spat from the array.

"Oh crap!"

Jack straightened in his seat. The nearest canyon lay too far away. His sonar picked up the incoming torpedo as it sped toward him. He found himself leaning forward, as if that would increase his speed. "Move it . . ."

Laughter sounded over his radio. "Adios, asshole!"

Jack realized he would never make the canyon. He searched for other options and spotted a large boulder resting on the seamount's summit. Slamming the left pedal, he dove at a steep angle toward it.

"Suicide, Jack? At least die with honor!"

Jack's gaze flickered between the speeding torpedo and the oncoming collision. He bit his lip, calculating. At the last moment, he blew out his ballast tanks and gunned his thrusters. The nose end of his sub slammed into the silty bottom in front of the boulder—and *bounced*.

With the increased buoyancy, the tiny vessel flipped over the boulder, like a gymnast flying over a vaulting horse.

But the torpedo couldn't.

The huge rock burst under the *Nautilus*. The blast shoved up the sub's stern, peppering its underside with shards. Jack whooped, riding the concussion while sucking up new ballast. The shock wave shoved him right over the edge of the canyon.

He dove, dropping like a lead weight straight into the next chute.

Near the bottom, he angled out, skimming along the seabed. Relief and excitement mixed, but it was short-lived. The dark waters above him soon grew lighter as David pursued, closing in with his faster sub.

Jack examined his sonar readings. A strange shadow showed up ahead. He kept his lamps lit, unsure what was coming.

He needed a place to hide—and soon!

Sliding around a slight curve in the canyon, he spotted the anomaly. An arch of rock spanned the chute, a high bridge of thin stone.

He glided under it. It was too small to hide him, but it gave him an idea. He slowed and settled to the silty bottom.

It was time to even the odds.

Situation Room, White House

Lawrence Nafe stood before the computerized strategy map glowing on the rear wall of the White House's Situation Room. Behind him were gathered the Joint Chiefs, the Cabinet, and the Secret Service.

On the map, the tiny island of Okinawa glowed red.

Destroyed. Hundreds of thousands killed in a blinding flash.

His Secretary of Defense spoke behind him. "We need to choose a target, Mr. President. Retaliation must be swift and severe."

Nafe stepped away from the map and turned around. "Beijing."

The men around the table stared.

"Burn it to the bedrock."

8:55 A.M., *Perseus*

On his belly in the sub's sleek pod, David sped around a curve. Sweat ran down his face, into his nose and mouth. He didn't bother wiping it away. He dared not release his grip on the controls. A heads-up display glowed across the poly-acrylic nose cone. Sonar lines were superimposed over the view of the real terrain.

Circling around the bend, David spotted his quarry. He smiled. So the bastard hadn't escaped the blast unharmed.

Under an arch of stone, Jack's darkened sub limped and teetered, clearly compromised. David watched as the desperate man fought to get his sub moving, sand and silt choking up, but with no success. His sub continued to founder.

Like a fledgling with an injured wing.

"Having problems?" he radioed over.

"Go fuck yourself!"

David grinned. He lowered the *Perseus*, adjusting his lights to illuminate the interior of the other sub's dome.

Inside, he saw Jack struggling.

Excited, David lifted his sub and angled over his enemy. As he glided under the arch, he adjusted the *Perseus*'s lights, keeping the focus on his trapped enemy. It gave him a thrill to see Jack fighting frantically for his life. As David passed directly over the damaged sub, the two adversaries faced each other.

Jack glanced up at him, while David grinned down.

That close, David saw no fear in Jack's eyes, only satisfaction. Jack lifted a hand and flipped him off—then the *Nautilus* blasted straight up.

Caught off guard, David couldn't get out of the way in time. The two vessels collided. David's chin cracked against the pod. He bit the tip of his tongue. Stars flared across his vision; blood filled his mouth.

For a moment Jack's dome ground against David's nose cone. Both men lay within an arm's reach of the other, yet remained untouchable.

Jack grinned up at him. "Time to even the odds, you bastard."

David glanced to his sonar array. He suddenly understood the trap—but a fraction too late.

The top of the *Perseus* struck the stone arch overhead. David swore a litany of curses. With a screech of titanium, the torpedo array struck the unyielding rock. One of the minitorpedoes ignited, shooting down the canyon and exploding against a distant cliff face. The remainder of the array broke off and tumbled away.

His trap sprung, Jack's sub sank away. "As you said . . . adios!" The *Nautilus* dove forward, aiming for the sheltering cloud cast up by the stray torpedo's explosion.

Spitting blood, David flicked a switch. "No you don't, asshole."

9:04 A.M., *Nautilus*

Jack's grin disappeared as the *Nautilus* suddenly lurched under him. He jerked hard in his harness as the sub's progress was halted in mid-dive.

Twisting around, he saw the *Perseus* had latched onto his sub's frame with a single manipulator arm, its pincers clamped tight. David was not letting him run. The titanium arm tugged; metal screeched.

Warning lights flashed red across Jack's computer screen. He was snagged and trapped. Caught from behind, his own sub's manipulator arms could not fight back.

Titanium continued to protest as the pincers on David's

sub crushed and tore. The computer flickered. The carbon dioxide scrubbers went silent. David had clamped the main power line. This was not good.

Thinking fast, he dove toward the bottom, taking on ballast, dragging the Navy's sub behind him, meanwhile beginning to circle during the descent. Flashing on his xenon headlight, Jack aimed at the mangled torpedo array on the seabed floor. His lights dimmed as the *Nautilus*'s power line was crimped. He ignored it, concentrating on his goal.

When he was close enough, Jack reached to the controls for his own sub's manipulator arms. He extended the right arm and grabbed one of the discarded torpedoes resting on the seabed.

By now David realized the danger. The *Nautilus* was jostled as David shook the vessel.

Rattled, Jack bobbled and dropped the torpedo, but he deftly snatched it back up with his other manipulator arm. Before he lost it again, Jack wound back the arm and whipped it forward, lobbing the torpedo against the base of the stone arch.

The blast blew out the support. The stone arch broke, falling toward them.

As Jack had hoped, David was not willing to risk his own skin. He freed the *Nautilus,* spinning away. But Jack spun the other way and grabbed the *Perseus*'s back frame, turning the tables, catching the shark by its tail.

"Leaving so soon?" he asked.

Overhead, the main section fell toward them.

"Let me go! You'll kill us both!"

"Both? I don't think so."

Smaller boulders landed around them, blasting craters in the silt. Jack monitored both his sonar and the tumble of rock. Using his other manipulator arm, he tore at the *Perseus*'s main thruster assembly, damaging the propellers, then released his pincers and backed at full throttle.

David's sub lurched, trying to crawl from under the fall of rock, but it was no use. Boulders crashed deep into the silt.

As Jack watched, a small burst of bubbles exploded from around the *Perseus.* He initially thought the sub had imploded, but as the bubbles cleared, a small pod of acrylic shot out from the external titanium frame. Spangler had employed his sub's emergency escape mechanism. The ejected glass "lifeboat" blasted away from its heavier external shell. The abandoned section was immediately pounded flat by tons of rock.

The bastard was escaping!

Jack scowled, climbing with his thrusters above the spreading silk cloud.

Under positive buoyancy, the lifeboat and its single passenger rose rapidly. A tiny red emergency light on its tail winked mockingly back at him. In his heavier sub, Jack had no hope of catching it.

He followed the escape pod's course with his xenon light as it cleared the canyon walls and climbed into the open sea.

Jaw muscles tense, Jack gripped his controls, unsure about what to do—then a flurry of movement to the side caught his eye.

A large creature stretched from a rocky den, reaching for the escaping glass bubble. The explosions, the threat to its territory, must have drawn it.

Jack touched his throat mike. "David, I think you're about to be dinner."

9:17 A.M.

David frowned at Jack's radioed message. What was he talking about? What harm could he do? Jack's sub could never catch him. Though his own lifeboat bore no weapons and had no maneuverability, it did have speed. The sleek torpedo of acrylic was light and extremely buoyant.

David tapped in a code on his computer, preparing to patch through to the sea base. He would order the anthropologist killed, slowly. Rolfe was a skilled "interviewer." He had loosened many a stubborn tongue. David would make sure her cries and pleadings were dispatched to Jack before she was killed.

As he typed in the final connection, the life pod was jolted, tossing David onto his side. He searched the water around him but saw nothing in the weak glow of the blinking emergency beacon in the stern. He rose up on an elbow. Then the lifeboat was jarred again, and suddenly dragged straight down. David's head struck the thick acrylic.

"What the fu—" Words died in his mouth as he glanced past his toes. In the light of the red beacon, he spotted a large dinner-plate-size sucker attached to the shell of the lifeboat. He watched a long tentacle wrap around the pod, drawing him back into the depths, reeling him in like a hooked fish.

A giant squid!

He had read the report of Jack's battle with the same monster. He pressed his palms against the glass, panic setting in. He had no weapons. He searched the sea around him. Strobed in the red light, other tentacles and arms flailed, descending on its trapped prey.

The pod was flipped around roughly. David rolled and found a huge black eye staring at him.

A small gasp choked out of him.

The eye disappeared as the pod spun in the monster's grip. David braced himself. All around was a blur of tentacles.

Staring past his toes, David suddenly sensed danger above his head. He jerked around—and screamed.

An arm's length away a huge maw opened, lined by razor-sharp beaks, large enough to bite the slender pod in half. Still crying out in horror, he was drawn head first into the hungry creature's mouth. It gnawed on the glass end, grinding its surface with its viselike beak.

David retreated, cramming himself into the stern half of the lifeboat. As he did, his elbow struck the communication system.

His eyes flicked to its palm-size screen. He still had communications! He could call in a rescue. Perhaps the bullet-proof glass would resist the creature long enough. Or maybe the squid would tire of its stubborn prey and simply let him go.

Clinging to this small hope, he forced down his panic, told himself to stay focused, in charge.

Elbowing his way forward, David reached the transmitter. As he called up topside, a horrible noise echoed through the pod.

—*crack*—

He stared overhead. Tiny cracks skittered across the glass. *Oh. God . . . no . . .* He remembered the way Dr. Cortez had died, crushed, his skull imploding.

The monster continued to gnaw. The threadlike stress cracks spiderwebbed around him. At these immense pressures, implosion was imminent.

David clenched his fists as his hopes bled away. He was left with only one desire: *revenge*.

His boss, Nicolas Ruzickov, ever paranoid, had built in a fail-safe system in case the pillar site were ever compromised. The CIA director had not wanted the power here falling into foreign hands. "Better no one get it than lose it to another," Ruzickov had explained.

David called up a special screen and typed in a coded sequence. His finger hovered above the Enter key.

He looked up. The beast's maw continued to grind against the glass. More cracks.

Monster or pressure . . . which death was worse?

He tapped the final key.

FAIL-SAFE ACTIVATED blinked for a brief second.

Then the lifeboat collapsed, crushing the life out of him in a heartbeat.

9:20 A.M., Neptune base

Sitting beside her captor, Karen knew time was running out. In a little over two hours the solar storm would hit. She had to contact the *Fathom* and let them know Dr. Cortez had been murdered. But her bodyguard had refused to let her out of his sight.

As she sat with her hands clutched in her lap, Lieutenant Rolfe leaned over the radio. A call had been wired down from topside. Though he whispered, she managed to make out two words: "evacuation" and "fail-safe."

Straining, she tried to eavesdrop on more of the conversation.

Finally, the lieutenant hung up the receiver and turned to her. "They're sending down the *Argus*. We're leaving immediately."

Karen noted the man refused to make eye contact. He was lying—he might be leaving, but she wouldn't be.

Feigning acquiescence, she stood and stretched. "It's about time."

The lieutenant got to his feet, too. Karen saw his left hand drift to the knife strapped to his thigh. No bullets. Not at these pressures.

Turning, she hurriedly crossed toward the ladder that led down to the docking bay. She mounted it first, keeping an eye on her adversary.

He nodded for her to climb down, hand leaving the hilt of his knife.

Karen quickly calculated. She'd been taught the safety systems as soon as she boarded here. Everything was automated. For her plan to work, she had to time this perfectly. She moved slowly down the ladder, a rung at a time. Rolfe followed, keeping close, as usual.

Good.

Halfway down, Karen leaped from the ladder, landing with a thud.

Lieutenant Rolfe frowned down at her. "Careful, damn it!"

Karen thrust herself to the wall and smashed her elbow into the safety glass, breaking the seal. Pushing through the glass, slicing her fingertips, she reached to the emergency manual override. It was a safety feature to lock down the levels in case of flooding.

Understanding in his eyes, the lieutenant, who stood halfway through the interlevel hatch, pushed off the rungs, dropping toward her.

Karen yanked the red lever.

Emergency klaxons blared.

The hatch whisked shut.

Karen rolled away as the lieutenant fell through the hatch, kicking at her head. But his attack was halted in mid-swing.

Twisting around, she saw him hanging from the hatch, gurgling, his neck caught in the sliding door. It closed with a pressure meant to hold back six hundred meters of water pressure.

Bones cracked. Blood splattered the deck.

She turned away as his body fell to the floor, headless, twitching.

She ran a few steps away and vomited, remaining bent over, her stomach quivering. She knew she had no other choice. *Kill or be killed*, Jack had told her once.

Still . . .

An intercom at the control station buzzed. A voice spoke. "Neptune, this is Topside Control. We're reading an emergency hatch closure. Are you okay?"

Karen straightened, heart thudding. The *Argus* must be on its way down. She could not risk being caught. Hurrying to the controls, she frantically tried to remember how to work the radio, moving toggles and dials. Finally, she thumbed the right switch and leaned to the mike. "Topside, this is Neptune. Do not attempt evacuation. I repeat, do *not* attempt evacuation. The station has been damaged. Implosion imminent. Do you copy?"

The voice returned, somber. "Read you. Implosion imminent." A long pause. "Our prayers are with you, Neptune."

"Thank you, Topside. Over and out."

Karen bit her lip. Finally free, she now turned her attention to more important concerns.

Where the hell was Jack?

9:35 A.M., *Nautilus*

Jack limped down the last canyon. He spotted lights ahead. It was the crash site! He was so close. He pumped the foot pedals, trying to eke a little more power from the drained batteries. The thrusters whined weakly.

If nothing else, the frantic chase through the seamounts had brought him within a quarter mile of the base. After watching David's lifeboat implode, it had taken Jack only eight minutes to reach the site. However, his computer screen was riddled with blinking warning lights in hues of red and yellow. Worst of all, the battery power level read zero.

The charge was so low that he'd been forced to turn off all immediately unnecessary systems: lights, carbon dioxide scrubbers, even heaters. After such a short trip, he was already shivering violently, lips blue from the icy cold of these depths.

And now with the lights of the base illuminating the last of the canyon, Jack turned off his sonar. This earned him another half minute of power to his thrusters. He glided the *Nautilus* forward. The sub's skids, bent and twisted, rode an inch above the sandy bottom.

At long last he pulled free of the canyons.

After so long in the dark, the lights glared. He squinted. The pillar lay twenty yards to his right, the sea base straight ahead, its three doughnut-shaped sections lit up brightly. He swore under his breath at the distance yet to travel. Why had they constructed the base so far away? He'd never make it.

Proving his words true, the thrusters whined down and stopped with an ominous silence. Jack pounded the foot pedals. "C'mon, not when we're this damn close!" He managed to earn a weak whine, but nothing more.

He settled back, thinking. He rubbed his hands together, his fingertips numb from the cold. "Now what?"

9:48 A.M., Neptune base

Karen wiped the blood from her hands onto her pants. She had climbed back up to Level 2 after disengaging the emergency lock-down. For the past five minutes, she had been fruitlessly trying to raise Gabriel.

Cut off, she felt blind and deaf. What was she going to do?

She stood up, trying to pace away her nervousness. She considered calling topside and coming clean. The fate of the world depended on someone taking action . . . anyone. But she knew her chances of convincing somebody in authority were futile. The disk with the data from the *Fathom* was gone, missing along with the body of Dr. Cortez. And who would believe a woman who had just decapitated a decorated member of the U.S. military?

Karen scratched her head, her heart pounding. There had to be a way.

As she paced, a small temblor shook underfoot. She stopped. The vibrations rattled up her legs. She held her breath. All she needed right now was a deep-sea quake. She moved to one of the portholes. As she peered out, the rattling died away. A fading light caught her eye. It was coming from the pillar.

Karen narrowed her eyes, studying it. Strange.

Suddenly, the light flared up in the pillar. The ground shook again. She gripped the walls, holding herself steady. For the briefest moment, as the light flared, she spotted the glint of something shiny and metallic.

Something was out there.

The quake ended, and the light faded.

She stared, straining, squinting—but could discern nothing more.

"What was that?" she mumbled to herself.

As she stood, arms tight around her, Karen thought of a way to find out.

10:18 A.M., *Nautilus*

Teeth chattering and weak from stale air, Jack struggled to grab another rock from the silt with the sub's manipulator arm. Of the first four stones, he had managed to hit the pillar twice. Not bad.

Earlier, as the sub had rested dead on the seabed floor, he'd remembered Charlie's lesson about the pillar's sensitivity to energy, even *kinetic* energy, like something striking its surface. He had just enough battery power to work one of the manipulator arms and lob stones at the pillar. The ground trembled, the pillar flared. But was there anyone to see his SOS? Had the base been abandoned already? He had no way of knowing.

He struggled to dig free another stone. His vision blurred. The cold and the carbon dioxide were taking their toll. As he fought to stay conscious, the manipulator arm froze up. He tugged at the controls. Not enough power.

He tried the radio one last time. The batteries' remaining dribble of juice was enough to power a final call. "Can anyone hear me? Charlie . . . anyone . . ."

Groaning, Jack collapsed back into his cold seat. No answer. He shivered and trembled all over. Waiting. The deep waters had sucked all heat from the small sub. His vision dimmed again. He began to swim in and out of consciousness. He fought it, but the ocean was stronger.

On his last flicker of consciousness, he spotted the large monster bearing down at him . . . then darkness swallowed him.

10:21 A.M., Neptune base

Karen sat before the control station on Level 1. She manipulated the joystick for the ROV robot named Huey, guiding its arms to grab onto Jack's sub. On the monitor before her, she watched her work from remote. The grips extended and latched onto a section of the sub's titanium tubing, clamping tight.

Satisfied she had a firm hold, she backed Huey along the path toward the base. The sub seemed to resist for a moment, then budged slowly. Karen wiped sweat from her eyes. "You can do it, Huey."

The Volkswagen Bug-size robot continued backing,

dragging the sub with it. As it retreated, Karen swiveled the remote camera's eye, making sure to avoid obstructions while ensuring that she didn't lose Jack and his sub.

Through the acrylic dome she watched Jack's form jostle around as the sub was hauled. His head lolled and his arms hung limp. Unconscious? Dead? She had no way of knowing, but refused to give up.

Working quickly, her eyes darted from the screen to the clock on the wall. Her grip grew slick on the joystick. Less than two hours. How could they possibly hope to succeed? On the screen, she watched Huey trundle backward, hauling the dead sub. Either way, she wasn't going to leave Jack out there.

Struggling with the joystick, she steadily drew the sub along the silt. Luckily, the track between the pillar and the station had already been cleared by workers. Even the stray bits of jet pieces had been vacuumed from the silt. Karen worked as quickly as safety allowed, praying for more time.

Then a familiar voice rose from the control station's speakers. *"Dr. Grace, if you can hear us, please respond."*

Karen cried out with relief. Keeping one hand on the joystick, she used her free hand to patch into the communication system. "Gabriel!"

"Good morning, Dr. Grace, please hold for the Deep Fathom."

On the monitor, Huey finally reached the station. Karen slowed the robot and carefully pulled Jack's sub underneath the base. She tilted the camera, coordinating to position the sub under the docking bay doors.

"Karen!"

"Miyuki! Oh, thank God!"

Before her friend could respond, a new voice came on. It was the ship's geologist, his Jamaican accent giving him away. "Professor Grace, time is of the essence. Have you heard from Dr. Cortez? What is going on?"

Karen gave him a summary as she initiated the docking bay pressurization. The two quickly compared notes. She learned the support ships topside were all leaving, steaming under full power away from the site and abandoning the *Fathom*. Once they were gone, communications had reopened.

"Why are they leaving?" she asked.

"Gabriel picked up a coded transmission. He was able to decrypt it. Apparently some fail-safe command was initiated. To wipe out the area. It seems they're not taking any chances on losing whatever resources lie down there to a foreign power. The place has been targeted for a missile strike."

"When?"

"Gabriel is still trying to work that out."

Karen suddenly felt faint, light-headed. From how many different directions could death aim their way?

"What about Jack?" Charlie asked.

Karen focused back on the monitors. "I'm trying to get him on board, but I don't know. The robot can't lift his sub into the bay. Jack has to do that himself, and I think he's out of power."

"I'll have Gabriel patch you over to the sub. See if you can wake him."

"I'll try."

As she waited, Karen leaned over and peered through the observation window. The bay was flooded and the doors were gliding open.

"*Dr. Grace, you are hooked up to the deep-water radio of the* Nautilus."

Karen spoke into the microphone. "Jack, if you can hear me, wake up!" She kept an eye on the monitor, focusing Huey's camera on the glass dome. She used the robot's arms to shake the sub. "Wake up, damn it!"

10:42 A.M., *Nautilus*

Jack swam through darkness, chasing a whisper. A familiar voice. He followed it up toward a bright light. The voice of an angel . . .

"Goddamn it, Jack! Wake your ass up!"

He jolted in his seat, groggy and blinded. He threw his head back. Lights shone all around him. He couldn't see.

"Jack, it's Karen!"

"Karen . . . ?" He wasn't sure if he spoke or if it was all in his head. The world swam with light.

"Jack, you have to raise your sub fifteen feet. I need you to enter the bay over your head."

Jack craned his head up. As his eyes adjusted to the light, he saw a large open hatch above his head. Understanding seeped through to him. "Can't," he mumbled. "No power."

"There must be a way. You're so close."

Jack stared up, remembering Spangler's death. Maybe there was a way.

Karen spoke, desperate. "Jack, I'll see if the ROV robot's arms are strong enough to push you inside."

"No . . ." His tongue felt thick and slow. He searched between his legs. His fingers found the release brake for jettisoning the external sub frame. He yanked on it. It was stuck, or he was too weak.

"Jack . . ."

Taking a deep breath, he grabbed it again with numb fingers. Bracing his feet, he used both his arms and his upper back to crank the lever up between his legs. He heard the muffled pop of the manual pyrotechnics. The external frame locks blew off, freeing the inner pilot's chamber.

Buoyant, the chamber rose from its shell, like an insect shedding its old carapace. Pressures thrust it upward through the open hatch.

Jack saw none of it, passing out again.

10:43 A.M., Neptune base

On the screen, Karen saw the sub appear to crack in half. She gasped with fright until she saw the inner chamber shoot upward—right through the open hatch. She hit a button on the controls, initiating repressurization.

She stepped to the observation window. Jack's escape pod bounced and rolled along the ceiling. Under it, the bay doors closed. The thump of the pumps began to sound.

Karen watched, holding her breath. Jack hung slack in his harness.

The five minutes to drain and equalize the pressure was interminable. She briefly contacted the *Fathom*, updating them. She learned that Charlie was working on some plan of his own with Gabriel.

Karen, afraid for Jack, barely listened.

At last the green light flashed above the door to the bay. She twirled the lock and hauled the hatch open. The pilot pod, half acrylic, half titanium, lay on its side. Karen had already been instructed over the radio by Robert on how to open it. Snatching an emergency oxygen bottle from beside the bay door, she ducked through the hatch.

She ran over to the pod, grabbed the manual screw pull, and began winding it around like a car's jack handle. She stared inside. Jack's face was blue. She cranked harder, pumping her arms. The seals peeled open with a hiss of escaping air. Karen smelled the foulness to it—stale, dead.

She reached to the loosened dome top and kicked it open. Kneeling down, she freed Jack's harness and hauled out his limp body. His skin was cold and clammy. She was sure he was dead.

Sprawled on the bay floor, Karen checked for a pulse in his neck. Faint and thready. His breathing was shallow. She slid on her knees and collected the small oxygen bottle, unhooking the tiny mask. She twisted the flow valve and placed the mask over his mouth and nose.

Leaning near his ear, she whispered, "Breathe, Jack."

Somewhere deep inside, he must have heard her. His chest rose and fell more deeply. She turned and zippered down his neoprene dive suit, freeing his rib cage.

As she did so, a hand rose and weakly took her wrist.

She looked down at Jack's face and found him staring at her.

He spoke through the mask. His voice was hoarse. "Karen . . . ?"

She began to cry, and hugged him gently around the neck. For a moment neither one tried to move.

Finally, Jack struggled to sit up. Karen helped him. He shoved aside the oxygen mask and minitank. His color was already improving. "Tell me what's happening," he asked, teeth chattering.

She did.

Jack rolled to his knees and coughed thickly. "What's this plan of Charlie's?"

"He wouldn't exactly say."

"That sounds like Charlie." Jack stood with her help, rubbing his arms. "How much time do we have left?"

"One hour."

20

Nick of Time

Jack sat buried in warm towels. He was finally starting to feel his toes. Charlie's image flickered on the computer screen in front of him. "First tell me about this missile strike. What's that all about?"

"A fail-safe mechanism was initiated from a radio transmission from below. I thought you might know more about it."

Jack glanced at Karen.

"It wasn't from here," she said. "I was with Rolfe at the time."

"Then it must have been Spangler," Jack said with a scowl. "His final attempt to kill me from the grave."

"He must have *really* hated you, Jack," Charlie chimed in. "A nuclear-tipped ICBM has our names on it."

Jack's eyes grew wide. He forgot about the chill in his limbs.

"How long do we have?"

"From Gabriel's estimation, fifty-seven minutes. One minute after the solar storm hits."

Jack shook his head. "So even if we can block this pillar and save the world, we still die in a nuclear blast."

Charlie shrugged. "Pretty much."

Jack sat quietly, stubbornly considering their options, then sighed. "What the hell. Heroes aren't suppose to live forever. Let's get this done. What's this new plan of yours, Charlie?"

"It's a long shot, Jack."

"Considering our current state of affairs, I'll take any damn shot."

"But I really wanted to run my calculations by Dr. Cortez first."

"Well, unless you have a Ouija board, that ain't happening. So spit it out. What's this plan?"

Charlie looked grim. "You gave me the idea, Jack. We overload the pillar with energy."

"Try to short-circuit it?"

"Not exactly. If we overload the crystal with *precisely* enough energy, pulse it at exactly the right frequency, it should fracture the crystal without a kinetic backlash, like shattering a crystal goblet by striking the right note."

"And you know the right note?"

Charlie nodded. "I think I do. But the hard part was finding a way to *deliver* the note. The energy has to be precise and sustained for three minutes."

"And you figured this out?"

"I think so." Charlie sighed. "That's what Gabriel and I have been working on since you left—and you're not going to like it, Jack. For this type of sustained power, we'll need a particle-beam weapon."

"How are we supposed to get our hands on such a thing?"

Charlie just stared at him as if he should already know the answer.

Then understanding struck Jack between the eyes. He jerked to his feet. "Wait . . . you can't mean the Spartacus?"

"Gabriel obtained its specs. It should work."

"What's this Spartacus?" Karen interrupted.

Jack sank back down. "It's a Navy satellite. The one I was putting into orbit when the shuttle *Atlantis* was damaged. Its equipped with an experimental particle-beam cannon engineered to knock out targets from space. Airplanes, missiles, ships, even submarines." Jack turned back to Charlie. "But it's defunct. Damaged."

Charlie shook his head. "Only its guidance and tracking systems —which, of course, makes it useless to the government. For it to work, they'd need an operator sitting up there aiming the thing by hand." Charlie paused. "But luckily, *we* have that operator right here."

Jack did not understand, but Karen realized the answer. "Gabriel!"

"Exactly. I sent him earlier to try to access the satellite's central processor. With the current global crisis and with the Spartacus classified as dead in space, he and Miyuki succeeded in slipping past the old firewalls. The satellite's processor is still active."

"You're kidding . . . after all these years?" Karen asked skeptically.

"It's solar powered. An infinite energy source."

As the others talked, Jack sat quietly, flashing back to the bright satellite lifting from its shuttle bay cradle, silvery solar wings spreading wide. He tried to close his mind against what happened afterward but failed. The explosion, the screams, the endless fall through space . . .

He shivered—not from cold, but from a twinge of superstitious dread. The Spartacus was cursed. Death surrounded it. Nothing good could come from the wretched thing. "It won't work," he grumbled.

"Do we have any other choice?" Karen asked. She placed a hand on his shoulder, then spoke to Charlie. "When can we try it?"

"Well, that's the clincher. We'll have only the one chance. The satellite won't come within orbital range until forty-eight minutes from now."

Jack checked the clock. "That's three minutes before the solar storm hits."

"Three minutes is all I'll need. Either it works or it doesn't."

Jack shook his head. "This is insane."

"What do we have to do?" Karen asked.

"To target the pillar, Gabriel will need an active GPS lock. Something upon which to focus the cannon. We're going to need you to place the *Nautilus*'s Magellan GPS homing device over by the pillar. It'll feed data to the *Fathom*, and in turn I'll send it to Gabriel."

Jack shook his head. "Then we have a problem. The *Nautilus* is still outside the sea base. I had to do an emergency jettison to enter the docking bay. There's no way to get to the Magellan unit outside."

Karen spoke up. "What about the ROV robot?"

"It's too crude to extract the Magellan unit without harming it. Someone would have to do it by hand."

No one spoke. Everyone sat sullenly.

Then Karen brightened. "I may have an idea."

11:44 A.M.

Standing in the docking bay, Jack watched the water level rise past the front port of his helmet. He moved his arms, acquainting himself to the deep-sea armored ensemble. It was one of the Navy diver's suits. The large helmet had four viewing ports: forward, right, left, and above. The bulbous helmet was so wide that it blended flush with the suit's shoulders, creating a bullet-shaped form with jointed arms and legs protruding from it. Small lights were mounted atop the helmet and at each wrist. There were also thruster assemblies built into the back, like the old rocket packs in sci-fi serials.

As Jack moved slowly about the filling bay, he found its operation fairly intuitive, similar to the EVA suits used for spacewalks.

"How're you doing?" Karen's voice came through the helmet radio. Through the seawater, he spotted her waving to him from the bay's observation window. After talking with Charlie, Karen had taken Jack down to the docking level and shown him the "garages" where the huge suits were stored. He had to give her credit. It was a clever solution.

He waved back. "Doing fine."

"Charlie is jacked into the radio system. He's monitoring also."

"Charlie?" Jack called out.

"Right here, *mon*."

"How's Gabriel doing?"

"The little bugger has finished troubleshooting the satellite's systems. They're powering up and awaiting our signal. Just get that GPS unit and haul ass. We're running out of time."

Jack's gaze flicked to the helmet's internal computer screen. *Sixteen minutes.* "I hear you."

Karen came back on line. "Careful. The docking bay doors are opening."

Jack bent a bit, peering down. A few feet away the huge doors slid open. The ocean lay beyond.

Jack stepped toward the opening. "I'd better get going." From across the way he spotted Karen's face through the window. She held a fist to her throat. Worried and scared. Jack sensed her fear was more for his own safety than the fate of the world.

With a last wave, he stepped from the bay and sank down to the ocean floor. Using a hand pad, he adjusted his buoyancy and settled in place. The remains of the *Nautilus* lay two yards away. Playing with the thrusters, Jack spun himself around until he faced the sub, then moved over to its side.

Bending at the knee, he searched the vessel. The Magellan unit was just forward to the portside thruster assembly. He shuffled around until he found it. Reaching with an arm, he used the three-pronged pincer grip to unscrew its cover plate. It took a little prying since it was bent inward from the hard use the sub had recently faced.

The plate fell away.

Jack kneeled lower, awkward in the bulky suit. He shone

the tiny wrist lamps inside. *Oh, shit . . .* The shoe-box-size device was smashed, its inner components open to the seawater. He groaned aloud.

"You okay, Jack?" Karen asked.

He straightened. "The Magellan is toast. The unit's fried." Hopelessness hollowed his chest. "Goddamn that asshole Spangler!"

Charlie's voice echoed through the tiny speakers. "But Jack, I'm picking up a GPS signal."

"Impossible. Not from the *Nautilus*."

"Step away," Charlie said. "Get clear of the sea base."

Using his thrusters, Jack skimmed between two of the steel support legs and out into open ocean.

"It's you!" Charlie said. "That Navy suit must be engineered with an automatic GPS homing device. A safety feature in case a diver gets stranded!"

Jack felt hope rekindle. "Then all I have to do is reach the pillar."

"You have eight minutes." Charlie paused. "But Jack, if the GPS is a part of the suit, you'll have to stay by the pillar."

Jack understood what Charlie was implying. It would mean his death.

Karen came to the same realization. "There has to be another way. What about that other plan? The last resort. To reset the explosive charges and blow up just the pillar."

Charlie argued. "The kinetic energy backlash—"

Fingering his controls, Jack goosed his thrusters. "Folks, either way, there's a nuke with our names on it already in the air. This is the only viable option." He swung around and flew across the seabed floor. The pillar lay fifty yards away. "Be ready."

11:58 A.M., *Deep Fathom*

Lisa stood with Robert and George by the bow rail. The sun overhead shone brilliantly. There was not a cloud in the sky. They had come up to the deck to await the outcome. With the other four belowdecks, the lab had been too crowded, too cramped. Lisa needed to feel the breeze on her cheek . . . if only for one last time.

George and Robert had accompanied her. George smoked his pipe. Robert had his Sony walkman over his ears. Faintly, Lisa could hear the tinny sounds of Bruce Springsteen singing "Born to Run."

She sighed. If only they could run . . .

But they couldn't. The *Fathom* needed to stay nearby to aid in the flow of transmissions between the station below and the satellite overhead. There would be no escape for any of them. Even if their plan succeeded, the area would soon be wiped out, destroyed in a decisive nuclear strike.

George removed his pipe and silently pointed its stem toward the horizon.

Lisa looked. A small contrail rose from the northeast, streaking higher as it arced into the sky. *The fail-safe missile.*

George replaced his pipe, his eyes on the sky.

No one said a word.

11:59 A.M.

Encased in his reinforced suit, Jack stood with his back to the crystal pillar. The ocean bottom lay dark all around him. A moment ago he had ordered Karen to turn off the grid to the lamp poles, plunging the seas back into darkness. He had also turned off his own suit lights. He could not risk exciting the pillar prematurely and interfering with his GPS signal.

"Are you registering me okay?" he asked.

Charlie answered from the *Fathom*. "Loud and clear. Transmitting data up to Gabriel."

He gazed around him. The only light came from the yellow glow through the portholes of the Neptune sea base. Though he could not see her, Jack felt Karen staring back at him. He sighed. He would have liked the chance to have known her better. His only regret.

He waited. There was nothing else for him to do. He was now just a living and breathing target for a space-based weapons system.

He glanced up through the upper port of his helmet, as if he could see the satellite—Spartacus. He had somehow known one day their paths would cross again. A destiny that needed to be fulfilled. He had escaped death once, the only survivor. Now he was standing in the crosshairs of the same satellite. Death would not be denied a second time.

He closed his eyes.

Karen whispered in his ear like a ghost, "We're with you, Jack. All of us."

He silently acknowledged her. All his life he had been surrounded by ghosts. Memories of the dead. Now, at this last moment, he let it all go, finally realizing how much power he had given to the shades of his past.

Well, no longer. At this moment he wanted only his flesh-and-blood friends at his side. He opened his eyes and his comlink. "Good luck, everyone. Let's get this done!"

Charlie's voice came next. "Here we go."

12:01 P.M., Low Earth Orbit, 480 nautical miles above the Pacific

Sunlight reflected off the wings of the brilliant satellite. Upon its flank, stenciled markings, as crisp as the day they had been painted, were easy to see: a tiny flag, identification numbers, and broad red letters, spelling out its name: Spartacus.

As it swept over the expanse of the Pacific Ocean, the satellite slowly rotated, an internal gyro spinning like a child's top. Pinioned solar wings tilted to catch more energy, in turn powering up the high-energy chemical laser.

It was a ballet of power and force.

On its underside, a hatch opened and a telescoping barrel protruded.

Around the awakening satellite, the upper atmosphere began to be peppered with ionized particles, charging the ionosphere with tiny bursts of radiation, like raindrops on a pond. Ripples began to spread. The satellite's communication system crackled.

Something inside listened and compensated, tuning away the interference.

However, these raindrops were but the first trickle of a coming flood. Overhead, past the orbit of the moon, the true storm rushed toward Earth, a raging gale of wild energy and particles, plunging through the vacuum of space at 1.8 million miles per hour.

Oblivious to the threat, the satellite finished its cascade. The chemical laser fed energy in microbursts to the particle-beam generator. Power levels rose exponentially, building to thresholds that could only be sustained by a whirling pair of electromagnets. Its shielded central processor registered the escalation, making one final adjustment, locking on a signal far below.

Power screamed between whirling magnets, seeking a way out.

At last a switch was opened—energy pulsed out in a narrow beam of neutrons, ripping through the atmosphere, striking the sea below and passing through the waters as easily as it had the air. Fed from space, the beam raced into the midnight depths of the ocean, where even the light of the sun could not penetrate.

12:02 P.M., Neptune base

Karen stood, face pressed to the cold window. Beyond the weak light of the portholes, she searched for some sign of Jack, but could see nothing.

A starless midnight.

Then, in a blinding flash, the crystal pillar burst with radiance.

Karen gasped, blinded. She closed her eyes, covering her face with an arm, but the pillar still shone, the image burned into her retina. She stumbled back, tears running down her face. It took several seconds before she could even open her eyes. When she did, each porthole shone with such brilliance that it seemed the sun itself had descended atop the sea base.

"My God!"

Shielding her eyes, she moved to one of the ports, trying

to see outside. Nothing was visible. Not Jack, not the seabed beyond. The world was just light. "Jack . . ."

12:02 P.M., Deep Fathom

Lisa continued to stand near the bow rail with George and Robert.

The old historian sighed out a long stream of smoke, seemingly unperturbed by the missile aiming across the sky toward them. By now its fiery tail was easy to see.

Lisa reached out and took George's hand. He squeezed her fingers in his grip. "Don't worry," he whispered, suddenly fatherly, his eyes on the sky.

As they watched together, the missile seemed to freeze in place, hanging as if caught in amber. Lisa stared, mouth hanging open. Surely it was an optical illusion.

One second . . . then another and another passed.

It still refused to move.

Robert spoke up, drawing her attention away from the strange sky. He was bent over the steel rail, looking down. He turned to them, taking off his headphones. "Guys . . . where's the ocean?"

"What do you mean?" Lisa and George joined the young marine biologist. She stared past the rail and gasped.

Beyond the keel there was no water. The ship was floating in midair, rocking gently on invisible waves.

Lisa bent over the rail. Far below, a fierce light shone. She looked around, turning. Inside a hundred-yard perimeter of the ship the sea was gone. Beyond this circle, the ocean was as normal as any day. It was as if the *Deep Fathom* were floating over a deep well in the ocean.

Only this well had a sun at the bottom of it.

"Look at the sky!" George called out.

Lisa tore her eyes from the wonders below to see something even more amazing overhead. In the sky, the small missile, once hanging in place, began to slide back down its smoke trail, as if it were retreating.

"What is going on?" she asked.

Jack stood with his arms blocking his helmet ports. He huddled against the light, mouth open in a silent scream. The power surging inches from his back vibrated his armor shell. His skin was flushed, hairs tingling. He felt the energy down to his bones. *God . . . !*

Before his sanity was burned away in the brightness, he sensed a change in the timbre of the energy. The light softened.

He lowered his arm.

Rather than blinding, the radiance from the pillar had become a silvery wash through the dark waters. The seamounts, the research station, the lava pillars, were all limned in stark relief, etched in silver, becoming mirrors themselves in the strange light.

A voice whispered in his ear, hopeless, scared. "Jack . . ."

As he stared, knowing death lay moments away, he spotted movement from the corner of his eye. He turned, searching out the helmet ports.

Then he saw them!

Reflected in the silvery surfaces of the nearby sea cliffs, he watched images of men and women kneeling, arms raised to the heavens. More gathered behind. Throngs of robed and cloaked figures, some with elaborate headdresses of feathers and jewels, others bearing platters laden with fruits, or leading sheep and pigs on leather tethers.

"My God," he whispered.

Searching around, he saw similar images in all the mirrored surfaces: warped figures moving across the curved skin of the sea base, fractured images on the broken wall of lava pillars, even on a nearby boulder, the reflection of a tall man, kneeling with his face to the ground.

It was as if the silvery surfaces had become a magical looking glass to another world.

"Jack, if you're out there, answer me!" It was Karen.

Jack's voice filled with wonder, his fear fading. "Can you see them?"

The kneeling figure lifted his face. He was bearded, with

piercing eyes, and strong limbs. He stood and stepped from the mirrored boulder.

Jack gasped, backing and bumping into the pillar behind him. All around him the procession of people moved forward, leaving their reflected surfaces. He now heard distant voices, echoing songs, chanting.

The figure from the boulder lifted his arms high, a shout of joy on his lips.

Jack found his gaze drawn upward. There was no ocean, only sky. A bright sun hung above, eclipsed by the moon. Glancing back down, he saw hazy mountains in the distance and dense forests. Yet, strangely at the same time, he could still sense the ocean, the sea base, the cliffs. . . .

He suddenly understood. These were the ancient ones, the people of the lost continent. He was glimpsing their world.

Karen whispered in his ear, barely audible past the growing songs and chants. "I . . . I see people around you, Jack."

It wasn't just him! Jack stepped forward to view the wonder better. As he did so, the tall bearded man crashed to his knees, a look of rapture on his face. He was staring right at Jack.

"I think they can see me, too!" he said, astounded.

"Who are they?"

Jack stopped and raised an arm. All around the ghostly clearing, men and women fell in postures of worship and prostration. "They're your ancients. The ones you've been looking for all these years. We're seeing back into their world through some strange warp. And they're in turn seeing into ours."

The kneeling man, some sort of leader or shaman, called loudly. Though the words were unintelligible, he was clearly pleading.

Jack had an idea. "Karen, are we still patched through to the *Fathom*?"

"Yes."

"Can you feed what this man is saying up to Gabriel? Can he translate?"

"I'll try."

There was a long pause. Jack gazed around in amazement.

Finally, a familiarly tinny voice, scratchy with distance, spoke in his ear.

"I will attempt to translate . . . but I have only begun to attach phonetics to the ancient language."

"Do your best, Gabriel."

Charlie spoke up. "You'll have to hurry. We're escalating to the peak pulse frequency in thirty-two seconds."

The man at Jack's feet continued to speak. Gabriel's translation overlapped. "Our need is great, spirit of the pillar, oh god of the sun. What message do you bring us that the land shakes and cracks with fire?"

For the first time Jack noticed the ground was trembling underfoot. At that moment, he realized not only *where* he was, but *when*!

He stood at the dawn of this continent's devastation.

Jack also grasped his own role here. He remembered the platinum diary's story: *The god of light stepped from his pillar. . . .*

Outfitted in his armored suit, basked by brilliance, he *was* that god.

Knowing his duty, Jack stepped forward and raised both arms. "Flee!" he yelled as Gabriel translated, his words echoing out to those gathered. "A time of darkness is upon you! A time of hardship! The waters of the sea will claim your homelands and drown them away. You must be prepared!"

Jack saw the shocked look on the other's face. The man had understood.

Charlie yelled through the speakers. "Get ready for the final pulse!"

The view of the lost continent began to flicker.

Hurrying, Jack stepped forward. "Build great ships!" he ordered. "Gather your flocks and fill the ships' bellies with food from the fields! Save your people!"

The shaman bowed his head. "Your humble servant, Horon-ko, hears and will obey."

A shocked gasp arose from the radio. *"Horon-ko,"* Karen

said. "The one who wrote the diary . . . the bones in the coffin."

Jack nodded, staring down at the man. Their shared stories had come full circle. As he stood, the images sank back into the mirrored reflections.

"Here it comes!" Charlie screamed.

Jack braced, tense, waiting for the coming explosion.

But it never arrived—instead, the brightness simply blinked away like a candle snuffed.

Jack straightened. After the intense light, the midnight seas were especially dark. The glow from the base's portholes appeared anemic and wan.

Karen yelled, fear in her voice. "Jack!"

"I'm still here."

She sighed with relief, then Charlie interrupted. "What about the pillar?"

Jack spun with his thrusters, thumbing on his suit's lamps. His lights spread far in the darkness.

Nothing.

The crystal pillar was gone. All that remained were bits and chunks scattered across the dark seabed floor, glowing in his beams like a sprinkle of stars. He moved forward, stepping among the shining constellations.

"Jack?" Charlie whispered.

"We did it. The pillar's destroyed."

Charlie whooped with joy.

Jack frowned. Charlie's happiness was hard to share. The world was saved, but what about them? "The tactical nuclear strike?" Jack asked. "Spangler's revenge. When's it due to hit?"

"I wouldn't worry about that, *mon*."

Deep Fathom

Charlie sat in the pilothouse, radio pressed to his lips. "Jack, you missed the eclipse the last time. You might want to get back up here so you don't miss it a second time."

"What the hell are you talking about?"

Charlie grinned at Jack's consternation. He couldn't resist stringing his captain along. His heart was too full of amazement and joy. He stood and stared out the wide window. The others were all gathered on deck, pointing up.

In the clear sky, a black sun shone down, casting the ocean in platinum.

Charlie checked his wristwatch. A little after twelve o'clock. He glanced back at the sun. It was low in the sky, too low.

Shaking his head in wonder, Charlie glanced to the satellite navigation system. Its clock and date were constantly updated with a feed from a dozen satellites in geosynchronous orbit. He stared at the digital time and date stamp. He had confirmed the anomalous results with the local weather band, too.

Tuesday, July 24
01:45 P.M.

"Goddamn it, Charlie, what are you talking about?"

Charlie sighed, letting Jack off the hook. "We ran into a little anomaly, Jack. Like I said before, I'm no expert on this new science of 'dark energy.'"

"Yeah, so? What happened?"

"Well, when we bombarded the pillar, the dark energy behaved as I had hoped—radiating straight back out, rather than down. But it had a side effect I hadn't anticipated."

"What?"

"Rather than stirring up the magma, the dark energy spike triggered a massive global time flux, *resetting* the Earth's battery to the moment when the dark matter had *last* been excited. Back to the solar storm two weeks ago. Back to the day of the eclipse."

Jack's voice was incredulous. "What the hell are you saying? That we've traveled back in time?"

"Not us, the *world*. Except for our local pocket here, the rest of the planet slipped back sixteen days."

Neptune base

In the docking bay of the research station, Karen helped Jack out of his bulky suit. She had listened in on the geologist's conversation with Jack.

A global time flux.

It was too wild to comprehend right now. All her mind could grasp was that they had survived. The pillar was gone. The world was safe. The mysteries of Einsteinian anomalies, dark matter, and dark energy would have to wait.

Jack groaned, climbing out of the unhinged armored suit. Karen held his arm, assisting him. Here was what she understood: *flesh and blood*. Jack had survived and returned to her as he had promised.

As he stumbled free, he straightened with a large smile. "We did it."

Karen opened her mouth to congratulate him—then their eyes met. She realized words were too weak to convey her true feelings. Instead, she threw her arms around his neck, knocking and pinning him back against the heavy suit.

Before either of them knew it, their lips sought each other out.

Karen kissed him hard, as if proving him no ghost. He pulled her closer. His lips moved from her mouth to her throat. The heat of his touch was electric, a dark energy of his own. She gasped his name, winding her fingers through his hair, tangling and twisting, refusing to let him go.

Their flaring passion was not love, nor even lust. It was something more. Two people needing to prove they lived. In the warmth of lips, the touch of skin, they celebrated life in all its physical needs, sensations, and wonder.

He pressed against her, urgent and hungry. She squeezed him harder, arms trembling.

Finally, he broke away from her. "We . . . we . . . not now, not this way. Not enough time." He sagged back, one hand vaguely waving up. "We need to find a way topside."

Karen grabbed his wrist. "Follow me." She brusquely guided him to the ladder. Climbing, she still felt the heat of his touch on her skin, a gentle warmth that spread through her limbs. Reaching the topmost tier, she helped him off the ladder.

"I was given a safety briefing when I first arrived," she explained. "There's a built-in emergency evacuation system." She hurried to a panel marked with large warning labels and pulled the door open. A large red T-handle lay snugly in place. "Help me with this."

Jack moved to her side, his shoulders brushing hers. "What is it?"

"The upper tier acts as an emergency lifeboat, sort of like the sub's evacuation system. This lever pops and separates the top level from the other two. Then, according to the specs, the positive buoyancy will float the tier to the surface. Ready?"

Jack nodded. Together they yanked the handle. A muffled explosion sounded, rattling the floor underfoot. The wall lamps blinked off as the tier separated from the main generators.

Karen found Jack's hand in the dark. In moments red emergency lights flickered on.

The floor swayed, then tilted. Karen tumbled into Jack's arms.

He held her snugly. "We're free. We're floating up."

After a moment he turned to her, eyes bright in the weak light. "How long till we breach the surface?"

Karen recognized the hunger in his voice. She matched it with her own. "Thirty or forty minutes," she said huskily. She slipped from his embrace and reached to her blouse. Freeing the top buttons, she stepped back toward the sleeping quarters. Her eyes never left his. "It seems I never did give you a proper tour, did I?"

He followed her, step for step. His hand reached to the zipper of his dive suit, tugging it down. "No. And I think it's long overdue."

Deep Fathom

Seven hours later, out on the open deck, Jack and the others sat around a makeshift dining table. Jack had broken out the champagne and pulled the last of the Porterhouse steaks from the freezer. It was to be a sunset dinner to celebrate their survival and the secret shared by the nine people gathered here.

Only they knew what had truly transpired.

Earlier, they had broken into teams to discover how the rest of the world had fared. Charlie discovered that this time around, with the pillar destroyed, the world had been spared the Pacificwide devastation. "Not even a tremor."

George, in the meantime, investigated if there was another *Deep Fathom* sailing the seas, the old timeline counterparts. There wasn't. "It was as if we were plucked from where we were and placed here." The historian also confirmed from the Hawaiian news wires that the Neptune sea base had vanished from its dock in the waters off of Wailea. He read aloud the news report with a smile. " 'The head of the experimental project, Dr. Ferdinand Cortez, spoke to authorities, expressing his dismay and bafflement at the theft.' "

Karen was especially relieved. "He survived?"

Charlie answered, "I guess the currents must have dragged his body beyond the zone around the pillar. When the flux occurred, he simply popped back into the old timeline, a timeline where he never came out here, never died."

"And he has no memory of what happened?"

Charlie shrugged. "I doubt it. Maybe somewhere deep inside. Something unspoken. More an odd feeling."

"But what about Lieutenant Rolfe? His body is still down there."

"Exactly. He remained within the zone. So he stays dead. I bet if you checked on him you'd find him missing from the real world, plucked out of the timeline just like the *Fathom* and the sea base had been."

Intrigued, Jack had taken it upon himself to check this angle. He had dialed Admiral Houston and found him still in San Diego. The admiral had been thrilled to hear from him after so many years. "Goddamn if I wasn't just thinking about you today, Jack. During the eclipse."

After exchanging pleasantries and a promise to get together, Jack hurriedly explained how he wanted to check into a friend's whereabouts—Lieutenant Ken Rolfe. After a couple hours, the admiral had called back, suspicious. "Jack, do you know something you're not telling me? A report came in an hour ago from Turkey. It says your friend went missing during a special ops mission at the Iraq border—along with another old friend of yours."

"An old friend?"

"David Spangler."

Jack had to cover his surprise and talk his way off the phone. Once free, he sat quietly for several moments. So David had stayed dead, probably still in the belly of the giant squid. The great beast must have nested close to the pillar. Jack felt a twinge of regret. Alive and free, he allowed himself the luxury of pity for the man. David had been warped by his upbringing, his father's unspoken abuses. So where did the true blame lie? Jack knew such answers were beyond him.

Later, as the afternoon had worn on, Lisa suggested the special dinner, to toast their survival. It was heartily agreed upon by all.

Now, with the sun sinking into the western ocean, Jack settled to the table and the celebration. From across the way, Kendall McMillan caught his eye. The accountant wore shorts and a loose pullover, extremely casual for the man.

"Captain," Kendall said, "I have a request to make."

"What is it?"

He cleared his throat and spoke firmly. "I'd like to officially join your crew."

This news surprised him. Kendall had always maintained an officious distance from the others. Jack frowned. "I don't know if we have the need for a full-time accountant."

Kendall glanced to his plate and mumbled, "You will when you're all millionaires."

"What are you talking about?"

He looked around the table, then spoke loudly. "I'm talking about the *Kochi Maru*. If Mr. Mollier is correct in his assessment that there were no quakes this time around, there is a good chance the previous volcanic eruption that swallowed the treasure ship may not have occurred. The ship may still be down there."

Jack's brows rose and his eyes widened. He remembered the ship's hold full of gold bricks. *At least a hundred tons.* Jack stood and reached across the table. He took the accountant's hand and pumped it vigorously. "Welcome to the crew of the *Deep Fathom*, Mr. McMillan. For that timely observation, you just earned yourself a tenth of the haul."

Kendall grinned like a schoolboy.

Jack lifted a glass of champagne. "We'll share equally. Everyone. That includes our newest shipmates: Karen, Miyuki, and Mwahu."

Kendall looked down the table. "But you said a tenth. There are only *nine* of us here?"

Jack patted the tabletop. The old German shepherd, squatting at his feet, jumped up, his paws on the table. He ruffled the dog's thick mane. "Anyone object to Elvis getting his fair share? After all, he did save all your asses from being blown to Kingdom come."

Kendall was the first on his feet, raising his glass. "To Elvis!"

The others followed suit. The old dog barked loudly.

Jack sat back down, smiling.

Slowly, as dinner became dessert, people began to wander away into private groups to discuss the day and their futures, all happy to still have one. Jack spotted Karen by the starboard rail. She stared into the sun's last glow.

He pushed to his feet, feeling slightly tipsy from the champagne. He crossed to the rail and put his arm around her shoulders, pulling her closer. As he did, he saw she held the broken shards of the crystal star in her palms.

She spoke, her voice melancholy. "With the revelations of these past days, my research is over. My great-grandfather was right. There *was* a lost continent. I now know the ancients truly existed." She looked up at him sadly. "But if we are to keep the secret of the dark matter hidden, then none must ever know the truth. Look how close we came to destroying ourselves with the mere power of the *atom*. Can you imagine what we'd do with the power of an entire *planet*?"

Leaning over, she tumbled the bright crystal shards into the dark sea. "Like the ancients themselves, we're not ready for such power."

Jack took her palms, cradling them in his own. "Don't worry. There are other mysteries yet to be discovered." Leaning down, he stared deeply into her eyes, his lips brushing hers, his voice low. "You just need to know where to look."

epilogue

Tuesday, July 24
San Francisco, California

Hours after the eclipse, Doreen McCloud left her office building. She stared down Market Street. The sun was a mere glow on the western horizon. As she stared skyward, she felt a surge of inexplicable joy. She didn't understand this sudden emotion. She had lost a critical client today, and the senior partners had scheduled an early morning meeting with her to discuss the loss. Where normally such a thought would fill her with dread, this evening all she felt was a simple appreciation of the cool San Francisco breeze.

As she walked toward the BART station, she noticed others glancing skyward, smiles on their faces, laughter.

Stopping atop the stairs to the station, Doreen glanced to the setting sun.

What a strangely wonderful day.

Aleutian Islands, Alaska

Jimmy Pomautuk climbed down the path, his malamute Nanook at his side. The noisy English trio clambered ahead of him, chattering nonstop, full of grins and jokes. Though the group had complained all the way up here, the eclipse had not failed to impress them. In fact, the sight had even touched his cynical soul: *the dark sun, the silver ocean, the brilliant borealis.*

He wished he could have shared it with his son, one generation passing a special heritage to another.

Glancing back, Jimmy watched the sun set beyond Glacial Point. For some reason, today he felt closer to his grandfather, his ancestors, even the old gods of his people.

Sighing, Jimmy patted Nanook.

"It's been a good day, boy."

Hagatna, Territory of Guam

In the garden atrium of the governor's mansion, Jeffrey Hessmire stood beside the Secretary of State. Together they watched President Bishop cross the courtyard. The festivities associated with the eclipse were dying away. People were returning to their normal activities.

President Bishop stepped in front of the Chairman of the People's Republic. He bowed slightly, a show of respect, and held out his hand.

After a short pause, the Chairman lifted an arm and gripped the President's hand. Off to the side there was a flourish of camera flashes as the press documented the momentous occasion.

"I know there is still much to settle between our countries," the President said, "but together we'll find a way to peace."

The Chairman bowed his head in agreement.

At Jeffrey's side, Secretary Elliot snorted. "This is just gonna kill Lawrence Nafe—both him and his hawkish cronies. After today, the Vice President's political support will dry up faster than a puddle in the Sahara. And though it may take some time for Nafe to realize it, his career just ended here today." Elliot clapped Jeffrey on the shoulder. "All in all, I must say it's been one hell of a great day."

Watching the ceremony, Jeffrey could not wipe the smile from his face.

No doubt about it . . . it was a day to remember.

An ancient angelic script.
Holds the secret to patterns in our DNA?
A great explorer in the jungles of Southeast Asia.
Discovered a fate so horrifying he never spoke of it.
An intrinsic basis for evil.
Buried in our own genetic code,
can mankind survive . . .

THE JUDAS STRAIN
Coming Soon in Hardcover
From William Morrow

Nothing stays buried forever—and it will be up to Sigma
Force to face what will be unearthed: a plague beyond any
cure, a scourge that turns all of Nature against mankind.

From the high seas of the Indian Ocean to the dark jungles
of Southeast Asia, from the canals of Venice to the crypts of
ancient kings, Sigma Force must piece together a mystery
that, unless solved, will end all life on our planet. But even
this challenge may prove too large for Sigma Force alone.
With a worldwide pandemic growing, Director Painter
Crowe and Commander Gray Pierce turn to their deadliest
adversaries for help, teaming up with a diabolical foe who
thwarted them in the past.

But can the enemy be trusted even now? Or will they
prove to be another Judas?

James Rollins—for the thrill of it!

> **"I have not told half of what I saw."**
> —the last words of Marco Polo,
> spoken upon his deathbed
> when asked to recant his stories of the Far East

May 12, 1293
Island of Sumatra
Southeast Asia

The screams had finally ceased.

Twelve bonfires blazed out in the midnight harbor.

"Il dio, li perdona . . ." his father whispered at his side, but Marco knew the Lord would not forgive them this sin.

A handful of men waited beside the two beached long-boats, the only witnesses to the funeral pyres out upon the midnight lagoon. As the moon had risen, all twelve ships, mighty wooden galleys, had been set to torch with all hands still aboard, both the dead and those cursed few who still lived. Flakes of ash rained down upon the beach and those few who bore witness. The night reeked of burned flesh.

"Twelve ships," his uncle Masseo mumbled, clutching the

silver crucifix in one fist. "The same number as the Lord's Apostles."

At least the screams of the tortured had ended. Only the crackle and low roar of the flames reached the sandy shore now. Marco wanted to turn from the sight. Others were not as stout of heart, kneeling on the sand, backs to the water, faces as pale as bone.

All were stripped naked. Each had searched his neighbor for any sign of the mark. Even the great Khan's princess, who stood behind a screen of sailcloth for modesty. Her maids, naked themselves, had searched their mistress, a maiden of seventeen. The Polos had been assigned by the Great Khan to safely deliver her to her betrothed, the Khan of Persia, the grandson of Kublai Khan's brother.

That had been in another lifetime.

Had it been only four months since the first of the galley crew had become sick, showing welts on groin and beneath the arm? The illness had spread like burning oil, unmanning the galleys of able men and stranding them here on this island.

With the cruel fire, the disease was at last vanquished, leaving only this small handful of survivors.

Seven nights ago, the remaining sick had been taken in chains to the moored boats, left with water and food. The others remained on shore, wary of any sign among them of fresh affliction. All the while, those banished to the ships called out across the waters, pleading, crying, praying, cursing, and screaming. But the worst was the occasional laughter, bright with madness.

Better to have slit their throats with a kind and swift blade, but all feared touching the blood of the sick. So they had been sent to the boats, imprisoned with the dead already there.

Then as the sun sank this night, a strange glow appeared

in the water, pooled around the keels of two of the boats, spreading like spilled milk upon the still black waters. They had seen the glow before, in the canals beneath the stone towers of the cursed city.

The disease sought to escape its wooden prison.

It had left them no choice.

The boats—all the boats, except one—had been torched.

Marco's uncle, Masseo, moved among the remaining men. He waved for them to again cloak their nakedness, but simple cloth and woven wool could not mask their deeper shame.

"What we did . . ." Marco said.

"We must not speak of it," his father said and held forth a robe toward Marco. "Breathe a word of contagion and all lands will shun us. But now we've burned away the last of the pestilence with a cleansing fire. We have only to return home."

As Marco slipped the robe over his head, his father noted what the son had drawn earlier in the sand with a stick. With a tightening of his lips, his father quickly ground it away under a heel and stared up at his son. "None must ever know what we found . . . it is cursed."

Marco nodded and did not comment on what he had drawn. He only whispered, *"Città dei Morti."*

His father's countenance, already pale, blanched further. But Marco knew it wasn't just plague that frightened his father.

A hand gripped his shoulder, squeezing to the bone. "Swear to me, my son. For your own sake."

He recognized the terror reflected in his fire-lit eyes . . . and the pleading. Marco could not refuse.

"I will keep silent," he finally promised. "To my deathbed and beyond. I so swear, Father."

Marco's uncle finally joined them, overhearing the younger

man's oath. "We should never have trespassed there, Niccolò," he scolded his brother, but his accusing words were intended for Marco.

Silence settled between the three, heavy with shared secrets.

His uncle was right.

Marco pictured the river delta from four months back. The black stream had emptied into the sea, fringed by heavy leaf and vine. They had only sought to renew their stores of fresh water. They should never have ventured farther, but Marco had spotted a stone tower deep within the forest, thrusting high, brilliant in the dawn's light. It drew him like a beacon, ever curious, brave with two score of the Khan's men from the galleys.

Still, the silence as they rowed toward the tower should have warned him. No bird calls, no scream of monkeys. The city of the dead had simply waited for them.

It was a dreadful mistake to trespass.

And it cost them in more than blood.

The three stared out as the galleys smoldered down to the waterlines.

"The sun will rise soon," his father said. "Let us be gone. It is time we went home."

"And if we reach those blessed shores, what do we tell Tedaldo?" Masseo asked, using the original name of the man, once a friend and advocate of the Polo family, now styled as Pope Gregory X.

"We don't know he still lives," his father answered. "We've been gone so long."

"But if he does, Niccolò?" his uncle pressed.

"We will tell him all we know about the Mongols and their customs and their strengths. As we were directed under his edict so long ago. But of the plague here . . . there remains nothing to speak of. It is over."

Masseo sighed, but there was little relief in his exhalation. *Plague had not claimed all of them.*

His father repeated more firmly, as if saying would make it so, "It is over."

Marco glanced up at the two older men, his father and his uncle, framed in fiery ash and smoke against the night sky. It would never be over, not as long as they remembered.

Marco glanced to his toes. Though the mark was scuffled off the sand, it burned brightly still behind his eyes. He had stolen a map painted on beaten bark. Painted in blood. Temples and spires spread in the jungle.

All empty.

Except for the dead.

The ground had been littered with birds, fallen to the stone plazas as if struck out of the skies in flight. Nothing was spared. Men and women and children. Oxen and beasts of the field. Even great snakes had hung limp from tree limbs.

The only living inhabitants were the ants.

Teeming across stones and bodies, slowly picking apart the dead.

Upon discovering what Marco had stolen from one of the temples, his father had burned the map and spread the ashes into the sea. He did this even before the first man aboard their own ships had become sick.

"Let it be forgotten," his father had warned then.

Marco would honor his word, his oath. This was one tale he would never speak. Still, he touched one of the marks in the sand. He who had chronicled so much . . . was it right to vanquish such knowledge?

If there was another way to preserve it . . .

As if reading Marco's thoughts, his uncle Masseo spoke aloud all their fears. "And if the horror should rise again, Niccolò, should someday reach our shores?"

"Then it will mean the end of man's tyranny of this

world," his father answered bitterly. He tapped the crucifix resting on Masseo's bare chest. "The friar knew better than all. His sacrifice . . ."

The cross had once belonged to Friar Agreer. Back in the cursed city, the Dominican had given his life to save theirs. A dark pact had been struck. They had left him there, abandoned him, at his own bidding.

The nephew of Pope Gregory X.

Marco whispered as the last of the flames died into the dark waters. "What God will save us next time?"

"Who wants another bottle of Foster's while I'm down here?" Gregg Tunis called from belowdecks.

Dr. Susan Tunis smiled at her husband's voice as she pushed off the dive ladder and onto the open stern deck. She skinned out of her BC vest and hauled the scuba gear to the rack behind the research yacht's pilot house. Her tanks clanked as she racked them alongside the others.

Her husband climbed up with three perspiring bottles of lager, pinching them all between the fingers of one hand. He grinned broadly upon seeing her. "Thought I heard you bumping about up here."

He climbed topside, stretching his tall frame. Employed as a boat mechanic in Darwin Harbor, he and Susan had met during one of the dry-dock repairs on another of the University of Sydney's boats. That had been eight years ago. Just three days ago they had celebrated their fifth anniversary aboard the yacht, moored a hundred nautical miles off

Kirimiti Atoll, better known as Christmas Island.

He passed her a bottle. "Any luck with the soundings?"

She took a long pull on the beer. "Not so far. Still can't find a source for the beachings."

Ten days ago, eighty dolphins, *Tursiops aduncus*, an Indian Ocean species, had beached themselves along the coast of Java. Her research study centered on the long-term effects of sonar interference on Cetacean species, the source of many suicidal beachings in the past. She usually had a team of research assistants with her, a mix of postgrads and undergrads, but the trip up here had been for a vacation with her old mentor. It was pure happenstance that such a massive beaching occurred in the region—hence the protracted stay here.

"Could it be something other than manmade sonar?" Professor Applegate pondered, drawing sigils with his fingertip in the condensation on his beer bottle. "Micro-quakes are constantly rattling the region. Perhaps a deep-sea subduction quake struck the right tonal note to drive them into a suicidal panic."

"There was that bonzer quake a few months back," her husband said. He settled into a lounge beside the professor and patted the seat for her to sit with him. "Maybe some aftershocks?"

Susan couldn't argue against their assessments. Between the series of deadly quakes over the past two years and the major tsunami in the area, the seabed was greatly disturbed. It was enough to spook anyone. But she wasn't convinced. Something else was happening. The reef below was oddly deserted. What little life was down there seemed to have retreated into rocky niches, shells, and sandy holes. It was almost as if the sea life here was holding its breath.

She frowned and joined her husband.

A sharp bark startled her, causing her to jump. She had

not known she was that tense. Apparently the strange, wary behavior of the reef life below had infected her.

"Oy! Oscar!" the professor called.

Only now did Susan notice the lack of their fourth crewmate on the yacht. The dog barked again. The pudgy Queensland Heeler belonged to the professor.

"I'll see to him," Applegate said. "Leave you two love-birds all cozied up. Besides, I could use a trip to the head before I find my bed."

The professor gained his feet with a groan and headed toward the bow, intending to circle to the far side—but he stopped, staring off toward the east, away from where the sun had just set.

Oscar barked again.

Applegate did not scold him this time. Instead, he called over to Susan and Gregg, his voice low and serious. "You both should come see this."

Susan scooted up and onto her feet. Gregg followed. They joined the professor.

"Bloody hell . . ." her husband mumbled.

"I think you may be looking at what drove those dolphins out of the seas," Applegate said.

To the east, a wide swath of the ocean glowed with a ghostly luminescence, rising and falling with the waves. The silvery sheen rolled and eddied. The old dog stood at the starboard rail and barked, trailing into a low growl at the sight.

"What the hell is that?" Gregg asked.

Susan answered as she crossed closer. "I've heard of such manifestations. They're called *milky seas*. Ships have reported glows like this in the Indian Ocean, going all the way back to Jules Verne. In 1995, a satellite even picked up one of the blooms, covering hundreds of square miles. This is a small one."

"Small, my ass," Gregg grunted. "But what exactly is it? Some type of red tide?"

She shook her head. "Not exactly. Red tides are algal blooms. These glows are caused by bioluminescent bacteria, probably feeding off algae or some other substrate. There's no danger. But I'd like to—"

A sudden knock sounded beneath the boat. Oscar's barking became more heated. The dog danced back and forth along the rails, trying to poke his head through the posts.

All three of them joined the dog and looked below.

The glowing edge of the milky sea lapped at the yacht's keel. From the depths below, a large shape rolled into view, belly up, but still squirming, teeth gnashing. It was a giant tiger shark, female, over six meters. The glowing waters frothed over its form, bubbling and turning the milky water into red wine.

Susan realized it wasn't *water* that was bubbling over the shark's belly, but its own *flesh*, boiling off in wide patches. The horrible sight sank away. But across the milky seas, other shapes rolled to the surface, thrashing or already dead: porpoises, sea turtles, fish by the hundreds.

Applegate took a step away from the rail. "It seems *these* bacteria have found more than just algae to feed on."

Gregg turned to stare at her. "Susan . . ."

She could not look away from the deadly vista. Despite the horror, she could not deny a twinge of scientific curiosity.

"Susan . . ."

She finally turned to him, slightly irritated.

"You were diving," he explained. "All day."

"So? We were all in the water at least some time. Even Oscar."

Her husband would not meet her gaze. He remained focused on where she was scratching her forearm. The worry in his tight face drew her attention to her arm. Her skin was pebbled in a severe rash, made worse by her scratching.

As she stared, bruising red welts bloomed on her skin.

She gaped in disbelief. "Dear God . . ."

But she also knew the horrible truth.

"It's . . . it's *in* me."

THE FALLEN
978-06-056239-7/$7.99/$10.99 Can

When an ex-cop-turned-ethics investigator is found dead, it's soon clear to San Diego homicide cop Bobbie Brownlaw that the dead man had hard evidence of sex, scandal and corruption in the local government.

CALIFORNIA GIRL
978-0-06-056237-4/$7.99/$10.99 Can

A hideous crime has touched the Becker brothers in ways that none of them could have anticipated, setting three brothers on a dangerous collision course that will change their family—and their world—forever. And no one will emerge from the wreckage unscathed.

COLD PURSUIT
978-0-06-059327-8/$7.99/$10.99 Can

California Homicide Detective Tom McMichael is a good cop determined to perform his duty to the best of his abilities—despite his growing feelings for a beautiful nurse who is the prime suspect in a brutal bludgeoning death of city patriarch Pete Braga.